The Wandering Harlot

INY LORENTZ

Translated by Lee Chadeayne

Text copyright © 2014 by Iny Lorentz

The Wandering Harlot by Iny Lorentz, represented by Verlagsagentur Lianne Kolf, Tengstrasse 8, 80798 Munich, Germany, was first published in 2004 by Droemer Knaur, as *Die Wanderhure*. Translated from German by Lee Chadeayne. Published in English by AmazonCrossing in 2014.

Published by AmazonCrossing, Seattle

ISBN-13: 9781477823347
ISBN-10: 1477823344
Library of Congress Control Number: 2013923613

Cover design by Lindsay Heider Diamond

AUTHORS' NOTE
THE MEDIEVAL PERIOD

This novel takes place at the beginning of the fifteenth century toward the end of an era referred to as the European Middle Ages. This era lasted approximately one thousand years, from the fall of the Roman Empire in the late fifth century until just before the end of the fifteenth century. During these ten centuries, many ancient accomplishments were lost, but consequently Europe quickly developed politically, socially, and culturally, laying the foundation for everything that makes up today's European and American culture and way of life.

In the center of Europe, the Holy Roman Empire of the German Nation was developing into an increasingly brittle colossus. Though its emperors regarded themselves as the successors of the Roman Caesars, their power was not great enough to fully control more than just a part of the empire. The imperial crown, however, came with such an aura of prestige that even Richard of Cornwall, the nephew of Richard the Lionhearted, aspired to it, though he failed in the attempt. The Habsburgs, whose dynasty reigned in Austria until well into the twentieth century, were more successful, but even they had to stand for election by the empire's seven electors, and they did not always win.

At the beginning of the fifteenth century, Sigismund, the count of Luxemburg, who was also king of Bohemia and Hungary, was crowned emperor of the Holy Roman Empire. One of his greatest problems was defense of the Hungarian borders against attacks by the Ottoman Turks. Two further serious problems concerned religion. The secularization of the Catholic Church had continued to grow, and the bishops had risen to become mighty lords. And so it happened that around 1415, three popes were fighting over who was the true pope. Each of these three ecclesiastic lords had his followers and was supported by a different part of the European empire. At the same time, the church's reputation had suffered grievously. For this reason, Kaiser Sigismund convened a council in the city of Constance in 1415, where the matter of the popes was to be settled once and for all.

At that time, Constance was a wealthy city with a population of about six thousand, well suited for such a council. Christendom was weary of the many popes, and so the usual negotiations began in which each party tried to keep the upper hand. Eventually it was agreed that all three popes would be deposed and a new pope elected. This was a success, and consequently antipopes were rare.

During the council, which lasted several years, up to sixty thousand visitors stayed in Constance—ten times the usual population. Most of them, chiefly belonging to the retinue of the ecclesiastic and secular lords, were men not accustomed to living chastely. Depending on the source cited, between eight hundred and fifteen hundred prostitutes were called to Constance, and moral standards in the entire city sank to such a low that the diplomat and minstrel Oswald von Wolkenstein declared: "Before the council, there were three whorehouses in Constance; afterward, there was only one, but it reached from one end of town to the other!"

This is the setting for the story of Marie Schärer, who is wrongfully condemned and then becomes a homeless prostitute.

Delegates from all over Europe—from England and Scotland, from Scandinavia, Spain, Poland, Italy, and, of course, from the Holy Roman Empire—attended the Council of Constance. During the council, the Bohemian reformer Jan Hus was arrested, condemned to death, and burned at the stake—despite the promise of safe passage. Kaiser Sigismund paid for this betrayal with an uprising in his kingdom of Bohemia that lasted nearly two decades. This cost him so much in money and men that despite favorable conditions at the outset, he could not extend his power in the Holy Roman Empire.

For a full six hundred years, the Frankish Empire, later East Francia, and the Holy Roman Empire had been the most significant powers in Europe. Now other empires were taking over, first Spain, then France, and eventually England. But this has nothing to do with the Middle Ages and concerns a new epoch.

And here, we meet Marie.

Iny and Elmar Lorentz

PART ONE
THE TRIAL

Constance,
in the year of our Lord 1410

I.

Marie slipped back into the kitchen guiltily, trying not to attract attention, and went about her work. Wina, the housekeeper, had already noticed her absence and now beckoned her over with an admonishing glance. Laying her hand on Marie's shoulder, Wina sighed deeply.

Ever since Master Matthis's wife had died in labor, Wina had tried to take the place of a mother to Marie. A small, broad-framed woman with an honest-looking but severe face and braids that were beginning to show strands of gray, Wina hadn't found it easy to raise Marie with the right mix of leniency and strictness, but until now she had been satisfied with Marie's progress. The once-inquisitive and often-boisterous child had turned into an obedient and God-fearing young woman of whom her father could be proud. As soon as Marie had learned she was to be married, however, she had changed. Instead of merrily singing and dancing her way through the house, she was behaving erratically and going about her chores gloomily.

Other girls would have been thrilled to learn that a man from a good family was courting them. She could hardly have done better: her future husband was Counselor Rupert Splendidus, the son of a count. Despite his youth, Rupert was a well-known lawyer with a brilliant future ahead of him.

Wina assumed that the nobleman had chosen Marie because he needed an energetic wife able to manage a house with many servants; she took pride in having raised Marie to be independent and hardworking. The thought brought her back to the present. Preparations for the wedding were far from complete, and night was falling. She quickly handed Marie a mixing bowl.

"Here, stir this well so there are no lumps. Now tell me, where were you, anyway?"

"Out in the yard. I wanted to get a little fresh air." Marie lowered her head so Wina wouldn't scold her for the look on her face, or give her a confusing lecture on conjugal duties.

Marie couldn't make Wina understand that she was terrified of the imminent change in her life. She had only recently turned seventeen, and, as her father's only child, she had previously brushed aside all thoughts of marriage. But the following day she would have to give herself to a man for whom she hadn't the slightest feelings, a man she'd met only once.

Rupert Splendidus was of medium height and thin, with facial features too sharp to be called handsome, though they were not outright ugly. But his eyes seemed to bore straight through everyone and everything, and when he'd greeted her, the limp feeling of his cold, almost lifeless hand had sent a shudder down her spine. Nevertheless, neither Wina nor her father would comprehend why the thought of marriage to the son of Count Heinrich von Keilburg did not send her into throes of ecstasy.

Since it appeared that Wina was about to launch into another lecture on proper behavior, Marie tried to change the subject. "The bales of Flemish cloth that the delivery wagon brought up today from the Rhine harbor are standing in the middle of the yard, and it looks like rain."

"What? I can't believe it! We've got to bring that cloth inside as soon as possible, and the porters are all down at the tavern celebrating your upcoming wedding. I'm afraid neither angry words nor flattery will bring them back. Let's see if I can find one of the house servants and get him to at least throw a cover over the bales. In the meantime, continue with your chores." The last few words were directed not just at Marie, but also at Elsa and Anne, the two maids who likewise were busy with wedding preparations.

No sooner had Wina left the kitchen than Elsa, the younger of the two sisters, turned to Marie, her beady eyes flashing. "I know why you sneaked off. You wanted to go see your sweetheart."

"Herr Rupert is a good-looking man," Anne added, batting her eyelashes.

As she put some wood on the fire, Anne gazed enviously at her master's daughter. Marie Schärer was not only heir to a fortune, but with her angelic face, wide cornflower-blue eyes, and long blond hair, she attracted the attention of all young men. Her nose was just long enough to appear distinctive, her rosy lips were gently curved, her hips were gently rounded, and her breasts were the size of two juicy autumn apples. Her narrow waist and perfect figure were accentuated by the tight bodice of her simple gray dress. Most other young women could only hope to look as charming in expensive velvet and silk.

Marie shrugged uneasily as she noticed Anne's eyes upon her. She didn't have to look in the mirror to know that she was strikingly beautiful. In the last two years, almost every man in town had told her so. The compliments had not gone to her head, however, as the priest had told her that only inner beauty really mattered. Nevertheless, ever since the solicitor had come into her life, Marie asked herself what she was really worth without the glamour of her father's gold. Rupert had asked for her hand even before he knew her, and she therefore assumed he sought her as a wife for reasons other than her appearance or virtues. Or had he seen her before and fallen in love? Things like that did happen, but if it that were the case, Marie thought he would have behaved differently toward her.

Meanwhile, Anne was looking at her own reflection in the shining top of the copper soup kettle and realizing that she was just as colorless and insignificant as her chubby sister. Most young men preferred brides who also came with a substantial dowry, yet the two of them owned little more than the clothes on their backs. Their only hope was to find suitors who would settle for a helping hand instead of physical beauty or wealth.

When Marie compared her fate with that of the two sisters, she was pleased and proud to be considered such a good catch. At the same time, how could she be happy with a man like Rupert Splendidus, who consorted with important councillors and princes of the church and was probably just marrying her for her dowry?

She tried to imagine what it would be like to live day after day with a man who didn't really love her and for whom she had little affection. Wina and the priest had assured her that love would come in time and all she had to do was to try to be a good wife. That shouldn't be so difficult, for she had never had strong feelings for a young man before, except perhaps for her childhood playmate Michel Adler. As the fifth son of a taverner, however, he was as poor as a church mouse and therefore out of the question as a husband. She did wonder why her father hadn't promised her to one of the other local men she knew from church, or to a business partner's son, as was done generally in well-to-do families in Constance. Instead, he was giving her away to a total stranger with whom she had barely exchanged even a few polite words.

Marie was ashamed of her timidity. Most girls were married to men whom they had scarcely known beforehand, yet they were happy brides and wives. She knew that her father wanted only the best for her and could certainly judge whether the counselor was a suitable match. She just wished he had asked her. With a soft hiss, she thrust the spoon into the bowl and pounded the dough furiously.

Just then, someone banged against the front door.

"Who wants something from us at this hour?" Anne said indignantly, then yawned.

The two sisters stared at each other, but as usual, Elsa lost the silent duel and left the room sullenly to open the door. Shortly thereafter she returned with Michel, who was struggling under the weight of a large beer keg.

He set the keg down on the table and breathed a sigh of relief. "Good evening! I'm bringing the beer for the wedding."

Elsa hissed angrily. "Couldn't you have waited until tomorrow morning for that? Now Anne and I have to drag the heavy barrel down to the storage cellar."

Her sister gave the young man a simpering smile. "Michel isn't such an impolite fellow that he'd make us weak girls haul such a heavy thing down to the cellar, would you? You'll be good enough to take it for us."

Michel folded his arms in front of his chest and shook his head. "That's not my job. I'm only supposed to bring it over here."

"What's gotten into you? You always used to be so helpful. Do you want to be like your stupid brothers?" Anne looked at him resentfully, and the two girls picked up the keg and carried it down the narrow stairway to the provision cellar, groaning and moaning. The last thing Marie heard was the trapdoor closing. Then she was alone with Michel.

"Do you love him?" he asked.

The question was so unexpected that Marie at first simply looked at him in astonishment. His face was pale, and he was clenching his teeth so tightly that his jaw muscles popped.

Three years older than she was, Michel had let her watch him fishing, played hide-and-seek with her sometimes, and told her wonderful stories. In return, she'd made him wreaths of flowers and idolized him like a king. But since his father was of a far lower social rank than her own father, she had been forbidden to spend time with him after she turned twelve. Since then, she'd only seen him in church.

Now, standing close before him, she noted his high forehead and square jaw and saw that though he'd gotten taller and his shoulders broader, he was unnaturally thin under his smock. Surely his father could feed him better. With a touch of sadness, Marie thought that Michel could easily become a handsome man. But that wouldn't be of much good to him, since as the fifth son, he counted no more than a servant and would never be able to support a family of his own.

His question was insolent, but for the sake of their childhood friendship, she replied. "Though I hardly know the counselor, he must be the right match for me since my father chose him."

She was angry at herself even as she spoke the words, wishing she had been honest with Michel. Eyes flashing, he didn't seem to like her answer, and Marie wondered if he was jealous. That wouldn't be very smart of him, she thought, because he surely knew that her father would never accept Michel as her suitor. Matthis Schärer had even turned away his secretary, Linhard Merk, who came from a good family of merchants. Marie still remembered how furious her father had been that Linhard had dared to ask for her hand in marriage, temporarily firing him before realizing he was indispensable and reinstating him.

Marie was glad that her father hadn't accepted Linhard's proposal. The secretary bowed and scraped to her father like a serf to his noble master, but he treated the coachmen and servants condescendingly. She knew she wouldn't have been happy with that unpleasant man, and in comparison considered herself lucky to be marrying a refined gentleman like Counselor Rupert.

Her abrupt words and dismissive manner did not dissuade Michel. "Does he love you?"

Offended by his tone, Marie responded brusquely. "I assume so. Otherwise he wouldn't have asked for my hand."

Michel stepped closer and looked at her earnestly. "Do you really believe you'll be content as his wife?"

Unintentionally, she smiled sadly. "How can I know that? Love and happiness come with marriage, so they say."

"I wish that for you," Michel replied, "but I doubt it. According to everything I've heard, Rupert is a cold, calculating person who would sell his own grandmother to get ahead."

Marie shook her head indignantly. "How can you say that? You don't even know him."

"I've heard things from travelers in the tavern. That counselor of yours is a well-known attorney who has helped his father, Count Heinrich von Keilburg, many times with legal tricks in order to take away other people's castles, land, and servants."

"Why is that so bad? The count only got what he was owed." Marie was irritated that Michel was spouting the idle talk of drunken tavern guests. He was apparently so jealous of her fiancé that he sought her out just to slander him. Disappointed, she turned and resumed working on the neglected dough.

Michel stormed away, but he got only as far as the kitchen door before he hesitated, turned around again, and walked back to the table. But Marie just waved him off and bent down even closer over her work. Clenching his fists, he searched for the right words to make her understand that she was headed for disaster if she married the notoriously crooked lawyer. The man had already brought misery to many people by doubling the possessions of his cruel father.

Michel started to speak several times, but Marie's grim expression told him he had no chance of convincing her. Now he was annoyed that he had bothered to lug over the beer keg instead of having one of his brothers bring it.

"I'll leave," he said, hoping she would ask him to stay a little longer, but Marie just ignored him and energetically worked out the lumps that had formed in the dough.

At the same moment, Wina returned, raising her eyebrows when she saw Michel.

"I brought the beer," he explained.

"So where is it?"

"Elsa and Anne took it down to the storeroom," replied Marie, answering for him.

"Those two are in the storeroom? I'll go check to make sure those thieving magpies haven't helped themselves to the smoked sausages." Breathing heavily, Wina headed down the stairs and opened the trapdoor.

Marie thought it unfair to call the two maids thieves just because they helped themselves from time to time to a mouthful of sausage or meat. But for the head housekeeper, it was a deadly sin that couldn't be absolved even by the pope.

Marie smiled to herself. Wina idolized the pope as a saintly figure, though that admiration was for the position in general, not for a particular individual. Idolizing a specific pope would have been hard, for at that time three princes of the church each claimed to be the head of Christianity. Marie didn't know much about these things, but her father and his friends frequently talked about the holy church when they were sitting around drinking wine, loudly proclaiming their hope that the emperor would strike the priests down with a bolt of lightning, putting them in their places.

Michel cleared his throat, bringing Marie back to the present. He was still standing there with pleading eyes, but she didn't want to hear any more from him. The next day she would become the counselor's wife and start a new life in which there would be no place for the insolent son of a taverner. From then on, her servants would deal with such people, as she would have to manage the household and devote herself to her husband. She didn't know where she would live after the wedding. Counselor Rupert didn't own a house in Constance but instead lived in Keilburg Castle, his father's home. She wondered if he would take her there.

Wina emerged at the top of the cellar stairs, shoving the scowling maids ahead of her. "You're still here," she snapped at Michel. Reaching into the leather purse she carried on a cord around her chubby waist, she pulled out a coin.

"I suppose you're waiting for your tip. Here, take it!" Michel thought Wina's gesture expressed the great difference in status between a gentleman like Rupert Splendidus and himself, and he was tempted to throw the coin at her feet.

Michel didn't know what he had thought he might accomplish by coming here. Marie had clearly long forgotten him and was looking forward to becoming an important man's wife. He knew she would never be happy with Rupert, but it wasn't within his power to save her from her fate. Sadly he turned around and left without saying good-bye. In the yard he dropped the coin on the ground in disgust.

II.

Master Matthis was feeling good about himself. Nodding proudly, he eyed his friends and guests. His two friends and business partners, the cooper Jörg Wölfling and the linen weaver Gero Linner, couldn't take their eyes off his future son-in-law, Counselor Rupert Splendidus, a respectable and mannerly man who knew how to behave in the presence of older and wiser people. Mombert Flühi also admired Rupert and didn't bother hiding how jealous he was of his brother-in-law's good fortune.

Rupert Splendidus appeared neither arrogant nor excessively proud, but behaved quite modestly despite his high standing. His clothing was made of good material but was not flashy or faddish like that of most young people. His overcoat hanging on a hook by the door was of the finest brown wool, and his gray jacket was simple. His forest-green trousers fit tightly but were not offensively loud or garish like the trousers worn by other men from the better families.

Indeed, in many respects Counselor Rupert was a man after Master Matthis's own heart. Considered quite young for a scholar at the tender age of twenty-four, he nevertheless was already one of the advisers to Constance's bishop, Otto von Hachberg. Most of the time, however, he was traveling on behalf of his father, Count Heinrich von Keilburg, one of the most influential men in the area and subject only to the kaiser. Master Matthis had seen the count only once, but he knew exactly which Rhine and Danube estates the man owned in addition to his ancestral castle in the Black Forest. Yet the difference in their social standings did not seem to trouble Master Matthis. As the bastard son of a servant woman, the counselor could not expect an inheritance, and all of the family possessions would instead be passed on to Konrad, the count's legitimate son. The situation created the perfect opportunity for the union of the counselor and Master Matthis's daughter.

Master Matthis's personal wealth made him feel pleasantly secure. In addition to his father's house in Constance, he owned an equally impressive estate in Meersburg, as well as some of the best vineyards on the lake's north shore and an excellent winery. His international trade had amassed him even more of a fortune.

His great wealth was evident in his home. As was commonplace in leading families' homes, dark wood paneled the walls, and the ceilings were brightly painted. A large table imported from Italy stood in his favorite room, where he regularly entertained his friends. It had elegantly wrought legs and a top inlaid with silver plates where elegant goblets stood ready to welcome his guests. The windows were hung with embroidered brocade curtains carefully selected to blend with the arched, yellow bull's-eye windowpanes.

Matthis Schärer raised his goblet again and toasted his guests. In contrast to the others, Rupert only sipped his drink. Though afternoon had not yet given way to evening, he could see how much Master Matthis had already imbibed, further evidence of the man's pleasures of good wine. His broad, somewhat uncouth face was flushed above his corpulent figure, and his astute gray eyes that usually searched for every business advantage were now dull and bloodshot.

Rupert's smile broadened as he handed Master Matthis two large parchment sheets full of writing. "I've prepared the contracts just as you wished, Father-in-law. Please make sure everything is proper."

Master Matthis admired the counselor's straightforward approach to his upcoming marriage, feeling that he could safely entrust his daughter and his wealth to such a man. Picking up the parchment, he read it through carefully and was not disappointed. Rupert had stuck to their verbal agreements almost word for word. He glanced at the part that guaranteed his daughter's virtue and virginity, something he could attest to without any qualms as his daughter had always been a good child. In addition, Wina had watched like a hawk to make sure no man had approached her too closely.

Master Matthis admiringly patted his future son-in-law on the shoulder. "Excellent! If you have no objection, we can sign the contracts at once."

"It would be a pleasure." Counselor Rupert bowed and spread out both copies in front of Master Matthis, who beckoned to his secretary sitting silently in a dark corner of the room. Linhard was a tall, haggard man with thin, light blond hair, a narrow face, and sharp features; his devotion to his employer seemed almost obsequious. But Master Matthis didn't notice and thought very highly of him.

The secretary bowed to Master Matthis and hurried to the office. Shortly after, he returned with a small tray on which he had placed a silver inkpot, a container of quills, a small knife, and some sealing wax.

Master Matthis picked up one of the quills, shaved it to a fine point, and dipped it in the inkpot. He glanced once more at the most important passages of the marriage proposal and signed his name on the parchment. Heating the sealing wax over a candle, he dripped the wax onto the document beneath his signature, then pressed it with his signet ring.

Linhard now handed the tray with the writing utensils to Counselor Rupert who then applied his own seal to the contract and passed it on to the other men to verify and sign.

Amazed, Master Jörg stared at the document. The bride's rich dowry was described piece by piece, followed by a listing of her father's assets that would be hers upon her father's death. At last he thought he'd solved the riddle of why the esteemed son of one of the mightiest noble families was wooing a girl whose grandfather had fled to the city as a bondservant and only later, through hard work and a favorable marriage, had acquired wealth.

Master Matthis watched his old friends as they read the document, and he took great satisfaction at their stunned expressions. Members of well-placed families had never viewed either him or his father, Richard, as their equals, but rather saw them as runaway slaves who were merely tolerated in the city despite their growing wealth. Richard Schärer had succeeded in amassing a fortune despite local opposition, and Matthis had increased it almost tenfold. Today, Matthis had finally outdone them all, and even the patricians of Constance would be envious of his son-in-law.

Matthis Schärer remembered how the nobleman had asked for his daughter's hand. At first Matthis had thought it was a bad joke. But Counselor Rupert had courteously reminded him that no one else in Constance or anywhere for many miles around could offer such a generous dowry for his daughter.

Jörg cleared his throat and turned to Rupert. "Excuse me for asking, Counselor, but I would be interested to know why your father didn't have you trained in the knightly arts, as is customary in noble circles, but instead made you a man of books."

Rupert's narrow lips broadened into a hint of a smile. "I was very frail as a child and not suited for training as a fighter, so my father judged it better to train me as his secretary and later have me study law."

It was apparent that the men were thinking that most illegitimate children of noblemen weren't given such preferential treatment, so Rupert had to be special. The counselor enjoyed their admiration even though it served as a painful reminder of his past.

From the time of Rupert's birth, Heinrich von Keilburg had taken no interest in him, and so he spent his unhappy childhood living in a remote, drafty corner of the castle with the servants. Only after the castle chaplain had reported to the count what a good head his bastard son had on his shoulders did his life change. Heinrich sent him to the Waldkron monastery, whose monks were known for their strictness, and inquired once a year about his son's progress. Rupert was instructed only superficially in theology but drilled in grammar, rhetoric, and the basics of law.

Count Heinrich had learned by painful experience that rules and laws could be more dangerous than swords, and he wanted a counselor who would support him in all matters. When he felt Rupert was ready, the count sent his illegitimate son to study law at the new university in Heidelberg. Rupert was aware that life would not give him such an opportunity more than once, and he did everything possible to succeed, surprising his father by graduating summa cum laude.

Later, Rupert served Count Heinrich and occasionally his friend Hugo, the abbot of the Waldkron monastery, as a legal counselor, winning one trial after another. His reward for this service, however, was far below his expectations, as Count Heinrich spent money only on himself. Even Konrad, his legitimate son, was given so little that he could not afford the trappings of his noble rank, but at least Konrad did not go hungry.

Now, the counselor turned Matthis's elegant, bejeweled wine goblet around in his hand and pondered the course of his life, allowing his gaze to wander over the remnants of the sumptuous meal. From now on he would live as he chose, indulging in pleasures of which he had only dreamed.

A knock on the door woke Rupert from his reveries. Standing in the doorway, Marie raised her hand shyly to get Master Matthis's attention, blushing as she smoothed her simple gray dress. "Excuse me, Father, if I disturb you. The carriage drivers left the bales of cloth out in the yard, and it looks like it may rain. Someone must put a canvas over them."

Master Matthis looked at his daughter gratefully. "The material is too valuable to get wet. Linhard, go and help the servant, and in the meantime Marie can fill our goblets. Mine is already empty again."

Marie filled the goblets without looking at the man with whom she would be spending the rest of her life and for whom she had an instinctive dislike. She felt like throwing herself at her father's feet and begging him to reject the counselor. But now it was too late—she saw the signed contracts on the table that bound her to the counselor. The wax seals looked to her like smears of blood, and she had to turn away. With lowered eyes, she served the men until Linhard and the servant returned, then left the room with a bow directed more to her father's friends than to her future husband.

Watching her leave, Master Jörg turned to Master Matthis with a twinkle in his eye. "Your daughter is a rare jewel. The counselor must be eagerly anticipating the joys awaiting him in the marriage bed."

The linen weaver had also partaken liberally of the good wine and told an off-color story that made them all burst out laughing. Rupert's face showed no emotion, however, and he let the risqué remarks about the coming wedding night pass without comment. Now and then he stroked his chin as if his thoughts were engaged with something quite different.

III.

Long after Marie and the maids had gone to bed, the men sat up celebrating. No one noticed that the counselor was only taking sips from his goblet while the other guests had theirs filled repeatedly. Master Jörg's words became almost incomprehensible, but that didn't keep him from telling long, tedious stories.

"You've got to admit you could have done worse than my niece," Master Mombert said, placing his arm around Rupert's shoulder and drawing him closer. "If I may give you some advice as an experienced man to someone younger . . ." He didn't finish sharing his wisdom, however, for at the same moment someone banged loudly on the courtyard gate.

"I'll go and have a look," Linhard said, leaving the room before his master could react.

Breathless, he returned shortly. "Counselor, there is a man downstairs who urgently needs to speak with you."

"Why didn't you bring him up?" Master Matthis asked angrily.

Linhard was trembling all over as if he'd seen a ghost. "The man wishes to speak privately with the counselor downstairs."

"If that's the case, I'll have to go down." Rupert arose and took his coat from the hook as protection from the cold night air. As the sound of his footsteps died away on the stairway, the remaining guests looked at one another questioningly. "It wouldn't be a messenger from his father, forbidding the marriage, would it?" The smirk on the linen weaver's face showed clearly how pleased he would be with this turn of events.

Master Matthis dismissed this possibility with a vigorous wave of his hand. "We have signed and sealed the marriage and inheritance contract, so Counselor Rupert has no choice but to marry Marie tomorrow."

His brother-in-law, Mombert, nodded in agreement. "It would also be foolish of Counselor Rupert to pull back. After all, my niece brings more wealth into the marriage than the dowry given by Count Eberhard von Württemberg to his daughter Ursula. And her bridegroom was, after all, the count of the Rheinburg district."

But when Rupert returned, his face was flushed with anger. He stopped in front of the master of the house and looked down at him with disgust. "Matthis Schärer, you're a wretched swindler! Your so-called virtuous daughter is nothing less than a loose, unprincipled hussy."

The effect of this statement was as strong as if the house had collapsed around the four men. Jörg Wölfling and Master Gero looked at each other in shock but also with a certain malicious satisfaction while Mombert's gaze wandered uncertainly back and forth between his brother-in-law and the counselor. Several times, the master of the house began to speak, but all the wine he had enjoyed now paralyzed his tongue, and he was unable to comprehend the significance of the accusation.

"Someone is telling you a pack of lies, Son-in-law. I'd stake my life on my daughter . . ." he finally said.

"And lose. I have a witness who can swear it is true." Rupert nodded at Linhard, who left the room and returned shortly thereafter with a powerfully built middle-aged man wearing a coach driver's rough clothing. His bright eyes darted over the room, stopping at Master Matthis.

Rupert pushed him forward to the table. "This is Utz Käffli, a carriage driver I know to be an honest and good man."

Openmouthed, Master Matthis staggered to his feet and stared. "Of course I know him. He also worked for me. What's the meaning of this, Utz? What is this all about?"

The carriage driver sneered at him and laughed. "May God strike me dead if I'm not speaking the truth. I never would have said anything critical of Marie, but I know Counselor Rupert is a noble and excellent man, and I do not wish to see him rush blindly to his doom." Utz glanced at the counselor, then looked back at Matthis. "I have slept with Marie several times myself. Moreover, I know a number of others who have slept with her and from whom she accepted money and trinkets in exchange."

Unobserved by the others, Utz Käffli poked Linhard in the ribs. Linhard swallowed, visibly shaken, then stepped to the table and raised his hand. "Excuse me, gentlemen, but my conscience . . ." He paused, took a deep breath, and spoke the following words so fast that those who heard him were stunned for a moment before realizing what he had said.

"I have also slept with my master's daughter!"

It became so still in the room that one could have heard a pin drop.

"Linhard?! You . . . you rotten scoundrel!" Master Matthis turned red and gasped for air, as if his collar were choking him. This just can't be, he thought frantically. Marie behaved like an angel and never showed interest in men. A pounding, searing pain coursed through his head. "How dare you both. These are lies, nothing but lies!" Master Matthis exploded in a fit of rage, and tried to grab the carriage driver by the throat.

The carriage driver stood up a bit straighter. "They are not lies, Schärer. I can prove what I say. The last time we were together, I gave her a mother-of-pearl butterfly."

Master Matthis sneered at him. "My daughter has no such jewelry."

"We will see." Rupert beckoned to Master Jörg and Master Gero. "Gentlemen, I suggest we go to Marie's room and look. If she should have a piece of mother-of-pearl jewelry in the shape of a butterfly, that would prove her guilt."

At Utz's command, the secretary fetched a tallow lamp and lit it over one of the candles. Master Jörg took the lamp from him and pointed in the direction of Marie's room. They stopped in front of her door and knocked. "Open the door, child. Your father wishes to speak with you."

Moments later Marie peered out sleepily, clad only in a thin nightshirt. "What has happened, Father?"

"Marie, there are serious accusations against you," said the linen weaver, answering for Matthis. "Some men here assert that you are no longer a virgin but have given yourself to the evils of the flesh."

Marie folded her arms over her breasts, for she was ashamed to be standing in front of the men so scantily dressed. "I swear by the Holy Virgin it is not true!" Marie looked at her father with pleading eyes, but Master Matthis ignored her, leaning against the wall and staring at the floor as if ashamed of his daughter.

"Father, why are you turning away from me? Do you really believe I did such a dreadful thing?" Marie tried to run to his side, but the counselor blocked her way and pushed her to the other corner of the hall. Then he pointed at her room. "We will soon have the proof. Meister Jörg, Master Gero, you are neither witnesses nor accused, and I ask you therefore to search the room."

Shocked, Marie didn't dare move as the two craftsmen entered the room and started searching her bed, the shelves, and her chest.

Suddenly Master Jörg raised his hand with a shout. A white mother-of-pearl butterfly sparkled between his fingers. "Here's the piece of jewelry! Utz Käffli spoke the truth."

Marie staggered forward and stared at the butterfly. "But it doesn't belong to me. I have never seen it before."

Rupert pulled her back. "Denying it won't help you now. You received this piece of jewelry from Utz Käffli for bestowing your favors on him."

"I swear that I never had an affair with that man!" Marie reeled in confusion at the unfolding scene.

Master Gero pushed Linhard forward from his hiding place in a corner into the lantern's circle of light. "Your father's secretary also confessed that he lay with you."

Trying to hold back her tears, Marie put her hands to her face. "But none of that is true! In the name of Jesus Christ and all the saints, I am still a virgin."

"Denial won't help you now! You besmirched my honor, and I insist on a trial in order to establish the gravity of your sin!" The counselor turned his back to Marie as if he couldn't bear the sight of her, and he pointed at Master Matthis.

"In accordance with the laws of the holy church and the kaiser, a woman accused of fornication is not allowed to reside with honorable people. Your daughter must spend the rest of the night in the dungeon. Master Gero, please call the steward of the castle and his bailiffs to take this fallen woman away."

The harsh words of the counselor broke the silence that had been spreading in Master Matthis's head, and he began howling like a wounded animal. "No! No! This is my house! I won't allow you to take my daughter away."

"Do you intend to disobey the law of the kaiser?" Although Rupert's voice had not become any louder, those standing around him winced as if being lashed by a whip.

Mombert Flühi attempted to mediate. "Moderate your anger, Counselor Rupert, and let us discuss the matter. I have known Marie her whole life and cannot imagine she would become a woman of loose morals without any of us noticing."

Rupert's face remained as frozen as a mask. "I will let the court judge."

Mombert wasn't ready to give up. "But if this is all a mistake . . . if Marie is indeed still a virgin . . ."

"I will have her examined by an honorable matron tomorrow morning, and if she is still a virgin, the carriage driver and the secretary will be cast into the dungeon as slanderers while I will have a glorious celebration of my marriage to Marie."

"We cannot object to that," Master Jörg affirmed. "Counselor Rupert is a man familiar with the laws and knows what should be done."

"Father! No! You mustn't allow them to take me away. Do you really think I am as evil as these liars assert?" Marie seemed to be struggling for air.

She didn't understand the turn her fate had taken. She desperately sought help from her father, but he just kept staring at the floor while mumbling something incomprehensible. Counselor Rupert seemed to take pleasure in damning her. Marie wondered in despair why he believed the statements of the two men more than he did her own.

She looked at her two accusers. Linhard turned his head away at once, but Utz grinned and ran his tongue back and forth between his broken teeth. The man frightened her, and Marie quickly turned away.

Master Gero returned almost at once with Hunold, one of the city bailiffs. Hunold stood more than a head taller than the men around him. His arms were bigger than the thigh of an ordinary man, and his abdominal muscles were as thick as ropes. He grinned broadly, seemingly enjoying the situation, and bowed to Counselor Rupert.

"Always at your service, sir."

"Carry this woman to the dungeon. I'll see to it that she is charged tomorrow."

Hunold glanced lustfully at Marie, then took a rope from his belt, tied Marie's arms behind her back, and pushed her toward the stairs. As he squeezed past her father, Master Matthis raised his head as if awakening from a bad dream and reached out to the bailiff.

"Take care of my daughter and see she has everything she needs. I'll repay you handsomely for that."

Hunold's gaze, however, wandered from the owner of the house to the counselor, whom he looked at questioningly. Rupert Splendidus nodded crossly and gestured vigorously for the bailiff to take the girl away, then descended the stairs. Stopping in the entryway below, he looked up at Matthis Schärer who was leaning on the railing and gasping. "You will understand that I can no longer be your guest. We shall see each other again tomorrow in court."

Master Matthis uttered a few incomprehensible sounds before his voice became clearer. "Go! Get out as fast as you can. And don't forget to take with you the swine who sullied my house, or I'll lose control of myself and throttle them."

He staggered toward Linhard who was still leaning on the wall, exhausted. At that moment Linhard sprang back to life, ran down the stairs as if the devil were after him, tore open the door, and disappeared into the dark night.

Rupert followed him at a leisurely pace. At the courtyard entrance, he reached for the lantern he had set there but didn't light it until he was outside in the street. Looking around, he saw Utz appear at the next corner, pulling Linhard after him.

An evil smile played around Rupert's mouth as he asked, "You know what you have to do now?"

Utz laughed. "We'll take care of everything, just as you wish, but first I'll have to convince this coward that he has to play along."

Rupert glared at Linhard. "Are you going to back out? Don't forget it was you who hid the butterfly in the girl's room. If you cross us, I'll have you broken on the wheel for perjury, fraud against your employer, and a few other crimes."

Linhard was visibly shaken and raised his hands, pleading. "No, sir."

"Then do what Utz tells you. Now go! I'll see you tomorrow in court."

The counselor turned around and walked off without saying good-bye. Utz lit a pine chip, held it up in his left hand, and with the other hand pushed the secretary toward the shore of the Rhine.

IV.

Marie felt as if she were a ghost hovering outside her body and looking down in disbelief at what was happening. Was she really being dragged and pushed through the dark streets, barefoot and in a thin nightshirt? This could not be happening.

Clenching her teeth, she prayed softly that she would wake up and find herself back in her own bed, but no Baby Jesus or saint came to her aid. At first she was relieved when Hunold pushed her to the floor in the tower dungeon and bound her arms in an iron ring, for she thought the nightmare had come to an end. Surely she was about to wake up in bed, cuddled in her warm quilt and thinking of something to dispel the terrible dream.

Time passed, though, and all she could feel was the damp cold creeping in from the hard-packed dirt floor, and all she could see was an impenetrable darkness without any moonlight. She slowly began to understand this was not a nightmare and that she really had been accused of immoral behavior. Since the rope around her wrists bound her to the ground, she pulled her legs up, put her head on her knees, and tried to pray, but her words were drowned out by her violent sobs.

Over and over she asked herself why the two men had lied. She had rarely had contact with the secretary, since he was usually caught up in business matters and was often traveling. Had the carriage driver thought all this up in order to humiliate her? But the two men knew they would have to swear to their assertions before a cross and a judge.

Thinking about what would happen the next day, Marie felt reassured. A matron would examine her in the morning and determine Marie was indeed a virgin. Linhard and Utz would be revealed as slanderers in court, and Marie would be exonerated.

Once she had convinced herself that she was not in danger after all, Marie wondered why Counselor Rupert had been so quick to believe the two men's assertions. Did he regret signing the marriage contract, and was now happy to have found this way to withdraw his offer? Or was he just stunned by the sudden accusations? No doubt he now realized his hasty reaction would lose him a fortune, and he would want the truth to come to light. It was in his own interest to help her now.

Just then, Marie heard someone sliding the bolt aside and inserting a key in the lock. It was her father and her fiancé coming to get her! So this was all just a cruel prank or horrible misunderstanding. The key turned very slowly, almost silently, and the door opened without a sound. Outside someone was whispering, and a light appeared as if several torches had been lit.

Marie looked expectantly toward the door. To her disappointment, Hunold appeared in the opening, grinning and holding a torch. Turning around, he pulled Linhard forward and gave him a shove that sent him stumbling across the room. The secretary's face was twisted in a terrified grimace. The bailiff stepped aside and Utz entered. The carriage driver placed his torch in a ring, looking at Marie as if he wanted to devour her with his eyes. Feeling ill,

Marie turned away as Hunold closed the door, locking it behind him. Then he placed the torch over Marie's head.

Marie was frozen with fear and sat up as far as her fetters permitted. "What do you want from me?"

Hunold bent over as if to grab her, but the carriage driver pushed him aside and looked Marie in the face. "You don't want Linhard and me to commit perjury tomorrow in court, do you?"

Marie crawled back toward the wall. "I don't understand . . ."

"Don't worry, you will in a moment." Utz forced Marie onto her back. Then Hunold walked over to Marie and ripped her nightshirt off as far up as her neck. At that moment Marie began to scream. "No! No! For the Mother of God and all the saints, you cannot do that! You are violating God's commandments."

Utz and Hunold nudged each other and doubled over with laughter. While the bailiff was still holding his belly, the carriage driver pointed up at a small opening just below the ceiling, warning Hunold against making so much noise. Then he stooped, slapped Marie in the face, and stuffed a dirty rag into her mouth so that now she could only whimper.

Still laughing, Hunold jumped on Marie.

Her world seemed to fall to pieces. Silently she called on God and all the saints. Why are you allowing this? she asked, What have I done that you are punishing me like this?

Hunold finished, rolling off her, and Marie doubled up, overcome by a wave of nausea before Utz forced himself on her. Afterward, her whole body was wracked with pain. The world around her seemed to have been transformed into a pitching and rolling ship, and all she wanted was for the surrounding ocean to open up and devour her. Through a veil of tears she could see Utz and the bailiff walking toward Linhard, who was holding on to the door and trembling all over.

"Now it's your turn," they told him.

When the secretary said nothing, Hunold grabbed him and forced him toward Marie.

"I don't know . . . I can't . . ." Linhard stammered.

"Are you going to perjure yourself tomorrow, or back out and betray us? Either you go along with us, or your corpse will be floating down the Rhine tonight."

Utz kicked him so hard, he fell down on top of the girl.

Marie struggled to catch her breath and tried to push Linhard away, but Utz placed his foot down so hard on her right leg that she thought the bone would break. Marie's feelings suddenly transformed. Just a moment ago she had been awash in a sea of despair, but now rage built up within her and she felt pure hatred for the first time in her life. The carriage driver and the bailiff were crude, conscienceless characters, but the secretary had served in her father's house for many years and was something like a member of the family. His betrayal hurt her so deeply that if she could, she would have torn him to shreds with her bare hands. At the same time, she wished she were dead.

Linhard stood up, turning his back to her as he buttoned up his trousers. Utz spat on the floor, ignoring Marie. "We're done here. What do you say we go to Guntram Adler's and share a tankard of beer?"

"Yes, but at your expense. The little secretary looks like he could use a stiff drink." Hunold opened the door, pushed Linhard outside, and waited until Utz had walked past him with the torches. Then he pulled the door closed and locked it carefully.

Inside, it was once more as quiet and dark as the grave. Marie could feel the cold creeping into her body, more so than before, but not enough to soothe the burning inside her. She struggled to sit up, laid her head on her fettered hands, and pulled her knees up to her chest to make the pain easier to bear.

She wondered anxiously what would happen now. People wouldn't ask if she had been violated, but they would instead issue blame and speak ill of her. Even if her father offered her weight in gold, no honorable man would seek her hand in marriage, not even a poor fellow like Michel. The best her father could do would be to marry her to some drunk like the sheepshearer Anselm, for whom the wine he could buy with her dowry would be more important than her virginity and reputation.

Marie kept thinking about the men who had first slandered her, then destroyed her life so brutally. She no longer asked why, but, almost choking on her hatred, she yearned to see the three men punished, whipped, and then driven out of town amidst shouts and jeers. Impatiently she waited for the morning to come when she would be examined by an old woman from Constance and the truth would come to light. She tried to seek solace from the Holy Virgin and the saints in order to escape the madness that had come over her. But her anger choked every prayer on her lips.

V.

The first rays of dawn shone through the window bars of her cell when she heard a key turn in the lock and the bolt slide back. When a powerfully built older woman entered, Marie began to cry with relief. It was the widow Euphemia who lived three doors away from them and had known Marie since birth.

The woman placed her torch in the ring above Marie's head, put her hands on her hips, and looked down at the figure lying at her feet. Without saying a word, she bent down, seized Marie's legs, and pulled her forward. Marie stiffened instinctively as the widow inspected her, then stood up with a cruel laugh. "Now you see what you get when a girl grows up without a mother."

Marie panted between clenched teeth. "Utz the carriage driver, Hunold the bailiff, and Linhard our secretary, came to the dungeon and violated me. Euphemia, you can see how much I was hurt. I was still a virgin until the men attacked me. You must testify to that in court."

The widow laughed bitterly. "I must do nothing of the sort! Your father should have been smart enough to marry me after your mother died. I would have seen to it that you grew up as a decent girl. But Matthis Schärer, the arrogant son of a runaway serf, thought he was too fine for a simple shoemaker's widow."

The shock triggered by these malicious words gave Marie the strength to sit up partway and look the woman in the face. "What are you saying? You can see what happened to me! Do you want the three men who slandered and violated me to escape their just punishment?"

At that moment the door opened again, and Hunold entered with a basin of water. Over his arm he carried a towel and a penitent's hair shirt.

Marie screamed at the sight of him, but Euphemia shrugged, dipped the cloth in the water, and began to clean her. Clinging to the hope that the judge would see through the web of lies and violence spun around her, Marie lay motionless. She didn't even resist when Euphemia put the hair shirt on her, then motioned to Hunold. "She's now presentable for the high court."

The bailiff bound Marie's arms behind her back as on the evening before and shoved her toward the door. She was so preoccupied with her misery that not until they were crossing the bridge did Marie realize that Hunold was taking her to the island's Dominican monastery, where the monks had a reputation for merciless severity.

VI.

The monastery's great hall was built to impress. The walls were made of precisely hewn stone blocks, their weight underscored by the unusually large woven tapestries depicting biblical scenes. Narrow, high, stained-glass windows told of the sufferings of Dominican martyrs. The ceiling was made of dark stained wood and decorated with fine carvings. The coats of arms of the bishops of Constance and abbots of the island monastery were displayed on the massive pillars. All of this gave the visitor the feeling of standing at one of the holiest places in Christendom.

Behind a solid rock table at the back of the hall was a seat as magnificent as the kaiser's own throne, and there sat the bishop's judge, Honorius von Rottlingen, dressed in the white-and-black habit of the Dominicans. Two steps to the side from the judge's table stood the prosecutor's richly carved chair where Counselor Rupert was acting as both prosecutor and plaintiff. Behind him, court bailiffs were positioned to carry out the judge's orders.

The spectators' chairs were empty, and Gero Linner and Jörg Wölfling sat on one of the sparsely occupied witness benches. At the other end of the same bench sat Utz Käffli and Linhard Merk. The carriage driver eyed his surroundings with a disrespectful smirk as if amused by the stiff dignity of this place, while Linhard half closed his eyes, visibly struggling with the aftereffects of the previous night's alcohol.

Matthis Schärer had taken a seat on the rear witness bench far from his daughter's accusers. His complexion was gray, his cheeks fallen, and one half of his face hung down slightly. Softly bewailing his misfortune, he clung to his brother-in-law.

Mombert also seemed shaken, but unlike Matthis, he was still able to think clearly. He was alarmed by the speed with which Counselor Rupert had been able to schedule Marie's trial and the aloof faces of the judge and the court bailiffs. It was a bad omen that Marie's case was being tried in the bishop's court and not before a local jury with jurisdiction over Constance citizens where he and Matthis could have presented a better defense for Marie. In this hall, where Counselor Rupert served as legal adviser to the bishop's court and was a frequently welcomed guest, they did not wield the slightest influence.

Mombert was also angry at Master Jörg, a member of the High Council of Constance, who should have insisted that this case be heard in a city court. But Jörg Wölfling remained quietly in his seat, neither speaking nor showing any emotion.

Honorius von Rottlingen cleared his throat to gain the attention of those present. "Bring in the strumpet!"

With those words, the judge seemed to have already made up his mind. Terrified of the fanatical monk, Mombert shuddered, tears rolling down his cheeks as the bailiff led Marie into the courtroom. Matthis felt ill and leaned forward, his face in his hands.

There were dark shadows under Marie's eyes. She shook violently, and her face was painfully contorted. None of that, however, detracted from her angelic beauty, and it was clear from the look in her eyes that her spirit remained unbroken.

A court bailiff led her to the prisoner's bench where she was forced to kneel. When the judge gave a signal, Rupert rose and walked to the middle of the hall, then accused Master Matthis of having knowingly deceived him into the engagement with his daughter. "But these two good men here followed the call of their conscience and warned me of Matthis Schärer's ruse and the immoral life of his daughter, Marie."

Marie bowed slightly and looked directly at the judge, speaking in a firm voice. "This is a wretched web of lies, Your Honor! Last night, Linhard the secretary, Utz the carriage driver, and Hunold the bailiff broke into my cell and violated me in order not to have to commit perjury here. I swear by the Holy Virgin and Jesus that until last night I was a chaste virgin."

Marie's father jumped up as if wanting to run to her, but then collapsed, groaning, and clenched his chest. Mombert held on to him.

"You have chosen a rather strange defense." The judge sounded doubtful. "If you are unjustly charging the three men, your punishment will be even more severe."

"I speak the truth," Marie affirmed. "I swear . . ."

Counselor Rupert waved her off. "Is she so scheming as to try to deflect criticism of her own crime with a baseless accusation?"

Mombert rose indignantly. "How can you say her accusation is baseless? I know Marie only as a pious, obedient child who never lies."

Rupert shook his head thoughtfully. "It honors you, Master Mombert, that you come to the defense of your relative, but you were present when Utz Käffli and Linhard Merk told us convincingly that they had engaged in immoral behavior with her. Her assertion she had not lost her innocence until it was taken from her against her will last night is really going too far. I hope the venerable father will consider this insolence in his judgment."

"What about the bailiff?" Mombert asked. "Not a word was mentioned of him last night."

"Naturally she must accuse him as well. Who but he could have given Utz and Linhard the key to the dungeon?" Rupert said, addressing the judge, who silently nodded his agreement.

"If you speak the truth, the matron who examined you will confirm your words, but if you have lied, the full force of the law will be brought to bear."

Marie could feel every hair on her body standing on end. She could only hope that Euphemia would obey her conscience in the presence of the cross. As soon as the widow was led in, however, Marie could tell that she didn't intend to testify truthfully.

Father Honorius called the woman forward. "You are Euphemia, widow of the shoemaker Otfried, ordered this morning to examine the virginity of Marie Schärer who has been accused of prostitution. Give the court your findings."

Euphemia scowled and blew air through her teeth. "Your Honor, I can hardly call the girl a virtuous virgin."

Father Honorius looked at her severely. "Euphemia Schuster, in the name of God and our savior Jesus Christ, I demand you tell us the truth. Did you see signs that the accused was violated during the night?"

The widow did not hesitate for a moment. "I saw no sign she had been violated. This I swear by God the Almighty."

Marie cried out loudly. "She's lying! She hates my father and is allied with those who defiled me!"

Father Honorius pounded the flat of his hand on the table so hard that the stone rang. "Bailiffs, gag the accused! She is not worthy of being allowed to raise her voice again."

The judge turned to Linhard and Utz. "You two have claimed that you fornicated with Marie, the daughter of Matthis Schärer. Do you swear by the cross that your testimony is true?"

Utz rose, walked up to the judge's bench, and placed his hand on the cross that the judge held out to him. "I swear by everything that is holy that I lay with Marie Schärer."

Seeing the judge's questioning gaze directed at him, Linhard broke out in a sweat. He held his head down, looking as if he expected to be struck down at any moment by a bolt of lightning. Clutching the cross in his trembling hands, he walked up to the judge's bench, and said the words that sealed Marie's fate: "I swear by all that is holy."

Satisfied, Father Honorius nodded. "The accused is hereby found guilty of prostitution and will be punished to the fullest extent of the law. Now we must decide the penalty. Counselor Rupert, since the godless actions of the accused have sullied your honor, it is up to you to demand an appropriate punishment."

The counselor bowed slightly. "I thank you, Venerable Father. According to the laws of the holy church and the Reich, if the guilt of a wayward woman has been proven and she admits and regrets her actions in a court of law, she shall be sent to a nunnery where she can pray for the forgiveness of her sins."

He paused and looked at the spectators, who nodded their silent approval. Then he turned to Marie. "Are you now finally ready to admit your sins?" he demanded. "Consider carefully. It is the only way for you to atone for your transgressions and save your soul from eternal damnation."

Marie hesitated. All she wanted now was to crawl away and hide behind the walls of a nunnery where she would be able to forget the cruelty of the world. But she knew she could be acquitted only by committing perjury and at the same time exonerating the three rapists along with the widow Euphemia whose vile slander had sealed her fate. She shook her head violently and uttered a sound that could be understood as "No."

Counselor Rupert turned a grim face to the judge. "If the girl remains unrepentant," he said, "and refuses to confess her guilt, she must be whipped and driven from the city."

Her father stood up, breathing heavily, and staggered forward. "Child, you don't know what you are doing," he said, whimpering. "Admit your guilt, and I will send you to the sisters of the Third Order of Saint Francis in Constance." Turning her head away, Marie gazed in another direction.

Marie could hear her father's pleas and saw her uncle Mombert's imploring look. Even the judge nodded his encouragement. It was as if the entire world had conspired against her, but she knew that if she took the veil, she would suffer the contempt of the noble nuns and would be punished for sins she had never committed. Worse, perjury was a deadly sin for which she didn't wish to atone. No, she was not ready to do that.

She looked at the judge and shook her head resolutely. Honorius von Rottlingen was visibly annoyed. "Since this hussy is stubborn and denies her guilt, she shall suffer the worst possible penalty."

He consulted briefly with his bailiffs, then rose and looked down at Marie.

"Marie Schärer, you are sentenced to thirty lashes with branches and eternal banishment from the city of Constance and its surroundings for having deceived the esteemed Counselor Rupert Splendidus and entered a marriage contract under pretense of being an honorable virgin as well as for slandering upstanding citizens." The judge was preparing to rise and conclude the session, when Counselor Rupert asked permission to speak.

"Excuse me, Venerable Father, for presenting one last request. None of your bailiffs should whip the whore. In my experience, most men deal more leniently with such a beautiful woman. I suggest that bailiff Hunold carry out the punishment. He will certainly not be merciful."

"No, he won't. Not after she accused him of this disgraceful crime," replied the judge, raising his hand to demand the attention of those present. "The judgment will be carried out today. Take the hussy to the marketplace and have the bailiff Hunold carry out the punishment. After that, two bailiffs of this court are to escort her out of Constance."

Marie could feel the last of her strength ebbing away. With a satisfied grin, Hunold approached, seized the rope with which he had twice dragged her through the city, and yanked it so hard, she fell to the ground.

"It won't do you any good to throw yourself at my feet and beg me to spare you," he sneered at her. "You should have thought of that before."

VII.

The day of Marie's court appearance was also market day in Constance. Farmers from the surrounding area had been streaming into the city since early morning with their vegetables, poultry, lambs, and pigs. By late morning, most of their goods had sold, and the farmers began taking down their stalls. Suddenly the hectic activity stopped. Even the city residents who had been running anxiously from stand to stand as if time were running out grabbed hold of their fully packed shopping baskets and stared openmouthed at the old granary.

Three court bailiffs stood there with scepters decorated with ribbons as a sign of their office. The visitors in the marketplace crowded closer, asking one another what was going on, but no one had an answer. An offender's punishment was usually announced days in advance by the town criers.

The spectators didn't need to wait long, as another court bailiff appeared soon after and politely asked the spectators to make room for the venerable judge Honorius von Rottlingen and his retinue. A passage quickly opened through the growing crowd for the monks coming up the hill from the monastery to walk toward the pillory's platform.

The judge, his bailiffs, and the secretary were met by expectant whispers and were followed by Counselor Rupert and his witnesses. Attracting the most attention, however, was Hunold who was pulling Marie along behind him like a calf on a rope. Two other men in the procession came several steps behind, barely capturing any notice. They were Mombert Flühi and Marie's father, who was leaning heavily on his brother-in-law and continually shaking his head.

As the judge and his retinue took their seats, Hunold dragged Marie to the pillory, a pole with iron fittings that had been anchored deep in the ground to resist even the rage of strong men. Blackened with time, the wood had become as smooth as polished stone from the bodies of the condemned who had writhed in pain there. Hunold pushed Marie toward the pole, tied her hands over her head, and with a violent tug pulled her dress down and threw it aside. Marie froze in shame.

Hunold untied the rope behind Marie's neck and ripped the gag out of her mouth. Then pulling a knife from his belt, he cut off her braids.

Marie turned her head to the side as much as she was able with her arms stretched over her head. "May God damn you to the darkest reaches of hell."

Hunold smirked and made room for the court bailiff, who stepped up to the pole and began reading the judgment in an ostentatious tone. In the meantime, Mombert had leaned his half-conscious brother-in-law against a cart and made his way to the front row of spectators. He didn't know what he thought he could do there. Didn't anyone see that an appalling injustice was being committed? Why didn't anyone intervene? The miracle he had hoped for did not happen.

The people around him didn't know what to think of the whole matter. Some of them knew Marie and affirmed they had considered her a virtuous young woman, but most proclaimed loudly that she had duped them all, and their voices sounded malicious and complacent. A few levelheaded citizens inquired about the kaiser's magistrate who was responsible for prosecution and punishment of crimes in Constance along with the city council, but they were informed that the magistrate had left town two days ago and was not expected back until the beginning of the following week.

The crowd quieted when a court bailiff handed Hunold three hazelnut branches. Marie clenched her teeth at the first blow. Again, the lash struck her back, and it felt like her body was in flames. The blows kept coming, and soon she could no longer think clearly, as every part of her body and soul was overcome with pain. Not even the torment of purgatory could be worse.

Finally, Hunold untied the ropes binding Marie to the post and watched as she sank to the ground. After a moment, he poured a nearby basin of cold water over her. Marie groaned and struggled to lift her head. "You are no longer human, Hunold. You are a monster."

He laughed and turned away, leaving her to the two court bailiffs who would lead her out of the city. The men pulled her to her feet. While one of them held her, the other dressed her in a bright yellow robe that only reached her thighs. More of a sack than a garment, the cloth showed two grimacing faces that represented fornication and lust. Then the bailiffs beckoned to the servant holding their horses.

"Come, whore! Now we're leaving town!" One of the bailiffs wrapped the end of a long rope around her tied hands and fastened the other end to a stirrup. Without giving her a second glance, he and his comrade leaped into their saddles and spurred their horses forward, Marie staggering along on foot behind them through a dense crowd of onlookers. As she passed through the Rhine Gate, the golden rooster perched on the cathedral ridge jeered a final farewell over the roofs of the old city.

VIII.

Matthis Schärer and Mombert Flühi had joined the crowd following the bailiffs. Marie's father had aged decades since her arrest,
but his strength suddenly seemed to return as he shoved his way
through the crowd so fast that his brother-in-law could barely keep
up with him. His mind still seemed to be clouded, however, as he
babbled incomprehensibly, stretching his trembling hands out to
his daughter. Mombert's eyes were also fastened on his niece, whose
yellow robe was turning red from her blood. He thought of his
daughter, Hedwig, who had just turned twelve, and he shuddered
to imagine her in Marie's place.

As the bailiffs were guiding their horses through the city gate,
Marie caught sight of Michel pushing his way through the crowd,
and their eyes met fleetingly. His face reflected his horror and help-
lessness, but also his sympathy and willingness to stand by her.
When she tripped over a protruding cobblestone and fell, he started
to hurry to her aid, but Guntram Adler suddenly appeared behind
him, seized him by the collar, and, cursing angrily, dragged him
back into the city.

Amidst the jeers of some in the crowd, Marie got back onto her
feet and stumbled on. Knowing that at least one person believed in

her innocence gave her new strength. The evening before, she had mistaken Michel's words for the angry prattle of a jealous young man, but now she realized she had done him an injustice. Michel loved her and had wanted to save her from this fate. She would probably never have the chance to thank him for that.

The only people who could help her now were her father and uncle. She hoped they would follow her and hide her from the world, allowing the wounds of her body and soul to heal. As she clung to these thoughts, her feet shuffled along behind the bailiff's horses mechanically.

As the last of the onlookers headed back, Marie could see Mombert speaking earnestly and softly to his brother-in-law as if trying to console him. Her father, however, vehemently waved him off, turned around, and tottered back toward town without even a last glance at Marie. Mombert spread his arms out wide in despair and kept looking back and forth between Marie and his brother-in-law. When he saw Matthis stumble, he hurried after him to steady him.

Marie stared at them in disbelief. Her own father was abandoning her! That was the last thing she had expected. Without the help of her relatives, without a coin in her pocket or a place to seek refuge, she wouldn't survive more than a few days. She was mired in shock and misery, sharp stones cut into the soles of her feet, her heart cramped at every beat, and the world around her turned so gray she could barely see where she was walking. *Were these the signs of the imminent death that would finally bring her relief?* she wondered.

She stared at the bailiffs and wondered if they would simply abandon her alongside the road. Marie didn't know that the bailiffs had an interest in sparing her and that for this reason they held their horses to a slow pace. If she died, they couldn't just leave her by the side of the road; it was their duty to bury the person in their care, digging a hole for the body with their bare hands. They wanted to avoid such an onerous task, and in any case no one was urging them on, so they chatted as if they were on a pleasant country outing, before finally stopping at the tavern in Wollmatingen.

Tying Marie next to the horses, the men gave her water from the trough, then went into the tavern for a hearty meal and some wine. Marie was young and strong, and the rest did her good. Her heart beat more calmly, and the veil before her eyes was lifting, so she could again see where she was. She didn't know whether to be happy or disappointed that she was still alive.

The bailiffs spent the night in Allensbach at an inn on comfortable straw mattresses while Marie slept inside a shed on the cold ground. Again, she was given only water. Not until the next morning did one of the bailiffs bring her bread crusts and a cup of the cheapest wine, pressing them both into her fettered hands. "Eat and drink," he ordered her. "This afternoon we will leave you, and you can go where you wish as long as it isn't in the direction of Constance."

Marie gripped the cup with both hands and drank so fast that she spilled some. The liquid burned as it slid down her throat, but she drank it all. She wanted to ask the man for a second cup, but he turned away as if regretting his compassionate gesture.

"Now get up. We don't want to waste the whole day hanging around here." He tied her again to his stirrup, and she struggled to her feet, stumbling along behind her guards. After a few hours, the bailiffs stopped again. One of the men jumped down, untied Marie's hands, and pushed her down the road.

"That is where you must go. Don't even think of showing your face again, as the venerable judge will not deal with you so mercifully the next time."

"Mercifully?" Marie almost choked on her hatred and struggled for breath. But before she could get her voice back again, the two court bailiffs had turned their horses and ridden off at a fast trot. For Marie, all that remained on this beautiful, hot July day were the dusty road and the blistering sun.

A few steps away, an ancient, storm-ravaged oak spread its shadow over the road where it forked, one route leading to Singen and the other to Radolfzell. For a while Marie stood there, uncertain which way to go. Finally, she decided on the road to Singen, the route shaded by old trees.

IX.

Ever since hearing the news of Marie's upcoming marriage to Counselor Rupert Splendidus, Michel had been tormented by fears. It had been clear to him that this betrothal could only bring unhappiness to Marie, but he could never have imagined that she'd be slandered and arrested, as her maid Elsa had breathlessly reported to him earlier that morning when he'd bumped into her on the street. Perhaps it would have been better if he'd recounted to Marie the story he'd overheard one night in a tavern, told by a family servant who had lost his position when his master had been driven away. The man hadn't minced his words and had spoken of Rupert's deceit, perjury, and forgery. His accusations were so serious that his table companion had advised him to keep quiet if he valued his life. Since Michel had heard other similar rumblings about Rupert Splendidus, he was angry at himself for not having been more insistent when he spoke with Marie. He was entirely convinced of her innocence.

Later that morning, as he was wiping down tables in front of the tavern, a passerby casually mentioned that Marie Schärer had been convicted and was at that moment being whipped. Michel dropped his cleaning rag and ran after the man. A large crowd had already formed to watch, so Michel had to settle for a place at the edge of the square where he couldn't see the pillory but could hear the snap of the whip. Every time Marie let out an anguished cry, he cringed as if the blows were landing on his back.

Not until the court bailiffs were dragging Marie behind them was he able to see her. With her short-cropped hair standing out like a halo around her head and with her pained expression, she looked to him like a statue of a Christian martyr that had sprung to life. This girl was as pure and innocent as an angel; he was more certain than ever about that. In that moment, he resolved to stand with Marie against all the dangers of the world. Without even thinking about having nothing but the clothes on his back and only his bare hands to earn a living, he let himself be carried along with the gaping crowd in order to slip out of town unnoticed and follow Marie.

Just then, his father spotted him, grabbed him by the nape of the neck, and dragged him back home. "So my high-and-mighty son chooses to abandon his job and run after a half-naked wench and leave all the work for his brothers. Get back to work, you wretched loafer, or I'll lose my temper."

Standing up to his father would only have gotten Michel a sound beating and a few nights locked in the cellar. If he wanted to protect Marie, he'd have to wait until his father and brothers were distracted by customers. He didn't know where the bailiffs would take Marie. They were on horseback, so they would certainly go beyond city boundaries, and that was more than a day's ride away. If he didn't want to lose track of them, he would have to follow before nightfall. He therefore waited, impatiently, for an opportunity to leave the house unnoticed.

Guntram Adler didn't tolerate idleness, least of all with his sons. Each of them had to do the work of two that day, because so many guests were crowded into the taproom that the tables in front of the building were all occupied, and others had to stand drinking their beer. Every time Michel tried to take a break, Bruno or his father had something else for him to do. To his annoyance, none of his tasks took him far enough from his family to allow him to run off. Late in the afternoon, Bruno gave him a short rest.

As he sat down for a few minutes, the first image that flashed into his mind was of Marie's pain-wracked face, and his thoughts focused on the girl he loved with every fiber of his being. Despising his cowardice, he told himself it would have been better simply to run off instead of giving in to his father. He knew he had to help her, and looking around carefully, he tried to think how he could slip out unnoticed.

But as he watched his sweat-covered younger brothers emerging from the cellar, Michel wondered if anyone would even miss him. After all, he had seven brothers and two sisters. In addition to Michel, there were three brothers living at home, and since only the eldest would inherit the tavern, the younger ones would have to stay with the oldest one as servants, without ever being able to start their own family.

A booming voice tore Michel from his thoughts. Standing over him was Guntram Adler, about to give him another slap. "Are you loafing around again? There are guests in front of the building who are waiting to be served."

His father turned away to answer a question from someone standing next to him, so Michel picked up some empty mugs and hurried out. A cluster of youths had gathered on the little green outside the tavern, and their main topic was Marie. The lads talked at great length about her outstanding physical features and bragged about bedding her.

Michel was seized with such anger that he dropped the mugs carelessly on the table and grabbed a young goldsmith by the arm.

"Liar! Marie would never have even looked at a wretch like you."

Startled, Benedikt looked up. "Hey, what are you doing? Let me go! Besides, what does it matter to you if I had my way with Marie?"

"Here are a few whacks for your lies," said Michel, hitting him so hard with two blows that he was knocked off the bench. Angrily, the boy jumped up and attacked Michel. He was two years older and heavier than Michel, always winning whenever they had wrestled, but this time neither his strength nor his agility did him any good. He was about to get the worst beating of his life, when Michel's father intervened and separated them.

"Stop! No fighting in my tavern." Benedikt tucked his torn shirt into his trousers and lifted his head up. "That son of yours attacked me for no reason."

Guntram Adler didn't even give Michel a chance to explain himself, but smacked him in the face with the back of his hand. Casting a furious look at his son, the taverner put his arm around Benedikt's shoulder, and smiled.

"Have a seat inside, lad. Bruno will get you a stool and bring you a big mug of beer. And you, Michel, won't show your face here anymore tonight. Is that clear?"

Without another look at Michel, he led Benedikt into the tavern, the other boys following.

Michel watched them leave, his fury at the boys' lies giving way to anger at his father. He wants me out of his sight? he thought. Very well, I'll do him that favor. Michel had been treated like an unpaid servant in his own home, and he figured he couldn't do worse elsewhere. But first he'd have to find Marie.

Without another thought, he climbed the narrow back stairs to the small attic room he shared with his two younger brothers. There were three straw sacks in the room with thin blankets on them as well as several wooden hooks for their few clothes. Michel wrapped his spare articles of clothing in a blanket, knotting it into a bundle. Then he quickly searched inside his straw sack for a small hidden package that contained his savings of customers' tips that he had carefully pocketed without his father or brothers noticing. He tucked the little package under his shirt, tied up his straw sack, and threw the bundle over his shoulder, quietly leaving the room.

Fate seemed to be on his side, for he didn't meet anyone as he sneaked out the side door and through the narrow space between the tavern and the neighbor's house. But he didn't dare take a deep breath until he had passed the weary guards at the Rhine Gate and crossed the bridge. Nightfall was approaching, but since the cloudless sky promised bright moonlight, he decided to press on and follow Marie as long as possible. His father or brothers wouldn't come looking for him until morning, and by then he wanted to be so far away that they would give up their search.

One glance at the moon rising over the trees reminded him how quickly time was passing, and he hastened his steps. He strode along until his legs became as heavy as lead and his stomach started to growl.

By daybreak he was so tired that he crept into some underbrush by the roadside to take a quick nap. He had hardly closed his eyes, however, when he was overwhelmed by nightmares in which Marie was lying dead in front of him. Starting awake with a shout, he jumped up and decided to continue on his way despite his exhaustion. In a tavern he bought a cup of wine and a piece of cold roasted meat for a few pennies. He stayed there only as long as it took him to gulp down the food.

During the day he passed drivers and travelers on their way to Constance, but he didn't greet anyone, much less ask about Marie. If one of those men went to his father's tavern and recounted meeting Michel, his relatives would know where to find him.

Just before dusk, he saw two riders approaching. He recognized the two bailiffs who had taken Marie out of the city and went to them. The two men had drunk many mugs of his father's beer in the past, and they greeted him with surprise. "Hello, Michel. Where are you heading so late at night?"

"Greetings, Burkhard. Greetings, Hannes. Have you taken Marie far enough away?"

"Of course, Michel. She won't show up again in Constance any time soon." Michael looked at Michel intently. "Why do you ask? I don't suppose you're running after her?"

Michel seemed so embarrassed by the question that the two bailiffs started to laugh.

"Did the little hussy get your blood boiling, Michel? Forget it, I'm telling you. She isn't worth getting a good fellow like you in trouble."

Michel shook his head stubbornly. "Nevertheless, you could tell me which way she went."

Burkhard hesitated, but his companion didn't have to be asked twice. "We left her where the road branches off to Radolfzell, and from there she headed south, probably down toward the Rhine. The boatmen and carriage drivers are always glad to welcome a new whore. Godspeed, Michel." Then he spurred his horse on and rode away. Burkhard followed him, shaking his head.

"Why did you lie to the boy? You saw yourself that she was heading for Singen."

His companion shrugged. "Do you want Michel to make a fool of himself because of a harlot? I don't. Let him go to Radolfzell and down to the Rhine. By then he'll get over it. Besides, the boatmen know him and will bring him back to Constance. In three days at most the lad will be home again. His father will be grateful and treat us to a cup or two of wine."

"I wouldn't mind a drink in Guntram Adler's tavern. He brews the best beer in Constance." Burkhard decided to see Michel's father as soon as they arrived the next day.

Meanwhile, Michel forged ahead, filled with new hope. Just before sundown, he reached the crossing to Radolfzell and headed south. He had missed Marie by less than a half hour. When he had reached the town of Stein am Rhein after a strenuous march over the Schienerberg Mountains, people just responded by shaking their heads when he asked about her.

But Burkhard and Hannes were wrong. Michel did not turn back home, and though his father complained for a while about the thankless brat, he finally shrugged and tried to forget him. He had enough other sons and didn't need to shed any tears over the loss of one. Every so often, however, a customer would ask about the boy and remind them all of the day Marie Schärer had been banished and Michel Adler had run off looking for her.

X.

Earlier on, Matthis Schärer had made a decision. Ever since his daughter had been accused, he had not been able to think rationally, but now his mind had cleared again. Watching Marie being driven from town as she stumbled behind the bailiffs, he had realized that despite any possible misdeeds, she was still his daughter, and he wouldn't allow her to suffer any more than she already had. He decided to return home, hitch up the wagon, and go to her aid.

He would take her to a beautiful place where she could live in peace and forget the horrible events of the past few days. Inspired by these thoughts, he shook the hand of his brother-in-law, bade him farewell, and hurried back to his house with renewed vigor.

"Pack some clothes for Marie and tell Holdwin to hitch up the wagon," he called to Wina who, looking pale and terrified, had received him at the door. He was halfway up the stairs when he noticed that the housekeeper was still standing stiffly in the entryway.

"What's wrong with you?"

"The counselor. He's upstairs," she whispered, as if afraid Rupert might hear her.

Matthis Schärer's face turned crimson. His hatred for the man who had destroyed his daughter's life made him so angry that his world seemed to spin, and he gasped for breath. Lowering his head, he stomped up the stairs and saw Linhard ducking into the living room. Matthis ran over and stormed into the same room where less than twenty-four hours ago he had been celebrating the marriage contract with Rupert and his guests. Here he found Utz Käffli and the counselor sitting at his desk, drinking his wine from his silver cups. Linhard, looking like the very personification of a bad conscience, withdrew behind the back of the carriage driver, as if hoping for protection.

Rupert lay sprawled out in Matthis's favorite chair, sneering at him.

Schärer shook his fists. "What are you doing in my house? I won't tolerate a scoundrel like you here. Go! Get out! And take this scum along with you."

Picking up a piece of parchment from the table, the counselor handed it to Matthis calmly. "In your house? Since I expected a large dowry and a considerable inheritance from my marriage with your daughter, the bishop's court in Constance awarded me all your possessions for the offense I have endured because of you and your daughter, and also, of course, for the loss of the future inheritance. Tone your voice down, since you are now a guest in my house."

Suddenly Master Matthis comprehended the extent of the conspiracy to which he and Marie had fallen victim. Too late, he realized that his daughter had never had an inappropriate relationship with Linhard, Utz, or any other man.

Misery crashed over him like a suffocating wave. His innocent daughter had been thrown in the dungeon and brutally violated. Matthis remembered her cries of pain as she was being whipped, and he was consumed with hatred for the arrogant man now holding this paper under his nose, leaving him penniless. It appeared that Counselor Rupert Splendidus had planned this all with such devilish perfection that he, Matthis Schärer, would not even be able to give his only child a piece of bread, to say nothing of a future.

"Now I understand. Your intention from the start was to destroy me. Because of you, my daughter is now an outcast, homeless, and perhaps even dead."

Rupert laughed. "You can blame it all on yourself. You came running to me like a bee flies to honey and bragged all over town about what a wonderful son-in-law you were getting. Do you really think I would lower myself to the level of a daughter of a foolish social climber?"

He stopped there, because Matthis had seized him by the throat, choking him as hard as he could. The counselor was power-less against the unrestrained fury of the heavy man, and his face was already flushed when Utz hurried to his aid. The carriage driver punched Matthis twice in the face but was still unable to stop him. Finally he seized Matthis's right hand and tore it violently away from Rupert's neck.

Head throbbing, Matthis tried to push Utz away, but the carriage driver took this opportunity to hit Matthis repeatedly with full force. Matthis stared at him with bloodshot eyes, trying to say something even as the blows kept coming, but his voice no longer obeyed him. Suddenly he tipped over like a sack of flour and lay motionless on the floor.

Utz kicked him several times in the stomach. "Thank God! That took care of him."

While Linhard looked at his master with an open mouth and eyes wide in horror, Rupert massaged his neck and looked angrily at Utz. "He almost killed me. Couldn't you have intervened a little earlier, you fool?"

The carriage driver answered with a shrug, then shoved Matthis with the point of his boot. "What will we do with him?"

Counselor Rupert looked at the prone man in disgust and pointed toward the door. "Toss the fellow out into the street."

While the carriage driver bent down to pick Schärer up, Linhard rocked his head back and forth in doubt. "I don't know if that's a good idea, Herr Counselor. If the neighbors find him, the whole city will be gossiping, and that wouldn't be good for your reputation. Remember, he has relatives here who might bring charges against you. Do you remember Mombert Flühi?"

The counselor nodded. "You're right, Linhard. Drag him out to the shed, and see that he doesn't run away. No one must know what happened to Matthis Schärer. If anyone asks about him, say he left the city to look for his daughter."

Matthis Schärer lived for three more days; then this man, until recently one of the wealthiest citizens in Constance, was secretly buried in a pauper's grave.

PART TWO
BANISHED

I.

Marie felt as if she were going to die.

The pain in her back spread through her body to the tips of each little hair, making every move torture. All she wanted was to lie down in the cool shadow of some dense underbrush and wait for her end. But fear drove her on. On both sides of the road were fields and meadows, only occasionally broken by dry clumps of bushes offering no protection from prying eyes. She was afraid she would be attacked if she simply lay down within sight of the road.

After a while she reached a little wooded area. She was just settling down on a cool bank of moss when she heard the rippling sounds of a nearby brook. After slipping into the refreshing water, she stood up, drank her fill, and crept back toward the bank, exhausted. There she rolled herself up in a weeping willow whose low branches lay on the ground. For a few moments she listened to the wind in the trees and the chirping of the birds, and thought she had found the proper place to slip gently into the arms of death. But only the darkness of a deep sleep came over her.

At dawn she awakened, trembling with cold, and crept back to the brook to again quench her unremitting thirst. *Why doesn't God let me die?* she despaired. She felt a burning, unrelenting hunger, and struggled to her feet. Weak and dizzy, she staggered forward until, a short while later, a small village came into view. She approached the first house, a small cottage where a young boy clothed in filthy rags crouched, chewing on a hard crust of bread. Two days ago, Marie would have thrown such a dirty crust to the pigs, but at the moment it looked like a priceless delicacy. Pleading, she went up to the child and stretched out her hand. "Give me a bit of your bread. I'm dying of hunger."

The boy looked first at her, then at his bread, thinking. Just then, a woman came out of the cottage. Shouting, she ran up to Marie. "Isn't there any respite from beggars and riffraff? Get out of here!"

"Please give me a piece of bread," Marie whispered. "God will repay you."

The woman examined Marie's yellow robe and spat in disgust. "For someone like you, I have nothing. Leave, or I'll give you a good thrashing." When Marie didn't react at once, the woman bent down, picked up a rock, and cried for help.

Marie saw several other women and men appear with ominous looks on their faces, and she fled. After a short distance, she discovered a bush bearing a small clump of berries, which she picked and ate quickly. The taste only made her hungrier, however, and she despairingly wondered if she would ever find help.

Because of her last experience, she didn't dare enter a village again, and she hid as soon as she heard travelers approaching. She breathed a sigh of relief when she discovered a large estate lying some distance off the road. If poor farmers wouldn't give her anything, she would have to try appealing to the sympathy of the landowner.

Here, too, she had no success, as several mangy-looking dogs ran toward her, barking loudly as she reached the garden. She turned around and ran back toward the street, but the dogs attacked her, and she could feel their bites. Suddenly a loud, penetrating whistle called the dogs back, and they wandered off, whimpering.

Weeping silently as she walked, she felt as if her head were hovering far above her pained body. She could hardly remember who she was and why she was stumbling barefoot along the road. In a final burst of will, she staggered on until she reached the shadow of a beech tree, where she slid down against the trunk, resting her head on a soft bed of moss.

II.

A group of travelers, dressed in colorful clothing made of patched rags, moved slowly along the road to Singen. Leading the procession was a rickety covered wagon pulled by two mares and guided by a haggard-looking, middle-aged man with a short black beard. Two young boys walked alongside with stout clubs in their hands, looking around as if guarding a valuable cargo. The rest of the people followed the wagon on foot. It was a band of street performers called Jossi's Jugglers, on their way to the fair in Merzlingen, a small city between Singen and Tuttlingen. A handful of other travelers of low social standing accompanied them.

At the end of the procession came a tall woman named Hiltrud, her hair bleached blond by the sun. Around twenty-five years old, she was not especially beautiful, but she had a pleasant face and sparkling light gray eyes. Her wide brown skirt was decorated with yellow ribbons that fluttered in the breeze, and a yellow linen blouse fit tightly around her full, well-shaped breasts. Accustomed to walking barefoot, the woman stepped lightly over the sharp rocks in the road without wincing. With a thin switch she guided two large goats hitched to a small, fully packed cart.

Men continuously shot furtive glances her way, at which the other women in the procession would shout and scold them. Hiltrud paid no heed to either the lewd looks or the ugly remarks. Women traveling alone were easy prey for men, something she had learned from painful personal experience, so she had joined the larger group for personal security; it didn't trouble her that the other women jeered at her. Some of the female street performers with loose morals viewed her as undesirable competition, and others feared their husbands and sons would succumb to temptation and spend the little money they had on her. Yet hardly any of the men ever paid for her services, expecting her to spread her thighs as thanks for their taking her along.

Hiltrud observed the fat wife of the group's leader waddling along amidst her swarm of children, and she wondered scornfully what the woman would say if she knew that just the night before, her husband had demanded the price for his protection. Hiltrud hadn't even minded doing it, for unlike most men, Jossi was a considerate lover.

Suddenly the leader's eldest son stopped and pointed toward a tree. "Look, there's a dead woman lying beside the road."

Soon the entire group had gathered around the lifeless body. Even Hiltrud left her goats and came closer, curious. At that moment, Hiltrud noticed the girl's lips moving slightly, and she shook her head. "She's not dead yet."

While the troupe eyed her doubtfully, Hiltrud bent over the motionless figure. Despite the layer of dirt and the pained look on her face, it was evident that she was strikingly beautiful. Her yellow robe suggested she had been driven from one of the nearby cities, and judging by her bloodstained shirt that clung to her back when Hiltrud tried to lift it gently, the girl had been whipped mercilessly.

In general, the behavior of maids and women of the lower classes didn't attract much attention in the cities. If they got out of hand, they would quickly be put in a penitent's robe and chased out of town, but they weren't whipped until they were half-dead. Puzzled, Hiltrud glanced at the girl's hands. Such smooth, delicate fingers didn't belong to a maid or day laborer. The girl had to be the daughter of a well-to-do citizen or even a nobleman. That made the matter even more mysterious, since if the daughter of a rich family got into trouble, she would usually be quickly married off to a willing liegeman, or sent to a nunnery. Hiltrud was intrigued and felt sympathy for the girl.

"If she isn't dead yet, she will be soon. We can't do anything for her." Shrugging, the leader of the group turned away and climbed back onto the coach box of his wagon. The performers were about to move on, but Hiltrud couldn't make up her mind. Though the girl was no concern of hers, it was against her nature to leave someone helpless by the side of the road. As the leader mounted his horse and clicked his tongue, Hiltrud stepped in front of him.

"Please wait a moment, Jossi. I want to bring the girl along."

The bearded leader shook his head. "If we dawdle, we won't get a good place at the fair."

"Just a few minutes," Hiltrud pleaded.

"You can stay behind if you want to deal with the dirty whore." The leader's wife emphasized the word *whore* in order to offend Hiltrud.

Hiltrud had been the target of so many insults that by now they just bounced off her. Annoyed, she watched as the leader raised his whip and drove his draft animals forward without waiting to see if she would get out of the way. After a short glance at the unconscious girl, she stepped aside and turned to one of the younger men.

"Please help me load her onto my wagon. I'll care for her after we arrive in Merzlingen."

With his help, Hiltrud lifted the girl onto her wagon, but while she was still thanking him, the leader's wife turned around and sharply ordered him to come back.

Hiltrud smiled as she gently prodded her goats to move forward, but her laughter died away quickly when she saw that her animals couldn't pull the wagon's additional weight.. She had to tie a rope around the wheel shaft and hitch herself up to the wagon as well.

That's what you get for having a soft heart, she chided herself in silent thought. Now you can play the part of your own draft animal, and all because of a woman who will probably die this very night. With this luck, you'll have to bury her with your own hands and pay the priest a few pennies to say a blessing over her grave.

With every step she took, her mood worsened. It was an arduous job, pulling the wagon in this heat. To get her mind off her situation, she thought about what to do with the girl if she survived.

I could use a maid to help me pitch my tent and cook for me. Besides, she's a pretty lass who will attract customers. When she's able to work I'll get good money from the men.

Now greatly concerned with making sure the girl lived, Hiltrud stopped briefly at a brook, soaked a cloth in the water, and dampened the unconscious girl's cracked lips.

She arrived at the fairgrounds, still thinking about how the girl could help make her money. A number of tents and booths were already standing, while others were being set up. As she was looking for the best place to set up her tent, the Merzlingen fair supervisor headed toward her to collect the prostitute's fee. His look suggested he also intended a payment in services later. She just hoped he would bathe beforehand.

While counting out the coins Hiltrud had given him, he pointed at Marie. "What about her?"

"I found her alongside the road and brought her along. You can't ask me to pay the tax for her as well." Hiltrud was going to turn away, but it wasn't so easy to evade the city finance representative.

"Judging by her robe, she's a whore, so you have to pay two pennies for her, too."

Hiltrud sighed. "Come back tomorrow, and if she's still alive, you'll get your money."

The supervisor laughed and held out his hand. Hiltrud didn't know whether she was angrier about man's greed or her own soft-heartedness. She took out her purse with another sigh and looked until she found two Haller pennies instead of the good Regensburg ones. He accepted the inferior coins with a surly glance and left to collect fees from another arrival. Hiltrud let out a relieved breath and went to pick out her tent site.

Jossi's Jugglers had set up their tents in the shadow of some tall trees, and Hiltrud found a place not far away. She pulled her wagon over, unhitched the goats, and tied them to two pegs she hammered into the ground with a stone. In the process of unloading the unconscious girl by herself, her cart tipped over, spilling all her belongings on the ground. Hiltrud cursed under her breath but set up her tent quickly, as usual, then dragged the battered girl inside and laid her down on a blanket. She cast a glance at the hordes of men milling about outside who feigned interest in the merchants' stalls and the performers. In truth, most of them were eyeing the prostitutes and, after short negotiations, disappeared with them into their tents or in the bushes down by the river. A client approached Hiltrud and spoke to her, but she turned him away, shaking her head. He cursed, spat on the ground, and moments later went into another woman's tent.

Placing her hands on her hips, Hiltrud looked down at the unconscious girl. "Do you have any idea of all the trouble you're causing me? Because of you, I have to pass up offers, so see to it you stay alive and pay me back every penny!"

She took a kettle and left the tent to fetch some water at the river. Then she found some dry moss, grass, and twigs; set up her trivet in front of the tent; and lit a fire. While the water in the kettle was heating, she cut the robe from the girl's body, leaving the parts that were stuck to the girl's wounds untouched. When the water started to boil, she took part of the robe, dipped it in the steaming water, and carefully started loosening and removing the remaining scraps of cloth.

As Hiltrud concentrated on her good deed, a short, scrawny middle-aged man appeared at her tent. He wore clean, gray trousers, a brown waistcoat, and leather shoes with copper buckles. Finding the tent flap open, he noticed the battered woman.

"Hello, Hiltrud. Who is this you've picked up off the street?"

Looking peeved, Hiltrud turned around, but her face brightened when she recognized her visitor, Peter Herbmann. The apothecary was a regular customer who looked her up whenever she came to the fair. She liked him, as he paid well and was a gentle lover who treated her better than most men. For a moment she was afraid she might lose him as a customer if she refused him.

Herbmann didn't demand anything of her or turn away offended, but instead knelt down and examined the girl. Hiltrud was happy to see that his eyes passed indifferently over the girl's especially well-formed body, expressing only a mixture of deep sympathy, anger, and a certain professional interest at seeing the bloody patchwork of lashes on her back.

Hiltrud looked at him despairingly. "I found the child at the side of the road. It didn't seem right to leave her there, but now I don't know what to do. If she doesn't receive good treatment, she will die, and then I'll have trouble with the fair supervisor."

She loosened the rest of the bloody robe from Marie's back and reached for a pot of salve, but found it almost empty. Before she could spread Marie's back with the little that was left, the apothecary reached out to stop her. "You have to use something else. I'll go home and get some fresh ointment and bandages along with something for the fever."

Hiltrud breathed a sigh of relief. "Thanks for your help, Peter. This time I've taken on too much."

The apothecary smiled, trying to cheer her up. "I'll be right back. In the meantime, can you make some broth? We'll mix it with some of my herbs and give it to her to drink."

Hiltrud looked down at Marie skeptically. "She's not conscious, and I don't think we can get her to drink anything."

"Don't worry, I know how to treat sick people." He patted her hand reassuringly and hurried off. He returned shortly, carrying a basket containing a full pot of ointment, a bowl, and finely chopped herbs along with a bottle he was handling like a fragile treasure.

"I've distilled this essence from various medicinal plants. It cleans the wounds and promotes the healing process," he explained to Hiltrud as he opened the bottle and poured the strong-smelling liquid over a clean cloth. Then he knelt down and cleaned the dog bites and the bloody welts.

The apothecary turned and looked up. "This stuff burns like fire in open wounds, but it keeps the welts from becoming even more infected. If the girl were conscious, she'd be screaming with pain now."

Hiltrud shuddered. "Just the smell of it burns your throat. Are you sure it won't harm her?"

The apothecary smiled. "It will only help. I'll put salve on the open wounds so they can heal. By God, I've seen many men who've been whipped, but hardly any whose backs were so badly lacerated. Whoever did this to the poor child was a beast, not a human being."

Hiltrud watched as he tended the wounds with skillful hands. Then he turned the girl around, set her up with Hiltrud's help, and patiently gave her the herbal broth one spoonful at a time. Though the young woman was still unconscious, she swallowed the soup like an obedient child.

Looking at Hiltrud, the apothecary pointed at his patient's badly swollen lower regions. "I think she'll recover, but keep an eye on her. The child fell into the hands of real monsters."

Hiltrud was angry at herself for not noticing earlier that the poor girl had been not only whipped, but also raped. Often contending with lovers who didn't care whether they inflicted pain, Hiltrud always kept a tincture in her bags that she had prepared for this kind of injury. She fetched some and poured the shimmering green liquid over the girl's abdomen.

"There, that should suffice for now." The apothecary cast a seductive glance at Hiltrud and slipped his hand under her shirt. "I think I've earned a little reward."

Hiltrud looked at Marie, who was taking up more than half of the tent. "You'll have to help me move the girl to one side to make room. And please wait a moment. I'm sweaty and would like to wash up first."

"Yes, do that. I like that about you. You are always so clean, whereas other women . . ." The apothecary didn't complete his sentence, but Hiltrud understood. Many women in her line of work didn't pay the slightest attention to their personal hygiene. She, however, cared for her body and therefore had regular customers from the well-to-do classes at every fair.

Hiltrud filled a leather pouch with water from the river, hanging it between two tent poles. Then she closed the entrance flap and disrobed. The apothecary's eyes lit up at the sight of her naked body under the stream of water, and she could see he wanted to pull her down onto the blanket at once. Nevertheless, she took time to wash herself from head to foot before lying down next to him.

III.

When Marie first regained consciousness, she thought she was back home in her room with the warm sun and street sounds streaming in through an open window. Groping about, however, she realized she was lying undressed and facedown on a blanket in the grass. Shocked, she tried to sit up, but felt a searing pain so severe that she almost lost consciousness again. Her back had swollen into a hard shell, her abdomen was burning, and her entire body was so tense that she couldn't move a muscle without agony.

Her eyelids were stuck together, and she struggled to open them and look around. She was lying on a frayed blanket scented with lavender, while a lighter but equally shabby blanket was thrown over her. She noticed the tent was faded with age and dappled by the interplay of sunlight and tree shadows.

Slowly and carefully, she turned over, sat up, and discovered a woman occupying the rest of the tent. Sitting cross-legged on a threadbare, patched blanket, the woman was sewing a yellow robe. Though she was large, everything about the woman seemed harmonious. Her sun-bleached hair and deeply tanned skin showed she had spent a lot of time outdoors.

The stranger felt Marie's scrutiny, raised her head, and looked her over with a cold, severe stare. "So you finally woke up? I'm glad to see you're in pretty good shape."

Marie drew back uncertainly and stared at the stranger. "Where am I? And who are you?" Her voice sounded like the cawing of a raven.

"In my tent at the Merzlingen fair. My name is Hiltrud."

"I'm Marie. But we're in Merzlingen? That's a long way from home."

Hiltrud pointed at the remains of Marie's robe carelessly tossed in the corner. "It appears that you don't have a home anymore. If you don't mind, I'll just burn that thing, and for now you can wear this robe. I hope it fits, as I had to take it in without being able to get your measurements."

Marie stared in horror at the shapeless article of clothing in Hiltrud's hands, but simply asked, "How did I get here?"

"I found you alongside the road and brought you with me."

Marie lowered her head. "I wish you had left me there to die."

"Why? I can use a pretty maid." Hiltrud had no desire to make things easy for Marie. The sooner the girl came to terms with her fate, the better it would be for both of them.

Marie looked around apprehensively. Everything around her was shabby and worn, and the cloth of the robe was of such inferior quality that Elsa and Anne would have rejected it indignantly. "A maid? Who are you that you need a servant?"

Hiltrud held up one of the yellow ribbons on her skirt that indicated her status for all to see. "I'm a courtesan."

She was immediately annoyed that she had used the euphemistic expression instead of saying openly and honestly that she was an itinerant prostitute.

In any case, Marie understood. Her face twisted in an expression of disgust, and she staggered back toward the side of the tent. "You have sex with men in return for payment?"

Hiltrud shrugged. "I have to make a living somehow."

"But anything else is better than that, even begging!"

Hiltrud reached back into the corner to fetch what remained of the penitent's robe, and held it up to Marie's face. "Now listen to me carefully, child, and get these foolish notions out of your head. After this judgment, you are unfit to be among proper townspeople, considered to be less than the garbage they throw on the streets. Usually they forbid us from entering their cities and curse at us even when we're cold and dying of hunger, whipping us if we dare to sneak in."

Suddenly Marie saw herself tied naked at the stake, mercilessly exposed to the gazes of the crowd. She spilled out her entire horrifying story, moaning in pain as sobs shook her body.

Hiltrud reached for a cloth, dipped it in water, and washed Marie's face. Then she placed the cloth across the young woman's forehead. "Stay calm, or the fever will return. You can do nothing to change any of that now and will have to put up with your new life, such as it is."

Marie took a deep breath and squeezed Hiltrud's hand suddenly. "No, no, I don't believe I will. Father is certainly on his way here and won't permit that to happen. I'm sure he will arrive at any moment."

Hiltrud looked at her skeptically. "That would be nice for you."

"I'm sure he'll arrive in the next hour or so, and he'll certainly reward you generously for having saved me. Perhaps you'll no longer have to . . . to run around." Marie pointed at Hiltrud's yellow blouse.

Hiltrud had gathered from Marie's story that her father had not been especially energetic in standing up for her, but since she did not want to hurt the girl's feelings, she did nothing to spoil her illusions. "I have no objection if your father wants to pay me a few coins, since I haven't been able to earn any while caring for you."

Marie didn't reply because at that very moment the apothecary stuck his head into the tent. "Greetings, my love . . . Oh! Our little patient is awake. I told you she had strong, healthy blood in her veins." He smiled, looked at Marie, and asked her to turn around so he could examine her back.

Marie shook her head and defiantly wrapped the blanket tighter around herself.

Hiltrud laughed. "Oh, don't be so prudish. This is Peter Herbmann, a local apothecary and a good friend of mine who helped me care for you. He's a better healer than the learned doctors who talk about devils bringing on hellish vapors and give their patients filthy things to eat. As you can tell by his name, Herbmann, he knows every plant and root, and has studied their effects on illnesses of the body and soul. He only wants to look at your wounds."

Marie relented and allowed the apothecary to take the robe off her back and probe her wounds with his fingers with Hiltrud's help.

"Excellent!" he exclaimed. "You're healing very well. All I need to do is treat a few welts with my extract, and also the dog bites, where poisons may have gathered. Sink your teeth into the blanket, child, because it's going to hurt."

Marie grumbled reluctantly, but she was sure she would be immune to almost any pain after the torture she had suffered already. But when the apothecary took the elixir-soaked cloth and dabbed it on her back, her eyes immediately welled with tears. Before she could scream, however, Hiltrud pushed a gag into her mouth.

"Go ahead, bite down on this and be still! Do you want half the marketgoers to come running when they hear your shouts?"

Peter didn't stop for a moment. "Relax, child. It will be over soon. My elixir will make the wounds heal fast and not leave behind any ugly scars."

He put the bottle down, and Marie spat out the cloth. If she was going to live, she was at least happy she wouldn't be forever scarred. She looked suspiciously at the pot of ointment Peter had just picked up, but as he applied it to her back, she noticed that the paste soothed the pains. With a small sigh, she easily submitted to the rest of the treatment, and when Peter was finished, he gave her an encouraging slap on the back of her thigh and stood up. "Let's look at the rest of your wounds now. Please turn over."

Marie clenched her teeth tightly and let the apothecary examine her lower parts thoroughly. "You are healing well here, too, but it will just take a bit longer than your back. For this, Hiltrud has her own, very effective mixture of herbs, and I have also brought you an ointment that will prevent scarring of the wounds."

Hiltrud stroked her hair, trying to comfort her. "Now you have been taken care of. Do you think you can sit outside for a while? Lean back against my wagon and look around a bit."

"I'll try." Her knees were shaking, but with Hiltrud's help, she was able to stand up. The apothecary straightened out a cloth he had put on her back and helped Hiltrud pull the altered dress on over her shoulders. Reaching almost to the ground, it hung on her like a sheet, but the apothecary nodded his approval. "For the next few days, that's the right thing for you to wear. It's loose on your shoulders and doesn't put any pressure on the welts."

Marie shuddered and broke out in tears as she looked at the yellow color that prostitutes wore to announce their shameful profession to the world. Now everyone who saw her would consider her a depraved sinner that no priest would allow to step over a church threshold. She thanked Peter, though, as he and Hiltrud led her outside, sitting her down on a folded blanket by the wagon so she could listen to the wind moving through the trees. But when she saw Peter laughingly reaching inside Hiltrud's blouse, she quickly turned away.

That didn't help much, since she could still hear the indecent exchanges between the couple and sounds that made her shudder. Horrified, she put her hands over her ears, but then dropped them quickly as pain flashed through her cramping muscles.

Marie told herself she had no right to feel ashamed or condemn Hiltrud for her way of life. The woman certainly had not become a prostitute by choice; circumstance had forced her to it. Just the same, it was disturbing to be only a few steps away from a pair of copulating lovers. Physical love was something men talked about, but only when no woman was present and their tongues had been loosened by wine. Women weren't even supposed to think of intimate acts, and Marie had strived all her life to do what was expected of a modest virgin. She felt betrayed and angry that the world would now label her a whore.

To take her mind off her pain and the activity in the nearby tent, she looked around at her surroundings. Marie was familiar with the church fairs in Constance, where her father or Wina had taken her since she was a small child. She recalled stalls overflowing with tasty bratwurst sausages and sweet cakes, and her mouth watered as she remembered devouring them while listening to adults haggling over pots, cloth, or entire shipments of wine. She always yearned to watch the gaily dressed performers, but Wina considered them bad people who stole chickens and little children—people a decent young girl should avoid.

Here in Merzlingen, the stalls and tents looked just like those in Constance, yet everything was quite different. Marie saw ragged women and their children bathing openly in the river, shouting to one another in shrill voices, while a fat woman in strange, colorful clothing lit a fire not far from the shore and poured some watery dough into a pan.

Marie buried her face in her hands. She longed for her old, well-ordered world in which she was a woman who didn't have to commit a sin to earn her daily bread. Seizing on the thought that her father would come get her, she again told herself that it wouldn't be long before he arrived, as there weren't many roads from Constance to Singen. She'd ask him to buy Hiltrud a little house with a pasture, and enough goats to make an honest living. She would give alms for the salvation of her soul, and she'd also generously reward the apothecary. Then her father could take her away somewhere she could slowly forget all the bad things that had happened to her.

As Marie sat pondering her future, the apothecary left the tent with a satisfied smile. He waved briefly to her and then disappeared in the direction of the gray walls that extended along the far edge of the meadow.

Hiltrud's head appeared in the doorway. "You can come back in, Marie. Would you like some breakfast? You like goat's milk, don't you?"

"I don't know . . . probably." Only now did she notice that the good smell of the fritters had made her hungry. As she tried to stand up, however, everything started spinning, and she sank to the ground in pain.

Hiltrud put a sheet over her, lifted her up, and led her into the tent. She helped her stretch out on the sheet, then took out two cups and left to milk the goats. When she returned, she was holding the cups of milk along with two leaf-wrapped fritters she had bought.

"Sleep a little while. You'll have to go outside again soon, as the first customers come at noon at the latest," Hiltrud told her between mouthfuls. "I've got to earn a lot of money if I want to survive the winter. I'll make a comfortable place for you under the willows so you can rest in the shade."

Marie had a lump in her throat. She regretted being such a burden on Hiltrud and at the same time was ashamed to eat bread that had been earned immorally. Her stomach didn't share her concerns, however, and only shouted for more. She clenched her teeth and asked Hiltrud for another cup of milk.

The tall woman left the tent and soon returned with half a cup of milk. "That's all the milk the goats have to give today, but you can help yourself to some water from the kettle. It's from the spring outside."

"I didn't want to drink all your milk," Marie whispered. "Thank you very much."

"You're welcome. I can't let you waste away, or you won't get any better."

Hiltrud stood up and fastened the tent flap on a crossbar. "Now, I've got to see if any worthwhile men come by."

Marie stared at her. "Why do you do this, anyway? With your strength, you could surely get some other kind of work."

Hiltrud shook her head. "No housewife would employ a prostitute as a maid, if only out of fear for the morals of her husband and her sons."

"How did you become a courtesan?" Marie couldn't bring herself to say "prostitute."

"My father sold me to a brothel owner when I was thirteen," Hiltrud replied without bitterness. "I worked there almost ten years until I'd saved enough to buy my freedom. Now I'm a wandering whore without a home, but at least I am my own mistress."

Tears came to Marie's eyes. "I'm sorry."

"Why? It's not your fault." Hiltrud saw a number of men dressed in city clothes approaching, and quickly put the cups away. "You've got to go outside again. These fellows look like the kind I can do business with." Without waiting for Marie's reply, she stood up and walked toward the men, swinging her hips.

Marie pulled herself up on a tent pole and staggered out. Her head started spinning again, but she wanted to get as far away as possible from the tent and the noises that would soon come from inside. First she clung to a tree, but she then walked slowly toward one of the willows along the shore. Looking back, she saw that Hiltrud had come to terms with one of the men, and Marie prayed to the Virgin Mary for her father to rescue her from this nightmare. But once again, her prayers were not answered.

IV.

As evening approached, wine was passed around, the men became boisterous, and Hiltrud was busier than ever. She was sorry that Marie was unable to work. Together they could have done a brisk business. The news that Hiltrud had picked up a beautiful girl at the side of the road dressed in a penitent's robe had made the rounds, firing the imagination of a number of men, and many customers had asked about Marie. To silence the persistent queries, Hiltrud had announced loudly that the girl was unable to work yet due to her injured back.

Marie was sitting outside again beside the wagon, because she was safer there than under a lonely tree. When she heard the sound of a man's moaning inside Hiltrud's tent, she put her hands over her ears. To escape the sounds, she stood up and joined the crowd of fairgoers, but the reaction of the people around her quickly made it clear that she was an outcast. Honorable women pulled in their skirts and drew back upon seeing her, shielding their children's eyes as she passed, and scolding the husbands who stared at her brazenly or tried to approach her. It was quite different from strolling through a marketplace, protected by a loving, generous father, while acknowledging the polite greetings of neighbors and sampling the delicacies that she could now look at longingly only from a distance.

Seized with fear, she hurried back to the outskirts of the market and soon discovered the tree where Hiltrud's goats were tied up. Along the way, she had passed a stand where an older man was selling fresh and dried fruit dipped in honey. It smelled so wonderful that her mouth watered, but as she had no money, she hurried past. She didn't get very far, as the owner of the stand ran after her and took her by the arm. "Don't you want a pear dipped in honey, girl?"

"I can't pay for it." Marie hoped he'd let her go, but instead he pulled her so close that their faces almost touched.

"I won't take any money from a pretty child like you. Come into the bushes with me, and I'll give you the best pear I have," he replied, shoving his hand down her dress. The shock was so great, it gave Marie the strength to pull back and run away.

To her relief, the man didn't follow but just shouted after her. "What's the matter with you? You're the little hussy who came with Hiltrud. If you want a pear, you'll have to earn it."

Marie shook herself and stumbled on until she arrived back at the tent, where she put her hands over her face. Did morals and commandments of the church mean so little outside city walls that they could be sold for a piece of fruit dipped in honey? Now she understood why her father had forbidden her as of her twelfth birthday from playing in the meadows outside the city walls anymore, or why he hadn't allowed her to leave the house without supervision. He really had watched over her carefully, at least until he had been so blinded by the counselor's enticing marriage proposal that he had thrown all caution to the wind, opening the way for slanders and lies.

Her former fiancé's face popped into her mind. It was strange how quick Rupert had been to believe her accusers. The more she thought about it, the more she realized it was his quick condemnation that had made the abuse possible. Linhard, Utz, and Hunold couldn't possibly have acted on their own, nor would Euphemia have committed perjury unless it was at someone's urging. She thought of Rupert's thin, self-controlled face. Even while courting her, he had never cast a friendly glance at her; indeed, he had entirely avoided looking at her. All the evidence suggested he had been the instigator, and the other four his accomplices. Though Marie couldn't understand why the man had ruined her life, by now she was firmly convinced he had purposely brought this misfortune down upon her. She could only hope her father would be able to explain everything to her when he picked her up the next day.

V.

Over the course of the following days, Marie avoided the stalls, instead sitting beside the road to Constance, keeping an eye out for her father. She wrapped herself in a blanket to hide her yellow robe. Hiltrud permitted it, as the girl seemed out of danger there and Hiltrud needed her tent for her steadily increasing flow of customers.

Due to the fine weather, an unusually large number of people visited the Merzlingen fair, and wagon drivers kept arriving with new goods far into the bright, moonlit nights. While the women looked at fabrics, pots, and other useful things, spending most of their time haggling over prices, the men cast lewd glances into the prostitutes' tents, examining what was available there. Despite growing competition, Hiltrud's attractive appearance and high standards of personal hygiene kept her in demand, and she was doing well.

On the last day of the fair, as the merchants started taking down their stands, Hiltrud sat down next to Marie. "Tomorrow I'm moving on. You should join me."

Marie shook her head emphatically. "I want to stay here and wait for my father. He'll be here sooner or later."

Annoyed, Hiltrud shook her finger at Marie. "You must be mad. What are you going to live on?"

"If necessary, I'll go begging."

"Oh, you will?" the other woman scoffed. "Do you know what that means? For the townspeople, you're nothing but a nuisance to be run out of town. And if you think begging will protect you from men's violence and impulsive behavior, you're wrong. And a pretty, young girl like you will attract every lecherous young fellow around, the way sweet fruit attracts wasps. The almsgiver in the monastery will drag you off into the hay as well as the stable boy at the inn where you go to beg."

Marie lowered her head and chewed on her lip. "My father will come," she repeated stubbornly. "At the latest, he'll be here tomorrow."

Hiltrud sighed when she saw the girl's pleading eyes. "Very well, I'll stay with you until the day after tomorrow. That's when a group of wagons will be leaving for Trossingen early in the morning. Their leader, Ulrich, is a decent fellow, and for the protection he can offer, I'm glad to spread my legs for him."

Tears welled up in Marie's eyes at Hiltrud's offer. "When my father comes, you'll never have to sell yourself again, I promise you."

Hiltrud pursed her lips and stared into the distance. Marie could sense her skepticism and felt her clinging hopes starting to vanish, giving way to a terrible emptiness. She no longer knew what to do. She knew that if she stayed with Hiltrud, she would have to take men into her tent sooner or later.

Marie shrugged and wrapped the blanket more tightly around her shoulders. "Yesterday, Erich, the spice trader, asked me if I'd like to work for him. He told me he had a cabin near Meersburg, where one of my father's houses is located. Perhaps I should go with him and have him send my father a message."

Hiltrud looked at her incredulously and began to laugh. "You're such a fool, Marie. Erich has a wife and a huge number of children he'll go back to in the winter. He'll use you, beat you just because he likes to, and finally sell you to someone else. If you work for one of these men, you'll have to do everything he asks without knowing when he'll toss you into the street without a cent. I must say, I prefer having them as customers. If one of them abuses me or smells too bad, I throw him out of the tent."

Marie stared at her, shocked. "Do you mean Erich, that friendly fellow, wants me to . . ." she stuttered.

"You can bet your life on that. He won't let such a tasty morsel as you slip away from him. Do you know how many offers I've had for you? Good Lord, girl, the fellows have only left you alone because you belong to me. Everybody knows I can be really mean when I'm crossed."

"I don't understand that. Why are they afraid of you?" A wicked smile passed across Hiltrud's face. "A few years ago, a coachman raped and strangled a young prostitute who was traveling with me and a few other courtesans, and he was never prosecuted. A few weeks later, he got into an argument with a Swiss mercenary, and in the ensuing fight he was killed. Only shortly before that, my companions and I had each invited the Swiss mercenary to our tents and pampered him for hours."

Lost in thought, Marie silently followed Hiltrud into the tent.

The next morning, many people left the meadow. The merchants packed their wares, hitched themselves or their scrawny mares up to their wagons, and moved out, along with the performers. Jossi walked past Hiltrud, looking questioningly at her. Since she was making no preparations to take down her tent, he shrugged reluctantly and gave his people the signal to leave.

By noon, Hiltrud's tent stood all by itself in the meadow, the surrounding grass faded yellow and trampled down where the tents and stalls had stood. The silence was oppressive. Shortly after the church bells pealed two o'clock, a bailiff from the city appeared and gruffly asked what the two were still doing there. To Marie's relief, he was satisfied with Hiltrud's explanation that they would leave for Trossingen the next day with Ulrich's wagon train.

Late in the afternoon, Peter Herbmann came by to have one last look at Marie's slowly healing wounds, nodding his satisfaction. "Very good, my child. The welts are healing and will probably not leave any scars." The apothecary smiled at Marie and pointed to a bundle he had brought along. "I packed a few articles of clothing for you that were in my attic. They belonged to my wife who has recently put on so much weight, she'll probably never look at them again. But they'll surely fit a slender girl like you."

"Thank you, Peter. You're a wonderful person." Hiltrud kissed his cheek and reached for the bundle. "I'll sew yellow harlot's ribbons on them right away so no one can object that Marie is wearing respectable clothing."

"Must you do that?" Marie wasn't pleased that she'd be publicly branded a prostitute.

Hiltrud snorted angrily. "If we don't do that, none of the wagon drivers will take us along, and if we travel alone, we'll be the victims of every mob of men we meet. Now would you please leave us alone, Marie? I'd like to say good-bye to Peter. Take your time as it may be a while."

Marie left the tent quietly and wandered across the deserted meadow to the road, where she sat down in her accustomed place and watched the many travelers still streaming past. For the most part they were people leaving Merzlingen, returning to their hometowns or heading to the next market. Only a few were heading into Merzlingen. Marie looked at everyone carefully, but neither her father, Uncle Mombert, nor anyone else she knew was among them.

Long after nightfall, she was still sitting at the side of the road with the cool night air stinging her legs and feet. Overwhelmed by disappointment, she couldn't understand why her father had abandoned her. Then it occurred to her that he couldn't know where Hiltrud had taken her. Perhaps he was looking for her down by the Rhine or had taken a road elsewhere. But sooner or later he would surely pass by.

What would happen if she went to Trossingen with Hiltrud? That city was across the Danube, and her father would never think to look for her there. On the other hand, according to everything Hiltrud and the apothecary had told her, she couldn't stay by herself. Even though it horrified her every time Hiltrud took a client into her tent, the woman was the only person she could depend on for help. Even Peter Herbmann could do nothing more for her, as his wife ran a tight ship. Marie really had only one choice: she had to go along with Hiltrud.

Suddenly she smiled. Her situation was not really all that bad. In the course of his examination of her wounds, the apothecary had told her she'd have to wait two weeks before her body would be healed enough so that she could sleep with men. At the time, his assumption that she would become a prostitute had angered her, her anger springing perhaps from fear that she might have no choice if she was to survive. But she realized now that by then her father would certainly have found her or she would meet a merchant who could take a message to him so he'd finally know where to look for her.

Her spirits briefly raised, they were suddenly dashed again when she realized she might meet someone who had witnessed her whipping. She wasn't sure she had the courage to approach someone from Constance, and her mood wavered between the hope of being rescued and the hopelessness of her situation, until she no longer knew what to think. Returning to the tent, she lay down without saying a word.

Hiltrud bent over her to wish her good-night and saw that Marie was silently sobbing, overcome with sadness. She wanted so much to help the girl, but she knew there were no words to ease her inner pain, so Hiltrud just pulled the girl close and held her.

The next morning, Marie and Hiltrud took down the tent and packed it loosely onto the wagon so that it would dry in the sun. After a scanty breakfast of goat's milk and dry bread, they hitched up the goats and silently strolled down to the road.

It wasn't long before a line of covered wagons appeared, each pulled by six strong oxen and with wheels almost as tall as a man. Hiltrud cleverly returned the drivers' grins and suggestive gazes cast in their direction. But the grim-looking armed guards who were protecting the train of wagons from robbers snorted and turned away, showing no interest in the two women.

Hiltrud went to greet the leader, a middle-aged, sturdily built man wearing the simple but durable clothing of a traveling merchant.

"Here we are, Ulrich, and thank you again for allowing us to come along with you."

Ulrich Knöpfli glanced derisively at the team of goats. "You'll have to hurry to keep up with us. We won't stop and wait for you along the way."

"Don't worry. We won't hold you up." Hiltrud laughed, tossing the towing rope over her shoulders in order to help her goats, and took her place at the rear of the procession.

VI.

Though dusk had not yet completely given way to night, sparks from the campfires flew through the sky like tiny shooting stars before vanishing into the darkness. Marie propped her head on her knees and couldn't help thinking how quickly her former life had vanished as well. She glanced at the four other prostitutes sitting around the fire, casting their flickering shadows into the grass. Hiltrud seemed as serene and calm as always as she held a stick into the fire with a piece of dough wrapped around the point.

When the crust had turned black, she broke off a piece and handed it to Marie. "Here's your share."

"Thanks." Marie reached out for it, then sucked in her breath. The piece was still glowing hot, so she juggled it back and forth between her hands while it cooled. The bread consisted only of flour and water, but Marie gulped it down hungrily. Aside from a cup of goat's milk that morning, it was the first meal she'd had that day, as the procession stopped only when the animals needed to drink.

Ulrich Knöpfli had wanted to reach the inn before nightfall, and now he sat inside the brightly lit tavern with other higher-class merchants and travelers while the wagon drivers and servants were drinking wine in the courtyard. Since Hiltrud and Marie were turned away with indignant looks, they set up their tents near a hawthorn hedge outside the gate where they were soon joined by these three other women.

While Marie was licking the last bread crumbs from her fingers, she observed the three strangers who, like Hiltrud, had been on the road for years. In recent days, she had begun to understand what it meant to be a wandering outcast, and she wondered how the women could tolerate such a life. On this short trip, they were not admitted into cities or inns, so they had to sleep outdoors or in Hiltrud's tent somewhere among the bushes and trees, protected from prying eyes only by the foliage.

A couple days earlier in Tuttlingen, Marie had been confronted with yet another kind of danger. A fat, bald man had approached them and warmly invited them to his inn. Laughing at the man, Hiltrud told him she had no desire to fall into the clutches of a brothel owner. In a rage, the man left and reported them to the city bailiff who then confronted them at their tent site with rude threats. That night, in the dark and in a rainy drizzle, they had to take down their wet tent and move it away from the city and down to the wetlands along the Danube where swarms of mosquitoes hovered.

Marie now looked around the campfire at the other women, assessing each one in turn. Pretty and quiet Fita, the youngest at just over twenty years old, had brown hair and freckles sprinkled over her nose and cheeks. She had been a housemaid for a well-to-do master craftsman who took advantage of her regularly. When she got pregnant, his wife denounced her to the priest as a whore and demanded strict punishment. The pious man of God saw to it that Fita was whipped and branded on both shoulders. Marie had seen the scars when she and Fita were bathing at the brook. Even though the marks had faded over the years, they still looked dreadful.

Fita's chubby traveling companion, Berta, a small woman with a round, red face and short black hair, had an easier past and was quite happy with her life. She always brought the conversation back to herself and only ever talked about her experiences with men, using expressions that made Marie blush. Her body was her business capital, her investment. Nevertheless, by her own admission, she wasn't especially fussy about her clients. Judging by her odor, she wasn't too concerned about cleanliness, either. Though only a little older than Hiltrud, she already seemed spent.

The third woman, Gerlind, was the oldest of the group. She had broad, matronly hips, but her face was as smooth as a young woman's. Only a full gray head of hair that reached to her hips revealed her age. Clearly proud of how good she still looked, she took care of herself. Hiltrud treated her with shyness and respect since Gerlind knew the secrets of many herbs and how to prepare healing drinks and tinctures and, as Hiltrud told Marie in a hushed voice, had even more experience in it than Peter Herbmann.

Berta, who was just telling another story, overheard Hiltrud's remark about Gerlind's herbs. "I could have used her potion to have been spared my four pregnancies. The poor little ones didn't live very long. But I'm not complaining, because I'm glad I have the stuff now. I shudder when I think of the poor things in the city brothels who have to spread their legs for everyone from the village policemen to the dean of the cathedral, and have a kid every year. I'm glad to live freely and independently."

Turning away, Fita waved dismissively. "I'd give almost anything to serve a master again who fed me twice a day and gave me a roof to sleep under. I hate this life."

Berta looked at her in disbelief. "What's so bad about being a wandering whore? We're our own bosses and do what we please. If we want to move to Bohemia or the Rhine, we just do it. We are better off than the oh-so-honorable wives who are defenseless against their husbands. There's no point getting worked up over these silly thoughts."

Despairingly, Fita raised her head. "I keep thinking about how it used to be, and it torments me that I must sin every day to survive."

Berta burst out in unkind laughter. "If you can't stand that men sard you, then you'll have to kill yourself."

Fita folded her hands as if in prayer. "People who kill themselves don't make it into heaven, and I don't want to take away my hope of making it there. God knows how I'm suffering, and didn't Jesus accept Maria Magdalene even though she was a whore?"

While the women continued their animated conversation, one of the carriage drivers exited the inn and looked at them. Berta stood up and headed toward him, swinging her hips. The others watched as she exchanged a few words with the man and then disappeared with him into the bushes.

Gerlind shook her head disapprovingly. "Berta makes it too easy and doesn't mind violating all the rules. She'll regret that someday."

Marie, who had been listening quietly, turned to her. "What rules?"

Surprised at Marie's ignorance, Gerlind raised her eyebrows. "The unwritten ones that make it easier for us to survive. In marketplaces, we're all competitors, and it's fine for Berta to approach any man there. But when we're traveling together, we make sure any eager man takes the one of us who has had the hardest time recently. This time it was Fita's turn."

"It's to make sure each of us has enough money," Hiltrud added. "Fights would break out if one or two women had to go hungry while the rest had enough to eat. If we get together in larger groups when we travel, we don't have to beg merchants or other group leaders to let us join them. We're pretty safe traveling about in groups of five." It sounded like an order to the other three.

Gerlind looked Marie up and down skeptically. "I wouldn't have any worries about you, Hiltrud. But what about your companion? She's not one of us."

"Marie is a poor child who was brutally raped and so badly injured, she will need a week or two to fully heal. As soon as she recovers, she'll work just like us."

Marie shuddered at Hiltrud's words. She would never do that, she thought. At the same time, her stomach cramped with fear that her father wouldn't find her and she would have no choice but to end her life in the next river. The water would certainly treat her more mercifully than people.

While Marie tried to come to terms with her fate, the other women discussed what to do next. Fita sided with Marie, seeing a kindred soul. Gerlind hesitated before finally giving a halfhearted promise.

"Let's wait and see what Berta has to say. Unless she has any objections, let's stay together at least to the next market."

Marie seemed dubious. "Isn't it dangerous if we travel without the protection of a group?"

"With five of us, it's worth a chance. After all, we're not defenseless little rabbits." Gerlind held up her walking stick, showing Marie the iron tip. "I can use this like a spear, Berta has a cleaver, and Fita carries a dagger under her skirt. We can certainly fight off pushy beggars or a few robbers."

"I told you, child, that courtesans are not helpless." Hiltrud smiled, pulling an ax out of her belongings. "Is this good enough for you? After all, you've already cut wood with it."

Just then, Berta returned to the fire, looking breathless and disheveled. As she stepped into the light of the campfire and looked into her hand, she flew into a rage. "Such a son of a bitch! Bangs me like a mad rabbit and cheats me out of the promised amount."

"You should have had him give you the money first," Gerlind replied dryly.

"He did show me the money, but in the darkness I couldn't see he was slipping me those cheap Hallers instead of the Regensburg pennies we'd agreed on." Berta snorted angrily and held the coins out to Gerlind.

"The first thing a prostitute has to learn," Gerlind replied, "is to check the coins with her fingertips. You were just too greedy, and I think it serves you right. It was actually Fita's turn."

Marie was silent and fought back her tears. Gerlind and Fita were very nice, but she dreaded having to travel with Berta, who perfectly matched a respectable citizen's image of a wandering prostitute. She was dirty, mean, and clearly thought only of herself. Ironically, it would be up to her to decide whether Marie and Hiltrud could join the three others. Ulrich's wagon train wasn't headed toward a market, and Hiltrud was worried about their safety without a group.

Gerlind looked at Hiltrud and smiled while poking the fire's embers until the flame rose high enough to illuminate their faces. "Hiltrud just proposed that the five of us continue on together. In the next few days there will be a number of fairs down the Danube as far as Ulm where we can earn good money."

Marie admired Gerlind's cleverness. She had brought up the proposal of traveling together without making Hiltrud look like she was pleading for it. Thinking it over, Berta put a few more branches on the fire. "I thought we were heading toward the Rhine. Hiltrud and Marie can come that far with us."

Gerlind sighed with relief, and Marie could see she was happy to have settled the matter without an argument. She looked at Hiltrud innocently, as if she had no ulterior motives. "What do you think of Berta's suggestion?"

"It's perfect! You can always make money in the harbors along the Rhine." Since Hiltrud had never really planned to travel along the Danube, she eagerly agreed.

"Very well, let's stay together." Berta nodded as if she had just gotten her way with the whole group, then stretched out her arms, yawning loudly. "I'm dog tired. Let's go to bed."

Fita looked around anxiously. "Wouldn't it be a good idea for one of us to stand guard? The men over there sound drunk, and frankly, I'm afraid of them."

Hiltrud nodded. "I agree. I wouldn't put it past those fellows to play a dirty trick on us."

"Marie, you're first," Gerlind announced, assuming the role of group leader. "She'll wake up Fita. Then it will be Berta, then me. Hiltrud can take the morning watch."

None of the women objected. Marie took the stick that Gerlind held out to her to defend herself if necessary. Since the weather was good, none of them had pitched their tents. Instead, the other four wrapped themselves in their blankets and lay down close together by the campfire in a place offering a good view of the inn's front door.

From time to time Marie stoked the fire with pieces of the half-rotted tree trunk that she and Fita had found in the nearby forest just before dark. For once she tried not to think about her dreadful experience in Constance. The memories were always lurking just below the surface, ready to burst forth and torment her. To take her mind off them, she looked at the sleeping women who would now be her traveling companions.

She already knew what she thought of Berta—she didn't trust her. The woman was only looking out for herself and seemed to actually enjoy being a wandering harlot. Fita, on the other hand, viewed her life as a sort of worldly purgatory, hoping that her suffering would earn her eternal salvation. According to Berta's snide remarks, the young woman contributed most of her earnings to the offertory boxes in the few churches open to them on market days. Since Fita wasn't a very shrewd prostitute and attracted fewer customers than the others, she often had to go hungry or accept customers who paid her with only a bag of flour or stale bread. Marie wondered if Fita welcomed these deprivations as a way to hasten an early death.

Gerlind was hard to classify. She was witty and had a dark sense of humor, but at the same time, she treated others coolly. Well over forty, she seemed still to have life in her, perhaps because she earned her living less from prostitution than from the elixirs and ointments she prepared from the various plants that she gathered. Indeed, other prostitutes paid her a small fortune for her medicine against unwanted pregnancies, since fat bellies drove away customers, weakened women physically, and burdened them with more cares if the children survived.

Fita suddenly became restless. She lifted her head, looked up at the stars, and threw off her blanket. "Go to bed, Marie. I'll take over the watch, as I can't sleep anyway."

Marie threw another stick on the fire in order to get a better look at Fita. "Surely not even half an hour has passed yet."

"More like a whole hour." Fita spread a handful of leaves on the fire and watched as the flames licked their way through them. Smiling sadly in the flickering red light, she seemed resigned, as if even purgatory would be a welcome relief from her current fate.

Marie pulled her blanket tighter around her shoulders, as a cool wind had come up. "I can't sleep, either. Perhaps we can talk a little to pass the time."

Fita demurred at first, but then let her hand drop and nodded. Marie moved closer to her and stared into the flames. After a while, Fita patted Marie on the hand.

"They ran you out of town in a penitent's robe as well, didn't they?"

Marie nodded. "Yes, but I don't know how it came to that. The evening before, I had gone to bed with the certainty of appearing before the altar as a bride the following morning, but that night I was dragged to a dungeon and robbed of my virginity. The next day, I was condemned as a whore, whipped, and chased out of my hometown. It was . . . No, it still is a nightmare without an end."

"A nightmare . . . That's how it seems to me as well, even though I must say, in my case it wasn't quite so unexpected."

In contrast to Marie, Fita's soft voice seemed to harbor no feelings of hatred. "There was nothing I could do about it. The master was so much stronger than I, and he took advantage of me as if he had every right to. Perhaps he did, because when I complained at home, my parents scolded me and told me not to be so prissy. The master's wife was harsh with me, but she let her husband do what he wanted."

Fita sighed, relaying how her mistress had taken her to court. "I suffered the full force of her anger and jealousy when I became pregnant. She must have hated me for the full belly her husband gave me while she was running to church every day, begging the Mother of God for a child that never came. But how was that my fault? The court condemned me for immorality and ordered the bailiff to be strict with me."

Fita stared at her intently. "Do you know what that means?"

"No."

"First they branded me with an iron, then beat me with no consideration for my pregnancy, and that's how I lost the child. All I could see was that it was a boy. The priest overseeing my beating said the child would go to hell anyway, so my baby was buried without being baptized. But I'm sure God took my little fellow into heaven, for he was the most innocent of us all."

Rocking his imaginary form in her arms, Fita continued to speak of the boy as if she were watching him frolic through heavenly fields. Marie realized that she lived only to atone for her unbaptized child and prepare her own way into the heavenly kingdom.

As Marie listened to Fita's life story, she envied her piety. Fita still believed in God's goodness and found consolation in prayer. But what would she herself have if her father didn't find her soon? She had lost her faith, even as she continued calling upon the Virgin Mary, begging her to send an angel to guide her father to her and release her from shame. But her prayers were empty words that gave her no hope.

Marie realized that miracles no longer happened in this world. She had heard many people say that all misfortune had been caused by the three men who had each declared themselves pope, fighting over which of them was Christ's true vicar on earth. This was a time of the devil and his demons, turning men into animals and making them violate all the commandments of God. Until just a short time ago, Marie hadn't taken an interest in this talk, but she was now convinced that people were right.

Suddenly Marie recoiled from these thoughts. She couldn't continue down this path. But she didn't want to end up like Fita, nor did she want to take her own life voluntarily. She knew that it wasn't easy for her father to follow her path, as she had already traveled a great distance and he couldn't know she had fallen in with a group of wandering harlots. In her heart, however, she firmly believed that her father would save her in time.

VII.

They spent the next day on the road and reached another inn shortly before nightfall. A simple fence surrounded the large front yard, and inside it many freight coaches stood around. The wagon drivers had already secured their loads and were sitting, relaxing in a circle.

Since the front part of the inn was not surrounded by a wall, there was no fortified gate and no servants to keep undesirables away, so Berta had been able to run ahead and easily approach the men. As her traveling companions came nearer, they saw that she was already shaking off the straw clinging to her from her roll in the hay with her first customer, and she came forward to meet them, waving cheerfully.

"We can earn good money here. There are two large wagon trains, one from Constance and one from Stuttgart."

"From Constance, you say?" Marie asked in a trembling voice. Without waiting for Berta's reply, she hurried over and looked around, seeing a wagon bearing the sign of a business she knew from home. Scrutinizing all the men sitting at tables relaxing and drinking their wine out of simple wooden cups, she hoped to see a familiar face. Perhaps she could learn something here about her father—or possibly, he might even be here himself. She soon spotted a man who seemed familiar even though he was sitting with his back toward her. For a moment she hesitated, but when he turned around to answer another guest's question, she was shocked and ducked back into the shadow of a freight wagon. She looked out again more carefully and realized she hadn't been mistaken. It was Utz Käffli.

Marie wrapped her arms around herself and doubled up with the pain that suddenly shot through her abdomen. The sight of the filthy man in his shabby coachman's uniform terrified her, and though she felt like running away, she stayed in the hope of learning something about her father.

Since Berta, Gerlind, and Fita had attracted the attention of the wagon drivers, nobody paid her any mind, not even Hiltrud, who had quickly tied her goats to the fence and also joined the men. So as not to be noticed, Marie stepped behind one of the shelters open on three sides where draft oxen and servants spent the night. Darkness was falling fast, concealing Marie from the gazes of others while she herself could see what was going on in the firelight.

She watched as Hiltrud came to terms with a well-dressed, middle-aged man and followed him under the canvas of a freight wagon. Fita was dragged off into the darkness by a heavily built man, and another coachman tried to grab Berta, but Utz got there before him and pulled the plump woman to him with a triumphant grin. Soon Gerlind had also found a customer and disappeared with him behind one of the large wagon wheels while the other drivers jealously looked on.

Visibly satisfied, Utz returned to his seat. Marie crawled back to the freight wagon and hid behind a wheel. She had to know what happened in Constance after she left, but under no condition did she want this devil to see her. The presence of the man who had slandered her and raped her prevented her from trusting anyone here, since he would turn anything she said against her and just add to her misery. Thus she had to be satisfied with what she was able to overhear.

Unfortunately, the wagon drivers only talked about everyday concerns and news they had picked up along the way. Their conversation soon turned to politics, and they discussed each of the three popes' having excommunicated the other two, sending their supporters with armies of mercenaries to fight and weaken their opponents, with no consideration for their believers who were thus embroiled in hopeless confusion.

Marie cared little about this matter and was afraid she wouldn't learn anything about her father. Just as she was about to leave and search for a half-safe place to sleep for the night, the well-to-do man who had been with Hiltrud returned, sat down with the Constance wagon drivers, and drank with them to the success of their trip. Judging by his clothing, Marie thought him a merchant who owned some of the goods in the caravan coming from Stuttgart and hoped he would change the topic of conversation. Indeed, he soon turned to Utz, who was the leader of the other wagon train.

"You're coming straight from Constance, so you must know the merchant Matthis Schärer, don't you?"

Utz grumbled something incomprehensible into his unkempt beard and nodded grudgingly.

The merchant didn't seem to notice Utz's deprecatory manner, as he smiled with relief. "Matthis Schärer ordered several wagon-loads of Flemish cloth from me and was going to send me a partial down payment. I've tried to contact him twice but haven't received an answer. Can you tell me . . ."

"You can't depend on that man anymore, sir," one of the other servants interjected. "Master Matthis's business closed after his only daughter was driven from town because of wanton behavior and other misdeeds. Schärer took it so hard that he sold his entire business and left the city. Some say he has crossed Lake Constance to join a group of pilgrims on the way to Rome or even to the Holy Land."

Another driver demurred with a contemptuous wave of his hand. "What nonsense! That's just a story that well-meaning people have been spreading. As far as I know, Schärer threw himself in the lake and drowned the very day his daughter was convicted."

An elderly wagon driver shook his head doubtfully. "I don't know what to make of all the gossip. Some say as well that Schärer sold everything he had to his almost-son-in-law and set out to find his daughter."

Marie was about to breathe a sigh of relief when she heard those words, but a traveler accompanying the wagon train from Constance who was, judging by his dress, a scholar from Lucerne, shook his head reluctantly. "That's not possible. I was involved in a legal matter a few months ago with Counselor Rupert Splendidus and his father, Count Heinrich. Rupert was as poor as a church mouse and couldn't even afford a decent counselor's robe. How could he have bought the property of a rich Constance citizen?" His voice sounded spiteful.

The older driver contradicted him vehemently. "You certainly got that wrong. The counselor now lives in Master Matthis's house and is always very well dressed. Hey, Utz, speak up! Weren't you there when the affair with the Schärer girl happened and Master Matthis disappeared?"

All eyes turned to Utz. Marie could hear her heart pounding so hard, she was afraid people would hear it. She pressed her hand to her chest and held her breath so not a single sound could escape her mouth.

Shrugging, Utz waved them off with his hand and spat into the fire. "Why are you asking all these silly questions? I don't know any more than you do. Master Matthis's daughter was convicted of immoral behavior and driven out of town. I have no idea what happened to her or her father after that."

"But you were a regular visitor to his house after Counselor Rupert moved in. Certainly you heard something," one of the drivers shouted, curiosity written all over his face.

Marie drew closer so she wouldn't miss a single expression on his face. Listening to him aggressively deny that he knew anything about the matter, she felt a shiver run up and down her back. Utz was lying, a fact that was even evident to some of the people at the table, and he angrily turned away any further questions. When the clamoring insistence of the others became too great, he stood up and went to one of the sleeping places without having finished his wine nor, as one of the armed escorts noted with annoyance, having assigned guard duties for the night. His curious behavior gave rise to wild speculation among those left sitting at the table, but since no one could shed any additional light on the issue, conversation soon turned to other topics.

For a while, Marie was so upset, she couldn't move. She wondered why Utz, whose false accusation had been the start of her misfortune, was now so strongly denying his part in the matter. There had to be something he wanted to keep hidden, and it couldn't just concern her. Utz alone couldn't have convinced Euphemia, the shoemaker's widow, to testify falsely. Only Rupert could have done that, with the wagon driver as his accomplice. She knew that if her father were alive, he would never have let the counselor set foot in the house, so had the two killed her father in order to take his property? Since government authorities immediately confiscated property without an heir, she couldn't imagine that possibility. With a start, however, she suddenly remembered that her former fiancé had good relations with the bishop and other high officials. It was indeed conceivable that with their help he had seized possession of her house.

Marie wanted to jump up and accuse Utz of rape and murder in front of everyone there, but she quickly realized it would only hurt her and the women she was traveling with. No one would believe her except Utz, and he would not hesitate to kill her, too, along with her companions. The surrounding forests could hide many dark secrets if a few itinerant women disappeared.

Carefully, Marie left the yard without being seen. Once outside, she crouched alongside the fence and petted Hiltrud's two goats, lost in her reveries. She knew two things for certain now: her father would not save her, and no one else was left to take an interest in her fate. In order to mislead her uncle Mombert and others, Rupert must have started the rumor that her father had left to search for her.

Listening to the sound of the nearby river Elta, she wondered if it was deep enough and its current strong enough to offer her a merciful end. She wasn't afraid to commit suicide, and she knew she'd never be able to travel the road as a harlot like Gerlind and the others. She struggled to her feet and began to head down to the river.

But at her very first step, it occurred to her that she was the only one who could confront Rupert for his treacherous misdeeds. He had stolen her father and had made her life worth less than that of a farm animal. If she killed herself now, he would have won everything.

Turning all this over in her mind, she wondered what she could do. As a dishonorable wandering prostitute, she had no possibility of seeking justice from a man like Counselor Rupert Splendidus, an esteemed citizen and son of the Count Heinrich von Keilburg. Give up, she said to herself. Do you want to become like Fita, where the rest of your life is one unending torture?

But something within her resisted surrender. Hadn't Hiltrud said that even prostitutes were not defenseless? Marie knew that she was still young and pretty, and if she stopped hiding that fact, perhaps a young man might fall so much in love with her that he'd kill Rupert, Utz, Linhard, and Hunold just to win her heart. Or perhaps, even better, she could save enough money to hire someone to murder the four of them. The thought of revenge was not exactly Christian, but the church had already condemned her to hell one way or the other, whether she became a murderer or spent the rest of her life atoning for a sin she had not committed. She decided it was better to live for revenge than to die now and enter the fiery gates without finding retribution.

Marie woke from her reveries with a start when the four other women returned. Hiltrud scolded her for daydreaming since Marie hadn't watered the goats, put up the tent, nor built a fire. But she didn't sound serious and seemed in good spirits from her business dealings. Berta also appeared pleased, humming a lively tune and jingling the coins she had earned. Even Gerlind chuckled happily to herself. But Fita groaned and bent over in pain, pressing her hand to her stomach.

"Why do men always have to be so coarse?" she complained.

Shaking her head, Gerlind sighed. "You let them take advantage of you and do anything they want. Look around for the right men, and then you won't have so many problems. Use some of Hiltrud's tincture, or better yet, the salve she gets from the Merzlingen apothecary. It doesn't burn as much."

Hiltrud went to her wagon to get the salve. "Gerlind is right," she told Fita, holding the balm out to her. "You have to learn to tame these ruffians, or you won't last long. Here, take this. It really helps. This stuff worked for Marie. She was badly beaten, and now the wounds are invisible."

Berta looked up and snorted. "Aha, so Marie is healthy again? I'm surprised you don't put her to work. She's your maid, and you have a right to most of her earnings. There were easily enough men with money in their pockets for all five of us today, and Fita could surely have done with one or two fewer. If Fita's as badly injured as she claims, it will be days before she's able to earn money again."

"I'll leave it to Marie to decide when she can start work." Hiltrud wanted to give Berta a tongue-lashing and tell her it was none of her business, as such admonitions didn't make it easier to convince Marie of the advantage of a prostitute's life. There was still a risk the girl would drown herself rather than be reasonable once she realized that none of her relatives would come to save her. But Hiltrud clenched her teeth to stifle any further discussion.

Berta didn't relent. "Then you really are stupid. I would have given that fine young girl to a brawny stud by force if necessary. If she wants to continue with us, she's got to adapt. I won't tolerate one more useless mouth to feed in the group." Her final words sounded venomous.

Gerlind pounded the grass with the flat of her hand. With these words Berta had attacked her authority, and she wouldn't tolerate that. "First of all, you don't have to feed Marie, and second, you should be happy you earned more money today than you could have if she had snatched away our best customers with her pretty face."

Fita stood up. "I'm going down to the river to wash up." She hated controversy and ran away from arguments. Gerlind and Hiltrud just nodded and went down to the river with her. As usual, Marie joined them to keep an eye on their clothing. After a short sulk, Berta also followed, but she had no intention of removing her clothes to wade into the water. She was still in a bad mood and hadn't gotten over Gerlind's reprimand.

"Be careful you don't catch cold down below, or I'll have to work all by myself for a while."

Gerlind laughed. "Haven't you always wanted to be the only whore for miles around?"

Even Berta had to laugh, and the tension among the women vanished as quickly as it had started. While Berta and Marie remained on the shore, Gerlind, Hiltrud, and Fita plunged into the water. In the light of the moon they looked like water sprites in a mysterious, shimmering kingdom. Finally, Marie also removed her dress and walked into the river. The cold water nearly took her breath away, and she had to force herself to go in as far as her shoulders.

"Very good, Marie. A prostitute should always be clean." Gerlind's expression showed her words were mostly directed at Berta, and they hit their mark.

"Some of the guys stank pretty bad," Berta said, snorting as she pulled up her skirt to wash between her legs.

Marie pushed her way against the current to Hiltrud and touched her on the arm. "I need to talk to you."

Surprised, Hiltrud looked up. She could sense Marie's inner struggle and understood that something must have happened. Marie no longer seemed so desperate; there was now a startling strength and determination in her eyes. Remembering that one of the wagon trains was from Constance, Hiltrud hoped that Marie had heard news to dispel any false hopes of salvation.

Passing her hand gently through Marie's hair, Hiltrud walked back toward the shore with her. "You can talk with me anytime, child."

Marie closed her eyes and felt the current in the river only tugging gently at her. No, she wouldn't find a fast, merciful death here, and surprisingly, she didn't long for it anymore. Instead, she wanted more than anything else to send Rupert and Utz—and especially Linhard, that spineless traitor—to hell, and she hoped they would get there long before she did. To do that, she would have to accept a fate that just a few hours ago had seemed worse than death. She looked at her companion and took a deep breath.

"I'm ready to work, Hiltrud. But there are a lot of things you'll have to teach me."

PART THREE
ARNSTEIN CASTLE

I.

Just after dawn, the market's streets of stalls were still empty and the booths were covered. Most of the merchants and travelers were asleep in their tents or beneath their wagons. A few early risers of both sexes were bathing unabashedly in the river, though most of the women blushed and moved away when some of the men started telling dirty jokes.

Marie had washed with Hiltrud long before the others had arrived. She was now sitting on a blanket in front of her tent, enjoying the warm sun and patching a rip in her dress. Before long, charcoal fires were lit, and Hulda put some bratwurst on the grill in front of her snack stand, the delicious aroma floating through the market. As Marie stood up to walk toward the tantalizing scent, Hiltrud came out of her tent.

"It looks like you can't wait for Hulda to have the first bratwursts ready."

"There's nothing better than a bratwurst in the morning, especially since the ones they make here are some of the best."

"They taste just as good everywhere," said Hiltrud, teasing her. "Don't worry, I'll bring you a few."

Marie watched her friend leave, thinking that bratwurst was one of the rare pleasures she could afford. More than three years had passed since Hiltrud had picked her up half-dead at the side of the road and taken her along with her. In those three years, Marie had learned to scorn the respectable world and appreciate the friendship of those the world cast aside. Ever since she'd been on the road with Hiltrud, she had learned to be happy with very little, and the memories of her earlier life seemed more and more like those of a distant childhood. But neither time nor anything else had been able to relieve the bitterness that had lodged in her heart after her shameful verdict.

Sometimes Marie had to force herself not to run off to Constance and denounce the venerable authorities there for their injustice. When an especially inconsiderate customer was lying on top of her, she clenched her fists and thought about how much money she would need to pay someone to kill her former fiancé and his conspirators. When she spoke with Hiltrud about it, she derided Marie's fantasy or even scolded her. But Marie could only tolerate her life by clinging to a hope that she could one day take her revenge on the men who had done this to her—and she would not forget the slanderous widow Euphemia.

"Are you still dreaming about wringing the neck of that fellow Rupert?" Hiltrud's voice interrupted her thoughts. Instead of answering, Marie took two of the bratwursts her friend held out on a serving board, juggling them in her hands because they were so hot.

"Glutton." Hiltrud looked at Marie and shook her head, then sat down beside her in the grass. Lost in thought, the two women ate breakfast. Hiltrud was concerned that Marie's obsessions would someday be her downfall. She had seen too many courtesans go mad or kill themselves because they couldn't cope with memories of their former lives and the real or imaginary injustices inflicted upon them. She hoped Marie would gradually come to her senses, but thus far neither Hiltrud's scolding nor pleading had made her friend see that the world was simply unjust—and that it was necessary to forget the past.

Marie regretted causing Hiltrud to worry, as she didn't want to make her friend unhappy. From the very outset, Hiltrud had been a good and caring companion, never treating her like a maid or forcing her to do anything intolerable. She remembered how the experienced courtesan had chosen Marie's first customer very carefully. He had been a pleasant and tender gentleman who had treated her very considerately. Nevertheless, she had submitted to the sex act with tightened fists, clenched teeth, and closed eyes. Without Gerlind's potion, which let her float in a cloud of indifference, she would have fled his embrace.

In the days following, she had used the drug every time until Hiltrud finally took it away, almost leading to their first big argument. But even then, Hiltrud showed great patience, repeatedly explaining that the drug was addictive and destroyed both the mind and body when taken regularly.

It was initially difficult for Marie to do without the medicine, and sometimes when she had an unpleasant customer, she still longed for the drug. Though she was in the fortunate situation of being able to select her customers, not everyone lived up to her expectations. Sometimes an outwardly polite and courtly man proved to be a depraved character for whom the woman underneath him was just an object he had bought for a few coins.

Marie couldn't help thinking of Berta, who would proudly display her black-and-blue marks if her pay was higher than usual. Inadvertently she glanced over at her former traveling companion's tent. She and Hiltrud had traveled the country with Berta, Fita, and Gerlind for two summers, but at the Rheinau autumn market, Berta had started a jealous quarrel that Hiltrud and Marie were attracting better customers, and she left the group. Fita, who clung to Berta like a dog, went with her while Gerlind stayed with Hiltrud and Marie.

That winter, Gerlind decided to give up her wandering life and stay behind in the cabin that the three had rented for a few pennies in the fall and had furnished comfortably. Gerlind's intention was to work there as an herbal medicine woman and, as she said with a giggle, take on a young girl as a maid and a source of income. Marie wondered if she'd ever see the old woman again. She hadn't expected to see Berta and Fita, since they had planned to head down the Danube to Bohemia, but they must have reconsidered, since they were now working here at this market. Berta had replied to Marie's and Hiltrud's warm greetings with just a grunt, and for this reason Fita didn't dare exchange even a few friendly words with them.

Marie thought that Berta's tent looked shabby and that the woman herself appeared more slovenly than when they parted ways a year and a half ago. No longer simply plump, Berta was now definitely fat. Fita, however, had become gaunt and seemed to have aged prematurely. Judging by the number of men who had visited their tents the day before, their business was good, but their clientele were for the most part humble journeymen and servants who had saved up a few pennies to experience the yearly treat of feeling a woman's warm body press against them.

Perhaps in a few years she'd have to be content with such customers, Marie thought with a sigh. But for now Hiltrud and she didn't need to take just anyone with three Haller pennies to spare. With her imposing stature, Hiltrud attracted many well-to-do men who wanted to prove their manhood.

As for Marie, she had her choice of many customers and could demand prices beyond the means of simple laborers. One of her most generous and loyal customers had on several occasions offered to set her up as his mistress in a fine home. A wool merchant from

Flanders, he wanted to take her back with him to his homeland. If she had gone with him, however, she would have had to abandon Hiltrud, and she would do that only if she saw an opportunity to exact her revenge.

Several times, Marie had tried to get information from her hometown, but the people who could have helped her were wagon drivers and merchants who had dealings with Utz, and she didn't dare approach them. Then one day she met a wandering minstrel on his way to Constance, and she gave him money to inquire about her father's fate. They agreed to meet two months later at the Basel fair, but to her great disappointment he didn't show up. She never saw him again, and she feared something had happened to him in the course of his investigations. Hiltrud thought that the man had simply taken the money, then fled to Italy or Lower Austria. Persuaded by her friend that the man had swindled her, Marie unkindly hoped that the fellow had contracted consumption.

All she could do was to wait for another opportunity, but so far, none had come along. Returning to Constance without permission as a banished woman could earn her double the number of blows and a possible brand. Even if she were able to sneak into the city without being seen, as soon as she started asking questions, she'd land in the tower. She didn't dare to imagine what Hunold would do to her then.

"Still so pensive?" Hiltrud finished her bratwurst and wiped her greasy hands on a nearby clump of grass. "Are you brooding over old memories? Please, Marie, just forget what happened, especially with your former fiancé. He's much too powerful and influential for you to pick a fight with."

Marie glared at Hiltrud. "If I can't think about getting my revenge on that scoundrel and his accomplices, then this miserable life isn't worth it."

Hiltrud shook her head thoughtfully.

"Our life isn't so bad. In fact, we're making pretty good money. I'll admit I owe at least half my earnings to your angelic face attracting well-to-do customers and their friends like bees to honey. But if you always look so angry, you'll drive men away and become prematurely old and ugly."

Hiltrud's pleased smile softened the effect of her admonition, but she couldn't help it. Marie had brought her luck, and without her stunningly beautiful friend, Hiltrud couldn't be as selective as she was.

Since Marie was still fuming, Hiltrud tried to divert her thoughts elsewhere. "I met Fita at the food stand. She looks bad, and an herb woman she consulted for her chest pain didn't give her long to live. I advised her to leave Berta, who treats her like a slave."

"I wouldn't object to Fita's joining us. We could no doubt nurse her back to health. But she's completely devoted to Berta, even though the woman shamelessly exploits her."

Hiltrud shrugged helplessly. "Nevertheless, I'll talk to Fita again and suggest she join us. Perhaps . . . " She stopped speaking when she saw a refined middle-aged gentleman striding quickly toward the tents.

"That fellow looks like his pants are on fire. Do you think he'd be good for us?"

Marie glanced at the man's military clothing and shook her head. "I don't like soldiers. They're too rough. Let him take Berta. She's well padded and can stand forceful handling."

Hiltrud laughed and nodded toward the penny prostitutes. "That's just what he's doing. Look! He's talking to her now. Well, military men often have strange tastes. I once knew an officer who could have afforded the best-looking courtesans, but he always patronized a fleshy old hag and was as happy afterward as if he'd bedded the most beautiful virgin."

Since there were no other customers around, Hiltrud and Marie watched as the man talked with Berta. But instead of disappearing inside her tent, he beckoned to Fita and several other prostitutes.

Hiltrud shook her head in amazement. "Maybe he wants to hire camp followers for the army."

"We'll know in a moment. I think he's coming over to us."

Hiltrud stood up as she always did when a potential client approached her tent. Marie remained seated, turning a cold shoulder to the man after glancing at his sullen face. As a rule, one could tell whether a customer was simply looking for a few agreeable moments in a woman's arms. That man was certainly no such customer. He stopped a few paces in front of them and glared at them furiously.

"You are courtesans?" It was more a statement than a question.

"Just say whore, if that's what you're thinking," Marie snapped.

The man growled like an angry bear. "I don't care what you women call yourselves. I'm looking for a pleasant and clean bedmate for my lord."

"If he wants one of us, tell him to come himself." Marie hated being appraised like cattle.

"That's not possible, as Sir Dietmar is at home in Arnstein Castle near Tettnang," he explained. "I am Giso, his castellan, and I have instructions to find an acceptable prostitute to keep his bed warm for the next few months, as he must avoid the bed of his pregnant wife."

Marie laughed in disbelief. "Then your lord must have a most generous wife, or has the lady no say at home?"

"That is none of your concern," the steward snapped back. "I have an order to find a useful woman, but your mouth seems a bit too fresh."

"With a harlot, normally it's another part of the body that matters." Marie had little desire to be confined for months in a drafty

117

castle just to serve a lord, then later be pushed aside and given to his liegemen.

Hiltrud had become curious. "What's in it for us?"

"The courtesan we select will leave with a full purse," the man replied.

Marie shrugged. "Full of Haller pennies? That wouldn't be enough for us."

Giso's face looked like he had bitten into a rotten apple. "I was given no specific sum. The woman who satisfies my lord's needs will have no regrets."

"Very nice for her. I wish you luck making your selection. You can find plenty of them over there." Marie pointed at Berta and a few other women looking in their direction and talking animatedly. Despite the distance, it was clear to see that Berta's face was contorted with envy.

Giso didn't seem put out by either the gazes behind him or Marie's snide remarks. "I look forward to seeing you all in my lord's tent. It's off to one side. You can't miss it, because an ascending falcon, my lord's coat of arms, is flying over it."

"I'll decline in advance, since my mouth, as you mentioned, is too fresh for your lord." Marie was about to turn away, but the man did not desist.

"I have my order to summon up all the prostitutes in the marketplace for inspection."

Marie bared her teeth. "If we come to your tent, we'll waste time when we could be earning money."

Giso clenched a fist, then relaxed his hand and placed it casually on his hip as if not wanting to be provoked. "All the prostitutes will be reimbursed for their efforts." Turning away without a farewell, he stomped away.

Marie tapped her forehead. "What a strange fellow! He acts as if we were chickens and he must select the fattest one for dinner."

Laughing at the comparison, Hiltrud nonetheless pointed at the empty lanes between the market stands. "If we get money just for showing up, we should go. It will be more than an hour until any decent customers come to the fairgrounds. The only ones to miss out on something will be Berta and her friends, since all the low-life servants are already starting to gather around their tents."

Marie scoffed. "I'm telling you there won't be more than a few pennies in it for us, but perhaps it will be enough for another bratwurst."

Hiltrud tilted her head to one side. "If you keep polishing off so many bratwursts, you'll get as big as Berta."

"Me?" asked Marie, smoothing her dress with both hands so Hiltrud could see her flat belly. "Where do you see any fat?"

Hiltrud grinned. "I didn't say you're getting fat, but if you keep stuffing yourself like that, it won't take long. As far as Giso's offer is concerned, it wouldn't be so bad to be taken care of over the winter. Remember the year before last when we were evicted from the cabin after the first snow? If we hadn't been lucky enough to find that abandoned shack, we would have really been in trouble."

"But he'll take only one of us to Arnstein for the winter."

"I'd never go to this castle without you," Hiltrud said emphatically. "Anyway, I think Giso will pick you. I'm probably too tall for his fine lord."

"Bah, I won't go there." Marie turned up her nose, jutted out her chin, and gave a half-dozen reasons why a castle was not a suitable place to spend the winter. Castle rooms were cold and drafty, full of poor relatives, servants, and warriors who spent nights on piles of straw in the halls and corridors. A prostitute wouldn't find a moment's rest there.

Hiltrud listened to Marie's reservations and then waved her hand. "Well, I don't believe all that. No soldier would even dare look askance at his lord's bed companion. The least he could expect for that would be a good beating."

Marie disagreed, and the two were soon so caught up in an animated discussion that they looked up in surprise when a soldier with the Arnstein ascendant falcon emblazoned on his chest suddenly stood before them and ordered them to come along. Marie looked at Hiltrud questioningly, then when Hiltrud nodded, reluctantly got up to leave.

"When we get such a friendly invitation, how can we refuse?" she said to the soldier, who gave her a look of complete disgust.

By the time they got there, Berta and the other prostitutes were already crowding around Arnstein's tent. Though it was relatively large, this tent had no fashionable embellishments save for the tattered flag bearing his coat of arms, unlike the richly decorated tents of other nobles. It had neither a wind deflector, nor a sun blind, nor gaily colored sidewalls. Instead, it was essentially a large square-shaped area covered in strong linen with a gently sloping roof for the water to run off during a rainstorm. The canvas in front of the undecorated entrance was tied up with leather straps, allowing an unobstructed view of the interior, and they could see that the rear third had been separated by a curtain.

Giso stood beside the entrance, observing the crowd of corralled women with obvious repugnance. An older woman in a housekeeper's austere costume exited the tent, and with a scowl at the jabbering prostitutes, motioned for the men to direct them inside.

Marie let the other women enter first, then stood next to the entrance, watching the curtain and wondering who might be behind it. From time to time, the curtain moved as if someone were peering out.

The housekeeper reentered the tent, then listened in the direction of the curtain. Marie felt her assumption confirmed. Dietmar von Arnstein's harlot would not be selected by either Giso or the housekeeper, but by the person concealed at the rear of the tent. She whispered her suspicions to Hiltrud, who cast a furtive glance at the curtain.

"I believe you're right. Who could it be? Count von Arnstein himself? Perhaps he's deformed and doesn't want to show himself until he's made his decision."

"I agree. Otherwise why would he go to so much trouble to pick someone to sleep with? Surely there's more than one castle maid willing to warm his bed for him."

Though the tent was large, it became quite crowded with the ten courtesans and the castle guards. When they had all assembled, two soldiers untied the leather straps and closed the entrance. Then Giso raised his hand and ordered everyone to be silent.

"I have had you all summoned here because my lord needs a woman who will fulfill his physical desires for the next few months. She must agree to move on after that so that she will not endanger the morals of the castle maids."

From the way he spoke, Marie concluded he was telling only half the story. It sounded like the mistress of the castle didn't want one of her maids to take her place for the next few months, perhaps making demands she would find unacceptable or proving a future temptation for her husband. A prostitute would take her pay and move on. Or maybe the lady simply wanted to avoid having one more illegitimate child to raise in the castle.

Giso addressed this point straightforwardly. "If the prostitute I select becomes pregnant by my lord during her stay at the castle, she will be allowed to stay until the birth of the child and be reimbursed for her time lost during this period. The lord promises to raise the child along with his servants' children and care for it thereafter."

Marie had no plans for a child, no matter who the father was. Gerlind's contraceptive potion had served her well so far. Hiltrud felt the same way. But some of the other women held out hope of even more money if they presented Count von Arnstein with a male offspring. Among them was Berta, who was standing in front, trying to hustle the other whores aside with her huge body.

Giso pushed her back angrily and ordered the women to form a half circle in front of him. "The woman must be healthy, clean, and have a pleasant disposition."

"That hardly describes Berta," Hiltrud whispered into Marie's ear.

"But it doesn't describe Fita, either," Marie replied. As if on cue, Fita began to cough, gasping for air.

The housekeeper turned up her nose. "That woman is sick. She can leave."

"Did you hear her? Leave." Berta pushed her loyal companion toward an exit that a soldier opened and then closed after her.

When Berta returned, Marie whispered to her, "You're a real bitch! After all, Fita is your friend."

Berta responded with a dirty look, and Marie gasped when Berta's elbow dug sharply into her ribs.

"Take off your clothes!" the housekeeper commanded.

Berta's response was so quick that she knocked one of the other women against the wall, causing her to fall. As the other woman struggled to her feet, Berta was already displaying her charms to the steward. Despite her huge size, she still looked pretty good. She had large but well-formed buttocks, and her firm, generously rounded breasts reached out invitingly to Giso.

The other women had also undressed and were looking at Giso. Retreating to the background, only Marie and Hiltrud kept their clothing on.

The housekeeper looked Berta over like meat of questionable freshness, sniffing at her distrustfully. "You can leave, too. I can't present my lord with something as dirty as you."

"I can wash up." Berta made no move to leave.

The housekeeper kicked Berta's dress. "What you need is something more than just a good washing. After you leave, I'll have to tell the maids to fumigate the tent walls, or lice and fleas will come here to nest."

Some of the women giggled while Berta pulled her dress over her head and smoothed it down, her face as red as a beet. "You're not going to get rid of me that easily. That fellow there," she said, jutting her chin out toward the steward, "promised us money just for coming here. I want it now, and so does my friend who just left."

Marie flared up with rage. "Now all of a sudden Fita is your friend again, even though you couldn't get rid of her fast enough earlier."

"That's none of your damned business." Berta held her hand out to Giso, and the steward took his purse from his belt, opened it, and tossed her a few coins.

"That's enough for you. Now clear out." Gathering up the coins, Berta slipped through a crack in the entrance that a soldier had opened.

"But don't forget to give Fita her share. I'm going to ask her later," Marie called out as Berta left.

"Why aren't the two of you getting undressed?" the housekeeper asked pointedly.

"Come, Marie. If these good people are going to pay, they should get a quick look." Hiltrud pulled her dress over her head, folded it carefully together, and placed it over her arm.

Marie hesitated for a moment, then did the same, but she stayed in the back of the tent while the housekeeper called up one woman after another, looking at their teeth and grabbing them between the legs to assess their condition. With most of the prostitutes, she shook her head and told Giso to pay them and let them go. The group quickly thinned out until only two other women remained. One was a rather dainty blonde and the other a brunette with an ample figure. Now the housekeeper stepped toward Marie and reached out toward her face with her right hand to examine her teeth, but Marie seized her by the wrist.

"I won't let you stick your fingers in my face after I've seen where they've been. If you want to see my teeth, here they are." She showed off her teeth and tapped them with her knuckles. "As you can see, they are white, healthy, and firmly in place. If you want to confirm that yourself, go and wash your hands."

"This one was difficult earlier as well." Giso looked ready to throw Marie out of the tent, and the housekeeper also seemed dismissive. But a few soft words could be heard behind the curtain, and the two hesitated. The housekeeper walked a circle around Marie, then turned to Hiltrud.

"For the time being, the two of you can stay, but I think we'll take one of the two other whores."

Marie had no objection to staying because she was curious how it would all end. The voice behind the curtain was clearly that of a woman. Again Marie observed the curtain's slight movement and pricked up her ears. She thought she heard the words "No, not that one, either," and wasn't surprised when the steward handed a few coins to the brunette.

The woman cursed in disappointment. "Your lordship probably thinks he's something really special. I've been mounted by counts and other great men, and they were all happy with me."

"Get out" was Giso's only comment. Flying into a rage, the woman was about to scratch his face with her fingernails when suddenly the entrance to the tent opened and a tall soldier grabbed the woman, throwing her out like a bundle of rags. Giso picked up her dress and tossed it out the door after her.

"What a bitch," he groaned in despair. Marie could see he wished he were somewhere far away.

The housekeeper beckoned the little blonde forward, asking her some questions. The woman didn't seem to know exactly how to answer and reacted so curtly to some of the questions that Hiltrud nudged Marie with a grin.

"It looks like it's going to come down to one of us." The mysterious person seemed to agree, uttering a short cry of disapproval of the blonde. After being paid by Giso and dismissed, the woman looked at the money that was certainly several times what she ordinarily received and shrugged disdainfully.

"They don't want to take any of us along to their castle," the woman said to Marie and Hiltrud. "No doubt a few lewd old men are sitting behind the curtain, getting a thrill out of looking at us, or perhaps the knight can't get it up anymore. But for this kind of money, I'll give him a special performance," she said, squeezing out a loud fart as she bent over to pick up her dress. Noticing Giso angrily raising his hand as if to strike her, she ran off, squealing in fright.

"Well, then, now to you two." Giso was clearly displeased that the only ones left were Marie and Hiltrud, but before he could continue, Marie raised her hand.

"I need to first make something clear. My friend and I have been traveling together for years, and we won't separate now. It's either both of us, or neither."

Giso pounded his fist into his hand. "You're the most impudent thing I've ever come across."

A strong female voice behind the curtain restrained him. "Be silent, Giso. It's their right not to want to part company."

"But we only need one whore for the lord," the housekeeper said hastily in support of Giso. "A second woman like this at the castle will just drive the men mad."

The lady simply laughed. "The two of them don't look that stupid. I think we can manage them."

The curtain opened and out stepped a lady. As tall as Marie, she was already in her midtwenties, and she wore a broad, embroidered dress that could no longer conceal her rounded, pregnant belly. Her face was neither pretty nor ugly, but seemed pleasant and friendly, and her long, blond braids gave her a majestic appearance.

"I am Mechthild von Arnstein," she said. "As you see, I am expectant and must avoid my husband's bed until after the delivery. But I don't want to leave him all winter long with no one to sleep with."

Hiltrud looked at her in astonishment. "You're looking for a whore for your husband? A farm girl would be much cheaper."

"My husband doesn't need a woman quivering and almost dying of fear in his bed, but he wants a healthy, robust woman who knows how to give him pleasure."

"If you're looking for a strong woman, take my friend Hiltrud," said Marie as her friend looked at her furiously.

An amused smile played at the corners of the lady's mouth. "Your companion is an imposing person, but my husband is . . . how shall I say, not the heroic warrior type. He would hardly allow me to bring him a playmate bigger than he is. But I like you, so I picked you out."

Marie held up her hands dismissively. "Me?"

"What is so strange about that?" the lady asked with a smile. "You are especially good-looking and have a quick tongue."

"You can certainly say that," Giso added sharply.

Marie struggled inwardly. Something didn't seem to be right here. "Why is a lady like you picking out a prostitute for your husband? That's no job for a Christian wife."

"That's no concern of yours, girl," the housekeeper interrupted, but her mistress beckoned to her to be silent. "I value harmony in my house, and an important part of that is to ensure that my husband won't become disgruntled because he can't prove himself as a man. But I also won't tolerate his flirting with the maids as my father did. Every time my mother was pregnant—as she often was—he bedded one of her maids. The fresh things thought they were important, shirked their duties, and were nasty to my mother."

Mechthild von Arnstein didn't look like one to tolerate such behavior from her servants. In fact, she seemed quite resolute. While Marie was thinking about how to answer, the lady continued.

"My husband laughs at me for my excessive caution and thinks he could do without a woman for the four or five months he has to avoid sleeping with me, but I know men. When winter confines them to their rooms and they find no comfort in bed, sooner or later they get the craziest ideas, or they become depressed."

Marie nodded, then did a quick calculation. "Five months, you say? That would be the middle of February, too early to be able to move on. We need someplace to stay until the middle of March, or if the weather is bad, the beginning of April. I don't care to be driven out onto snowy roads."

"That won't happen," Mechthild von Arnstein promised. "You will be our guests until spring even if I no longer need your services."

As Marie was thinking it over, Hiltrud nudged her furtively. "The idea isn't really that bad. We'd be under cover all winter and wouldn't need to spend anything on room and board."

Mechthild von Arnstein smiled encouragingly at Marie. "Your companion appreciates the advantages of our offer."

Marie sighed, already half-convinced. "What kind of man is your husband? I usually look men over carefully before I take them into my tent and avoid coarse ones who hurt women."

The lady smiled. "You don't need to worry about that. My husband is always very tender and gentle in bed with me."

"Why are you being so fussy, Marie?" Hiltrud asked gruffly. "Such an opportunity doesn't come often."

Marie closed her eyes briefly and tried to think. Hiltrud was right. If she agreed, they would have a roof over their heads for the winter and wouldn't have to spend their hard-earned savings. Perhaps she'd even earn enough to send someone to Constance again in the spring. She'd just have to find a more reliable messenger than that wandering minstrel who'd cheated her last time.

She took a deep breath and nodded. "I accept."

II.

Marie was accustomed to traveling on foot, and she would gladly have done so this time as well, for the wagon she and Hiltrud were sharing with two maids and a dozen crates, baskets, and barrels creaked and groaned worse than a barge on the Rhine. Every bone in her body ached, and she envied the servant walking beside the draft oxen. Hiltrud's goats had been tied to the back of the wagon and ran along happily, stopping from time to time to pull up a few tufts of grass or bleating to gain Hiltrud's attention.

Up in front, Mechthild von Arnstein's closed carriage sank into a pothole every two or three paces, then rose again, pitching and rolling. Though the servants bedded the mistress down on soft pillows to protect her from the jolting wagon, the trip must have been painful for the pregnant lady. This concerned Marie. Everything now depended on the health of the lady. If the child was stillborn, the master of the castle would view two itinerant prostitutes as useless baggage and throw them out.

Marie sighed and grabbed hold of the wagon side as an especially hard jolt threw her off balance. She sent a brief prayer heavenward that they would really arrive at the castle that evening, even though she had no illusions about what she'd find there. Since they had visited some imposing fortresses before and even spent the night at a few of them, Marie's notions of what they were like had been completely confirmed. Knightly castles were drafty, cold, damp, and swarming with people. Judging by experience, Hiltrud and she wouldn't be nearly as comfortable in the castle as they had been in the old cabin they had come across the winter before. Marie thought longingly of the thick floor covering of dry leaves where they had slept, and the fire in the hearth they kept burning constantly with grass and twigs so they could cook and have enough heat.

Suddenly Hiltrud kicked her, snapping her out of her gloomy thoughts.

"What's wrong?"

Hiltrud pointed to the soldiers escorting the wagon train as they tightened the buckles on their suits of armor and held their weapons at the ready.

Directly in front of them, the road continued over a narrow wooden bridge where several dozen men on horseback had taken up position, clearly intending to block their way. As their wagons drew closer, Marie could see the coat of arms on the men's breastplates— a red tower topped with battlements and a hovering black boar's head. She knew the sign, but couldn't place it, which didn't surprise her since she had seen many different shields on the breastplates of vassals and knights loyal to various lords on her travels. But at the sight of this coat of arms, her hair stood on end, and she wasn't sure why.

Shortly before the bridge, Giso ordered the wagon drivers to stop, trotting his bay horse slowly toward the highwaymen. He paused just before reaching the first man, so that the head of his horse was almost touching the man's nose.

"Clear the way at once!" he barked at the men.

"Why should we?" replied their leader belligerently. "Just so you know, Arnstein's riffraff aren't welcome on this land anymore."

Giso jutted out his chin. "This is Sir Otmar's land, and Keilburg's scoundrels have no place here."

With his loud pronouncement, Giso's voice drowned out the oxen's restless lowing and stomping. Marie swallowed hard and pressed her hand to her pounding heart, for now she remembered where she had first seen that coat of arms. It was the signet on the ring Rupert wore, the symbol of his father, Heinrich von Keilburg. Her father, in his attempts to stress the generosity of her fiancé, had spoken often about the count. Marie waited tensely for the Keilburg leader to answer.

"Where have you been hiding? Everyone knows that Sir Otmar bequeathed his possessions to my lord, Count Konrad, then renounced the world and withdrew to a monastery."

Giso laughed scornfully. "That's another one of those lies your master likes to spread. If Sir Otmar in fact has retired to a monastery, then his land now belongs to my lord, because Sir Otmar made a contract of inheritance with him and cannot transfer his belongings to anyone else."

"Apparently he can," the Keilburg knight replied in an impassive voice. "In any case, my lord's claim is documented and sealed. Friedrich von Zollern, the new bishop of Constance, and Abbot Hugo von Waldkron signed the contract as witnesses, and the kaiser himself ratified it."

Giso was about to grab his adversary by the throat, but he held back in view of the drawn swords of the Keilburg mercenaries. "That's a lie! Get out of our way! I must bring my mistress home. She is with child and won't survive a long detour over bad roads."

The leader of the Keilburg horsemen laughed scornfully. "Then she ought to stay home, as any respectable lady would. You won't pass through here unless you get on your knees and beg me to make an exception for your mistress."

His face turning beet red, Giso raised his sword. His men rushed forward to join him, and it appeared that a fight was inevitable. Since the Keilburg warriors outnumbered Giso's people three to one, Marie feared the worst, but at that moment Mechthild von Arnstein drew back the curtain on her wagon and called out.

"Come back, Giso! I won't allow armed conflict without an official declaration of hostilities, and I won't sacrifice good men without knowing what has really happened. Come, we'll turn around and find another way. But you, sire," she said, turning to the leader of the group, "can tell your greedy master that we Arnsteins will defend our rights."

Giso shook as if a cold bucket of water had been poured over his head. "Mistress, we cannot withdraw like whipped dogs. Look at these scoundrels. They'll spread the word that the Arnsteins are cowards."

"That's just what you are," the Keilburg knight sneered.

For a moment, Giso appeared about to disobey the command of his mistress, but then he placed his sword back in its sheath and ordered his men to do the same. As his men returned to their wagons, Giso slowly pulled back his horse while keeping a close eye on the Keilburgs.

"Your master will bitterly regret this," he finally shouted, then guided his horse to his mistress's wagon, speaking in lowered tones.

Marie could see Mechthild von Arnstein shake her head briefly but emphatically through her window. "We're turning around, Giso, even if it offends your honor. Count Konrad will pay for this, I swear."

Even though her voice was calm, there was a determination in her words that earned Marie's respect. Giso was unable to see any farther than the point of his sword, but she seemed to be looking far into the future. In Mechthild von Arnstein's eyes, drawing back here was the intelligent thing to do, and despite her anger, she appeared a bit mischievous, as if pondering her next move.

The castellan accepted his mistress's decision with a curt bow and shouted a command. Immediately, some of his men began to unhitch the oxen, while the rest formed a defensive line against the Keilburg warriors.

It was hard work turning the wagons around on the narrow road. Since the animals were in danger of sinking in the swamp-lands or river flanking the road, the heavy wagons had to be turned by hand. Following the example of two maids, Marie and Hiltrud jumped down from their wagon to help. Mechthild von Arnstein also wanted to assist her men, but Giso allowed only Guda, the housekeeper, to leave the lady's wagon.

"My lady, you don't want to give the riffraff over there even more reason to heap scorn on us."

"Who are these people, anyway?" Marie asked Giso, who was standing beside her to help pull the wagon out of the mud.

"Leaderless mercenaries and robbers that Count Konrad von Keilburg has hired."

"I've heard of a Count Heinrich von Keilburg," Marie persisted. She was curious to know if Rupert Splendidus was connected in any way with the people on the bridge.

Giso happily vented his anger. "Heinrich was the father of the current count. When, thank God, the devil took him away, we were all very relieved and thought everything would improve. But his son, Konrad, is even greedier and more unscrupulous than his father, and now he's trying to steal property belonging to Sir Otmar von Mühringen. But I swear, he's finally bitten off more than he can chew."

Taking a deep breath, he gave the wagon one last push so the men could hitch up the oxen again. Since Marie kept looking at him expectantly, he stopped to explain to her how the Keilburgs were attempting to increase their wealth at the expense of their neighbors.

"They presented Gottfried von Dreieichen with his uncle's last will, demanding a third of the family castle and treasure. When refused, Heinrich von Keilburg secretly obtained a declaration of hostilities and seized Dreieichen Castle. They also took Walter vom Felde's land by presenting him with a sealed document signed by witnesses in which his father had pawned his property to the Keilburgs. Walter swore over and over that this was not possible, and the only thing he gained by trying to defend his castle was a place in the Keilburg dungeon. These two men are not the only ones to have suffered losses at the hands of the Keilburgs, who will seize half the Duchy of Swabia if no one stops them. At present, Heinrich is trying to seize the inheritance of Sir Otmar from my lord, but Sir Dietmar and especially Lady Mechthild aren't going to give up that easily."

Giso winked at Marie, then turned serious again and shouted at the men who were energetically turning the lady's wagon around. "Careful, you fools! Are you trying to drive Lady Mechthild's wagon into the river?"

The wagon had tipped alarmingly to one side and looked about to slide down the embankment, but at the last moment the men were able to get it back onto the road. A soldier quickly placed a large stone under the wheel and vigorously wiped the sweat from his brow.

"If we don't pay these fellows back soon for this outrage, I'll choke on my anger."

"You are not the only one," Giso replied, gesturing as if he wanted to throttle the forty horsemen on the bridge with his own hands. He didn't trust them and was afraid they might consider seizing his lady as a hostage to extort her husband. He breathed an audible sigh of relief when the last wagon was hitched up and they were able to move on.

At first they made good progress, but before long they turned onto a rough road overgrown with grass and small bushes that forced them to move slowly. After a while, they came to the river again, but it was wider than back by the bridge and the current was slower. Previous travelers had placed stones in the water to create a ford, and even Mechthild von Arnstein had to get out of her wagon here. A burly soldier carried her across the water, set her down carefully on the other side, and remained guarding her with drawn sword.

After the column of wagons had made the crossing, the sun was approaching the western horizon. Both the men and animals were so exhausted that the drivers scarcely had enough strength to lift their whips, and Giso reluctantly gave the order to set up camp for the night. It was evident he was going to hold the Keilburgs to account for their having to spend this night out-of-doors as well.

Mechthild von Arnstein and her housekeeper settled down comfortably in their well-padded carriage while Marie and Hiltrud, accustomed to sleeping outside, wrapped themselves in their blankets and lay down under a tree. The soldiers didn't make a fuss, either, bundling up in their coats and falling asleep almost as soon as they hit the ground. The two maids, however, were trembling with cold and fear and whimpering pathetically. At their lady's command, Guda handed them blankets and pillows, ordering them to crawl under the wagon. They didn't quiet down, however, until they saw Giso, who was still seething with rage and had therefore taken the first watch of the night, circling the camp like a guard dog.

At dawn the next day, they broke camp with the prospect of a good meal only when they reached Arnstein Castle. The sun stood at high noon as the beech forest thinned and a long valley with fields and meadows opened up before them. Shortly thereafter they passed through a village that appeared completely abandoned.

Visibly nervous, Mechthild von Arnstein urged them to hurry. Turning back onto the main road, they finally saw Arnstein Castle towering above them.

The castle had been built on a ridge jutting out over the valley with flanks falling off steeply on both sides. Above the steep slopes were sturdy defensive walls with towers spaced along the wall and two larger corner towers in the front. Marie had learned from the maids that the castle had two open spaces enclosed by the walls and that the main buildings had been positioned so they could be defended even if the outer walls were overrun by the enemy. The entire complex looked like a bizarre gray mass of rock to Marie, and she couldn't imagine feeling comfortable there.

When a guard spotted the lady's caravan, he sounded a horn so loudly that it echoed throughout the valley. A few people emerged from the battlements guarding the entrance to wave at the new arrivals, and only moments later a group of horsemen led by a nobleman in light armor rushed toward them. Ignoring Giso and the others, the nobleman hurried to the traveling coach, pulled back the curtain, and stuck his head inside.

"Thank God for your safe return!" he cried joyously.

So that was Dietmar von Arnstein, Marie thought. Well, for a knight, he certainly didn't cut a heroic figure. He was at most two or three finger-breadths taller than she. It appeared he'd been worried about his wife. Marie liked him for that, edging her way forward so she didn't miss anything. The knight disregarded the impish smiles of his men, speaking to his wife in almost childish terms of endearment and making amply clear how worried he had been about her.

"Everything went well, Dietmar." She smiled, stepping down from her wagon and pulling him to her like a little boy. Then she graciously greeted the other horsemen, who Marie gathered were friends and neighbors of the Arnsteins facing similar problems with Count Konrad von Keilburg and who had come to the castle to discuss a shared strategy. Marie trembled with anticipation. Her meeting with Mechthild von Arnstein seemed like a sign from heaven, for if she was lucky, she would find allies at the castle to help carry out her revenge on Rupert and his henchmen.

Lady Mechthild's next words reminded her of her position here, however, and brought her back to reality. "This is Marie, the whore I picked out for you. Do you like her?"

Dietmar von Arnstein cast a perturbed glance her way. "How can you be thinking about her right now? What's important is the wrong the Keilburgs have inflicted on us. Konrad and his repulsive half brother harassed old Otmar until he finally gave in and signed an agreement favoring Konrad, but it won't do him any good this time."

One of the noblemen came forward. "You should be glad, my lady. Your husband told us he gave Abbot Adalwig at Saint Ottilien a copy of the countersigned testament for safekeeping. Even Count Konrad won't be able to contradict the word of Abbot Adalwig."

Marie didn't think it wise to mention such things where anyone could hear. The lady seemed to be thinking the same thing as she cast a peeved glance at her husband and gave the order to move on. Quickly approaching the castle, the wagons wound their way toward the left tower, clattered across a bridge over a deep moat, and passed beneath a menacing row of machicoulis through which molten lead or boiling oil could be poured on an approaching enemy. At the other end of the wall, the road turned sharply to the right toward the gate in the second tower.

As Marie walked through the gate, she looked up with some dread at the imposing iron bars of the portcullis. Behind the gate was the outer ward between the outer castle wall and an almost equally strong inner wall. From here, the only way leading farther into the castle was another strongly fortified gate. In peaceful times, the outer ward was used for grazing cattle, but it was now occupied by men and animals from the abandoned village.

The lord of the castle informed his wife that the Keilburgs had made a number of forays from Mühringen Castle, which they had taken from Sir Otmar, to menace the village belonging to the Arnsteins. This fact, along with their blocking of the road, pointed to an as-yet undeclared feud. Marie found herself in the midst of events linking Rupert with her own fate, and she wondered how she could use this situation to her advantage. As a wandering harlot, she could hardly expect support from the noblemen, but no one could prevent her from keeping her eyes and ears open. Perhaps she could gain the lord's confidence and explain to him the insidious ways in which Counselor Rupert had been deceiving people.

In the meantime, the column of wagons had reached the interior ward, only a third the size of the outer one and surrounded by houses and stables constructed of large, rough-hewn blocks of stone. In the middle stood another gated tower protected by moats and a drawbridge just like the outer tower. The three wagons passed through this gate as well, finally stopping in a small courtyard between the main buildings of the castle. The lady of the castle was lifted out of her carriage by her husband, who instructed the servants to take her luggage and purchases to her rooms. Before she entered the tower, Lady Mechthild beckoned to Marie.

"Guda will show you and your friend to a stable for your goats and then take you to your rooms. You will reside adjacent to my quarters so that I may reach you at all times."

Before Marie could reply, the lady turned away. The housekeeper, not pleased with the extra work, shooed Marie and Hiltrud off in front of her like farm animals.

III.

Marie had expected to be shown to a modest room just large enough for two sacks of straw, but Guda instead took the two women to a clean, spacious room larger than the one her father had at home for visitors. There was a bed for two people and a huge trunk big enough to fit all of Hiltrud's and her things several times over. The floor was carpeted with strips of cloth sewn together, promising warm feet in the winter. The most unusual thing, however, was the elaborately decorated tile stove with a bench running around it covered with little woolen cushions. There was also a table, its top fashioned from a single piece of beechwood, and three chairs of the same wood. The value of the furnishings was only surpassed by the two narrow windows of shimmering yellow glass that bathed the room in soft daylight. The wooden frames could easily be opened—something that Hiltrud tried right away—with a view into the castle courtyard as well as over the walls and out into the countryside.

"This is magnificent," Hiltrud said, visibly impressed. "I've never lived in such elegant surroundings. I really hope we can spend the winter here."

"What would keep us from doing that?"

"Well, maybe this damned feud. As long as Dietmar is fighting with the Keilburgs, he won't be looking for caresses from you."

Marie shared this concern. If Sir Dietmar decided he didn't need her anymore, he could throw her out onto the street. Under different circumstances, this wouldn't have worried her at all. As long as the autumn was still somewhat warm, they could get along fine, but she would now lose the first chance she'd had in nearly four years to learn something about her former fiancé's plans.

For the next two hours, Marie fretted about how she might be evicted from the castle on a moment's notice. The view out the window was anything but encouraging, as Dietmar's people and his allies' horsemen were everywhere. Marie tried to count the soldiers, but she couldn't tell the men apart in their war costumes, and she stopped trying when she noticed she had counted some of them twice. She was certain, however, there were more than a hundred armed warriors in the castle. Finally it became too much for Hiltrud. "Won't you sit down? Your running back and forth is driving me to distraction."

Marie perched on a chair, wrapping her arms around her knees, as if she had to hold on to something. Jumping at every sound, she alternated looking between the door and the window even though the sky was all she could see from where she was sitting.

Putting her hands on her hips, Hiltrud finally walked over to her. "Why are you so worked up? You're acting like a chicken whose eggs have been stolen from her nest."

Marie shrugged and wrapped her arms around herself even more tightly. "It's about Count Konrad von Keilburg. I have to learn more about him."

"What is it about him that interests you?"

"About him, nothing. It's his half brother who concerns me."

Hiltrud, puzzled, stared at her for a moment with raised eyebrows. "Tell me, is this your former fiancé, Rupert Splendidus, of whom Giso spoke?"

Marie clenched her fists. "I'm sure of it. Do you understand now how terrible it would be for me if we had to leave right now?"

"Can't you think of anything but your revenge?" Hiltrud sounded somewhat amused. She'd had to remind Marie often enough that a wandering harlot was powerless against such a high-and-mighty nobleman, but now she felt like she'd been banging her head against a brick wall.

Marie had heard Hiltrud's reservations so often over the past few years that she could rattle them off by heart. "I know what you're going to tell me. But I've got to think it over."

Dwelling on Rupert's trickery, she wondered how she might win over Lady Mechthild and her husband as allies.

No longer able to stand the tense silence, Hiltrud went to the door. "I'm going to see if we can get something to eat. Last night there was nothing but water, and nothing this morning, either."

Just as she was about to step into the hall, two maids approached, carrying trays. A tempting aroma of warm bread and other delicious smells emanated from one tray; on the other stood a clay mug and two cups.

"With best wishes from the lady," one announced cheerfully. "Lady Mechthild regrets you had to wait so long, but first she had to attend to her husband and his honored guests."

Hiltrud's mouth watered when she saw the thick slices of smoked ham, enormous sausages, and the large piece of cheese that lay on the tray next to half a loaf of bread. After one of the maids had filled the cups, Hiltrud opened her eyes wide in astonishment. "That looks like wine."

The older maid nodded proudly. "This is the wine from the vineyards that Lady Mechthild brought to her marriage in her dowry." Remembering her father's vineyards near Meersburg, Marie felt a wave of grief wash over her. Swallowing her tears, she trembled with hatred, her fingers squeezing tightly shut. Rupert and his accomplices had taken so much from her! She struggled to return the maids' parting farewell, and despite her gnawing hunger, it took her a while before she took a first bite.

Hiltrud forgot Marie's distress as she happily dug into the food. "This may be the best meal I've ever had. Isn't it glorious?" When there was no reply, she nudged Marie with her foot. "Say something, won't you? Or aren't you hungry?"

Marie took a deep breath, and a reflective smile crossed her lips. "I think we'll stay, unless Lady Mechthild is just making our farewell more bearable with these treats."

"A little bowl of stew from the servants' kitchen would have been enough for that. No, I'm sure they'll keep us here. If you're smart and don't annoy the lord and lady with your sad story, we might just spend the most pleasant winter of our lives here."

Marie wanted to tell Hiltrud how many agreeable winters she had spent growing up, but she didn't want to spoil her friend's good mood. Curious about what would come next, Marie looked at the door anxiously every time she heard steps in the hallway. But no one seemed to be interested in her. After a while, the two maids returned and cleared the table. Since the wine pitcher was almost empty, they brought in a new one.

Hiltrud asked the maids where the toilet was and learned it was right around the corner. "As far as I'm concerned, it can continue like this until the spring."

Marie shrugged. "Remember, we're not here just to eat and drink wine."

"I hardly believe Sir Dietmar will call for you tonight. He seemed too angry to be interested in the joys of life."

"Just the same, I want to be ready."

"Do as you like. I'm going to the stable to check on the goats. It's time to milk them. I'll ask the maids if the lady likes goat's milk. It's supposed to be good for pregnant women."

Marie watched as she left, then sighed deeply. She really liked her companion, but her wordy enthusiasm sometimes got on her nerves. She poured herself more wine, diluted it with three parts water, and took little sips. She mustn't get drunk, as she wanted to make the best possible impression on Sir Dietmar and Lady Mechthild.

When the door opened after a while, she thought at first that Hiltrud had returned, but it was the two maids bringing a tub of water. The younger one, a perky girl who only reached Marie's chin, ran out again and came back shortly with a wash rag and a piece of soap.

"The lady said you must wash up."

Marie wanted to wait until the two had left, but they stood unmoving. Shrugging, Marie pulled her dress over her head. What difference did it make if the two maids saw her naked? She was accustomed to that at home. But in the last few years she had always tried to wash early enough in the morning that no one would see her, and she only undressed in front of her customers if they paid extra.

The maids followed Marie's every move as if to check that she had washed herself thoroughly.

The younger one beamed with joy. "You're as beautiful as an angel. Come, let me help you wash your hair."

Untying Marie's braid, they discovered the fine white scars on her back and let out shocked cries.

"Someone beat you pretty badly." There was a tone of disgust in the younger maid's voice, as if someone had debased a saint.

Marie laughed brightly but soon turned serious again. "They tied me to the pillory and whipped me. If there hadn't been a good apothecary to treat me with ointments and tinctures, my back would look like the bark of an old pine tree today."

"You are surely very thankful to the friendly gentleman for that."

"Oh, indeed I am." Marie smiled to herself. Every time she went to the Merzlingen fair, she took the apothecary into her tent. He enjoyed it, but remained loyal to Hiltrud. Just then, Marie saw that Guda had entered the room. The housekeeper sniffed at the two maids standing around.

"Keep working, you lazy wenches. The lady ordered the courtesan to be brought to the master's bedroom."

After wrapping Marie in a sheet, the maids were leading her out when Guda stopped them and pulled a little bottle from her bag. When she opened the bottle, the entire room smelled of roses. She dabbed a drop behind Marie's ear, then closed the bottle again carefully.

"That is the lady's perfume. She wants you to smell just like her when she takes you to her husband," the housekeeper declared, pushing her toward the door.

Marie remembered the salves and spices that her father had traded. Sometimes he had opened one of the bottles and let her take a whiff. Then he would tell her that he would buy her only the finest fragrances when she was grown up. Now, for the first time she was experiencing how rose oil felt on her skin, but instead of bringing her pleasure, it was only part of her job. She was here to satisfy the wants of Sir Dietmar. Or were they those of the lady? The thought amused her.

The knight's bedroom was at the other end of the hallway. When Marie was led in, Dietmar von Arnstein and his wife were standing in the middle of a room furnished much like the room she and Hiltrud were in but slightly larger. The carpeting here was more richly ornate, and a number of intricately painted wardrobes stood along the walls. In one corner was a pile of things that Lady Mechthild had obviously purchased at the fair but hadn't yet had time to put away. Marie wasn't surprised, as most of the lady's time seemed occupied with trying to care for and calm down her gloomy husband.

He turned his back to Guda and Marie and snapped at his wife. "Damn it, Mechthild. I don't need your whore!"

Smiling softy, his wife caressed his face. "But you do, now more than ever! You're a strong man who can't do without a woman for long. I was gone for two weeks, and even before that I couldn't satisfy you as much as you deserve."

"I am completely satisfied with you," Dietmar protested, "and I don't want any other woman."

Lady Mechthild rubbed her cheek against his well-shaven chin. "I know that, my dear. No woman has a better husband than I. So allow me for once to think of your own good. It will be better for me and for our child that I'm carrying if I know you are happy."

"How can I be happy when a neighbor like Keilburg is just outside my gates?" the knight snorted.

His wife just smiled and turned his head around so he would have to look at Marie. "Isn't she beautiful?"

She said it with such pride that her husband had to laugh. "You're playing a dangerous game, Mechthild. What will you do if I keep the beautiful whore and send you back to your father?"

"You certainly won't do that, as I would be taking your unborn son along."

The knight took his wife's hand and kissed it. "I love you, Mechthild, and don't wish to offend you by sleeping with another woman."

"You'll offend me if you don't sleep with Marie. I picked her out especially for you." Lady Mechthild sniffled a bit and pretended to be offended, while giving Marie a conspiratorial wave.

Mechthild's husband was fooled by her act, and looked like a chastened puppy with his tail between his legs. "All right, then, I'll take her, if only to make you happy. But I have to go back to my friends in the great hall soon. They're waiting for me."

"Oh, the gentlemen there are already consoling themselves with a few drops from our wine cellar, and I don't think they're ready for serious discussions this evening." Mechthild stood on her toes, kissed her husband on the tip of his nose, and walked toward the door. "I'll leave you alone now but will be back later."

Dietmar von Arnstein nodded and was about to undress when something else occurred to him. "Tell me, woman, how are you so sure the child will be a boy?"

"I lit a candle for the Madonna of Saint Ottilien, asking her to send us a son. Abbot Adalwig assured me that the Madonna would hear my prayers."

The knight threw back his head and laughed. "I'd have nothing against a son and heir, but when I see you like this, it makes me wish it's a girl. That would put a crimp in your pride, woman. Recently you've had your nose pretty far up in the air."

The deeply loving look he gave his wife as he said that made Marie envious, for she realized she'd probably never know that kind of affection.

Mechthild gave her a sign, and Marie removed her sheet, presenting her full glory to the knight. Dietmar's eyes sparkled, but instead of pulling her down onto the bed, he jokingly asked his wife to help him remove his shirt. With agile fingers, Mechthild untied the laces, kissed him, and quickly left the room before he could detain her again.

The lord of the castle turned to Marie and pointed with his chin to the bed. She lay down, and he passed his hands over her body, examining her, while she fought the usual feeling of being just an object that anyone could use for a few coins. It was clear to her, however, that she was doing the knight an injustice with such thoughts. He said nothing but didn't hold her as roughly or as lustfully as other men did.

When he lay down on her, he supported himself with his elbows and didn't use his weight to press her into the pillows. Dietmar wasn't as gentle as Herbmann, but he also wasn't thinking only of his own pleasure. Marie felt nothing but was simply happy he didn't hurt her, and she pretended to be excited in thanks for his consideration.

Just as he finished with a gasp of relief, the door opened and Lady Mechthild slipped in.

"You see, dear, this is better," she said with a smile.

Dietmar rolled away from Marie and lay on his back, the guilty look on his face making his wife smile.

"Kiss me," Mechthild demanded. He did so and looked relieved when she passionately reciprocated his tenderness.

"In a few months we will be able to once again enjoy the pleasure of our conjugal bed. Until then, Marie will take my place," she explained, getting her breath back. "But we will continue to sleep side by side at night and talk with each other. Now that you are relaxed and not so much in the grip of your anger at the Keilburgs, we need to consider what to do. Simply starting a feud and going into battle, as Hartmut von Treilenburg demands, doesn't seem the right thing to do."

Dietmar threw his hands up helplessly. "But we have to do something. If we don't stop this rogue knight, he will destroy us all."

"Of course we have to oppose him in some way," she agreed in a gentle voice. She slipped under the bedcovers and gently pushed Marie aside. "You have done me good service and can retire to your room," she ordered, then turned back to her husband.

Quickly leaving the bedroom, Marie didn't realize until she was outside the door that she'd forgotten her sheet. Though she was embarrassed to run through the castle naked, she didn't dare return to the bedroom. Covering herself with her hands as best she could, she hurried down the corridor, happy that no one saw her.

She couldn't know that in fact someone had been watching. Behind a slightly ajar door, a haggard man in a shabby monk's robe was peering out into the hallway to check on all comings and goings. He saw Marie for a moment in all her beauty, watching as she disappeared into her room. When the door closed behind her, he seemed to want to follow her, but his feet stood rooted to the spot and he flailed the air with his hands as if struggling to control himself.

Listening to check that the coast was clear, the man tiptoed down the hallway to the lord's bedroom and placed his ear against the door while keeping an eye on the corridor. His face was tense with anticipation, and his lips twisted into a disappointed grimace as if he heard things that displeased him.

IV.

Since Marie only had to be available for one man, she had plenty of time to listen, look around, and think about things. She often considered the relationship between the lady and the lord of the castle, marveling at how Lady Mechthild wielded astonishing power over her husband. But Marie didn't realize just how great the lady's influence was until the next day, when she hid in the stairwell leading down into the knight's hall and overheard one of the conversations between Dietmar and his allies. There he used exactly the same words Lady Mechthild had put into his mouth just the evening before.

When Marie told Hiltrud, her friend laughed at her. "The mistress is, as we both know, very smart and at least as assertive. It's no wonder Sir Dietmar follows her advice."

"But I still don't understand how she can put another woman in his bed and still lead him around like a horse on a bridle. Don't priests always say that women must be subservient and obey their husbands? That's what a burgher's daughter is taught even before she learns to walk."

Hiltrud demurred. "You should accept things as they are and not pry into the way other people act. I think you have too much free time. Ask Guda if she has something for you to do, because if you keep sitting around here like this, you'll go mad. I enjoy helping in the stables. Do you know they have a whole herd of goats here? Thomas, the boy who cares for them, promised me he'll let his best buck mate with my two nannies, so when we move on, we'll have two little kids again." Hiltrud's eyes sparkled.

"Nice for you, but I'm not concerned with goats at the moment. If I ask Guda for work, I won't have any time to listen in on the conversations in the great hall, and I won't be able to learn more about Rupert."

Hiltrud looked anxious. "You should stay away from there. If they catch you, they'll think you're spying for the Keilburgs, and they do away with traitors pretty quickly here."

Marie waved her hand dismissively. "I won't be so easy to catch. The stairway is rarely used, and if someone does come by, I can just pretend I'm looking at the weapons and hunting trophies."

Hiltrud pounded her hand on the table. "You're not just putting yourself at risk. If they catch you, they'll suspect me, too, and we'll consider ourselves lucky if we're thrown out onto the street in the middle of winter. It's more likely we'll rot in the dungeon."

"You're too pessimistic," Marie replied, relieved to see the maid enter with the evening meal, then stay for a short chat. Hiltrud kept the easily frightened girl occupied by telling her a few horror stories, so Marie was able to dwell on her thoughts.

Hiltrud was right. If she spied on the noblemen, she would risk losing not only their comfortable winter quarters but also their lives, because the men were so incensed that they would take it out on anyone. Nevertheless, she felt a desperate need to find out what was happening. In the beginning, with emotions running high, it looked as if the Arnsteins would declare a feud against Konrad von Keilburg and dispatch him to hell along with his illegitimate brother, Rupert. But these hopes quickly disappeared, as Sir Dietmar insisted that an attack on the count could only be successful if they found additional allies.

Though the Keilburgs had more than twice as many soldiers as Sir Dietmar and his allies, Count Konrad seemed hesitant to start a feud with the knights. Through her snooping, Marie learned a lot about the feudal laws that restrained the Keilburgs from attacking a knight without warning, and she learned all the things her host had to do, and to avoid doing, in order not to give the count any pretext for officially declaring a feud.

Indeed, Count Konrad von Keilburg was obligated to show consideration for his neighbors, and in his case also that of the higher nobility. Marie thought through the names of those whom Rupert's half brother had to fear the most, among them Count Eberhard von Württemberg, one of the most influential nobles in the now-nonexistent old Duchy of Swabia. Together with Margrave Bernhard von Baden and Friedrich von Habsburg, Count Eberhard had an important role to play in the unstable power structure that the Keilburgs so ruthlessly exploited.

All of the noblemen currently convened at Arnstein feared their powerful neighbors and continually talked of entering into an alliance against the growing influence of Count Konrad von Keilburg. The next evening, as Marie took her usual place on the stairway peering through the balusters, Dietmar von Arnstein returned to this topic. "We have to align ourselves with either the Habsburgs or the Württembergs, or the Keilburgs will devour us one after the other."

"I'm for Duke Friedrich—he's the most powerful." Degenhard von Steinzell, who was staying at Arnstein Castle with his son, Philipp, as usual stated his preference for the Habsburgs.

Rumold von Bürggen grimaced. "That's just the reason I'm against this alliance. If we ally ourselves with Friedrich, we'll be reduced to insignificant vassals who'll be at his beck and call. We'd have to take part in wars that don't concern us, depriving our own lands of able-bodied men for months. No, friends, we have no other choice than to rely on our own strength. With any luck, an alliance of all the independent knights and lords would be able to stop the Keilburgs in their tracks and put an end to their hunger for land once and for all."

"That's just exactly how I feel," replied Hartmut von Trellenburg, turning to Rumold. "Why should we bow our heads to the Habsburgs or the Württembergs? I say we need to stand up for ourselves. It shouldn't be hard to put together an alliance against Konrad von Keilburg. After all, he has angered many others, including the abbot of Saint Ottilien whose Steinwald hills Keilburg just seized. Gottfried von Dreieichen had donated the forest to the monastery as a place for prayer and meditation, but when Abbot Adalwig demanded the land back, he was scorned and reviled. Some even say Keilburg threatened him."

Sir Dietmar put his head in his hands. "If Count Konrad is intimidating the abbot of Saint Ottilien, then things look bad for me. After all, Adalwig is the guarantor of my contract with my uncle Otmar."

Hartmut von Treilenburg nodded approvingly. "Don't worry about Adalwig. He'll stand with us if it comes to a feud with the Keilburgs."

Wearily, Sir Dietmar waved off his comment. "I'd feel better if Abbot Adalwig could support us with armed men or was rich enough to hire mercenaries, but his seventy friars won't be much help in a battle."

"That's why we need to throw our lot in with Duke Friedrich," Degenhard von Steinzell insisted.

"No, that's why we need to join forces with Eberhard von Württemberg," Rumold von Bürggen insisted, pounding the table. "He doesn't have nearly as many men as Duke Friedrich, but some of his vassals up north are the Keilburgs' neighbors. Count Eberhard has to be careful that Count Konrad doesn't get the best of him."

"In my opinion, we're talking too much," Hartmut von Treilenburg interrupted. "Are we mice or men? Every one of our horsemen is worth two or three times as much in battle as Keilburg's paid mercenaries."

Sir Dietmar raised his hand, asking for silence. "I oppose an open battle. It would cost us good men who till our fields in peacetime. A battle, however, benefits Count Konrad since his paid soldiers don't earn anything if they fall in battle, whereas he currently has to spend a small fortune housing and feeding them while they wait for a possible feud. As long as we don't break any laws and give him a reason to declare a feud against us, peace will financially hurt him much more than a fight."

"Are you against a battle, Dietmar, or is your wife?" Rumold von Bürggen asked with unconcealed sarcasm. "We all know that Lady Mechthild has a good head on her shoulders, but waging war is something she should leave to the men."

Dietmar's face flushed at his words, and he jumped up, glaring furiously at Rumhold. "You've crossed the line! I won't let anyone call me a coward or unmanly."

"Then don't act that way," Rumold replied, undeterred. Degenhard von Steinzell spoke calmly, trying to smooth things over. "Why are we having this stupid argument? Your quarreling only helps Keilburg to bring us down. Remember, we have to stick together!"

Clenching his fists, Dietmar had to force himself to sit down. "I won't let anyone call me a coward."

Rumhold von Bürggen waved him off with a look of contempt, angering his host further.

"Degenhard is right," Hartmut von Treilenburg asserted, addressing them both. "If we don't stick together, we'll meet again sooner or later in Keilburg's dungeon."

Marie didn't hear whether his appeal was well received, as she heard steps behind her. Jumping up, she ran back down the corridor and hid in a doorway. But it was too late. Jodokus, the monk who served Sir Dietmar as his scribe and priest, blocked her way, baring his huge yellow teeth and twisting his mouth into a grimace.

"Good day, Fräulein Marie. I'm so delighted to meet you."

Marie stepped back a bit. "Fräulein? It's nearly four years too late for you to call me that."

Sir Dietmar thought highly of the monk, and Lady Mechthild had publicly praised him several times. But Marie didn't like him, regarding him with distrust. She found his pale gaze as repellent as the unctuous way he always tried to engage her in conversation.

Smiling gently, as if to calm her down, Brother Jodokus placed his hand on her shoulder and drew her closer. "You're ashamed of what life has made of you, Marie, yet you're as beautiful as an angel of the Lord. A loving and experienced hand could lead you safely to paradise."

Marie understood the monk meant a very earthly type of paradise, as his other hand slid down gently past her breasts to her thighs. She shoved him away and tried to sneak by him, but he seized her so tightly, she could feel his fingernails digging through the heavy wool cloth of her dress.

"Why do you turn away from me when any man can have you for a few pennies?"

Marie was terrified. The monk looked ready to push her into the nearest empty room and take her by force. In another setting she would have fought back and shown him not to touch an unwilling woman. But here she couldn't anger him, because it was entirely within his power to make the rest of her stay miserable or to have her and Hiltrud thrown out of the castle. Thinking fast, she looked at him boldly.

"At present I'm not available. The lady brought me to the castle for the sole use of her husband and would be angered if I granted my favors to another man."

Brother Jodokus made a face like that of a child whose toy had been taken away. "Lady Mechthild doesn't have to learn about it."

Laughing, Marie pulled his limp hands from her dress. "Does anything happen inside these walls that Lady Mechthild doesn't learn about? At a fair, you could buy my body for a few pennies, but here the lady's will doesn't allow it."

The monk groaned, grabbed her again, and pressed himself against her so tightly that she almost lost her breath. "I don't want just your body. Since I saw you naked as God created you, I've known I must possess you."

Confused, Marie pushed him away. When did he see me naked? she wondered in shock. She took great care to protect her privacy. Jodokus's remark led her to wonder if there was a peephole in her room that the monk could look through to see her. Shivering, she resolved to thoroughly inspect the walls.

"It's true I am a whore, but I don't offer myself to everyone," she answered sharply.

Her rejection seemed only to inflame the monk's passion. "Don't turn away from me, sweet child. Together we could achieve the greatest happiness on earth or in the hereafter."

"How so? As beggars on the open road?"

Jodokus smiled. "Don't underestimate me. I will soon be a very rich man, and if you come with me, you'll live like a noble lady."

In great detail he explained how he would shower her with jewelry and clothing. Even the merchant from Flanders had never offered her such expensive finery. Pretending to listen, Marie was just waiting for a chance to escape. Even if he was telling the truth, she didn't want to get involved.

As a monk he had taken a vow of celibacy, and probably also of chastity, but he seemed not to adhere to his vows any more than most other men of the church. The morality of priests and monks had been steadily declining ever since Popes Gregory, John, and Benedict had been fighting for the leadership of Christianity. Marie remembered a facetious remark she'd overheard in her travels. "Why shouldn't a priest marry?" a street performer asked her one day, providing his own answer. "Because all the women in his congregation are available to him anyway."

Marie had laughed, but it was true. Nevertheless, it was far different for a priest to bed women or for a bishop to keep a mistress than for an ordinary monk to keep a woman or even marry. Doing so would turn people against Jodokus, and they would make short shrift of him and the woman he kept.

Marie shuddered at the brazenness of the man's lust. Yet even if he wasn't a cleric and a marriage with him could elevate her standing to that of an honorable woman, she wouldn't do it. Jodokus disgusted her, and it made her furious that she couldn't tell him that to his face.

"Excuse me if I don't understand you. I'm just a stupid woman," she mumbled in a desperate attempt to win time.

For a moment it seemed the monk was going to speak, but he just pressed his lips together as if to guard against saying anything rash, instead devouring her with his hungry eyes and breathing heavily. After a few moments, he released her and stepped aside. "I desire you, and I will have you."

It sounded like a threat to Marie. Curtsying quickly, she flew down the hallway, but even after she had bolted the entrance to her room, she felt his eyes boring into the back of her head from behind the door.

Jodokus watched her until she disappeared from sight. Then he leaned against the wall, trembling and pressing his forehead against the cold stone. The harlot was right. Lady Mechthild would never allow anyone but her husband to touch her. He was consumed with jealousy, thinking of how the young woman was at the knight's disposal even though Dietmar didn't make much of it. The monk wouldn't give up, though. In three months at the latest, Lady Mechthild's child would be born and she would again take her place in the lord's bedroom. The monk would then carry out his plan, putting him in a position to buy Marie and make her completely his own. Then he would make sure no other man ever came near her. Thinking about the future, Jodokus smiled so contentedly that Guda looked at him in astonishment as she passed by. Whenever she'd seen the monk before, he'd always been wearing a sour face.

V.

In Marie and Hiltrud's first few weeks at Arnstein Castle, their interests and attentions diverged. Hiltrud enjoyed life in the castle more than she ever could have imagined. They lived like nobility in their large room with a fireplace that was always stocked with wood; even their beds were as exquisitely soft as the clouds on which angels slept. They were given the best food and allowed to do as they pleased. All that was asked of them was that Marie respond to the lord's needs and that Hiltrud not entice other men.

The maids who waited on them treated them like exotic creatures, but they were always friendly and chatty. The other servants didn't dare criticize them because it would anger the lady, and the men left Marie alone. Though the men didn't dare lay a hand on Hiltrud, either, they did puff themselves up like roosters when she walked by, and, every now and then, she slept with a few of them. Giso, the sharp-tongued castellan, paid twelve pennies for her service, and she was pleased with the easily acquired money.

In contrast with the others, Thomas, the goatherd, didn't have to pay. A year older than Hiltrud, he had been born deformed and was thus unable to become a warrior. He had a slender face with deep-set gray eyes surrounded by a full head of light brown hair and bore a slight resemblance to Sir Dietmar. Apparently, the former lord of the castle also took comfort in other women during his wife's pregnancy, and Thomas had been born about seven months after Dietmar. What Hiltrud liked about Thomas was his wonderfully gentle and friendly behavior toward her, along with his skill in raising animals. He accepted her attentions as a precious gift and enjoyed her friendship.

Hiltrud found it hard to restrain her emotions, but as she had learned through bitter experience, it wasn't smart for her to have special feelings for a man. Their love would only survive the winter; then she would have to resume her old life in the spring and once again take to the roads. For this reason, she wasn't ready to give up her professional favors for Giso and other men just for love.

She had even slept with the monk Jodokus once, though he smelled bad and had offered only a few Haller pennies for her services. Normally she would have turned someone like him away, but in the castle she didn't dare say no because his words carried weight with the lady. Since the monk had no experience with prostitutes, the sex act was brief, but afterward he questioned her for more than an hour about Marie. Later that evening, she had joked with her friend about it, but Marie was aloof, grimacing and muttering curses when the monk's name was mentioned.

One evening, Hiltrud was in bed with Thomas in the little shed over the goat stable that served as his home. Bark still hung from the unfinished wallboards, and the room was perched in the rafters like a bird's nest. Thomas had constructed a bed, a small table, and two stools out of wood scraps, and a few hooks made of forked branches completed the furnishings. There wasn't room for anything else there, but the goatherd was content with its snugness.

While Hiltrud lay lost in thought, he sat up and looked at her breasts that, despite their size, were still firm. "You are beautiful."

"Marie is beautiful," Hiltrud contradicted. "I'm just acceptable."

"You're hiding your light under a bushel," Thomas remonstrated gently. "To me you are the most beautiful woman in the world, and I'll be very sad when you leave me."

"I'm not a woman you should fall in love with. Even now I'm not too faithful, as you know."

"You're making a living, just as I am caring for the goats."

Thomas's voice caressed her as gently as a spring breeze, and Hiltrud couldn't help thinking how happy she could be if she weren't so worried about Marie. The goatherd seemed to read her thoughts, for he pulled the blanket over her and stroked her cheek.

"What is troubling you so much?"

"Oh, it's only Marie. Why can't she be happy in the present, like we are? All she ever thinks about is getting revenge on the man who destroyed her life. She might as well take a handful of snow and throw it at the sun to put it out."

Thomas smiled dreamily. "Sometimes all it takes is a handful of snow to put out a fire."

Hiltrud shook her head in annoyance. "Don't encourage her with this foolishness."

"I won't do that, but you should warn her that people are talking about how she sneaks into the great hall when the noblemen meet there. If Lady Mechthild hears about it, she'll think your friend is a spy and have her locked in the dungeon."

"I'll keep an eye on her," Hiltrud promised, and snuggled up closer.

Planning to give Marie a scolding when she left Thomas's room, she saw that the guests and their retinues were preparing to leave, and breathed a sigh of relief. Now she didn't need to fear for her friend anymore.

The noblemen's faces looked strained as they said their hearty farewells to Sir Dietmar. Despite the danger they were all in, their neighborly relationships had grown even more tense. Hiltrud watched as the horsemen left, and she crossed herself three times.

Lady Mechthild, standing in a green dress in the residence tower doorway, laughed with relief. Her hands had been full keeping her husband and his hotheaded friends from doing things that would surely have turned out badly. Nothing could be gained by a feud using brute force against the Keilburgs, and it would have only turned other nearby castle owners against them, as wars disturbed trade and reduced income.

Mechthild waved and smiled at her husband who had escorted his guests on horseback for a short way, and he returned the greeting sullenly as he rode back into the castle.

When he dismounted, she hurried toward him and lightly pressed his hand to her cheek. "I know that allies are important, but I'm happy to have our castle to ourselves again. After a while our guests were a bit of a strain."

Dietmar took his hand away and tossed the reins to a stable boy, then stared at her with a mixture of anger and despair. "In their eyes I'm a coward because I don't want to assert my rights by force."

"A right that you assert by force is like a law of the jungle," she lectured him gently. "Our only chance against Count Konrad von Keilburg is an appeal to the Imperial Court of Justice. Even Konrad von Keilburg isn't powerful enough to oppose the will of the kaiser. Until then, we'll have to look around for a friend who is more powerful than Keilburg."

"So you still think I should ally myself with Count Eberhard von Württemberg?" Sir Dietmar didn't sound entirely convinced.

Smiling widely, she nodded and embraced him, then gave him a big kiss.

Catching herself eavesdropping, Hiltrud ran back into the tower. Entering their room, she found Marie sitting at one of the windows, staring into the distance. Hiltrud placed her hands on her hips and shook her head disapprovingly. "You brood too much, Marie."

Marie looked as if her friend had wakened her from a deep sleep. "I can't help myself. Ever since I've been here, I constantly think of Rupert, and I long for the day he and his scoundrels get their just punishment. For a while I'd hoped Sir Dietmar would declare a feud against the Keilburgs and that Rupert would lose the protection of his aristocratic half brother. Then all I would have to do is hire an assassin to dispatch the monsters who ruined me."

"You're dreaming. Lady Mechthild will never allow hostilities to develop."

Marie nodded somberly. "I know. After all, I overheard the conversations."

"Yes, and that was a very risky thing to do. The servants are already talking about it, and Thomas asked me to warn you."

Marie shrugged and thrust out her lower lip. "What does a goatherd like him know?"

"He's very bright and knows better than most what's going on in the castle. You need to pull yourself together and forget your silly ideas. Enjoy the time we spend here. This is the easiest money we've made in the last three years."

"I'd rather be a camp prostitute in an army hell-bent on destroying the Keilburgs," Marie exploded. "Here I'm not getting anywhere. Perhaps Sir Dietmar and his friends will get a favorable ruling from the Imperial Court, but that won't help me. No court in the world will give me satisfaction!"

Marie broke out in tears of despair, and Hiltrud put comforting arms around the young woman. Marie clung to her like a little child, but the words she spoke revealed a hatred that made Hiltrud shudder.

VI.

Shortly after the noblemen departed, it started to snow heavily, and Arnstein tucked itself in for the winter. Only rarely did anyone enter or leave the castle. Twice a messenger from an ally came struggling through the snow, and Marie watched as, completely exhausted, he was lifted out of the saddle and brought into the castle. Unable to overhear the conversation, she had to rely on rumors circulating among the servants.

It was said that neither Dietmar nor his allies had succeeded in finding support. The Keilburgs also seemed paralyzed by the winter, however, and the count had apparently dismissed some of his mercenaries, sending the rest of his army to their winter quarters. His men still controlled the main highway to the north but allowed a few wagon trains and travelers to pass. Only the horsemen and vassals belonging to Arnstein Castle or Rumold von Bürggen were forced to take the dangerous route through the swamp.

Marie rarely spoke with Hiltrud, who spent most of her time with Thomas. When the two did see each other, Hiltrud talked mostly about her goats. Thomas had supplied his best ram, and Hiltrud was thrilled about the young kids on the way. Greatly enjoying this life, Hiltrud struggled with tears when she thought about leaving in the spring.

Meanwhile, Marie was helping the maids in the sewing room to prepare and decorate with fancy embroidery clothes for the child that Lady Mechthild would bear in a few weeks. Marie had once been adept with needle and thread, sewing and decorating her own dowry, and Lady Mechthild was so pleased with her work that she gave Marie enough remnants and good thread to make two dresses, two scarfs, and a few undershirts for Hiltrud and herself.

Marie enjoyed the sewing as it took her mind off her dark musings, but one morning after an especially bad night plagued with nightmares, she had no desire to do anything. Pushing some ribbons aside, she put her hands in her lap and stared out the window. Just a few bare trees with snow-covered crowns and part of the road to the castle were visible, but the view let her feel less confined.

She suddenly blinked in astonishment. For more than a week, only residents of the castle or small nearby village had entered the castle gates, but now strangers were approaching on horseback. Since they were weaving through the trees, she couldn't see their exact numbers, but she guessed there were at least a dozen men.

When the tower watchman sounded the alert, the maids excitedly hurried to the windows to see, but the horsemen had already disappeared behind the castle wall. Since Guda had left the room to assist the lady in preparing for the unexpected guests, the women ran down the hallway like a swarm of chicks until they arrived at a window overlooking the inner courtyard. As the first rider passed through the gate with a pennant proudly raised, one of maids cried out in astonishment. "That's the Keilburg coat of arms. What are they doing here?"

Heart pounding, Marie didn't even try to glance out the window, but instead ran outside to look for a place from which to secretly view the travelers' reception. Since the visitors hadn't yet reached the last gate, she ran over the drawbridge into the inner part of the castle and hid in the feeding aisle of the noblemen's horse stable. Pushing a crate under a small barred opening, she climbed up and was able to see everything happening outside.

No sooner had she settled down in her observation post than the new arrivals entered the courtyard. They were in fact Keilburgs, as the coat of arms on their cloaks made clear. Judging by their dress and their behavior, however, these ten armed men were not ordinary horsemen but hired mercenaries escorting a nobleman. Marie glanced at the eleventh man and the blood in her veins ran cold. It was none other than Counselor Rupert Splendidus.

Only ten steps away from her hiding place, he stopped his horse and looked around. He appeared to be counting the warriors deployed in the castle courtyard and on the battlements. He was biting his lip and looked troubled. She surmised that he clearly hadn't expected so many soldiers. A triumphant smile lit her face. Rupert had been fooled by Lady Mechthild's trick, planned weeks ago, in which she had weapons and uniforms made for all the servants to make the castle's armed force seem much larger than it was. Even Thomas stood armed with a long spear atop the walkway where no one could see his hunched back.

Marie's triumphant smile faded when she looked more closely at Rupert. The last three and a half years had been good to him. Stouter than she remembered and better dressed than a man of his position could ordinarily afford to be, he was wearing a beaver skin cap and a coat of the finest Flemish wool trimmed with wolf's fur to protect him from the cold. As he dismounted and removed his gloves, she saw half a dozen golden rings glittering on his fingers.

"I wish to speak with Sir Dietmar!" His voice filled the courtyard.

"What do you want from me?" The lord of the castle had stepped onto a balcony from which he could get a good look at the uninvited guests without having to fear a surprise attack.

Turning his head upward, Rupert faced Dietmar. "I come in the name of my esteemed brother, Count Konrad von Keilburg. He has ordered me to negotiate with you."

This reply was so surprising that at first Sir Dietmar didn't seem to know how to answer. Resting his hands on the balcony, he looked closely at Rupert. "If Count Konrad wishes to hand over my uncle's inheritance, you are welcome to talk. Otherwise, anything you have to say is superfluous."

Rupert's smile was inscrutable. "I can't offer you that. Sir Otmar may once have promised to leave Mühringen to you, but he since changed his mind and bequeathed his castle and land to my brother in a signed agreement. Count Konrad does not wish to quarrel, however, and has sent me with a message of peace. I would prefer not to present my message out in the cold in front of everyone but would appreciate coming indoors to savor a cup of the excellent wine from your wife's vineyard."

Rupert seemed to be trying to position himself as an equal and give Dietmar some hope of settling the dispute through negotiation. Based on her own unhappy experience, Marie suspected that a conversation with Rupert could prove more dangerous for Dietmar than a thousand armed soldiers standing before Arnstein's walls. But knowing Dietmar as she did, she was certain he would take Keilburg's offer as a sign of weakness and agree to talk.

Breathing quickly, Marie didn't want to miss a word. She jumped down from her crate, ran through the servants' quarters and up some stairs into the stronghold of the castle, then continued into a gallery above the great hall. Since everyone was preoccupied with the visitors, she managed to reach her observation post on the upper staircase without being seen. She was sure Sir Dietmar would receive Rupert here, where the pictures of his ancestors and many battle trophies displayed his impressive power and lineage.

She was right. Crouching on the stairwell, she barely had time to wrap her dress around her legs to ward off drafts before the lord of the castle led his visitor in. Dietmar sat down first, looking like a king on his elaborately carved throne at the head of the large table. He had his cup filled with wine while Rupert stood like a supplicant until a servant brought him a chair. Since the counselor's thin smile didn't waver, it was hard to tell if he was offended. Taking the offered chair, Rupert waited until a servant had filled his cup as well, then drank to Dietmar as if they were best friends.

"So what does your brother have in mind?" Sir Dietmar was gruff, but Marie was angered that Rupert had succeeded in impressing him, as the knight was now addressing the counselor as an equal.

"Count Konrad regrets the bad feelings between you two and would like an amicable settlement."

"All he has to do is to give me what is mine," Dietmar replied curtly.

Once again Rupert's lips twisted into an inscrutable smile. "Unfortunately, my brother sees matters differently. He has an iron-clad contract awarding him Otmar's possessions and sees no reason to relinquish it."

"Is that so?" Sir Dietmar called loudly for his scribe.

Just then, a door opened in the great hall as if someone had been waiting outside, and the monk entered. In front of him he was carrying with great care a long leather roll that he handed to his lord.

Sir Dietmar took the roll, pulled out a parchment sheet, and handed it to Rupert with a triumphant expression. "Read this yourself! Here, signed and sealed, it states that my uncle has bequeathed his possessions to me and cannot change his will without my approval."

Rupert glanced at the contract and briefly grimaced; then his face once again became blank. "That's a matter of interpretation. According to current law, a newer testament supersedes an older one. Even if you go to court, this contract won't gain you more than a small compensation out of all proportion to the costs and trouble that a trial incurs." He put the document down in front of him on the table and crossed his arms over his chest. He didn't even look at his wine while Dietmar was having his glass filled again.

"But in order to be a good neighbor, and to put an end to this disagreement," said Rupert, stressing the words *good neighbor*, "my brother offers you the Steinwald Forest."

The lord of the castle pounded the table furiously. "He stole that property from Saint Ottilien's monastery. Does he want to sow the seeds of discord between me and the abbot?"

"You shouldn't be so hasty. It wasn't my brother who took Steinwald from the monastery, but Sir Gottfried himself who unlawfully went to war with the justified claims of my father, Count Heinrich."

For a moment, Marie felt like she was again in the Constance courtroom, hearing Rupert's merciless voice condemning her to her ruinous fate. She realized that Rupert was an insidious enemy who knew how to beat his adversary with the power of words. Now he was aiming to drive Dietmar into a corner. The lord of the castle was still mulling over Rupert's words when the counselor raised his hand and continued speaking.

"Before you say or do things that you will later regret, please hear me out. My brother is not your enemy. He is only defending what is lawfully his. You, too, would not have permitted it if your uncle had bequeathed his property to you and another neighbor presented an older will to contest it."

Sir Dietmar nodded instinctively as if to agree, but then raised his head. Rupert noticed the motion and smiled. "Why don't you accept the situation as it is? Take the hand that my brother extends to you in friendship and ally yourself with him. In return, Konrad will cede Felde Castle to you along with a third of the land that once belonged to Sir Walter. The property would better round out your holdings than the property of your uncle."

Marie could feel the almost hypnotic power in Rupert's words and feared for a moment that Sir Dietmar would succumb.

Lady Mechthild, who had silently appeared at Marie's side, seemed to feel the same way. "My husband will never do that!" she called down into the hall. Before Marie could jump up, she felt the lady's tight grip on her shoulder.

"You have some explaining to do later!" she whispered angrily to Marie, barely moving her lips or taking her eyes off her husband and Rupert.

Since neither of the men replied, she addressed Rupert. "Tell your brother that Arnstein will never cower before him. To accept this offer would be a disgrace. We demand our rights and will fight for them."

Rupert's face darkened with fleeting anger. Raising his wine-glass as if trying to conceal a scornful grin, he looked at the knight over the rim of the glass. "So it's true what they say about you, Sir Dietmar. Your wife wears the pants here."

For a moment the lord of the castle looked sheepish, but then brought his fist crashing down onto the table. "No one gets away with talking to me like that, least of all the miserable illegitimate son of an even more miserable father. Leave, knave, or I'll have my servants throw you out."

Rupert had not expected this. His eyes darting nervously between the knight and the signed parchment, he reached for it without thinking.

Sir Dietmar seized the valuable document. "You'd like to have that, wouldn't you, scoundrel! Your reaction shows me that my chances are good of retrieving my property in the kaiser's court without an armed conflict."

"We'll see about that!" Rupert snapped as he sprang up and left the great hall without saying good-bye.

Sir Dietmar turned away and looked up at his wife, shaking his head. "What if Keilburg's peace offering was meant seriously?"

"If you'd accepted, it would be stabbing our neighbors in the back. Your friends would rightfully take such an agreement as a betrayal. Then we would be left without any allies, completely at the mercy of Count Konrad."

"But I'd have Felde Castle and a nice piece of land."

"Something Konrad von Keilburg could take back from you whenever he wanted without anyone lifting a finger to stop him. No, Dietmar, we don't have much more than our honest name, and we mustn't risk it for a mess of pottage."

"Woman, I'm afraid you're right again! But I need some fresh air to think it all over." Dietmar took a deep breath, drank the rest of his wine, and left the great hall, shoulders drooping. Lady Mechthild stood shaking her head as he left the hall, waiting until the doors had closed behind him. She then turned to Marie.

"Now, as for you. Why are you eavesdropping on my husband? I know this isn't the first time. Are you spying for Count Konrad?"

Tears streaming down her cheeks, Marie wiped them away with the back of her hand. "No, my lady. I have nothing to do with Keilburg, but all the more so with his scoundrel half brother."

Lady Mechthild raised an eyebrow. "What do you know about Counselor Rupert?"

Marie groaned as the lady's fingers dug into her shoulder. "He was my fiancé! He stole everything I had and made me what I am today."

Though Mechthild loosened her hold slightly, doubt as well as interest showed in her face. "Tell me everything you know about him. Come along!"

She led Marie into her private room overlooking the courtyard. Aside from the well-padded stone bench that ran under the three windows, there were a diminutive closet, a matching sewing table decorated with inlaid work, and an upholstered footstool. The floor was covered with sheepskin, which along with the old woolen wall hangings made the tiny room feel like a cave. This was where the lady retreated when she wanted to be alone.

Lady Mechthild ordered Marie to take a seat. Then she took two cups from the little closet, filled them with wine from a clay pitcher, and sat so that her face was in the shadows while Marie sat in the light of the slowly setting winter sun.

"Speak now. But I warn you! If I feel you are lying, I'll make quick work of you."

Looking down at her hands, Marie tried to swallow the lump in her throat. Overwhelmed more by memories than the lady's threats, she spoke haltingly at first. But as Mechthild quietly listened and didn't interrupt, Marie's confidence increased, her words tumbling out faster and faster. She held nothing back, not even her plans to murder the counselor.

As she was about to relay her experiences on the road, Mechthild raised her hand and changed the topic back to Rupert. She had Marie repeat everything she knew. Finally the lady stood up and put her hand on her back as if to keep from collapsing with the weight of all her duties. "If what you say is true, our enemy is even more dangerous than we had assumed."

"I swear by all the saints that I have spoken the truth," Marie said calmly, despite the emotions raging within her.

"For your sake, I hope so. I will send a trusted man to Constance who will ask around. Until he is back, you will not leave the castle."

Lady Mechthild rose and opened the door, then closed it again and put her hands on Marie's shoulders. "If your report is true, Counselor Rupert's treatment of you is more than shameful."

Marie pictured herself again in the dungeon, and sobbed. "He wasn't the only one."

"Pull yourself together!" Lady Mechthild didn't give Marie time to wallow in misery, but instead ordered her back to her room to prepare herself for the lord. When Dietmar returned from his walk still out of sorts, he felt little desire to sleep with Marie, but he was helpless against the will of his wife.

VII.

Mechthild von Arnstein took Marie's report so seriously that she sent her trustworthy castellan to Constance. The heavy snow had let up over the past several weeks, but now cold gripped the land and icy winds swept over the hills. Despite the freezing weather, Marie walked around the battlements every day and climbed the tower to watch for Giso's return. She was thankful that Mechthild had not imprisoned her, but even with this daily routine, she was barely able to contain her mounting tension.

Trying to distract her friend, Hiltrud took Marie along to the goat stables. Thomas showed her his animals, introducing them by name and telling her funny stories. For a few days Marie enjoyed her visits, as Thomas was very entertaining, but she soon felt like she was intruding. She could see that these two very different people had forged a bond of affection that went far beyond ordinary friendship, but when she suggested that Hiltrud ask Lady Mechthild if she could stay at the castle, Hiltrud vigorously shook her head.

"No, that wouldn't work out, even though we both care very much for each other. Thomas is a vassal and can't lift a finger without asking his master's permission, and people would always make me feel shameful. We're just enjoying this time together from which we'll always have beautiful memories. That's all we can hope for."

"That's a shame. Your Thomas is a good man and would be a caring companion." When Marie saw the tears in Hiltrud's eyes, she could tell how hard this was for her friend, and she resolved not to bring up the subject again. After that, she only occasionally accompanied Hiltrud to see the goats. Lady Mechthild's pregnancy kept her busy, and she also spent time on the castle walkway or in the sewing room.

In the weeks before Christmas, it began to snow hard, and for a while it looked like the castle might be completely cut off from the outside world. Finally, during a raging snowstorm, Giso returned. Lady Mechthild, who was now very large with child and had difficulty moving, nevertheless hurried down to the courtyard to greet him. Marie followed close behind with a cup of hot mulled wine and was pleased that the lady was awaiting Giso's report as eagerly as she was.

The castellan took the wine Marie offered and gulped it down without so much as a glance. Knocking the snow from his coat, he threw it to a servant in the hall and rubbed his freezing hands. "This is no weather for traveling, my lady, but I think my trip was worthwhile. I apologize for making you wait and wonder for so long, but I had to stay for the results of some important inquiries in Constance, or I would have been here before the snowfall."

Lady Mechthild looked at him with some annoyance. "Was it so difficult to learn something about Marie?"

Giso demurred. "Certainly not. After three days, I knew everything there was to know about her. But there is news, my lady, that will interest you and your husband more than the fate of this woman. Kaiser Sigismund will be coming to Constance and staying there for three or four months. That gives you ample time to travel there and present your dispute concerning Sir Otmar's testament."

"That's the best news I've heard in a long time." Breathing a sigh of relief, Lady Mechthild momentarily folded her hands in prayer. The kaiser resided in Prague most of the time, but often traveled to his various other estates in the Reich. In order to present his case, Sir Dietmar would have had to search for him, taking along a large retinue for protection. Doing so would have deprived the castle of many battle-ready men and given the Keilburgs the opportunity to storm the fortress in a surprise coup.

Giso nodded and smiled encouragingly. "The kaiser plans to hold a council in Constance that will sweep through Christianity like a storm and remove all the filth, especially the three unworthy popes."

"A council, you say, in Constance?" This news surprised Lady Mechthild so much that she forgot why she'd sent Giso there. She asked him for details of everything he'd learned and then paced back and forth in the hallway, mulling it all over. Marie couldn't curb her impatience and finally dared to address Giso.

"Did you learn anything about my father?"

His face darkened. "Your fate created a great stir in Constance. Everyone I asked had something to say. In retrospect, some people feel appalled at how you were treated. A handful of city council members protested to the kaiser's governor about the speedy sentence in the Dominican court since your case should rightly have been heard by the city council. But no judicial steps were taken because your father disappeared the day you were driven from the city. Various rumors were circulating, but finally, after I bribed a drunken sheepshearer named Anselm with two cups of wine, he told me a story that sounds the most likely. A few days after you were expelled, he said he'd helped a gravedigger bury a corpse in potter's field. When they threw the body into the hole, the blanket covering the dead man slipped, and the sheepshearer recognized him. Anselm swore to me by all the saints that it was your father, Matthis Schärer."

That wasn't unexpected. Marie lowered her head, waiting for tears to come, but her eyes remained dry. She listened almost indifferently as Giso told Lady Mechthild about Marie's unusually short trial and her immediate sentencing. He also told of how Rupert had all of her father's property, which the bishop's court awarded to him. The counselor also won several trials against her uncle Mombert who had protested the shameless confiscation of the property.

"The whole matter seems to me like a wicked trick of Keilburg's illegitimate brother," Giso said in conclusion. His face turned so dark that he appeared to want nothing more than to personally throttle the counselor.

Lady Mechthild patted Marie gently on the head. "I am indebted to you, girl, because I now understand the counselor's true deviousness, and I am certain we can soon present our case to the kaiser. My deepest sympathy on the death of your father. Even though the fiendish counselor did not personally lay a hand on him, he's responsible for his death."

Marie thanked her in a few polite words, but her thoughts flew back to that day nearly four years ago when she had first been accused. It suddenly became clear that she would never see her father again. Now she could seek to silently beg him for forgiveness because she thought he had abandoned her. Nevertheless, any tears she might have felt were staunched by her deep hatred for everyone who had anything to do with his death along with those who had left her abandoned and miserable.

"Rupert is now living in my father's house, putting on airs and acting like a nobleman," she said bitterly.

Giso nodded sympathetically. "Alas, that's so! He has become a respected citizen of Constance and enjoys the favor of the new bishop. It is said he will also play an important role in council preparations."

Lady Mechthild threw her head back. "Then maybe things don't look as favorable for us there as I had thought. If he stands in such high favor, he might be able to convince the kaiser to recognize the new will that Count Konrad von Keilburg presents. I wish we could speak with my husband's uncle. Though Sir Otmar intended to enter the monastery at Saint Ottilien, he never arrived there and left no trace of his whereabouts."

"It's possible Count Konrad had him killed," Giso growled.

Lady Mechthild crossed herself. "God forbid. I fear I may have made a mistake in keeping my husband from forming an alliance with the Keilburgs."

Giso looked disgusted. "Getting involved with scoundrels such as Count Konrad and Counselor Rupert would be a sin before God."

"I can only hope my husband sees things that way," Lady Mechthild responded with a touch of anxiety.

Marie reached out for Mechthild's hand and was happy the lady didn't draw back. "Sir Dietmar loves you very much and would never say anything bad about you, especially not just before your child comes."

"Now I really hope it's a boy, or my husband will be bitterly disappointed." She sighed and asked Marie and Giso to excuse her.

Marie watched anxiously as Lady Mechthild, deeply discouraged, struggled with ponderous steps out of the hall. After the doors had closed behind her, Marie turned to Giso again, who was just finishing his third cup of mulled wine. "Did you learn anything about the others I told you about? What happened to our housekeeper, Wina, for example, or the two servant girls, Elsa and Anne?"

"The old woman Wina is now working for your uncle Mombert. The maids have likewise found other work, one in Constance and the other in Meersburg. None of the servants in Rupert's house are from your time there."

"What became of Linhard Merk, the secretary?" Marie spat out the name as if something disgusting had gotten stuck in her teeth.

"Linhard now calls himself Brother Josephus. He entered the Scottish monastery in Constance a few months after you were driven out of town."

Marie laughed bitterly. "A murderer and rapist wearing a monk's robe? The good citizens trust such a man and think they will get to heaven faster with his help? What about his two accomplices?"

Rubbing his nose with his finger, Giso thought for a moment. "Hunold is still one of the city bailiffs, and Utz enjoys the confidence of business people in Constance, traveling the world as a leader of wagon trains."

"The two didn't make much from their vile deeds. I would have expected Rupert to richly reward at least Utz. What happened to the widow Euphemia?"

"Her betrayal of you did even less for her, as she was found dead in bed only three months after your trial. The strange thing is that she was healthy, and shortly beforehand had boasted around town that she would soon be very rich."

"Perhaps she was going to blackmail Rupert, so he or one of his cronies killed her." That gave Marie little satisfaction. She could only assume Euphemia had received her just punishment and hoped the woman was suffering all the torments of hell that the church reserved for perjurers.

She also asked Giso about her relatives, but all he knew was that Mombert and his family were in mourning because the son they had long yearned for had died shortly after birth. Marie suddenly thought of Michel, but she hadn't asked Giso to make inquiries about him, so she thanked Giso and promised to tell Hiltrud he had returned.

VIII.

Giso had only just returned before a whole series of events took place that kept the residents of the castle holding their breaths. The sun was standing high in the sky when a tower lookout announced the sighting of a man on horseback who was driving his horse at a full gallop up toward the castle despite the icy road. The horse slipped several times, but instead of dismounting and leading it by the reins, the rider whipped the poor animal and spurred it on.

Opening the castle gate and approaching the man, Giso intended to reprimand him for the mistreatment of his mount. But before Giso could say anything, the horseman fell from his saddle, and the castellan was only just able to catch him. Ice crystals were stuck to his eyebrows, and he was trembling so violently, he could barely speak.

"I must see Sir Dietmar. It's of the utmost importance."

"It's Philipp von Steinzell!" shouted one of the guards at the gate.

Only now did Giso recognize the squire, and he wondered what new misfortune Philipp was there to announce. Seizing the unexpected guest under his arms, he dragged him toward the living quarters. Remembering the horse, he turned around to see the exhausted mount standing under the entryway, trembling, with lacerated shanks and bleeding sides. Calling to the guard, he issued a brief order.

"Take the nag to the stable and call the goatherd. Tell him to make herbal compresses for the animal and nurse it back to health."

In spite of the man's considerable weight, Giso carried the young Steinzell into the great hall, giving him some of the same mulled wine that had revived his own spirits just a few hours earlier. Giso then listened in horror to the bad news that Philipp had brought.

"Rumold von Bürggen betrayed us!" Giso cried out to Sir Dietmar as the knight strode into the hall with the lady. "He made a pact with the Keilburgs, and in return was given Steinwald Forest as well as Felde Castle and part of the surrounding land."

Turning red with anger, Dietmar stood there as if struck by lightning. "What are you saying? That would be a betrayal! No, I can't believe that."

Philipp von Steinzell nodded grimly. "Unfortunately, it's the truth. My father sent me as soon as he heard the news. I'm to tell you that there is only one way out for us, the way my father has always suggested. We must offer ourselves as vassals to Duke Friedrich immediately and pledge our allegiance. Since the duke has reached an agreement with the Keilburgs, Count Konrad will not attack us anymore."

While Sir Dietmar was trying to regain his composure, Lady Mechthild questioned the young Steinzell further. His report left no doubt: the alliance of the four castle lords had fallen apart even before it had gone into effect. From now on, Rumold von Bürggen would be added to the list of Arnstein's enemies. Philipp confirmed several times that his father would enter into an alliance with Friedrich von Habsburg and pleaded with Sir Dietmar to do the same.

Now that she was allowed to stay in the great hall with the family instead of being forced to eavesdrop from the top of the stairway, Marie saw how Sir Dietmar was tormented and in despair. Rumold von Bürggen's property sliced deeply into Dietmar's land like a wedge separating Arnstein Castle and his two remaining allied neighbors. Rumold's betrayal seemed to seal Dietmar's fate, since his land would now be surrounded on three sides by that of the thieving Keilburgs.

As soon as the Steinzell squire had finished his report, Sir Dietmar began angrily shouting. "If I had known what a traitor Rumold was, I would have taken Count Konrad's offer myself, and today we'd be much better off."

Shaking her head, Lady Mechthild said something that sounded like "Don't trust him." But her words were lost in her sudden groaning and wheezing as her face contorted with pain and she placed both hands on her stomach. "It hurts so much," she whispered through tears. A moment later, her screams echoed throughout the great hall, brushing aside all other concerns.

Guda immediately came running to help, leading the lady up the stairway to her bedroom. "The child is coming. Pray that everything goes well!" she called back to Sir Dietmar while hurriedly yelling out instructions to the remaining servants.

The great hall emptied out so quickly that soon only Marie remained behind with the young Steinzell. As Marie was wondering whether to offer Guda her help, Philipp held out the empty wine pitcher.

"Bring me another cup of your mulled wine, girl. I could use another drink." Marie ran to the kitchen, poured a fresh pitcher from the pot that was kept warm over the fireplace, and quickly returned to fill the young nobleman's cup. Her thoughts were with Lady Mechthild, and she didn't notice the young man's eyes lighting up when he saw her. Paying no attention to the wine, he pulled Marie down and forced his right knee between her legs.

"I've had my eye on you since my last visit to Arnstein, but I haven't been able to approach you because Lady Mechthild has always had her people watching me. But now she's busy and can't keep me away from you. So don't make a fuss, or I'll take you by force."

Marie could see he was serious and tried to call for help, but he pressed his gloved hand to her mouth. Though she struggled and fought to escape, he dragged her to a corridor at the other end of the great hall and pushed her into the room used for guests' luggage. In the room were several chests large enough to serve as makeshift beds. Surrounded by thick walls, it was so far away from the residences that no one would hear her screams. Now Marie realized why one of the younger maids had been so careful to stay out of Philipp's way during his last visit. In despair, she remembered what Hiltrud had taught her and resolved not to resist in order to avoid serious injury.

At that moment a key turned in the lock and the bolt slid aside.

"Who the hell . . ." The squire cursed, sat up, and saw Jodokus standing before him. His voice completely calm, the monk seemed uninterested in the goings-on, but instead stated his errand. "Marie, the lady wishes to see you."

"You damned monk, can't you see we're busy? Get out!" Philipp added an obscene curse, and pinned Marie to the ground. Jodokus quickly grabbed him and pulled him off. Despite his gaunt frame, the monk had astonishing strength.

"You've lost control of yourself, Herr Philipp. As a guest, it's unseemly to seize the lord's property."

"Leave me alone, monk! This woman has already been violated by so many fellows that one more doesn't matter."

The monk didn't retreat. "The lady of the castle wants Marie to be the lord's companion, and his alone."

Jodokus's severe tone left no doubt that he would report Philipp if he didn't take his hands off Marie.

Philipp von Steinzell looked as if he wanted to strike the meddlesome monk, but he had come here to convince Dietmar von Arnstein to become a vassal of Friedrich von Habsburg, and if he didn't achieve that goal, he would garner his father's wrath. Thus, he reluctantly backed off, hissing at Marie.

"You'll see me again, whore. Once Sir Dietmar tires of you, I'll ask him to send you to me."

"Your mouth will run dry waiting for that day. I am neither Sir Dietmar's vassal nor yours." Marie smoothed out her dress and ran past him through the door. Following her, Jodokus gripped her arm tightly.

"I hope you won't forget I saved you from this fool," he whispered hoarsely in her ear.

Marie nodded silently. Jodokus was one of those especially stubborn people who would wait until Lady Mechthild released her from service and then demand his reward. Just the same, she was thankful to Jodokus. She preferred to give herself to a man as a prostitute rather than to be taken by force, and she tried to smile gratefully at him. "Did the lady really call for me?"

"Yes, she wants you to calm down her husband and keep him out of the maids' way." Jodokus's jealous tone made Marie shudder, and for the first time she longed for the day she could leave Arnstein Castle. For the time being, however, she was happy to run to Lady Mechthild's room and didn't see the monk grinning maliciously as he waited for Squire Philipp. The man soon appeared, looking around for a maid who might cool his passions. But all he found was Brother Jodokus.

"The sky has cleared, and it will be a bright, moonlit night. If you hurry, you'll get home today. You can't stay here in Arnstein, as the servants have no time to care for guests. Send my greetings to your father and tell him I'll try to convince Sir Dietmar to join Duke Friedrich."

Philipp angrily rejected this idea. "I will wait here until your lord has committed to the alliance with Duke Friedrich."

The monk smiled softly. "As long as his wife is in labor, Dietmar will be thinking of nothing but her and the child. When he is ready to speak with you depends on how the birth goes. Do you wish to keep your father in the dark for that long?"

Philipp didn't want to do that and mumbled his assent. The monk helped him into his overcoat, handing him his gloves while calling for a stable hand to saddle a fresh horse. Accompanying Philipp to the outer gate, the monk watched as the squire vanished into the growing darkness. Then he returned to the great hall.

At the bottom of the staircase Jodokus stopped and listened for any sounds coming from the lady's bedroom. Everyone was attending to Lady Mechthild, and even the lord wouldn't be thinking of anyone else, and least of all taking advantage of Marie's charms. The monk jealously imagined bedding the young woman. He dreamed of her all night, and during the day, he was almost consumed by desire. It was only because of her that he was still at the castle, since he had long ago carried out his mission. Now, it was time for him to mysteriously disappear.

If he wanted to succeed, he'd have to strike in the next few hours, and he knew that there would never be a second chance. But if he went away, he'd run the risk of never seeing Marie again. The thought weakened his resolve, but he then slapped his forehead. If he didn't act now, his dreams of wealth would be gone forever. He knew he was destined to find the young prostitute again, and the day would come when she would belong completely and only to him.

The monk silently climbed the stairs to the upper floor, darting like a shadow down the corridor and stopping for only a minute in front of Lady Mechthild's door to listen to her screams and the maids' nervous voices. It didn't sound good. The knight would likely lose his wife as well as his still-unborn child.

Jodokus almost said a brief prayer, but reminded himself that the lady's fate was of no concern to him, and hastened on. Moments later, he reached the door to the room where Sir Dietmar kept his most precious things. Only four people had the key to this oaken, double-hinged door—the lord of the castle, the lady, Castellan Giso, and Brother Jodokus as the knight and his lady's scribe and confidant.

Sliding the key out from under his robe, the monk inserted it into the lock just as a maid came running out of Lady Mechthild's bedroom, hair flying, and rushed past him. Though she ignored him, Jodokus was startled to the core, and he pressed himself against the wooden door, waiting until the maid had disappeared down the hallway. Finally opening the door with trembling hands, he slipped inside. Not wanting to attract attention, he closed the door behind him, then leaned against the wood for a moment, breathing deeply. He next walked over to a chest with silver fittings and three locks standing in a niche off to one side. Initially Jodokus had had only one of the three keys, but it hadn't been difficult for him to borrow the other two for long enough to make their wax impressions. On a trip to Saint Ottilien's monastery, he had met an accomplice who gave him perfect copies of the other keys before he headed back.

Opening the locks, he raised the lid carefully, taking care not to let the unoiled hinges squeak. With an experienced hand, he quickly found the leather binding containing Sir Otmar's testament and removed it from the chest. He unfastened its silver clasp and spread out the leather in front of him. Taking a little glass bottle from a pouch hanging on his belt, he removed the stopper and carefully poured the bottle's contents over the testament. Closing the binder, he secured the clasp so it wouldn't fall apart, and placed it back in the chest.

His hands were trembling so much that he was barely able to close the three locks again. If anyone discovered what he'd done, it would be all over for him. After listening for sounds in the hallway, he stepped out of the room, quickly closing and locking the door behind him. Shortly thereafter he left Arnstein Castle by a side door and strode off at a quick pace in order to reach Felde Castle as soon as possible.

IX.

When Marie arrived in Lady Mechthild's quarters, the lady was lying on her bed, screaming with pain, eyes tightly closed and fingers clenched. Nevertheless, she seemed to know what was going on around her, for as Marie bent down, she grabbed her by the shoulder and looked at her with wide, anxious eyes.

"You must try to comfort my husband. I don't want him to be too worried about me. Recently, he has suffered more misfortune than even the bravest of us can bear without God's help."

"Very well, I'll try." Marie nodded, then quickly slipped out through the side door into the anteroom leading to Sir Dietmar's bedroom. The lord of the castle was standing against the wall near the door, staring at it as if he expected to see the devil.

Marie brushed past him, picked up a goblet that had rolled across the floor, and wiped it off with a cloth. With trembling hands, she refilled it with wine and handed it to him. "Drink, my lord. It will do you good. Then we must kneel down and ask the saints to stand by Lady Mechthild in her hour of need."

Time crawled by as Marie searched her memory for suitable prayers for a woman in childbirth and recited them for the knight. As she did so, she listened to the sounds coming from the next room in the hope of hearing the shouts of joy and praise that would announce a successful delivery. All she heard, however, were soft whimpers, the tiptoeing of many feet, and the lady's cries penetrating the thick walls and drowning out all other sounds. Sir Dietmar cringed each time he heard his wife's voice, pressing his fists against his stomach as if sharing the pain she had to bear. Finally, he could stand it no longer and jumped up to run to his wife. Marie tried to hold him back, but he pushed her aside. At the door he bumped into Giso who struggled to keep his master from rushing into the neighboring room.

Dietmar shouted angrily at his vassal. "Let me go, you scoundrel! I must see my wife!"

Marie tried to help Giso and pleaded with the lord. "You can't help her. The midwife is with her, and if you disturb her, you will just make everything worse. So be sensible and stay here!"

"God will not be so cruel as to take my wife from me?" he asked Marie, his eyes wide with fear.

"Certainly he will not," Marie swore, hoping that all would be well. She shuddered as she imagined what the lord might do in his anguish if Lady Mechthild did not survive the birth.

"I love her so much. Without her I am only half a person. She is my strength, my . . ." Sir Dietmar broke out in tears that neither Marie nor Giso viewed as a sign of weakness. The liegeman adored the lady of the house and would have given his life for her, but in this difficult hour no one but God could help.

She didn't dare leave the lord alone, so she had no choice but to stare at the door, waiting for any news. Only two heartbeats later the door handle moved. Marie held her breath and clung to the knight's trembling arm. The door swung open and Guda entered, cradling something wrapped in one of the cloths Marie had embroidered. With a broad smile, she held the bundle up to the knight.

"You have a son, my lord, and he's as happy and healthy as can be." As if to confirm her words, the infant let out a robust wail.

Disregarding the baby, the knight looked anxiously at the housekeeper. "How is my wife?"

"She's very tired, but she survived the ordeal."

Dietmar broke out in a cheer that frightened the child into another loud cry. Dietmar glanced only briefly at the red, wrinkled little face before he pushed Guda aside and ran into the next room. Relieved, Marie and the housekeeper followed. Lady Mechthild lay in her bed, looking tired and worn out, but very happy, and she smiled as her husband knelt down beside her.

"I told you it would be a boy," she whispered.

"The most important thing is that you survived," Dietmar replied. He kissed her and nodded to Marie who remained at the foot of the bed while he congratulated Lady Mechthild on the blessed occasion.

"To show our thanks to the Holy Virgin who has spared the life of my wife and son, I promise to go on a pilgrimage to Einsiedeln and light a candle on her altar," he said solemnly. "But first we shall have my son baptized."

"What name will you give him?" Marie asked curiously.

"Grimald," the knight answered with a sparkle in his eye. "And I already know who his godfather will be." He looked at his wife and laughed out loud as if all his cares had suddenly been swept away.

X.

The next morning, Giso took a few men to bring the news of the birth to Sir Dietmar's friends. Marie also learned that he was going to seek the man who the lord hoped would be the child's godfather, but no one knew who that was. Even the lady was dying to know, but the knight wouldn't tell her. Curiously, the castellan took pack-horses as if he were setting out on a long trip.

Marie was less interested in the godfather's identity than in what happened to Brother Jodokus. Now that she was indebted to him, she despised him even more and didn't want to run into the man in a dark corner. Tiptoeing past the chapel, she was surprised at how quiet it was, so she peeked inside. As a sign of heavenly gratitude for the birth of the son and heir, three candles were supposed to be lit in honor of the Trinity, and one candle should have been burning before the statue of the Holy Mother. But Marie was puzzled to see only the almost-horizontal rays of the sun coming through the windows illuminating the totally empty ornamented vault.

One of the maidservants told her that Jodokus hadn't gone to congratulate the lady after the birth, nor was he in the great hall where Sir Dietmar and his liegemen were celebrating the birth of the castle's heir. Marie learned that Philipp von Steinzell had returned to his father's castle the previous afternoon, and she wondered guiltily if the young squire had killed the monk out of anger for helping her. When Jodokus didn't show up for supper, she pointed his absence out to Guda.

The housekeeper seemed not to care where the monk might be. "Brother Jodokus is an old homebody. To tell you the truth, it's fine with me if that *man* stays out of our way. I don't like how he creeps up on you, and I'd advise you to stay away from him, because I don't trust him."

Guda stressed the word *man* as if she knew about the monk's obsession with the young prostitute. Somewhat mollified, Marie later mentioned the monk's disappearance to Hiltrud, who teased her. "Do you miss your admirer? I didn't think you cared for two-legged goats."

But after Marie had told her about the incident with Philipp von Steinzell and the monk, Hiltrud became serious. "You'd better keep your mouth closed if you want to stay out of trouble. The favor of the mighty is fickle, and who's to say what the lady will think?"

When Jodokus had still not shown up by the next evening, Sir Dietmar began to worry.

He ordered a search within the castle walls, which proved unsuccessful. Finally, he sent servants out with torches to search the surrounding area, as he thought that the monk might have had an accident while out on a walk. Though there was little hope of finding him alive in the bitter cold, not even a trace of him could be found, and the monk's disappearance remained a mystery that no one at Arnstein Castle could solve.

A few days later, Hartmut von Treilenburg and Abbot Adalwig of Saint Ottilien's monastery appeared in person to offer their best wishes to the knight and his wife, promising to come back for the baptism. After more than a week, Giso returned and handed his lord some documents covered in official seals, and all the lord's worries seemed to disappear in an instant. Beaming with pride, Dietmar ordered his people to prepare a great feast and hurried to his wife's room to deliver the good news.

Marie was free sooner than expected of her duties to the lord. After the birth of his son, the knight firmly rejected making use of the beautiful young woman, preferring instead to wait longingly for the day when his wife could again share his bed. Marie still had plenty to do, since Guda needed every available hand to prepare for both the baptismal feast and the Christmas holiday that had been postponed by the betrayal of the Bürggens and overshadowed by the birth of the heir.

Even though the baptism was still several weeks off, it didn't initially seem that things would be ready in time. But Lady Mechthild was gaining strength every day, and after she recovered enough to leave her bed and take charge, the servants sprang back into action, laughing and joking despite the hard work. Even the soldiers pitched in, although they usually regarded servants' work as beneath them.

January passed and Candlemas arrived. Since Brother Jodokus was still missing, the abbot of Saint Ottilien said the Mass. The abbot was a good friend of Sir Dietmar's and a determined foe of the Keilburgs. Everyone assumed that Sir Dietmar had chosen Abbot Adalwig as his son's godfather, but Sir Dietmar postponed the baptismal service and asked forgiveness of his guests for postponing the feast because one important guest had not yet come. But he didn't say who that was.

Two days later, the tower watch announced the approach of a large group of men on horseback. Hartmut von Treilenburg and some of the other nobles feared a surprise attack by the Keilburgs and called their men to arms, but Sir Dietmar reassured them and ordered the gates to be opened to receive the visitors. Dressed in festive attire and protected from the frigid air by nothing but an overcoat lined with fox fur, he strode into the courtyard to greet their guests. Lady Mechthild joined him, along with a maid carrying a pitcher of warm mulled wine and some goblets for the new arrivals.

"Am I mistaken, or is that Count Eberhard von Württemberg's coat of arms?" a soldier standing near Marie cried out in surprise.

The man was right. The banner depicted the leaping stag of the Württembergs. The horsemen were wearing sheepskin greatcoats over their capes to protect them from the cold, and their beards were encrusted in ice. The horses had been wrapped in blankets, their legs partially bandaged, and white clouds of steam puffed from their nostrils.

"Sir Dietmar must stand high in the favor of Count Eberhard if he makes the long trip here from Stuttgart in the middle of winter," one of the guests whispered to Hartmut von Treilenburg. The latter nodded with his mouth hanging open, but he also looked a bit doubtful, as if he didn't know yet what to think of it all.

Count Eberhard rode through the gate, stopping before the lord and lady of the castle. Two servants ran forward to help him out of his saddle, as he was almost frozen stiff despite his blanket and fur-trimmed coat. Gratefully he accepted a goblet of mulled wine from Lady Mechthild and emptied it at once.

"That tastes wonderful," he said while the maid poured the warm drink for his companions as well. Count Eberhard knocked the rest of the snow from his coat, removed his gloves, and leaned forward to shake Dietmar's hand.

"Best wishes on the birth of your son, Sir Arnstein. Nowadays one cannot have enough brave men."

"I thank you for coming, Count von Württemberg." Sir Dietmar sounded relieved, as the count treated him as an equal, apparently spared from the bitter cup of vassalage that Degenhard von Steinzell would have to swallow under Friedrich von Habsburg. Hartmut von Treilenburg's dark face quickly brightened. He went to Count Eberhard and took his outstretched hand. "I am greatly pleased to see you, Count Eberhard."

"I feel honored to be invited," Eberhard replied, quickly glancing around the interior of the well-fortified castle. What he saw seemed to please him, and he patted Dietmar on the shoulder to show his approval as the servants stepped forward to help the men take off their capes and heavy winter coats.

Marie now got a better look at the visitor and guessed that Eberhard was in his midforties. Though he was tall and imposing, he had remained slender in contrast to many others his age. His face was framed by a dark blond beard speckled with gray, and his eyes sparkled with cheerfulness. His jerkin was of the black and gold colors of Württemberg, though the yellow seemed a bit faded, reminding Marie with amusement of a courtesan's yellow ribbons. The count's trousers were dark blue and the codpiece generously padded to suggest his noble rank.

Everything was ready for the guests in the great hall, and the maids were already bringing in warm food for the count and his men. Marie helped with the serving until Lady Mechthild beckoned her over.

"Let the maids do the work and sit here with me since I can see you're dying of curiosity. In any case, I have a job for you." The lady sounded happier than she had in a long time.

Marie quickly accepted, setting the bowl of pork roast that she was carrying down on the table in front of Eberhard. Untying her apron, she handed it to a maid and took the seat near the lady. Hiltrud, who was also serving the guests, looked on in astonishment.

Looking admiringly at his new seatmate, Eberhard leaned forward and tugged on her sleeve. "You're a damned beautiful woman. By what name may I call you?"

"This is Marie," Lady Mechthild answered for her. "She's a courtesan and will satisfy your needs if you wish."

Count Eberhard's eyes flashed with desire, and Marie knew that by evening she would be lying in his bed. For a moment she was infuriated, as she didn't expect Lady Mechthild to pass her around like a shiny plaything; then she laughed at her own naïveté. She'd been brought there as a courtesan, and why should she suddenly be treated like something else?

The count was an enemy of Konrad von Keilburg, and she knew that Lady Mechthild had arranged this pairing so that Marie could get close to Count Eberhard and relay all that she learned back to the knight and the lady. In any case, the count was certainly more affable that Philipp von Steinzell, and he didn't share Jodokus's repulsive odor.

She listened carefully to the conversation around the table, remembering what she knew about Count Eberhard von Württemberg. Along with Friedrich von Habsburg, who ruled over large holdings of land that spanned countries, Count Eberhard was one of the most powerful and influential noblemen in the old Duchy of Swabia, whose title had been vacant since the previous duke died. Until now, none of the noblemen in Swabia had succeeded in gaining a duke's title or rank, which would give them power over the other noble houses. Marie wondered if Eberhard wanted this position for himself, but nothing of what she heard suggested that.

At first Eberhard and Sir Dietmar talked about ordinary things such as the unusually cold winter and the council that would begin in the fall. Count Eberhard would be attending, and he invited the lord and lady of the castle to come with him to Constance. Only later, after the maids had cleared the table, did the men get around to discussing their problems with the Keilburgs. "I hear that Count Konrad seized a castle that belongs to you," Eberhard began.

"Indeed," declared Sir Dietmar, and told the count about his uncle's alleged second testament that supposedly awarded Mühringen to the Keilburgs. "Konrad took the castle in a surprise attack and refuses to recognize my claims," he concluded with a grim expression.

Eberhard von Württemberg puffed out his cheeks. "Can't someone ask Sir Otmar what convinced him to make up this new will?"

"Count Konrad asserts that my uncle entered a monastery, though he doesn't know which one, or I would have asked him long ago." Sir Dietmar's expression clearly indicated he considered this a lame excuse.

Supporting his bearded chin in his right arm, Eberhard fiddled with one of the ornamental silver buttons on his jerkin. "I can't say I like the situation. In any event, I'll present your case to the kaiser. You say you have your uncle's document, signed and sealed before witnesses?"

"I do indeed, and in two copies," Dietmar replied with a contented smile. He fumbled with a key on his belt while holding out his other hand to his wife, who gave him the second key. Taking another key from his belt, Giso gathered all three of the keys and left the great hall to fetch the document. Soon after, he returned, holding a leather binder in front of him.

"Here is the contract, sir. But I can't say it smells very good."

The lord of the castle looked up in irritation and sniffed the leather. Its odor made him cough. "There's something wrong here," he said, regaining his breath. Carefully opening the cover, he stared dumbfounded at the shreds of parchment inside, all of which were illegibly stained and emitted a foul stench.

Eberhard had a servant bring him a cloth to protect his hand while he picked up one of the pieces. The parchment seemed burned, and it was impossible to read a word. Shaking his head, the count handed it back to Dietmar. "It looks like Keilburg played a dirty trick on you. Someone poured acid over this and destroyed it. I'm afraid you have a spy in the castle."

To her horror, Marie saw several people look her way. Meanwhile, Sir Dietmar stared at the leather as if he couldn't believe his eyes. Then, with a curse, he flung the stinking mass on the ground and started pounding the table.

"That won't help Keilburg. The second copy is stored safely in Saint Ottilien's monastery, certainly beyond the reach of Count Konrad's people."

"No, Sir Dietmar!" Abbot Adalwig, sitting on the other side of Dietmar, cried out in shock. "You had the testament picked up a few weeks ago by Jodokus, your scribe."

The lord of the castle stared at the abbot wide-eyed. "That's not possible. I never . . ." Grinding his teeth, he paused. "So that's the reason Jodokus disappeared. First he destroyed this testament with acid and then he went to get the second copy in the monastery. Oh, fool that I am! Why wasn't I suspicious right away when that damned monk disappeared?"

Silence descended over the great hall following the knight's outburst. People looked at one another, their faces showing fear of an enemy whose power was strong enough to destroy contracts stored behind thick walls in heavily locked chests. Some in the group crossed themselves.

Count von Württemberg felt that something had to be done to dispel people's evident fear of the seemingly unlimited power of Konrad von Keilburg. Taking a long gulp of wine, he placed his hand on his host's shoulder.

"Didn't you invite us for the baptism, Sir Dietmar?" The latter nodded in surprise. "Yes, but . . ."

"No buts!" Eberhard said in a thundering voice. "We're not going to let Count Konrad ruin this event! Lady Mechthild, bring my godson and some holy water. But no, wait . . . no holy water.

That has been sullied by the traitorous monk. Speak your blessing for the child, Abbot Adalwig. That will certainly be pleasing to God."

"Now? Here, in the hall?" the abbot asked, stunned.

"Why not?" the count replied. "Most children are not baptized in a church, but at home. Furthermore, it's warm and comfortable here whereas the child would be cold and miserable in the chapel."

The abbot exchanged uncertain glances with the lord and lady. Nodding in agreement, Lady Mechthild sent Guda to get the boy. She immediately understood that Eberhard wanted to dispel the threatening shadow of the Keilburgs with the sacrament of baptism, and she was so grateful to him that she resolved to have three masses said in Saint Ottilien for the salvation of his soul.

By the time Guda returned with the baby, everything was ready for the baptism. Giso and a few of his people had not only brought in the gilded crucifix from the chapel but also the heavy baptismal font that took six strong men to carry it.

Eberhard approached the housekeeper and took the boy in his arms. "A splendid child," he said with a smile, watching as Lady Mechthild's cheeks glowed with joy. "Speak your blessing, Venerable Abbot," he said to Adalwig, who still didn't quite understand what to do. Finally the old man stood up and took his place alongside the baptismal font. He hesitated a few times while trying to remember the words, but he recited the blessing without error and finally made the sign of the cross over the child with a relieved "Amen."

"Amen," came the resounding reply of all present.

Most of the guests thought the dinner would resume, but Eberhard raised his hand to speak.

"In view of the honor I have been afforded as godfather of this child, I wish to present my gift," he called out in a voice that filled the room. "To strengthen the bonds between his clan and mine, I am bequeathing Thalfingen on the Neckar to my godson Grimald."

Holding the baby in his arms, he turned to gauge the impression his gift had made and smiled inwardly at the crowd's reaction.

Mouth wide-open in shock, Sir Dietmar stared at him with gleaming eyes. It didn't trouble him in the least that the gift made his son a vassal of the Württembergs, because this connection would protect Arnstein from any further Keilburg attacks. Count Konrad would think twice before threatening an ally and vassal of the Württembergs. Lady Mechthild also looked overcome with joy, and Abbot Adalwig sent a prayer of thanks heavenward, realizing that the mighty guest would now hold a protective hand over his friend Dietmar. Hartmut von Treilingen, who had been holding his breath, let out a huge sigh and raised his goblet to the health of the count and his godfather. He, too, would gain from the Württembergs the protection he so desperately needed.

Indeed, Eberhard's visit had infused Arnstein Castle with hope, and the overall mood lightened. Even Marie was optimistic that Counselor Rupert would one day receive his just punishment. She briefly wondered whether she should tell Eberhard her story and ask him for help, but since her injustices had not happened in his jurisdiction, she dropped the idea at once. Count von Württemberg had no influence in Constance and could do nothing for her. It was also not very likely that the nobleman would care about a courtesan's concerns or put any credence in her story.

Count Eberhard von Württemberg stayed at Arnstein Castle for two weeks, and many people laughed that his visit was so lengthy because an extraordinarily beautiful woman was adding spice to his nights. As a farewell gift, he tucked a handful of golden coins embossed with the leaping stag of Württemberg in Marie's bosom, then kissed her in front of all the assembled guests. Riding out on a clear winter's day, the count left relieved and happy guests behind.

PART FOUR
DANGEROUS TRAVELS

I.

"Won't you even consider my offer, Marie?" Lady Mechthild sounded peeved.

Marie bit her lip and shook her head.

"I only want to help, you stubborn thing," Lady Mechthild continued. "A marriage to one of our farmers would make you an honorable woman. I discussed it with my husband, and he is ready to give you and your offspring property in the domain of Thalfingen. Moreover, since you were born free, I will give you a signed and sealed letter that ensures that your children will likewise not be serfs."

Heart pounding, Marie felt something within pleading for her to accept the generous offer. The prospect of being a free landowner with her own property was exactly what Anne and Elsa, her father's two maids, had dreamed of in Constance. It wasn't an easy life, as a farmer's wife worked hard, and Marie knew that she would first have to learn everything that country girls had been taught since early childhood. But with the help of a loving husband, she could do it.

But if she agreed, for the rest of her life she would be bound to a piece of land that she could leave only briefly when she traveled to the nearest market town or went on a pilgrimage. Her home would be far from Constance, and she would never be able to take her much-desired revenge on the counselor and his cronies. No, she couldn't give in now and accept the gift, or she would never find peace of mind.

She took a deep breath, choosing her words carefully so as not to offend Lady Mechthild. "Your offer is more than generous, but I grew up as a merchant's daughter and have spent little time in the countryside. I could never manage a farm properly."

Lady Mechthild laughed. "You don't know what you are saying. Do you think you will ever again have a chance to escape the squalor of your wandering ways? To find a place where you can save your soul through a decent life pleasing to God? No, girl, once you leave here, you will end up back in the gutter where the half brother of our enemy cast you, and you will wander the roads for the rest of your days."

Through the lady's window, Marie could see Hiltrud in the courtyard, hitching up her reluctant goats and three kids to the little cart with Thomas's help. For a moment, she considered asking the lady to permit Hiltrud and Thomas to marry, giving the farm to them instead, but if the lady agreed, she would have to move on by herself, and she was fearful of that. She despised herself for being selfish and for disregarding her friend's future happiness. Fighting the tears welling up within her, Marie threw her head back.

"I realize what I'm turning down, my lady, but there is nowhere on earth that I can truly find rest." She almost added, "As long as Rupert Splendidus is still alive," but she held her tongue just in time. Her plans for revenge didn't concern Lady Mechthild. Clearing her throat, she curtsied to the lady without meeting her eye.

"It is time for me to say good-bye, my lady."

"As you wish," the lady replied reluctantly. "You have already received your wages. Accept my thanks and best wishes for the help you have given me. I will pray for your soul."

Marie curtsied again, then abruptly turned and walked slowly through the castle to the courtyard where Hiltrud was waiting, taking leave of the place that had been her home for the past several eventful months. She brought with her all that she had learned in her time there, along with a purseful of money that Lady Mechthild had paid for her services.

Marie also carried Count Eberhard's gold coins in another purse she kept hidden deep inside her clothing. She didn't yet have enough money to hire an assassin for such a high-placed nobleman as Rupert Splendidus, but it was enough in coins to murder the scoundrels who had raped her. She couldn't have the men killed yet, however, or Rupert would be alerted, and she didn't want to risk that.

Standing next to the wagon, Hiltrud was caught in animated discussion with Thomas. Her cheeks glowed and she looked well fed, unlike her appearance after earlier winters. For a wandering harlot, this had been an excellent winter. She had new clothes, coats, and undergarments, and she hadn't had to spend coins for either rent or a cabin. Instead, she'd enjoyed some very pleasant months and earned good money. A woman of her standing really couldn't ask for anything more.

"Can we leave?" Hiltrud's question awakened Marie from her reveries.

"I'm ready. How are things with you?"

"I said good-bye to Thomas." Hiltrud's misty eyes belied her feigned composure, but since they had no choice but to return to the dusty roads, Marie didn't respond. Hiltrud would have to deal with her grief just as Marie struggled with her own inner conflict.

Once they had reached the outer gateway, Marie looked at Hiltrud questioningly. "Do you have any idea where to go? We shouldn't travel too far all alone."

"Let's head to Saint Marien am Stein. It's not far from here, and Thomas told me there's a pilgrimage to that site on Palm Sunday. We'll find plenty of customers there to help us get used to the old routine."

"I agree. We'll certainly find other women there with whom we can travel unmolested. Do you know the way? I'd prefer not to travel through lands belonging to the Keilburgs or Steinzells."

"Then there aren't many roads to choose from," Hiltrud joked. "But your fear is not entirely unfounded since Thomas has spotted Philipp von Steinzell around Arnstein on a few occasions. The scoundrel still dreams of getting between your legs, but we'll spoil his fun."

Hiltrud laughed a little too loudly and clicked her tongue. As they passed the gate watchman, he waved and joked a bit with them. He chuckled as Hiltrud replied in kind, though her voice didn't sound as cheerful as her words for she seemed about to burst into tears. Leaving the castle behind them, Marie wondered if she should point out Thomas waving at them from between the battlements of one of the towers. But her friend was staring ahead grimly and didn't once look back as they followed the serpentine path down into the valley.

Meanwhile, Thomas stayed at his observation post until well after the two women had disappeared into the trees on the other side of the valley. Finally, with drooping shoulders, he returned to his goat stable to pour out his grief to the animals.

II.

The pilgrimage church of Saint Marien am Stein was built on a peninsula, embraced by the arms of a little lake. Most of the year this place was filled with only the sounds of birds chirping and waves lapping the shore. But once a week, these sounds were drowned out by the bell tolling as monks from the nearby monastery came to the old white stone church to care for it and say their prayers. On pilgrimage days, as on this Palm Sunday, the narrow peninsula was scarcely able to hold all the faithful. Dressed in their Sunday best, men, women, and children made their way toward the church's open gate to gaze at the miraculous Virgin Mary statue and to pray for her mercy and intercession for the forgiveness of their sins.

When Hiltrud and Marie first arrived, it disturbed them that the women eyed them distrustfully and the men looked them over while calling out suggestive remarks. Soon, however, they had gotten used to the usual routine and they were pleased they'd have a chance to earn good money there. With only four threadbare tents with faded, pale yellow ribbons fluttering in the wind, they didn't have much competition.

It was obvious that the women in those tents were already hard at work, as the entrance flaps were drawn shut and a few men prowled around them impatiently, waiting their turns. Marie and Hiltrud saw some hopeful gazes directed their way and hurried to set up their own quarters. Since neither a bailiff nor a monk showed up to assign them a place, they chose a dry part of the meadow on a little rise near the river shadowed by weeping willows. The trees' low branches draped over the water, offering them a somewhat private place for early-morning baths. While they were still busy tying the canvas to the poles, one of the other prostitutes stepped out of her tent and looked over at them.

"What a surprise! It really is a small world."

"Gerlind, what are you doing here?" Hiltrud called back in surprise. "I thought you'd retired."

Squinting, the old woman approached them. "I tried," she said with a bitter laugh. "But I was too successful for the procurers in the area, and they sent the priests and bailiffs after me. Believe me, there can't even be as many laws as they said I broke. They took away the two girls I'd spent so much time training, gave them to a local procuress, and remembered to steal my hard-earned savings. Then they whipped me and chased me away. Now I'm back to wandering the roads and training a new girl. Märthe isn't the brightest star in the sky, but she's good with the men."

Hiltrud embraced Gerlind joyfully, appearing not to notice how dirty the toothless, gaunt woman was. "So great to see you! Now we can go back to traveling together."

"Of course! Of course! Then our old group will be back together again. On the way here, Märthe and I met Berta and Fita, who are also looking for company. With six of us, we'll never have to beg any traveling group for protection."

Hiltrud nodded enthusiastically, but Marie made a sour face. Berta wasn't exactly her dream company, but it was still better than joining a group of street performers or a wagon train whose leaders would demand their bodies night after night. She was glad, however, that she might learn more from Gerlind about the effects of various herbs, and she was also curious about the girl that the old harlot had taken on as a maid.

The arrival of two new prostitutes, especially such a pretty one as Marie, attracted men like moths to a flame. Some of the monks who came running to stare at her were still wearing their choir robes. Physical lust clearly meant more to them than serving God and the souls of the pilgrims, as they had obviously abandoned the pious singers whose Latin hymns could be heard coming from the little church. One of the monks accosted Marie while she was busy trying to tie down her tent with a heavy rope.

"Welcome to Saint Marien am Stein, dear child. Your soul will be saved and your sins forgiven if you humbly satisfy my needs."

Pausing in her work for a moment, Marie looked at him scornfully. "Humbly means for free, but only death is free, and even that costs your life."

The monk didn't give up so fast but gave his voice an even more unctuous tone. "Don't be so haughty, dear child. When you arrive in heaven someday, the watcher at the gate will remind you of your sins and send you off to purgatory, but if you serve us pious monks, the hands of Satan's servants will be tied so they can light only a small fire that will at most feel like a warm bath to you."

Marie sniffed him briefly and laughed. "What you need is a warm bath yourself, Brother. God created me with such a sensitive nose that I can't help you."

When Marie turned away, he spat on the ground and approached Hiltrud. To Marie's surprise, her friend nodded and let him into her tent, even though she hadn't finished hammering her tent pegs. It was a riddle to Marie why the always-clean Hiltrud had let in the stinking monk. She had little time to think about it, however, as the crowd of men in front of her tent kept growing.

Marie looked the customers over and felt a lump in her throat. After his son's birth, Sir Dietmar had refused to even look at her, so she hadn't had to give herself to anyone since the Württemberg count. Only now did she recall how nice it had been to be left alone. All she wanted was to crawl back into her tent and tie it closed from the inside, but in the long term she couldn't afford to turn away customers, and the longer she waited, the harder it would be for her to resume her business.

A well-dressed farmer came forward with a swagger. "Name your price, girl."

Marie didn't like his pompous attitude and answered, "Five shillings." Taken aback, the farmer waved her off contemptuously. "Twelve good pennies? You should be made of gold to demand that much."

Pointing to Berta's tent, which she recognized by its dirty spots, Marie informed the men of her business practices. "If you're looking for a penny whore, you'll find her down there. I give my favors only to men who can afford me."

Some of the men standing around laughed, while the farmer snorted and left, muttering rude words. He didn't go to Berta's tent, however, but headed for Hiltrud, who had just dismissed the monk and was now walking toward the farmer, swinging her hips. They settled on a price within a few minutes and disappeared together inside her tent.

"Five shillings is what you ask? I think I can afford that," someone said in Marie's ear.

Turning, she saw a man wearing a broad, soiled pilgrim's cloak. Though his coat was frayed and bleached by the sun and his shoes had been patched often, the pilgrim did not look poor. Indeed, his broad, muscular shoulders and the calluses he had on his hands meant that he was used to wielding a sword and suggested that he was a knight. Marie assumed that he, like many others, had given his property to a son and gone on the pilgrimage. Since he kept himself cleaner than most of the other men, Marie pushed the tent canvas aside to let him in. "If you would please follow me . . ." Setting his walking stick down in front of the tent, he squeezed past her. As he removed his shirt, she saw he was an old man, with white hair on his wrinkled chest. Yet his face showed nothing of the serenity of old age nor a pilgrim's blissful otherworldly glow, but instead shone with undisguised lust. Before Marie could settle down comfortably, he jumped her.

Marie was repelled by the man, by herself, and by what had become of her. An eternity seemed to pass before he collapsed on top of her with a dissonant groan. Relieved, she struggled to stand up, then smoothed out her dress and held out her hand. "Five shillings, please."

The pilgrim just snickered. "Take this blessing from Saint Jacob, which I have in my body, as a reward. I won't pay any money for a whore."

Marie cursed herself for being such a fool and for forgetting to get paid in advance. At the same time, boundless rage welled up inside her. She wasn't prepared to let the old man go without doing something about it. "That wasn't our agreement. Either you pay or . . ."

"Or what?" he sneered, leaving her tent. But Marie was faster than he was. Picking up his walking stick, she knocked the man down, much to the amusement of everyone standing around. Before he could struggle to his feet, she reached for his purse and ripped it off his belt.

"You can keep your blessing from Saint Jacob. We agreed on five shillings, and that's what you're going to pay." She opened the purse, took out the agreed-upon amount, and counted the coins for all to see. The old man cursed her as a thief, and called upon the crowd to help him with the shameless whore, but most of the men jeered at him and pushed him around, jealous that he got to sleep with such a beautiful woman.

Marie threw the visibly thinner purse on the ground in front of him and glared at the other men. "The old goat probably thought he could graze around here for free, but I changed his mind about that."

Another man came up to Marie and counted out five shillings in her hand. To judge by appearances, he was a rich merchant who had come here less out of piety than for business reasons. Marie cast a final triumphant look at the old man who had tried to cheat her and disappeared with the merchant into the tent.

Somewhat later, as she was looking around for another customer, she learned that rumors had spread of the incident involving her and the old pilgrim. All the men at the festival now seemed to know her price, and the number of people approaching her tent had greatly decreased. Naturally, a few tried to get her to lower her price, but in the end they all paid their five shillings. She was happy she'd earned good money even though that meant fewer customers.

Hiltrud, on the other hand, seemed unable to find enough clients and ignored every rule that she had taught Marie. Taking every interested man into her tent, she paid little attention to their appearance or body odor, and didn't even seem concerned if they couldn't pay, as Marie saw entering her friend's tent some monks who clearly didn't have a cent to their names. Marie became worried about Hiltrud's welfare.

Later, when things had quieted down, Marie walked to the riverbank with her friend and spoke frankly about her concerns without receiving a reply. Hiltrud's gaze was fixed far in the distance, and her face showed a bone-tired weariness. When Marie pressed further, Hiltrud angrily shook her head. "Leave me alone. I know what I'm doing."

Marie didn't let herself be brushed off so easily. "If you keep up like this, you'll soon be as run-down as Berta, who spreads her legs for any dirty fellow, and of whom demanding customers steer clear. In any case, you ought to wash thoroughly and check yourself for lice and fleas. Some of your customers looked like they were well acquainted with vermin."

Hiltrud smiled sadly. "Don't worry about me. I'll pull myself together soon, but today I had to remind myself who I am in the world. Our time at Arnstein Castle didn't do me much good."

"You're tormenting yourself because you couldn't stay with Thomas." Marie put her arms around her friend and pulled her close. "I understand how much you miss him, but you shouldn't punish yourself. You'll become like one of those penny whores, and well-off customers will avoid you. They don't like it if the man before them was a lice breeder."

Even Hiltrud had to laugh at that. Raising her hands, she conceded. "You're right—I was a fool. I solemnly promise never to neglect myself like that again. Now are you happy?"

Marie nodded, and Hiltrud stood up. "Come, let's undress and go take a bath. First, though, I want to hang my blanket and dress over the fire, as I'm afraid I really did inherit a few fleas from my recent clients."

Hiltrud entered her tent to change, fetched the soap she had made from fat and ashes, then waved to Marie to follow her away from the pilgrims. They walked along the shore for a while until they came to a gathering of sharp rocks that projected far out into the water. There, Hiltrud undressed, then energetically set to work washing herself, scrubbing so hard, she seemed almost intent on scraping off her skin. Still wearing her dress, Marie walked into the water where she cleaned herself and her clothing while keeping an eye on her friend in the moonlight.

Even though Hiltrud's grief at leaving Thomas was still strong, she was grateful to Marie for having given her such a severe scolding. It was unfortunate when any woman let herself go, but with a prostitute, it was the beginning of the end. To salvage her reputation, Hiltrud would have to choose her clients more carefully for a while even if it meant not making as much money.

When Marie and Hiltrud returned to their tents, they found the four other prostitutes sitting around a campfire eating some sort of nondescript soup. Though they didn't recognize the young blond girl sitting next to Berta, she was obviously Gerlind's new maid, Märthe. She was already well padded around her breasts and thighs, but judging by her moon-shaped face, she couldn't be older than sixteen. Gerlind waved to them, calling out, "Here you are finally. Feel free to help yourself to some of the soup."

Walking over, Hiltrud shook hands with Berta, Fita, and the new girl. "Nice to see you again. We'll have plenty to talk about once we set on our way." Berta and Fita assured Hiltrud it would no doubt be a lively trip, but Märthe only looked up briefly, giving Hiltrud an unfriendly look before returning to spoon her soup without taking any more notice of the new arrival.

Marie had gone back to her tent to change and hang up her dress to dry, and was thus able to observe the women sitting around the fire without being seen. Märthe's chilly attitude toward Hiltrud puzzled her, though it was hardly disturbing. The girl fit in well with the other three, however, for they all looked unkempt and bedraggled.

Sitting down by the fire, Marie realized that the women were even filthier than she had thought, and she was repelled by what she saw. Gerlind used to groom herself carefully, and she had made sure that Berta and Fita didn't run around looking slovenly, either. Now all of the women reeked of the same sharp smell, and their clothes were dirty and full of spots. Gerlind's hands and face appeared not to have been washed for weeks, and Marie suddenly felt ill at the idea of eating something she cooked.

Hiltrud apparently shared her reluctance, and the two friends instinctively stepped back a bit from the pot. "We won't be having supper with you this evening, Gerlind, as we still have provisions that have to be used up."

"We'd be glad to help you with that," Berta called to them as they left.

Marie and Hiltrud returned to their tents and sat around their small, smoky fire, trying to think what to do next. If they didn't want to cause problems, they'd have to at least share some of the ham that Guda had packed for them before they left Arnstein Castle.

Hiltrud cast a glance at Marie and shuddered. "I hope we'll be able to get Gerlind to wash her hands, or we'll have to insist on eating separately."

Pouting, Marie looked at her friend. "I'd prefer to do without the company of these four entirely."

"So would I, believe me, but it's too risky to travel with the pilgrims on our own. There are too many men among them who'd throw us on our backs alongside the road without paying. And if we wait until they all leave, then we'll have to deal with the monks who quickly forget their fear of God when they see two women traveling alone."

Marie broke off a piece of Arnstein bread and put it in her mouth. "Why did we have to bump into these slobs, of all people? Couldn't we have happened upon nicer whores?"

"Don't talk with your mouth full unless you want to look like Berta," Hiltrud shot back.

III.

The first of the pilgrims left the next morning, but there was still work left for the six prostitutes. Since Marie was considered too fussy, she had just two customers. Hiltrud kept her promise and let into her tent only those customers whose appearance and odor corresponded to the rules she had drilled into Marie almost four years before. Some of the men she turned away cursed her and then lined up before the tents of the four other women who bedded anyone with three Haller pennies to spend.

Over the course of the day, more and more pilgrims said their last prayers in the chapel and departed. As the crowd grew smaller in front of the prostitutes' tents and the church also emptied, Marie suddenly felt the need to say a prayer there, which surprised even her, for ever since that dreadful day in Constance, she had not entered a church nor found any consolation in faith. Wrapping a shawl around her shoulders in an attempt to hide at least some of the yellow ribbons, she walked over to the pilgrimage church.

As she was about to enter, an old monk stepped in front of her. "This is the house of the Holy Virgin. Whores have no place here."

For a moment Marie wondered whether to bribe him with a few coins, but then all her anger at her treatment before the Constance episcopal court boiled over. Drawing the shawl tighter around her shoulders, she dodged to one side to escape the monk as he reached out to grab her. She saw both the disappointment and the lust in his face, and knew he wanted her to use her body to pay the cost of entering the church. But she was not about to do him that favor. Of what value was her prayer if she had to prostitute herself to enter? According to the rules of the church, that was a crime for which a woman could expect at least several lashes.

The monk didn't give up easily, but instead followed her for a distance over the meadow. Several pilgrims stopped him and pleaded with him to bless the devotional articles they had bought at the fair, allowing Marie to finally slip out of his reach.

Breathing a sigh of relief, she directed a silent prayer to the patron saint of courtesans, as prostitutes called Mary Magdalene. Then she sat down in the grass beside Hiltrud's goats, running her fingers through their fur.

Hiltrud came over and joined her. "You were right, Marie. I earned less today than usual, but I feel much better."

Marie leaned her head on Hiltrud's shoulder. "I'm glad. Even if we're only whores, disrespected even by those regarded as dishonorable in the cities, we still have our dignity."

Hiltrud stared at the waves gently cresting in the lake. "We shouldn't have gone to Arnstein. I could see there the future I gave up because my father valued the coins of a whoremonger more than his own child. Even the lowest serfs have it better than we do."

"You mustn't think about the past, or about what might still happen," someone answered for Marie.

Looking up, the two women saw Gerlind standing there. She grinned at them toothlessly, but her voice sounded bitter.

Marie understood what Gerlind meant. The old woman had dreamed of a quiet place where she could spend the last years of her life in peace and a small degree of happiness, but just when she had attained her goal, she had been forced back out onto the street. Marie was about to say something to cheer her up, but then Gerlind started waving her walking stick at them. "First, I want to make something clear. I'm the leader of this group." Gerlind directed her words less at Hiltrud than at Marie, and her voice sounded shrill. "I heard from Berta that you spent last winter as a nobleman's bed warmer. Don't try to make anything out of that. You're no better than any other whore and will have to do things the way we do."

Unlike the woman Marie had known four years before, Gerlind was now an old hag consumed with envy. Marie felt like lashing out, but she knew that for the time being, she'd have her hands full just trying to avoid a fight.

"Neither Hiltrud nor I dispute your right to be leader. Since we'll be traveling companions for the next few days, we need to get along with one another."

A thousand wrinkles spread across Gerlind's face as she smiled smugly. "It's good you see it that way, but before we let you join us, I have something to tell you. The four of us—Berta, Fita, Märthe, and I—have decided to put a fourth of what we earn in a common travel fund that I will manage. If you come along, you'll have to do the same."

Gerlind knew that two prostitutes traveling alone wouldn't make it safely to the next marketplace, and she was making the most of that fact. About to flare up in anger, Hiltrud caught herself, bit her lip, and stared into the water. Marie also had a sharp retort on the tip of her tongue. Since Hiltrud and she made a lot more money than the other four combined, this requirement was nothing less than extortion.

Raising her stick, Gerlind spoke again. "I'm not finished. The four of us also agreed that we should stay together until the fall. So don't get any ideas that you can take off at the next opportunity, or we will tell all the other whores how malicious and deceitful you are, so no one will ever take you on again as traveling companions." Marie looked at Hiltrud questioningly. Gerlind's intent was obvious. The old woman knew that she and her companions would have trouble making enough to get through the coming winter, and they wanted to have these two cash cows around to pull them through as needed.

"It looks like we'll have to accept your conditions, Gerlind, but don't think that we're happy about it." Hiltrud glared in contempt at the old prostitute, then turned around to pet her goats. Gerlind moved away from her former friend and stepped closer to Marie, reaching for her as if she wanted to shake her. "How was it in that castle? Did you earn a lot?"

Pushing aside Gerlind's cramped, clawlike hands, Marie shook her head. "Free food and drink and a few shillings when we left, that was all." That wasn't quite true, as Lady Mechthild's payment would at least cover the rent for a simple cabin and provisions for the coming winter, and in addition to those savings, Marie still had the gold Württemberg guilders, but she saw no reason to taunt Gerlind.

In the meantime, Märthe had joined the group. "I was just at church," she said with a blissful gaze. "It's beautiful. The altar is richly decorated, and I felt as if the Holy Virgin statue was about to step off her pedestal and embrace me."

Marie looked up in amazement "How did you get into the church? A monk at the portal turned me away."

"Well, the venerable brother standing there also told me that it wasn't appropriate for a fallen woman to enter through the portal of a sacred house, but he was kind enough to let me in through the vestry."

"What did you give him for doing that?"

Märthe gave her a blissful smile. "We spent a few minutes in the vestry relieving the pain in his loins. That, too, is a deed pleasing to God."

Marie wondered if Märthe was really so stupid as to believe that. Perhaps she was simply pious in her own way, like Fita, who had once served a whole monastery full of monks just so she could pray before the statue of the Mother of God.

Märthe nudged Marie with her foot. "By the way, the righteous brother asked me to send you his greetings. He said you could come to him anytime he's not busy with the pilgrims. As a reward for your compliance, he'll let you into the church."

Marie clenched her fists. Märthe wasn't just dumb; she was also as annoying as a fly. Refraining once more from blurting out what was right on the tip of her tongue, Marie explained to the girl that she had no intention of going to church.

Märthe stamped her foot angrily. "Then the pious brothers will be very disappointed."

I can imagine so, Marie thought scornfully. No doubt the monks in this remote place suffered from a lack of submissive women. A compliant prostitute who believed their glib talk was just what they were looking for.

IV.

The next morning the six women bid farewell to Saint Marien am Stein. Before leaving, Fita and Märthe quickly ran to the massive church to kiss its walls one last time. Since they were gone for a while, Marie assumed they had encountered a few of the monks suffering from pain in their loins. The phrase amused Marie. In her opinion, most men suffered from this illness, or there wouldn't be any prostitutes. Since the others had already taken down their tents, Märthe and Fita had to hurry upon their return, but the few things they had were quickly packed and the group left shortly afterward. At the top of the first hill, Marie turned around to look at the lake and the church down below.

From above, the pilgrimage site looked like her image of heaven as a child: calm, peaceful, and untouched by the human hand, a place where angels dwelled. The willows along the shore gleamed white in the splendor of their flowering branches, and the pilgrimage flag flew atop the church steeple. Across the peninsula stood the monastery, looking like a fortress with its massive walls and small narrow windows. The monks even called it a fortress of belief.

Marie wondered to which of the three reigning popes these monastic orders belonged—Rome, Avignon, or Pisa. No matter which it was, the monks didn't take their obedience to the church as seriously as their own needs, as if the hell they always preached about was reserved only for others. Marie thought about the great church council scheduled for Constance in the fall. Perhaps a divine wind would arise to sweep away the depraved monks and priests who called themselves servants of God but had only malice instead of consolation for those dealt a hard blow by fate.

"Are you brooding about your former fiancé again?" Strangely, this time Hiltrud didn't sound facetious. Her face looked tense, and she didn't wait for Marie's answer. "I was really happy to see Gerlind again, but the change I see in her troubles me. If I start becoming like her, I'll take a rope and hang myself, no matter what the priests say. Purgatory can't be worse than living the way she does now."

Marie glanced at the front of the procession, where the four other harlots were mingling with a small group of pilgrims who had also set out that morning. "We've got to look around as soon as possible for other traveling companions. If we drift around with these fleabags much longer, no respectable customer will ever look at us again. I'm more afraid of that than of incurring Berta's wrath."

Laughing, Hiltrud shook her head. "How are you going to prevent the others from coming along with us? I'm afraid those four are going to stick to us like glue and scare away any other prostitutes who might be willing to travel with us. The only way we'll get rid of them is if the devil comes and takes them."

At nightfall they arrived at a courtyard inn set behind a wall. A servant told them they were not allowed inside the wall and would have to set up their tents at the other end of the meadow so the night watchman could make sure there was no trouble. Marie and Hiltrud were happy with this arrangement, but Gerlind, who approached their campfire after nightfall, was annoyed.

She made a few snide comments about servants at the inn ruining their business, but when Hiltrud disagreed, saying that the innkeeper's rule wouldn't keep interested customers away, Gerlind got nasty. "You lazy riffraff, you're only standing up for him because you don't want to do anything. Do you think we're here just for the fun of it?"

Hiltrud glanced up at her with a studied look of innocence. "I don't understand what you mean."

Gerlind's face turned dark with rage. "You understand me very well. It's time you two came up with some money. Or do you intend to live at our expense?"

Marie wanted to slap the old hussy in the face for this outrageous remark. But since they needed to stay with the other women for protection, there was nothing she could do but clench her fists under her clothing and answer as coolly as possible.

"First of all, we have our own provisions and don't take any food from you. Second, you are not our whoremonger. When it comes to choosing our customers, we're on our own. I don't just offer myself to anyone with a few pennies."

Gerlind hissed furiously. "If you don't earn something pretty soon, you'll have to give up some of your savings to pay your share of the travel fund."

Putting her hand on the ax she'd been using to cut up dry twigs for the fire, Marie glared at Gerlind, jutting out her chin. "Try to come and get it."

The old woman stared at the ax, spat on the ground, and snorted angrily as she left. Soon afterward, Hiltrud and Marie could see her talking quietly with Berta and casting glances back at them.

Sparks flew as Hiltrud poked around in the fire with a stick. "We'd best take care, as I'm afraid Gerlind and Berta have it in for us."

Nodding bitterly, Marie took the pan off the fire and dripped some bacon grease onto their bread. "The next few days won't be easy," she said, chewing on the bread. "Except for a bit of flour, we've used all our provisions, and I have no intention of touching Gerlind's stew."

"I heard one of the pilgrims say there's a little market in the next small town we'll get to tomorrow. Perhaps we can buy something there."

Marie gave a cynical snort. "If we can convince the guards at the gate with two Hallers that we mean to spend money there, they'll certainly let us in."

"Indeed, if we come to spend money, the honorable towns-women will be glad to overlook the yellow ribbons, but that won't keep them from asking outrageous prices for bad goods. That's the lesser of our problems, though. The larger one is that if Gerlind and the others notice we're buying food, they might come along with us and try to have us pay for their provisions."

"That would be just fine by them," Marie cackled contemptuously.

"In any case, the others mustn't find out how much money we have and where we've hidden it."

Marie nodded silently, as she knew how tricky Berta was and how that had cost a number of her clients. Several times Hiltrud had told the fat harlot that one of these days she'd be caught stealing from the men, and have her nose cut off as punishment. But Berta would have the last laugh if she stole things from other prostitutes.

"We'll have to take turns keeping watch. We have more to fear from our traveling companions than from the fellows in the inn, because if one of them bothers us, he'll have to deal with the inn-keeper. He's got a reputation for keeping order."

"That's sad but true." Marie sighed. "Lie down. I don't feel much like sleeping."

Hiltrud put another log on the fire and looked at their meager supply of firewood. It wasn't enough to last the night, as they had had to share what they gathered with Gerlind and the others. She reminded Marie again to keep the fire burning slowly without letting it die.

V.

The next morning, Marie found some dry grass and bushes near their camping site and was able to rekindle their fire, cooking a few pancakes with the remaining fat, flour, and honey. Berta, who had a good sense of smell, raised her head and sniffed. Her persistence was rewarded, as Hiltrud finally handed her one of the pancakes even though there weren't enough for both Marie and herself. Berta's gratitude went no farther than telling the others that Marie and Hiltrud had nothing left for them.

As the two broke camp, packing up and preparing to move on, Märthe stepped in front of Hiltrud and placed her hands on her hips. "Normally traveling companions share everything. But you seem to be saving all of the goodies for yourselves."

"You get back what you put into the common pot." "Hiltrud replied. "You want to take advantage of there being four of you in order to take a quarter of our earnings. You can't expect us to thank you for that."

"Then it's about time you started earning some money," Märthe shot back.

Berta reared up alongside Märthe, trying to look fiercer than she was. "And you should hand over a quarter of what you earned in Saint Marien am Stein."

Hiltrud couldn't be intimidated. "Our association began the moment we left Saint Marien. I don't see any reason to give you money we already earned there."

Making a face, Gerlind pounded her walking stick on the ground. "As you will." It sounded almost like a threat.

Hiltrud shrugged and walked around Berta and Märthe without saying a word. The goats followed her, bleating, so the other women had to jump aside so the cart wouldn't roll over their feet.

Shortly after noon, they arrived at the little city of Wallfingen. Gerlind and her companions set up their tents and waited for customers. Marie and Hiltrud did the same, but more to ensure privacy than to entertain customers, as the market in Wallfingen was too small to attract many travelers, and the townspeople had access to girls in the local brothels. The two friends were nonetheless in a good mood and weren't even annoyed that the market supervisor immediately swooped down on them like a falcon to collect their market tax.

Marie and Hiltrud smiled at each other when the sound of Berta's cursing drowned out even the bellowing of the animals. She was offended because the market supervisor refused to accept the taxes in the form she offered.

"I'd prefer money," she heard the man reply, laughing. "And as far as your merchandise is concerned, I'd rather take the goods from that young woman." He pointed at Marie and raised his eyebrows in question. Marie didn't take him up on his offer, however, handing him tax money rather than letting him into her tent.

Taking her basket from the cart, she headed through the city gate and continued down the busy street to the market square. While most people gave her a wide berth after glimpsing her yellow ribbons, the market women and merchants at the stands were not averse to exchanging a few friendly words. Marie took her time, enjoyed the shopping, and returned with an overflowing basket and a sack of flour over her shoulder. When she arrived at their tent, the unpleasant expression on Hiltrud's face told her that something had happened, but before she could ask, Gerlind came running toward them. She had a middle-aged craftsman in tow, judging by his expensive beaver-skin cap and long, fur-lined coat.

"Here you are finally! Get to work, Marie. The gentleman here wants a pretty bed companion, and I advised him to wait for you. Hurry to your tent so he can sleep with you."

Marie stared at her in disbelief. "What did you say?"

"Sleep with him. He has already paid, and you'll get your share later."

Gerlind started pushing her toward her tent, but Marie was having none of it. She pushed back and raised her hand as if about to strike the old woman.

"Have you gone mad? I choose my own customers. And they pay me and no one else, do you understand? If the man wants a roll in the hay, let him take you or Märthe. In any case, he's not getting into my tent."

The man listened to the argument with visible displeasure. "What's this all about? They promised me a pretty whore, and that's what I paid for. So hurry up, girl. I don't have all day."

He grabbed Marie's arm with a tight grip and started pulling her into the tent. Furious, she reached into her skirt and unsheathed the sharp knife she carried, holding it against the man's stomach.

"Take your hands off me if you ever want to sard a woman again!" she snarled at him.

The man looked at the knife and let go. Stepping back, he opened his mouth, about to explode with anger, but then stared at Marie wide-eyed. Closing his mouth, he made the sign of the cross.

"By the Holy Virgin and Saint Pelagius, this can't be true. Is it really you?"

Blankly, Marie looked at the man who had turned as white as a sheet. But then it dawned on her. "You . . . You are Jörg Wölfling, the cooper from Constance."

"And you are Matthis Schärer's daughter, Marie, who was driven out of Constance."

"After they slandered, raped, and whipped me," she added bitterly.

This was the moment she had feared most. She was so ashamed at being seen as a prostitute by one of her father's friends that she wished the ground would open up and swallow her. But she quickly got control of herself and shook off her trepidation. After all, she wasn't here through any fault of her own but because Rupert had ruined her, and Master Jörg hadn't lifted a finger to help her.

The cooper pointed at the knife Marie was still holding threateningly in her hand. "Put that thing away, and let's talk like reasonable people."

Marie nodded and slipped the little knife back into its sheath.

"Tell me how you've been doing. We've thought a lot about you in the last four years." Wölfling sniffled like a child and wiped his nose with the back of his hand. Marie did not know what to say. She wanted nothing more than to run away, but at the same time she had a thousand questions.

Using his sleeve, Wölfling dried the tears now running down his cheeks. "My God, Marie, it's a miracle you're still alive! How happy Mombert will be."

Marie stiffened and shook her head vigorously. "I don't want anyone to learn about me. No one needs to know I still exist, do you understand?"

Master Jörg reached for one of the yellow ribbons on her skirt and nodded sadly. "I understand, but nonetheless your uncle would be thrilled to hear from you."

"It would be better if you'd keep our meeting to yourself, but I would be grateful if you could tell me how my relatives are."

"I'd be glad to do that." Master Jörg took Marie gently by the sleeve. "Come, let's take a seat over there by the wine stand in the shade. It'll be easier to talk with a pitcher of red wine."

"I don't think they'll allow me to sit down there."

Master Jörg dismissed the thought in consideration of the important person he was and led Marie toward the stand. As they walked up, the barkeep frowned and murmured that the master should take his whore elsewhere.

Wölfling opened his purse and gave the barkeep several coins. "A big pitcher of your best wine and two cups."

The barkeep couldn't resist the look of the shining silver pieces. "Take a seat over there," he said, pointing to a bench off to the side where they could talk without being disturbed. Taking the pitcher filled to the brim with the best Rhine wine and two cups, they walked to the bench, lost in thought.

Wölfling raised his glass to Marie with a sad smile. "It's really just by chance that we met today. I would never have come here if the kaiser hadn't ordered the three popes to come to Constance to settle the problems of Christianity with a council. Because of that, we can't keep up with barrel orders, and the Constance coopers' guild asked me to come here to negotiate with the makers here for the delivery of more."

Marie nodded congenially even though she wasn't really interested in the barrel makers' problems. "It's surely an act of fate. But do tell me, Master Jörg, how is my uncle?"

Wölfling raised his hand hesitantly. "He is well, and his business is doing better than ever since word got out about the council."

"He wasn't doing so badly beforehand, either."

Master Jörg sighed deeply. "That was before your misfortune. After that, things looked bad for him for a while, as his trials against Counselor Rupert Splendidus almost financially ruined him. Of course, you can't know that your former fiancé confiscated all of your father's possessions with the episcopal court's help. Mombert lost each of the three times he took Rupert to court. Finally he tried to retrieve your mother's dowry, but Rupert kept presenting documents to dispute Mombert's claims."

Marie wasn't surprised as she had heard enough about how Rupert dealt with his opponents, but she continued asking questions. "What do you know about my father? Back then I hoped he would look for me and pick me out of the gutter."

She looked at him intently, as she still hoped the sheepshearer had lied to Giso to get more wine out of him.

Helplessly, Master Jörg spread out his arms. "I'm terribly sorry for you, child! No one saw your father after that dreadful day. Master Rupert claimed that Matthis Schärer had bequeathed him all his possessions and gone to the Holy Land to atone for your sins. Some said he had left on a pilgrimage to Rome, and others said they had met him somewhere in Flanders, still looking for you. I tend more to believe what the sheepshearer Anselm said before he drowned in the Rhine."

Marie felt a tightness in the pit of her stomach. "Anselm is dead?"

"Yes, it was bound to happen. A few foolish wagon drivers were plying him with drinks, and on the way to Gottlieben he fell into the Rhine. If his corpse hadn't been found floating in the water, no one would have ever known what happened to him. But apparently, shortly before he died, he had told a stranger he'd helped bury your father in potter's field. Marie, child, I'm so sorry for you, but I'm afraid the old drunk may have been telling the truth."

Marie gasped, sure that the stranger was Giso. And she knew that Anselm's death was no accident. Even though most people in Constance paid no attention to a drunk's blatherings, she was convinced that Rupert and his accomplices had silenced him. She wondered if Utz was involved, having goaded a few friends into plying the old man with alcohol.

Shuddering, Marie dried a few tears. "My father never would have left his possessions to Rupert, so I can assume he's dead."

Wölfling placed his hand on Marie's shoulder. "Master Matthis loved you very much, Marie, and he would never have abandoned you. I'm ashamed to say that I was jealous of your father and the wealth he had accumulated as a bondsman's grandson, while my family had to fight for survival even though we had played a leading role in the last civil war against the nobles. That was the reason I didn't lift a hand to help you, and I have been severely punished for that.

"The reputation of my ancestors had secured me a city council seat, and I lost that forever because of you. The other council members accused me of allowing Counselor Rupert to take you before the episcopal court instead of the city courts, as was your right. But it all happened so fast. Before I could clear my head, you had already been driven from town, your father had disappeared, and Rupert had taken possession of your house."

Judging from his bitter tone, Wölfling was less concerned about her misfortune than about the loss of his council seat, which came with all kinds of honors. She was unforgiving enough not to lament his fall from the ranks of the privileged, as she hadn't forgotten how elated he and Master Gero had been to find the incriminating piece of jewelry in her bedroom.

Keeping her feelings hidden, she continued questioning Master Jörg, learning a bit more about what had happened in Constance since her banishment. "Mombert and his wife feel blessed to have

Hedwig, who has turned out to be a very pretty girl. She looks like your younger sister, Marie, though I must say you have become even more beautiful in the last few years. If I had enough money, I'd buy you a house on the Rhine and keep you there as my lover." He shook his head and sighed, wondering what was left to tell Marie.

"By the way, do you remember Michel, the son of the taverner? The boy must have really loved you since he left town that terrible day to follow you. But the two bailiffs played a trick on him, sending him in the wrong direction. His father went to search for him but lost track of him in Diessenhofen, and it's said he signed onto a ship headed for Holland."

"At least one person believed in me!" Marie exclaimed.

She tried in vain to picture Michel's face. Though she couldn't remember what he looked like, she could still clearly remember his voice that evening when he warned her about Rupert. The boy must have understood her fiancé better than her father, who had been blinded by the honor of having his daughter marry the son of a count. Marie silently hoped that Michel had been led astray, forced to wander homeless along the highway; at the same time she feared he might have paid for his loyalty to her with his life, as sailors were a notoriously rough crowd and the Rhine had pulled many down into its depths. Or Rupert might also have had Michel killed. Shedding a few tears for her former playmate, Marie nodded at Master Jörg. "I thank you for the news and ask you to please leave me to myself now. I need to think about all that I've learned today."

"I understand. I'm sorry I couldn't bring you better news. Do you really not want me to tell your uncle about our meeting?"

Marie nodded. Wölfling wondered if he should tell Mombert anyway, then decided it was better to keep quiet. He knew that if he spoke about seeing Marie, Counselor Rupert might get wind of it, and he didn't want to have anything to do with that man.

He poured the last of the wine into his cup. Since Marie had only a little to drink, most of the wine had disappeared into his portly paunch, making him sentimental. He remembered all the meals to which Marie's father had invited him, and he was struck by a bad conscience. Suddenly Marie seemed as beautiful and pure as a saint. What a virtuous and exemplary citizen she could have become! He despised himself for his weakness. Since his negotiations in Wallfingen had made him a nice sum, he impulsively undid the clasps fastening his full money bag to his belt. Opening the purse, he handed everything in it to Marie.

"Here, take this. You can surely use it." He stood up quickly, as if afraid he might regret his generosity. "I believe I had better go now. May the saints protect you, Marie."

"It's about time they do," she replied, standing and shaking his hand in farewell.

Master Jörg briefly embraced her and then suddenly let her go. Marie watched until he disappeared beyond the city gate, and then she returned to her tent. On meeting Gerlind, she was about to demand the money Master Jörg had paid the old harlot, but Marie shrugged and walked past her. At the moment she had no wish to quarrel. Moreover, Master Jörg's purse contained far more than the few shillings Gerlind had taken for herself.

VI.

Marie's meeting with Wölfling weighed so heavily on her mind that for a while she forgot about the new argument between Hiltrud and Gerlind. The old woman wanted to go over to Baden and then to the Rhine, where she thought there were better chances of making money, whereas Hiltrud thought it better to first go down the Neckar River to the Rhine. Mechthild von Arnstein was related to the House of Büchenbruch, and Hiltrud had heard at Arnstein Castle that there would be a feud between the Büchenbruch clan and the House of Riedburg. Hiltrud thought it dangerous to follow the route Gerlind suggested and possibly find themselves caught between the two warring factions.

Gerlind demurred with a scornful look. "That's just foolish talk. If there were really going to be a feud, we'd have heard about it by now. I say we head straight for the Rhine, and then we'll arrive early enough to meet the Black Forest raftsmen taking their logs down the river. They've still got plenty of silver jangling in their purses from the advances their bosses gave them upon taking the job, and they'll be happy to relax with us after their hard days of work."

Puffing out her chest, Berta tried to look down on Hiltrud, which was rather ridiculous given their difference in height. "I agree with Gerlind, and so do Fita and Märthe. So it's four against two."

"Against me and Marie, who also heard about the feud and would no doubt take my side," Hiltrud replied, her face strained as she turned to look for her friend. She was nowhere to be seen, however, so Hiltrud gave in. "Very well, then, let's go with your plan. I hope it's safe for us."

"And why shouldn't it be?" Berta asked derisively. "If a fellow gets too fresh, I'll whack him on the head so hard with my big knife that he won't get up again until the last trump sounds." She waved her weapon in front of Hiltrud's face amidst general laughter.

Hiltrud stepped back instinctively, which made Gerlind laugh even louder, her belly and breasts bouncing up and down. "Six determined women like us don't even need to fear God."

Fita suddenly turned serious and crossed herself. Then she folded her hands and asked God for forgiveness for this blasphemy. Bertha walked up and shoved Fita headfirst into the grass. "Don't act as if God doesn't understand a joke. He's certainly not as strict as the priests want to make us believe. Haven't you figured out yet that they tell us so much about hell in order to get inside our skirts for free?"

Opening her mouth, Fita prepared to deliver one of her religious tirades, but Gerlind snapped at her before she could speak. "See those fellows hanging around over there? Go get one of them, or for the next few weeks you won't be able to put a penny in an offering box or light a candle for the Virgin Mary. You've fallen behind recently in your earnings, and I don't intend to let you live off us."

Staggering to her feet, Fita wiped away her tears with the hem of her dress and ran over to the three men. Two of them gave her a contemptuous look and stared lustfully after Marie who was feeding the goats with her back turned to the other women. The third fellow let Fita take him to her tent from which a loud groaning and moaning could soon be heard.

"If the fellow's banging her up as badly as it sounds, he'll really hurt her," Berta joked, and swinging her hips, she walked over to the two other men, waving at Märthe to follow.

Disgusted at the way the four other women acted, Hiltrud knew that their behavior diminished their value and made the better customers avoid them like the plague. She herself had been so fussy that day that she didn't even earn enough to cover expenses. Nevertheless, rather than looking around for another customer, Hiltrud sat down with Marie in the grass and petted her goats.

"We'll have to stay with Gerlind's group until we get to the Rhine, but then I swear we'll go our own way, even if we have to sleep with every single servant in the wagon train," she said to Marie, telling her about the route Gerlind planned to take. Marie was only half listening, however. "I don't care where we go, as long as we lose the four of them."

VII.

The six women left at dawn the next morning. Gerlind and her companions carried a lighter load than before, as Hiltrud had allowed them, after a fierce dispute, to put some of their things on her cart. As a result, the goats had to strain a bit more, and even the kids were hitched up, tugging vigorously on the reins. As the road steepened, however, it became too much for the animals, and Hiltrud was forced to help pull the wagon while Marie pushed from behind. By the third hill, Marie suggested hitching up Berta or Märthe as well.

With a contemptuous wave of her hand, Hiltrud demurred. "They would just force Fita to help us, and she'd collapse like a tottering old nag after three steps."

Marie heaved an angry sigh. "Four years ago I never would have imagined that I'd long for the day we could part ways with Gerlind."

She would always be grateful for how friendly Gerlind had been, taking her in and helping her with such care over those first hard days. But this bitter woman in a filthy dress hobbling in front of them was no longer the Gerlind that Marie had gotten to know and admire. Nevertheless, she felt bad that she no longer was thankful to the old woman. Struggling with her guilt, she tried to shake off her feelings.

"What's the matter?" Hiltrud asked, concerned.

"I was thinking about Gerlind. Tell me, who has changed more, me or her?"

Hiltrud laughed out loud. "That's obvious. You've both changed, you for the better and she for the worse. I must say, I'm looking forward to soon saying good-bye to her for the last time. It makes me feel wretched just to look at her anymore."

Marie nodded silently and started pushing again.

The following days were mostly uneventful but not apt to soften Marie's and Hiltrud's hostility, now directed less at Gerlind than at Berta, who did everything she could to make their lives harder. The first night she told Marie and Hiltrud that they weren't welcome at their campfire but that they instead needed to set up their tents some distance away. Nevertheless, Berta insisted that they take half of the night watch while helping herself to some of the wood that the two had gathered for themselves.

Hiltrud didn't object to the guard-duty assignments, since she didn't trust the others and was afraid she'd lose her goats to a bear or a stray wolf. Marie just prayed that the wild animals would spare her, for her knife was not a suitable weapon. Even Gerlind's iron-studded stick was no longer what it used to be. Its point, once so sharp, had worn down and become bent. That first night, however, they had set up camp near a large farm, and Marie was happy that the noise of the barking dogs was so loud, it would keep beasts of prey away, even if it kept them awake.

On the second day, Berta caught six fat hens that had wandered into the street, and she wrung their necks. Marie's mouth watered at the sight of the birds, as she'd always liked chicken, especially the way Wina used to prepare it, crispy brown with tasty stuffing.

Unfortunately, the four other women had no intention of sharing their meal with their two companions.

Instead, Hiltrud prepared a little dough cake with flour that she baked on a stone in the fire along with onions and wild fennel. Marie kept an eye on other women, shuddering as she watched them hastily scorch the chickens in the campfire, then hungrily devour the half-cooked insides. She preferred Hiltrud's crispy dough cakes to that.

By the next day, they could see the forested summit of Mount Fürstkopf in the south, and their path merged onto a wider road where fresh hoofprints of large horses, deep wheel ruts, and trampled grass were visible. The tracks suggested that a large merchant's convoy had recently passed through, and Gerlind and Berta became extremely excited, as there were no doubt plenty of men in the group willing to spend their money on women. Gerlind therefore didn't look for a campsite in the late afternoon, but instead quickened her pace and hurried her companions along so they could set up their tents and collect firewood before nightfall.

"The wagon train is at most an hour ahead of us, and if we rush, we'll soon be sitting by a warm fire with a cup of wine in our hand . . ."

"And a man between our legs," Berta interrupted with a giggle.

By the time they finally spotted a blazing bonfire in the valley ahead, the hour had long passed, and darkness had descended over the land. Gerlind pointed triumphantly. "There they are! In no time at all their silver pieces will be jangling in our pockets."

As they turned off the road, they could hear loud laughter and voices, as if a big party were going on. Distrustful, Marie stopped and listened. She had spent the night close to many wagon trains, but these noises were unusual. It was also strange that the people were camped out in the middle of the forest rather than staying at an inn. Merchants and wagon drivers traveled from one inn to another if at all possible, because they could otherwise easily fall prey to robbers out in the forest or be attacked and robbed by knights or townspeople. At night, with no witnesses to report the attack, even a safe-conduct letter purchased at great cost was of no value to the merchants.

Marie warned other women to stay away, but it was too late, as rough male voices were already calling out to Gerlind and Berta.

"Hey, what are you women doing out on the road at night?" Two men holding torches walked toward them.

"Look! They're whores!" the second one shouted, waving the torch excitedly. "Men, the evening is saved. Whores are coming our way."

At that, more than three dozen men came running through the forest toward the women, cheering. Some held up their torches while others boldly grabbed and groped them, pinching their bottoms and breasts.

"Stop that!" Marie shouted furiously, punching one of the men, and he grabbed her by the chin, forcing her to stare into the light.

"You're a damned pretty little bird. I think I'll help myself." He was about to throw her on the ground when a powerfully built fellow lay a hand on his shoulder.

"Keep your hands off her. This fine girl is something for the noblemen, or do you think they'd want to let you take her away from them?"

As Marie reached under her skirt and grabbed the handle of her knife, the man snorted angrily and let her go. She tried to withdraw inconspicuously and disappear into the bushes, hoping to slip away under the cover of darkness. Gerlind had led them straight into a camp of mercenaries, and Marie knew from talking with other prostitutes what they could expect there.

These were roving mercenaries of the worst sort: Swiss deserters, Swabian lance bearers, and people who'd rather cut throats than earn an honest living. Even in the torches' flickering light it was clear that their equipment was anything but uniform. There were no coats of arms on their surcoats since they didn't belong to a nobleman's army, and some of them were wearing shirts with faded marks on the chest from where they had removed a nobleman's insignia upon leaving his service.

Thinking only of escape, Marie had slipped away from the torchlight and was about to disappear into the pitch black of the undergrowth when a huge man grabbed her and pressed her against his chest. "Here's the little bird for our Sir Lothar! Now you owe me something," he called out to the large man.

Understanding the seriousness of their situation, Gerlind tried to negotiate. "Don't be so rough with us, fellows. We have no objections to spreading our legs for you. This pleasure costs only a few pennies, and we'll see that each of you gets his turn." Though she tried to sound cheerful, her voice trembled with anxiety.

One of the men began to laugh loudly. "If you can find a Haller in our purses, old lady, you're lucky. Our spare change has long ago been spent in drinking and whoring, but we'll take you just the same. Don't you agree, men?" Those standing around grinned and nodded vigorously.

The men dragged the protesting women back to their camp, which was inadequately lit by the bonfire in the middle but where Marie could see two wagons heavily laden with barrels and war supplies, and another wagon with two dismantled cannons. Directly in front of the wagon with the cannon was a tent presumably belonging to the group's leader, since the mercenaries had set up their beds of blankets and coats under the open sky.

Marie had heard many times that wandering prostitutes were often raped. She herself had been lucky up to now, but it looked like her luck had run out. The entrance flap of the tent was turned up, and a young man dressed like a nobleman stuck his head out. Marie began to hope it wouldn't be as bad as she'd feared.

"Why all this noise?" he asked sharply.

"We have visitors," a mercenary replied with a grin. "We ran into a few whores, and we've reserved the prettiest little bird for you, Squire Siegward, a treat that will certainly be to your taste."

Shocked, Marie knew whose hands she'd fallen into. Old Siegbald of Riedburg Castle was the declared enemy of Lady Mechthild's relatives at Büchenbruch Castle. He had a reputation as a highway robber—and his sons, of whom Siegward was the eldest, had even worse reputations. If this man learned that Marie had spent the winter at Arnstein Castle, he'd probably kill her out of anger toward Lady Mechthild, who had sent help several times to her relatives in their fight against the Riedburgs.

Siegward von Riedburg licked his lips and looked her up and down as if she were a calf being delivered for slaughter. He was tall and broad-shouldered, with a warrior's build that would make Sir Dietmar envious. His dull, pale blue eyes revealed that he wasn't very bright, however, and his jutting chin suggested a domineering personality.

The squire pinched Marie's breast and nodded to his people. "Well done, men. This is exactly what I need tonight. In the meantime, amuse yourselves with the other whores."

"We will, sire," replied the soldier, nodding vigorously. "But to do that, we need to fill our bellies with something more than the porridge we had for supper. Hey, fellows, how about roasting those goats?" He pointed to Hiltrud's animals standing on the nearby roadside where they were eating grass.

"Hands off my goats!" shrieked Hiltrud, but the men only roared with laughter as one of them drew his sword and chopped off a goat's head. Hiltrud tore herself free and rushed at the perpetrator, clawing at his face with her fingernails. Several of the soldiers grabbed her immediately, however, and threw her to the ground.

Turning away from the scene, Squire Siegward lifted Marie in his arms and carried her into the tent. A simple but bright oil lamp lit up the interior, where two men playing cards looked up expectantly. Judging by the younger one's resemblance to Siegward, Marie assumed he was one of Siegward's brothers. The other man was stocky and broad-shouldered with long arms and short, crooked legs.

The beds were filthy, as if the occupants had wallowed in dirt before getting in, and strewn with clothing and weapons. On the folding table in the middle of the room were three cups alongside a pile of playing cards and stacks of coins, and beneath the table an empty wine jug. The men must have had a wild party, for when Siegward forced a kiss on Marie, she could smell the strong, acrid odor of wine.

He tore open her dress and pulled her toward him, his younger brother dancing nervously around him to ask if he could also grab the girl. "The whore is for all of us." Siegerich von Riedburg let out a demented laugh as Siegward pushed Marie back onto one of the beds.

The look on his face was not promising. He jumped on Marie, and as Hiltrud had taught her, she went completely limp. She felt the pain caused by his lack of consideration, but in her mind's eye another scene was playing out, one that she had repressed as much as possible in recent years. Suddenly it was no longer Siegward panting and groaning on top of her, but Utz, the wagon driver. Instinctively she stiffened and opened her eyes, then was brought back to the present by the sight of the young squire rearing up over her, his face flushed, while his brother stood over them, awaiting his turn.

"I'm next," Siegerich begged his brother like a young boy after a piece of candy.

Siegward answered without pausing in his violent contortions. "But only with the armorer's approval, lad. You know we have to humor Gilbert. After all, he's the one with the job of destroying Büchenbruch Castle with his artillery."

"I'll go and enjoy myself somewhere else for a while and let your brother go first." The armorer raised the canvas over the opening and stepped outside.

Finally, bellowing loudly, Siegward finished and made way for his brother. Siegerich tried to compensate for his inexperience with vigorous movement, but after a few breaths he collapsed on top of her. At that moment the armorer returned, a contented look on his face. "The fellows broke open a barrel of wine and started drinking. If you don't do anything to stop them, you'll never get them moving again in the morning."

Siegward waved him off with a laugh. "One day doesn't matter, so let them have their fun." His gaze fell on the empty wine jug, and he pushed it over to his brother with his foot. "Bring us something to drink, too. We shouldn't have to enjoy a tasty little chick with a dry throat."

Siegerich grabbed the pitcher and ran out.

After a long while, Gilbert sank down on top of her, overcome by wine and exhaustion, and began to snore. The three had abused her so much that it felt like every bone in her body was broken, and she struggled to crawl out from under the armorer.

As she tried to get up, her knees buckling with exhaustion, her first impulse was to run away. However, the laughter and savage groaning outside the tent made her realize that the other mercenaries were still busy. Not wanting to fall into their hands as well, she collapsed on a stool and thought about what to do next. She felt horribly dirty, but she couldn't find any water, so she dipped a corner of her underdress in the wine still remaining in the pitcher and washed herself with it. The alcohol burned like fire, but that didn't bother her nearly as much as the shrill screams of the women outside.

As she sat tying her shirt together with strips of cloth ripped from the knight's clothing, an almost unbearable hatred welled up inside her. Searching for her knife that Siegward had torn from the sheath on her leg and weighing it in her hand, she considered slitting the three men's throats, running her fingertips along the knife's sharp blade. But as she approached Gilbert, she caught sight of his purse that was full to the bursting point with coins.

In the meantime, her anger had subsided somewhat and she was reluctant to commit murder, so she simply used her knife to cut the armorer's purse from his trousers, then likewise seized Siegerich's purse. It took her a little longer to cut Siegward's purse from his belt, since it was attached by a broad, strong leather strap. Unfastening the strap holding the leather bag closed and looking inside, she almost forgot her misery. The first two men's purses were full of good silver coins and smaller pieces of gold, but Siegward was carrying golden ducats and guilders of considerable value. This was even enough money to hire an assassin to murder a nobleman, to say nothing of an illegitimate offspring like Rupert.

Marie clenched her fists triumphantly. If this money helped carry out her revenge, then the disgrace, fear, and pain she had endured that evening had been unexpectedly worth it. Raising her dress, she made a belt with long, hanging strips of cloth to which she attached Siegward's money pouch, her own little bag with the Württemberg guilders, and Master Jörg's purse. She then tied all three purses around her thighs with additional strips of cloth so they would not reveal their presence by jangling. Later she would sew pockets into her dress so she could serve her customers without first having to remove and hide the purses. As for Gilbert's and Siegerich's purses, these coins she would share with the others, as they were also entitled to compensation for this dreadful night.

VIII.

Several hours passed before the last mercenary finally succumbed to the wine and their wild orgy. Marie didn't want to imagine what would happen if her own torturers awoke to discover she had robbed them, but luck was on her side, and Siegward, his brother, and their armorer remained fast asleep. When it became quiet outside, with only the sound of a sobbing woman, Marie snuffed out the oil lamp's wick and carefully exited the tent.

Only a few glowing embers still shone in the campfire, and the moon appeared in the clear sky as a thin crescent, so Marie had trouble putting one foot in front of the other. Her eyes slowly becoming used to the faint light, she saw sleeping men everywhere before she discovered a woman wandering around naked.

"Hiltrud? Is that you?" Marie asked in a whisper.

"Marie?" She sounded both surprised and relieved as she embraced her. "I hurt so much, I can scarcely walk. How are you feeling?"

"I feel like a pack of rabid dogs attacked me. Where are the others? We must get out of here as soon as possible."

"Not until I have slit the throats of the men who murdered my goats," she replied, her entire body shaking. Marie grabbed her arm so tightly that she groaned.

"That won't bring them back to life again," Marie said. "Be reasonable and come along with me. We've got to put a lot of distance between us and these fellows before morning, as I've stolen their leaders' purses. The money will help compensate for your goats and everything they did to us here."

Hiltrud clenched her fists, then quickly opened her hands again. "Well done. But you're right—we must get out of here as fast as we can, because when they discover the theft, they'll want to cut us up into little pieces."

Putting on what remained of her dress, Hiltrud looked at Marie. "Hurry and get the others. In the meantime, I'll get a few things from our cart that we can take on our backs, since we'll unfortunately have to leave most of our possessions behind."

Heading toward the sound of sobbing that she heard earlier, Marie found Märte slumped along one of the large wagon wheels. Even though she shook and cajoled the young girl to get ahold of herself, Märte only cried louder when she saw Marie. Not until Gerlind came staggering toward them like a pale, haggard ghost did Märthe calm down enough to stand up and pull together the tattered shreds of what had once been her dress.

Gerlind said nothing, but the furious kicks she gave to some of the sleeping drunks showed that her anger was greater than her fear. Her dress was so torn that it wasn't even fit for a scarecrow, but since she had nothing else, she tied what was left of it together. Gerlind's cursing attracted the attention of a completely naked Berta who was wandering around with a torch in her hand and examining the mercenaries lying on the ground. Finding a man who matched her in size, she took his shirt for herself.

"I wasn't even treated this badly when I was an army camp follower," she complained, straightening up and looking at Gerlind. "That was a fine idea, leading us into a camp of mercenaries. You're such a great leader! From now on, I'm in charge, do you understand?"

Though her face contorted in a furious grimace, Gerlind didn't try to defend herself against Berta's accusations. Instead, she quietly suggested patting down the sleeping soldiers to search for anything valuable. Turning her back on the three quarreling women, Marie joined Hiltrud who had spread out her possessions and was picking out things to take along by the light of a burning stick. Marie also chose her most essential possessions; then they put everything else in the cart and pushed it into a marshy area behind the camp. There the two women came upon a whimpering Fita. Apparently she had been trying to get to the water, but was instead lying helplessly in the reeds.

She didn't react to Hiltrud's urgings to stand up, and when Marie bent down to touch her, she raised her head slightly and said, "Let me die."

"You're not going to give out on us now, Fita," Marie replied with feigned cheerfulness, but the woman just rolled over feebly.

Hiltrud picked up a stick she had just stumbled over, placed it in the still-smoldering campfire, and blew on the stick until the point had caught fire. In the light of the flame, she and Marie could see how badly Fita had been beaten.

Hiltrud looked back at the camp and shook her fist. "These aren't men. They're beasts. I hope the devil takes them soon." She and Marie carried Fita down near the swampy pond to a clear brook where they washed her.

"It's a shame we already sank our cart in the swamp," Hiltrud said. "We could have used some clothing for her."

"I can give her my spare skirt," Marie suggested.

"By the way she looks, she doesn't need a dress—no doubt she's going to die soon," said a voice behind them. It was Berta who had come down to the water with Märte to wash, and they did so more thoroughly than Marie and Hiltrud had ever seen before. They even used a rounded stone to remove the clinging filth on their bodies.

Holding up the torch, a smirk passed over Marie's face. "I made sure we had a little reward from this mess. I took the men's purses. But if we don't get out of here quickly, they'll kill us."

Berta laughed loudly and started walking toward Marie. "You're going to share your spoils with us, as we agreed."

It sounded like a command, but Marie nodded eagerly and patted the two purses on her belt. "I will, but not here. We've got to be far away by the time these fellows wake up."

She put her extra skirt on Fita with Hiltrud's help. Then the two women fastened their bundles on their backs and stood Fita up between them. Berta cursed at the waste of time, bluntly telling Marie that it was stupid to bring a half-dead person along with them.

Marie reared back. "One more remark like that and I won't give you anything of what I stole."

Her threat had an immediate effect. Berta closed her mouth and turned grimly silent, steering clear of Marie, Hiltrud, and Fita for the rest of their night's journey. Gerlind, too, didn't say another word to them and paid no attention to their injured companion, though she did light the way for Hiltrud and Marie with the burning branch she was holding. Märthe hobbled along behind them, constantly moaning to herself, though she seemed the least hurt of them all.

Tired and sore and with clenched teeth, the women staggered through the night that was gradually giving way to a new day. Afraid of being pursued, they headed deeper into the forest, avoiding the main roads and paths. Not until the trees had become almost impenetrable around them did they stop, sinking to the ground with exhaustion.

"The mercenaries certainly won't find us here," said Berta, groaning and feeling her feet. Though she was accustomed to going without shoes, her bare feet were so stung by thorns that she said she wouldn't be able to walk for three days. Since none of the other women were any better off, no one paid attention to her whining. Looking up, Gerlind told her to stop complaining and go to sleep, and after grumbling a bit more, Berta lay down, her arm under her head.

Soon after, they were awakened by Fita's soft whimpers. Berta rose again and nudged Hiltrud. "You should have brought along some food rather than that half-dead girl over there."

Marie responded angrily. "Berta, you are the most heartless person I've ever met. Remember, I'm going to share the money!"

Hiltrud sighed. "Let's not quarrel. I've packed something to eat."

Evidently she'd thought ahead, and she took a package from her bundle, spreading out the contents in her lap. Berta, Gerlind, and Märthe practically tore the food from her hands, and Hiltrud had to be careful that there was enough left for the three other women.

After Hiltrud had eaten, she vainly tried to coax some food into Fita's mouth while Marie went to a nearby stream to fill her leather water pouch. Fita drank almost all of it, then leaned back with a barely audible thank-you. Hiltrud sprinkled the rest of the water on a cloth that she applied as a compress on Fita's bleeding abdomen.

In the meantime, the sky had brightened and was beginning to turn red in the east with the promise of a beautiful day. Gerlind and Berta looked around anxiously, realizing now that the thicket in which they had spent the night was really rather open and that there was nothing to shield them from prying eyes. Beyond the thicket was a sparsely wooded stand of oaks and beeches through which horsemen could easily pass; Berta even thought she could make out a trail. Shortly afterward, the women were terrified to hear ringing and clattering.

"That sounds like a swineherd leading his pigs in our direction. If he sees us and betrays us to the Riedburgs, we'd be in terrible trouble." Gerlind picked up her bundle and was about to run quickly away, but Hiltrud held her back.

"Marie and I sat up with Fita half the night. Now it's your turn."

"We should take her a bit farther into the forest. No one would see her there, and we'd be rid of her. I'm not going to go along with her." Jutting out her chin, Berta placed her arms on her hips provokingly.

Gerlind gave her a contemptuous look and told Märthe to help Fita walk. Hiltrud also lent a hand while Marie walked ahead, clearing a way for them with her stick. Berta, on the other hand, stomped sullenly along behind them, and only Gerlind's sharp words finally made her hide their tracks using a birch branch. They continued on like this for hours, losing the path behind them.

As the day drew to a close, Marie found a place that they all agreed looked secure. It was an area where a storm had mowed down the trees as if they were grass. Since then, new growth had appeared, but the lower vegetation was so dense that no reasonable person would even attempt to enter. Hiltrud and Gerlind checked the surroundings for bear tracks, but to their relief they found only a deer path leading into the new growth. All six of the women slowly followed the path until it ended in a dry spot beneath two huge overlapping tree trunks lying on their sides.

Marie and Gerlind gathered some moss and branches and set up a shelter where they could care for Fita. Even though the bleeding had stopped, her abdomen still looked battered, and her stomach felt hot and as hard as a stone.

Helplessly, Marie waved Hiltrud away from Fita and spoke quietly. "Do you think we can help her?"

"It doesn't look good, but maybe my salves and tinctures will help." Hiltrud went to get her medicines and began to treat Fita.

Meanwhile, Berta had been talking quietly but intensely with Gerlind and Märte, and she finally approached Marie with an outstretched hand.

"Now we can divide up the booty. Hand over your purse!"

Putting her hand on the two leather pouches, Marie wanted to tell Berta to go to hell. She regretted she hadn't hidden the money, but now all she could do was to try to put on a good face, for Berta and Gerlind would give her no rest until they had gotten their share.

"We'll divide up the money, but only under the condition that we'll all stay in this hiding place for a few days, or at least until we can be sure that the mercenaries have left," Marie told her.

Gerlind agreed impatiently and sat down next to Marie. "Yes, yes, we'll do that. Now hand it over."

Marie shook her head so hard that her hair flew in all directions. "First I've got to see how much I have, and then I'll figure out what everyone's share is."

Hissing like a snake, Berta stepped closer to Marie and reached for the purse. "Each of us, of course, gets the same."

Marie pushed her away. "Hiltrud lost her goats and her cart, so she deserves more."

"And you get a larger share, Marie, because you took the money," added Hiltrud, who tended to be generous but was repelled by the others' greed.

Berta pouted and stepped back a few paces, but she didn't take her eyes off Marie's belt. "Well, fine, but you don't need to include Fita in the calculations, as she's not going to be around much longer, and she'd just take her share to a church offering box before she kicks off, anyway."

"Fita will get her share, and what she does with it is her business." Marie had to tamp down her fury, for she saw how Fita, who had been Berta's companion for many years, quivered at hearing the nasty words. Under Gerlind's and Berta's watchful eyes, Marie emptied the two purses in her lap and counted out the money. The total was more than she'd expected, as there were no coins of lesser value among them. She made four equal piles from the first purse for Gerlind, Berta, Märthe, and Fita. The second purse was distributed equally between Hiltrud and her. Gerlind was visibly unhappy even though the sum that Marie put into her hand was at least five times as much as what she earned in a good year.

Berta wrapped her coins in a strip of cloth she had ripped from her shirt, and put them away without saying a word. Then she reached for Fita's share, as if to pocket that as well. "After all, we were always comrades."

Marie slapped Berta's hand away. "I'll keep Fita's money for her until she's back on her feet. That way, I can be sure she'll really get it."

"You're a disgusting wench! I'm not going to let you cheat me." Berta jumped up and lunged for Marie while Hiltrud tried to hold her back, grabbing her from behind, but before they could exchange blows, Gerlind stepped in.

"We're not going to fight over a few pennies, are we?" she said.

Hiltrud, who was ordinarily very even-tempered, flushed with anger. "You got your share, and I'm not going to let you cheat a sick companion. Berta should be ashamed of herself. That's more money than she's ever held in her hands at one time, but now she also wants to steal money from Fita, whom she's always exploited."

Gerlind put her left hand around Hiltrud's shoulder and patted her cheek with her other hand. "You're right, dear. Berta has no reason to complain, and I don't, either." But she kept staring at the money Marie had piled up, as if she wanted to devour the coins with her eyes.

Forcing a laugh, Gerlind finally turned away. "Do you know what? I was able to save a few of my things, too, and I'll make us all a strong cup of tea to help us get our strength back."

She winked at Berta. The fat whore made a face, but she did as Gerlind asked and fished out the tin cups they'd taken from the camp. Gerlind and Märthe beckoned for Berta to help them gather enough wood to make a little fire, and before long, the tea water was simmering in Gerlind's battered kettle. The old woman sniffed at the brew several times, sprinkled the contents of a little bag into the liquid, and let it steep for a bit. Finally she filled the six cups, handing Marie and Hiltrud theirs.

"Here, have something to drink. It will do you good. It's strong enough to get Fita back on her feet as well."

"That would be nice. Thanks, Gerlind." Hiltrud gave a sigh of relief and watched as Märthe, who had silently remained in the background until now, bent down and also gave Fita some tea. Then Hiltrud nodded at Gerlind. "I'm happy we're all getting along again. Now let's find a stone we can use to bake some biscuits. I have enough flour left to make a batch."

She started to stand up, but Gerlind put a hand on her shoulder and pushed her down again. "Not yet. Go to sleep and give the medicine a chance to work, or it won't help. In fact, we should all lie down and sleep. The biscuits can wait."

Relaxing back onto the grass, Hiltrud nodded her agreement, trusting Gerlind's advice since she knew the old woman was knowledgeable about herbs, and she slowly sipped the strong brew that left a bitter aftertaste on her tongue. Though her first inclination was to toss the pungent liquid away, Marie didn't want to provoke any further conflict, so she drank the tea in short sips, Leaning her head back against the rotted, crumbling wood behind her, Marie stared dreamily at the piles of coins for a moment, then glanced over at Berta who had withdrawn into a corner, pouting. Gerlind went to join Berta, and they got into what looked to be an animated discussion. Finally Marie put aside the coins intended for Fita, counted out both her share and Hiltrud's share into the two purses she had stolen, and handed one to Hiltrud.

Stretching out, Hiltrud gave a long yawn. "Your warm tea feels good, and the medicine already seems to be helping. You'll have to give me the recipe sometime, Gerlind. It even relieves my stomach pain."

"It will relax you a lot more than this," Berta sneered.

Hiltrud felt Gerlind poking her and wanted to say something more, but her tongue suddenly became as heavy as her eyelids. She saw Marie sinking to the ground before she herself drifted off into a dense, dreamless cloud. The last thing she heard was Berta's laughter. "That was an effective drink. The two of them are sleeping like logs."

Gerlind stared at the two women slumped on the ground and spat as if disgusted with herself. "We've got to get out of here as fast as we can since I don't know how long the potion works. Come on, Berta, take the money from them."

Berta didn't need to be asked twice. Quickly grabbing Fita's share, she then took the leather pouches Marie and Hiltrud were carrying, as well as Marie's smaller purse of recent earnings, and handed some of the gleanings to Gerlind.

The old woman was visibly struggling with her conscience. "We shouldn't take everything from them."

Berta waved her off with a snort and put the purses in her pockets. "Bah, it's each one for herself!" Then she pointed at Hiltrud's and Marie's bundles. "What is this stuff? Shall we take it along, too?"

Gerlind shook her head. "We have enough to carry. Come on, let's go."

Berta's face contorted into a spiteful grin. "With the greatest of pleasure. As long as I live, I'll never forget how happy I am to have played this trick on these two snotty bitches. Now that they have no more money, they'll have to bed every stinking old goat that comes along."

She turned around without even a brief glance at Fita, and stomped off with a contented look on her face. Märthe followed in her footsteps, while Gerlind hesitated. Only after the other two women turned to call back to her did she make up her mind, leaving the drugged women behind and unprotected.

IX.

When Marie woke up, it was shortly before noon. At first she was confused, for it seemed like it had just been late afternoon. A bitter taste in her mouth reminded her of Gerlind's tea, and she realized she had been sleeping almost a whole day. Struggling to her feet, she looked around and had to shake herself several times before she was fully awake. An arm's length in front of her, Hiltrud still lay in a deep sleep.

"What's wrong?" Hiltrud groaned a short while later as she, too, slowly awoke, holding her head in her hands.

"Gerlind drugged us with her tea."

Hiltrud glanced around drowsily. Except for Fita, who lay rigid on her nearby bed of moss, there was no one to be seen. Gerlind, Berta, and Märthe had disappeared, and with them the purses that had been hanging on their belts.

Hiltrud let out a curse that would have made even a hardened sailor's hair stand on end. "Those filthy whores stole all our money."

In disbelief, Marie looked down and discovered the remains of the leather straps that had been attached to both her small purse and the divided spoils. Chills ran up and down her spine, and she quickly reached under her dress to see if Siegward's gold and the rest of her savings had also been stolen. She let out a shout of joy when she found that those little bags were still there.

Hiltrud stared at her as if she'd lost her mind. "What's gotten into you? We've been looted, and you're happy?"

"It's not as bad as I thought." She raised her dress and showed her friend the hidden treasure. "The money here is at least ten times more than what they took. I'm so glad they didn't think of searching us."

Breathing heavily, Hiltrud felt an anger at the robbers far greater than her pleasure at seeing Marie's little fortune. "Those thieving women will pay us back every penny, with interest! Come on, Marie. We've got to find their tracks and follow them. I'll beat the hell out of Berta."

"But first, we have to take care of Fita." Marie didn't wait for Hiltrud's reply, but steadied herself on her still-shaky legs and went over to where the sick girl was lying. When she saw Fita's face, however, Marie realized there was nothing more they could do.

She turned aside and wiped the tears from her eyes. "Fita is dead. The only thing that consoles me about it is that because of Gerlind's sleeping potion, she didn't have to suffer."

Hiltrud placed her hands on her hips and looked grimly at the body. "Hah! Gerlind's brew probably killed her."

"The tea only hastened her death. I don't think Fita would have survived much longer. She was too badly injured and had lost her will to live."

Kneeling down, Marie stroked the dead woman's emaciated face. "Good-bye, Fita! If there's a just God, he will finally unite you with your child."

"May God give her eternal peace." Hiltrud shifted restlessly from one foot to the other. "What shall we do with her? We can't just leave her lying there."

"We've got to bury her."

Marie gave Hiltrud no time to object but took Fita's knife and started digging. Hiltrud grumbled about Berta getting away, but she also set to work energetically using a small rock. The afternoon passed as they dug a hole in the ground with their makeshift tools, and by the time they had placed the last stone on Fita's grave, the sun was already setting.

Stretching her stiff muscles, Hiltrud sighed. "We must say a prayer for her, but I don't know the right words."

Marie tried to remember the prayers she'd heard in the Constance cathedral. She used to attend Mass almost every day, listening to the choirboys sing. Since Hiltrud was visibly nervous and wanted to look for a new campsite before the last light of day, Marie recited the words quickly.

"Take Fita into your everlasting hands, dear Lord. Her heart was too good for this world. Amen," she said, throwing a handful of dirt on the grave, while Hiltrud picked a few flowers and scattered them over the grave. They then made a simple cross from two branches and a strip of cloth, and set it in the ground.

They were relieved to see that Gerlind and the others had at least left behind their packs containing some essentials. Between their two bundles, Hiltrud had another dress, and Marie a smock to change into, and there were also two blankets, cooking utensils, two wooden cups, and a few other useful items like flint, tinder, and the ointments they urgently needed after every bad night. Taking their bundles, they left the campsite as quickly as they could, as if they were running away.

More than an hour later, the two friends stopped under some low pine boughs to set up a makeshift camp for the night. Taking out her pack, Hiltrud was astonished to find her small leather bag, and she laughed as she looked into it.

"Those thieving magpies didn't find my spare purse, either. It's not much, but at least we won't have to start out by paying for our bread with one of your gold pieces. Things like that attract bailiffs, who are usually nothing more than more-adept thieves. They'd say we'd stolen the money and immediately take it from us."

Marie sat up and placed her hand reassuringly on her friend's arm. "First of all, there aren't just gold coins in the purses, but there are also a few shillings and Regensburg pennies. And second, we can borrow Gerlind's tactic of trading favors in our tents for some bread, a pitcher of wine, or some fat and honey for pancakes."

"Thanks, but I prefer to use silver." With a glum face, Hiltrud said good-night, lay down, and turned her back to Marie.

It was clear to Marie that Hiltrud was obsessed with finding the trail of the thieves and catching up with them as soon as possible. She herself wasn't so keen on the idea because she wouldn't be surprised if Berta sent the Riedburgs out to get them. For this reason she was glad to be away from the previous campsite, and she agreed with Hiltrud that for the time being they shouldn't light any fires.

As Marie had expected, her friend woke her at the first light of day the next morning and barely left her time to get herself ready. While washing at a nearby brook and rubbing ointment on her recent wounds, Marie temporarily lost sight of Hiltrud who had run a short distance ahead. But then she heard her voice.

"Hurry, Marie! Come quickly!"

Tossing her pack over her shoulder, Marie quickly followed her friend.

Hiltrud was standing by a small path, pointing excitedly at a muddy puddle that had almost dried up. Between the tracks of deer and wild pigs, the impression of a naked, human foot was clearly visible. Hiltrud placed her own foot alongside it in the mud, and when she removed her foot, her print was a bit longer and narrower than the other.

"If this footprint isn't Berta's, I'll let every priest take me free of charge in the future," Hiltrud crowed.

Marie nodded, then raised her hands, trying to cool Hiltrud's enthusiasm. "These footprints are definitely Berta's, but I don't know if it's a good idea for us to follow the three of them through such open country. The Riedburgs are still too close."

Hiltrud shook her head angrily. "I'm not going to let those wenches off so easily. I always expected the worst of Berta, but I'm really disappointed with Gerlind. I traveled with her for years and never imagined that one day she would ruthlessly drug me and rob me. I'm going to pay her back for her betrayal!"

"Then we'd better be careful. Siegward von Riedburg won't accept the loss of his money kindly."

"If you're so afraid of him, you shouldn't have stolen it. What can he do except seethe with outrage?"

Hiltrud kept moving, and Marie realized her friend was too angry to pay any attention to reasonable arguments, so she had no choice but to follow her and keep her eyes and ears open. The necessity of staying alert soon became clear. They had been following a seemingly endless path, winding through a dense growth of trees, and walking on ground damp enough to show the footprints of the three women who had passed there the day before. At one point, the path crossed another, wider path, and Marie could hear the distant clatter of metal.

She grabbed hold of Hiltrud. "Hurry—we have to get back into the forest!"

Hiltrud followed her, puzzled. "What's the matter?"

Just then, Hiltrud also heard the loud voices and muffled sound of hooves on the soft ground, and she followed Marie into the underbrush without objection. Terrified, they threw themselves on the ground, curled up into tight balls, and barely dared breathe. As the men passed by not far from them on the path they had just been on, the two women carefully raised their heads.

As Marie had assumed, Siegward von Riedburg was leading the procession, accompanied by four horsemen, and followed by a dozen mercenaries marching in double time. They seemed to have a specific goal, for they hurried past Marie and Hiltrud without even looking up from the path. Before long, the men had disappeared into the forest as quickly as they had come. Only then did the two women dare to breathe again, looking at each other in fright.

"That was close. If you didn't have such good ears . . ." Hiltrud left the rest of her sentence unspoken. They had both seen Siegward's furious face.

Hiltrud pressed her hand against her pounding heart. "Shall we go deeper into the forest or go back the way the men came? I'd like to have a good day's march between us and the Riedburgs, but the trees will slow us down."

Marie wrapped her arms around herself as if she were freezing. "But what will we do if more men are following him?"

"We'll hear them early enough, too." Hiltrud tried to sound more courageous than she felt. It seemed safer to have Squire Siegward far behind her than somewhere nearby where he could surprise them at any time. Marie had nothing to say in response, so they crawled out of the bush and set out again silently, startling and clutching each other at every sound.

But they proved lucky. Dusk was falling, and neither a solitary walker nor any of Siegward's soldiers had yet crossed their path. Finally reaching a crossing, they stopped to consider which direction to go. Suddenly Marie let out a shriek, and Hiltrud quickly covered Marie's mouth with her hand.

"Quiet!" she said anxiously.

Hiltrud took her hand away, and Marie choked and nodded, pointing to the bloody, disfigured mass on the ground that had once been Gerlind. A wave of nausea came over her, and she staggered, bent over and retching, until nothing was left in her stomach except bile.

Hiltrud could do nothing to help Marie, because she was paralyzed by complete horror. "Gerlind was a thief and betrayed us, but she didn't deserve to die like this," she said as Marie walked toward her.

"No human being does." Marie groaned, then hunched over again as she hobbled away, pain radiating from her empty stomach.

Hiltrud ran after her and discovered the remains of Berta and Märthe less than ten steps away, also both badly mangled. Marie's stomach had settled down a bit, but tears continued to run down her cheeks. "How can people be so cruel? This is all my fault," Marie whispered. "If I hadn't stolen the money, our friends would still be alive and well."

Hiltrud straightened up, dried her face on her sleeve, and placed her hands on Marie's shoulders. "Now listen to me! If those three hadn't drugged and robbed us, they would be alive now, and we would all be safe. Where do you think Siegward and his killers were going? They're headed to the camp where those harlots left us. One of the women must have told the killers, and if the men hadn't spent so much time slaughtering them or if the effect of Gerlind's potion had lasted longer, we'd both be dead, too. And our last moments would have been even more torturous, as Siegward would have found his purse on us."

Marie nodded, but she also didn't want to completely condemn their former traveling companions. It was easy for her to imagine that one of them, fearing for her life, had betrayed the location of their camp to the Riedburgs, and Marie tried to get Hiltrud to understand that as well.

"That may well be," Hiltrud interrupted dourly, "but all I'm interested in right now is saving my own skin. Let's get out of here and run away as far as our feet will take us. And don't try to convince me to bury these three thieves."

"No, there's no time for that. When Siegward finds our tracks, he'll return, and, at the latest, that will be after he doesn't find us at the campsite where Fita's buried."

Marie straightened up, pressed her hand to her aching stomach, and followed Hiltrud into the gathering darkness. She was ashamed of her weakness and at the same time struggled with self-reproach. No matter how she looked at it, she felt guilt for the death of her three former companions. Though she tried to console herself with Hiltrud's admonitions that the three women had sealed their fate through their own greed, she already suspected that the horrible sight at the crossroads would follow her in her dreams for a long time.

X.

Later that night, Marie couldn't begin to work out how far they'd traveled, and even the next day she couldn't figure out what direction they had taken. The land around them seemed more rugged and wild. Dark forests of trees overgrown with moss stretched far to the south, and when they reached the top of a bare hill, all they could see around them was more forest, unbroken by either tilled land or villages.

Turning to look in all directions, Hiltrud frowned. "We must be in the Black Forest. That's both good and bad."

Marie nodded dejectedly. When she lived in Constance, she had heard a lot about this part of the country, a place where you could walk for days without meeting anyone. More bears and wolves were said to live under these ancient oaks, beeches, and pines than there were residents in all of Constance.

Hiltrud looked at it a bit more optimistically. "Siegward certainly won't find us here. Come, let's look for a place where we'll be safe from wild animals. I'm so tired, I'll soon fall asleep standing up."

Marie slipped out of her shoes, each consisting of a wooden sole held on by a wide leather strap, and examined her sore feet. "I wouldn't recommend sleeping that way, but I have nothing against finding a dry shelter with a brook nearby where I can take a drink and cool my feet."

Grumbling something that sounded like "spoiled kid," Hiltrud started walking down the hill in front of them. At the bottom, they found a brook that passed through a deep cut in the rocks where Marie could quench her thirst and fill her leather water pouch. Stepping out of the brook onto the opposite shore, she found a copse of trees suitable for setting up camp. Though their hungry stomachs were growling loudly, they were too tired to look for firewood and were also afraid that the fire would reveal their location. Sharing their last piece of bread, they washed it down with water.

With heavy eyes, they summoned up their last bit of strength to weave together a wall of branches so that they could hear any approaching man or beast. Finally, they wrapped themselves in their blankets and stretched out on the rocky ground.

Exhausted, Marie and Hiltrud slept until late afternoon. Stiff and frozen from lying so long on the cold, hard ground, they clambered down to the brook to drink. Unfortunately, there weren't any ripe berries or mushrooms so early in the year, but Hiltrud found some wild celery that they wolfed down voraciously. Though it filled their stomachs, it wasn't satisfying, and they knew that they wouldn't survive long on that diet. Since they also wanted to put more distance between themselves and Siegward, they waited until the moon had risen, then continued down through a gorge in the half-light.

In the course of their travels over the next few days, they lived on raw roots and tree mushrooms and chewed on tree gum if they couldn't find anything else, since they still didn't dare build a fire to cook what otherwise might be their last meal. At last, however, their exhausted legs wouldn't carry them any farther, and they sought refuge in a thickly forested ravine.

Protected by an overhanging ledge, they wove branches together to make a simple shelter and covered the roof with thick layers of moss and tufts of grass. At first their mood was as gloomy as the weather, but they quickly brightened up after they had lit a little fire in their hideout and were nibbling on a supper of baked flour cakes and a soup of wild grass and tree mushrooms. Their first hot meal in a week, it seemed like a banquet.

Judging by the view from the bare hilltop above the ravine, the next human settlement was several hours away on the other side of the mountains in the direction of the Rhine. Though the Rhine was their ultimate goal, Hiltrud didn't want to leave the forest until dust had settled over the matter with the Riedburgs. Instead, she wanted to head a bit farther south to put more even distance between themselves and the Riedburgs' castle. Marie agreed with all of Hiltrud's suggestions, as she was still too wrapped up in her own worries. The close encounter with the mercenaries and the gruesome consequences weighed heavily on her mind.

When the women heard the sound of a swineherd's horn a few days later, they left their shelter, plunging deeper into the ever more desolate and gloomy forest. Occasionally, they came across shelters used by swineherds or woodsmen, but they didn't dare use the cabins for fear of being followed, and instead built makeshift shelters of brushwood or birch twigs in the evenings. Hiltrud had made a snare to catch wild animals, and they sometimes added meat to their menu, enjoying rabbit stew and even venison once, along with their daily diet of roots, tubers, and tree mushrooms. Still, they desperately longed for bread, and their desire grew so strong that Hiltrud was dreaming of fresh loaves of bread, swearing she'd give herself to any man for just one slice. Marie laughed at her but had to admit she was thinking almost exactly the same thing.

Though they avoided all human contact out of fear of Riedburg and his mercenaries, Hiltrud demanded that they both still wear their yellow ribbons; the danger of being caught without that sign of their social status was simply too great. Prostitutes traveling alone without their ribbons of immorality were often charged by city bailiffs, then whipped after a speedy trial before a compliant judge.

Marie, on the other hand, thought that her friend's caution was extreme, especially since she knew that their ribbons made it impossible for them to buy provisions in any of the scattered forest settlements without attracting attention. Indeed, she had come to believe they had nothing to fear anymore, since after their time in the forest, both women were now almost unrecognizable. Plant extracts and tree funguses had darkened their hair, and their faces had turned brown due to their constant application of plant oils.

After they had climbed up through the Schönmünztal Valley in the northern Black Forest and looked down at the Rhine from atop Mount Hornisgrinde, Marie decided it was time to return to the civilized world. For days they had been following a well-traveled path, judging from the other sets of fresh footprints, and Marie hoped it would eventually lead to a small city or even to a pilgrimage site. She was ready to take the risk of bribing a gatekeeper with a shilling just to be able to shop again.

As the roofs of a city appeared, Hiltrud gave in to Marie's plan to go into town, but since she was afraid the two of them together would attract too much attention, Hiltrud decided to wait for Marie in the forest near town. Despite Hiltrud's disapproval, Marie covered her yellow ribbons with the tattered cloth that she used to carry her possessions and took only a handful of coins along to buy bread and provisions.

Hiltrud hovered over her friend, worried. "I don't feel good about this. What if you are molested or run right into the arms of Riedburg's people?"

Marie laughed and shrugged off her concern. "No one is looking for a dirty old hag with brown hair. Hiltrud, we have to eat something other than wild plants and tree funguses. And if we don't make ourselves some new clothes soon, we'll have to run around naked, as these rags we're wearing are falling apart. If we get to the Rhine dressed in these old sacks, no man with a full purse will even want to come near us."

"I know you're right, but . . ."

"No buts, Hiltrud," Marie interrupted. "Make yourself comfortable here, and I'll go on alone."

Hiltrud's shoulders slumped. "Very well, if you don't want to listen to my advice, then go, for God's sake."

Up close, the city was larger than Marie had expected. Built on a gently sloping mountainside, tall dark wooden houses had straw-covered roofs that reached to the ground. The largest building in the city was an inn with a "Welcome" sign visible for miles, its massive size demonstrating the importance of the trade route it marked, leading from the Rhine over the last peaks in the Black Forest, and then onto Stuttgart. In front of the inn, Marie could see the canvas coverings of merchants' stands, and she breathed a sigh of relief. Evidently it was market day in town.

Her heart was pounding as she approached the city gate. The guards didn't turn her away, but one of them bent down and tugged at an unruly yellow ribbon that had slipped out from under her dress, demanding a gate tax of four pennies. When Marie looked at him angrily, he sternly pointed at the guardroom with an unambiguous wave of his hand.

Marie didn't want to trade her services as payment for entering the city, and she stared at him with grim determination. "I want to go to the market to buy bread."

The guard's expression showed that he hadn't meant his threat seriously, but he was still disappointed she hadn't accepted. To her great relief, he simply accepted three pennies from her and even wished her a good day and God's blessing.

Marie pushed the ribbon back under her dress and hastily walked through the dense crowd toward the marketplace. After the long, lonesome time in the forest, Marie found it awkward to be among people again. She startled every time she heard a loud voice, and it took her a while to realize that no one was paying any attention to her. Finally, she went over to a market stand to see what was for sale.

Marie didn't know exactly how long she and Hiltrud had been living in the forest, but seeing the fruit and vegetables for sale— cherries, pears, and already the first plums shipped in from the Rhine valley—she thought it must have been weeks. Her mouth watered, and for a while she resisted temptation, but she finally gave in when she passed a sausage stand a few moments later. She bought four of them, looked for a quiet corner in which to enjoy them, and almost felt like she was cheating her friend. After she'd eaten and licked the fat off her fingers, she set about buying some essentials. Before long, she had bought two loaves of bread, a piece of ham, sewing needles and thread, and two pieces of cloth from which she and Hiltrud would be able to sew new clothing. Finally, she bought a large shoulder bag in which to carry her purchases.

At first she spoke very little, limiting herself to just the basics, but when a smiling wine merchant gave her a friendly yet respectable greeting, she asked him to fill the jug she'd just bought with Rhine wine and struck up a conversation. "My good man, could you give me some news?"

"Of course," he responded with a laugh. "But what do you want to know, woman?"

"What do you know about the council in Constance? Have the noblemen arrived yet?"

The man shook his head. "Far from it. Before princes and bishops meet, there are all sorts of things to consider. They don't just get on the road the way people like us do, but because they rarely trust one another, they first have to exchange messages and make all kinds of agreements. Then they send people ahead to inspect the inns along the way and find suitable accommodations where they give instructions for receiving their masters. That's a very difficult thing, woman, as the kaiser must not live in poorer accommodations than the pope, and vice versa, and a bishop's lodging must be equal to that of a prince or a count. It takes many months before that's all arranged."

The man loved to talk, and he told in great detail about the noblemen who would be going to Constance. Soon Marie's head was spinning with all the names. Along with the noblemen and dignitaries from the Reich, many nobles and church authorities would be coming from faraway places like Scotland, Spain, and Italy. He also told Marie about the preparations being made in Constance for this great event.

"The Holy Father will travel there by ship directly from Rome," he stated with an ecstatic look, marveling at the splendor of the pope's great ship. At that point Marie interrupted and asked the merchant about any recent feuds between noble houses.

He stopped to think for a moment. "Indeed, there was a big feud in the spring between the Riedburgs and the Büchenbruch clan. That was a bad situation, I tell you. Old Siegbald had secretly sent his eldest son, Siegward, to the Rhine in order to hire mercenaries and purchase those hellish things called cannons, monstrous metal devices whose roar causes walls to collapse and makes the hearts of courageous men stand still. The Riedburgs must have paid a fortune for them, but they didn't help. While Siegbald's eldest son was away, Lothar von Büchenbruch boldly attacked and conquered the Riedburgs' castle. When Siegward returned home with his mercenaries and cannons, Büchenbruch ambushed him. Not wanting to surrender even though the situation was hopeless, young

Riedburg counterattacked, and he, along with his brother Siegerich and most of the mercenaries, died in the battle."

Marie listened wide-eyed to the merchant's account. If he was right, then she and Hiltrud had been hiding in the forest for nothing. Thanking him for his information, she moved on, a full wine jug in her left hand and her other purchases on her back. She bought some dress trimmings from a brash merchant in order to confirm the Riedburg feud, and the man gladly told her what he knew without too many embellishments. Indeed, it seemed that the wine merchant had not been exaggerating. Riedburg Castle had in fact been stormed by Lady Mechthild's relatives, and the two eldest Riedburg sons had fallen in battle not long after they'd murdered Gerlind, Berta, and Märthe. The merchant even knew that Gilbert Löfflein, the famous cannon maker, had also perished in battle.

XI.

Later that afternoon, head spinning, Marie returned to where Hiltrud was hiding. She found her friend anxious and annoyed.

"Did you have to keep me waiting so long? I was afraid you'd fallen into the hands of the Riedburgs' mercenaries, and I've already died a thousand deaths worrying about you."

Marie threw her head back, laughing. "I didn't see any mercenaries, and even if I had, he wouldn't have paid any attention to me. Hiltrud, do you know we've been hiding out in this forest for weeks for no reason? Most of the men who abused us are dead."

Hiltrud stared at Marie disbelievingly. "Repeat that again."

Marie told her what she'd learned at the market and swore she'd spoken with two different people about it. Hiltrud kept shaking her head in amazement and finally burst out laughing.

"I told you God loves us more than the priests want us to believe, though rarely have the sinners been so thoroughly punished as in this case."

Marie chuckled as she unpacked her purchases. Hiltrud's eyes nearly popped out of her head upon seeing the loaves of bread and the ham. She was even happier to see the golden Rhine wine. While Marie gladly gave her most of the refreshing drink, she hurried to help herself to some of the ham, as Hiltrud was wolfing it down and didn't stop until she'd enjoyed the last piece. Wiping the grease from her mouth, Hiltrud smiled with contentment.

"So it's true? We really don't need to fear Siegward anymore?"

"Only as a ghost." Marie's little joke didn't please her friend.

"Don't say that. It's already too much to bear that Gerlind returns in my dreams to say how sorry she is that she betrayed us."

"It's easy to be sorry in hindsight. Gerlind made her choice, and in so doing, almost ruined us as well."

Marie poured herself some wine, staring pensively into the amber liquid. Though the murder of the three women had initially upset her far more than it had her friend, its memory was already fading for her. Hiltrud, however, was still dreaming at night about her former traveling companions and remained deeply shaken by their fate. The only faces Marie remembered from her nightmares were those of Rupert and his cronies.

Hiltrud knew Marie so well, she could almost read her thoughts. "You're thinking about your former fiancé again! Just let it go. It would almost have been better if you hadn't learned about Siegward's death, because then your fear of him would help you forget those old memories."

Though Hiltrud sounded unkind, Marie didn't hold it against her friend. Hiltrud thought that revenge was a plaything of the nobles and not for people like them, but Marie didn't agree. If there was a just God in heaven, she believed that he would put a weapon in her hand to use against Rupert. This hope was her sole motivation in life. In a sense, the stolen money felt like a gift from heaven, for now she finally had enough money to hire an assassin. But Marie kept her plans to herself, and only regretted she couldn't talk with Hiltrud about it.

The jug of wine was now empty, and since Hiltrud rarely had the opportunity to indulge in such strong drink, her head fell onto her chest, and Marie wasn't faring much better. Struggling to their feet, they found a hiding place in the thick underbrush and slept the rest of the afternoon all the way through to late the next morning.

When they finally awoke, they discussed what to do next. Since they had nothing to fear from the Riedburgs anymore, they could finally go down to the Rhine and get to work again. But first they needed to improve their appearances.

Hiltrud thanked Marie for remembering to pick up cloth and sewing supplies, but in the same breath she criticized her failure to bring back any yellow material or white bands to dye yellow since their old, tattered ribbons would prove an odd contrast on their new clothing. After some muttering, though, Hiltrud removed them and freshened them up with a mixture of turmeric and dandelions, hanging them on a branch to dry. Marie chose the blue linen for her dress, while Hiltrud decided on the ocher-colored woolen material. Because they didn't have scissors, they cut the materials to size using Marie's knife, and went to work zealously.

Marie stopped sewing for a moment and looked at Hiltrud's hair. Though she had dyed it dark in the forest, her light blond roots were now showing. Marie pulled one of the dirty brown strands of her hair up to her face. "What shall we do about this? Dye it again or try to wash out the filth?"

"I'm for washing it out," replied Hiltrud, who was proud of her blond hair and had dyed it only to disguise herself from the Riedburgs.

"Then we should start right away. I want to return to the Rhine looking just like the Marie people once knew." Marie took a pot and hurried to the brook to fetch water.

Since the weather remained fair and they didn't have to build a hiding place, their preparations took only three days, during which they wrapped their hair with cloths dipped in a plumbago solution. Though they only had primitive tools with which to work, they were more than happy with the results. Now they were presentable again and no longer ran the risk of being viewed as penny prostitutes. Hiltrud had even decorated the neckline of Marie's dress with a strip of trimming, which she told Marie would magnetically draw men's eyes to the two alabaster hills underneath. Finally, Hiltrud sewed the yellow ribbons on both dresses while Marie watched sadly.

"The dress looked a lot nicer without the ribbons." She sighed.

Hiltrud gave her a gentle bump on the nose. "Let's go, and don't pretend you're tired! Pack up your things. I'd like to get started today."

Marie seemed to have been waiting for these words, as for once she had finished tying up her bundle before Hiltrud and was watching her friend impatiently. Hurrying along, they softly sang a lilting tune as they followed the setting sun westward. The weather remained fair, and since they had a full moon to brighten their way, they made good time. Hiltrud hoped to reach Strasbourg within a few days, where clean and hardworking harlots could make a good living near the harbor.

Marie listened patiently as Hiltrud rambled on about the big markets taking place that year, speculating on their chances of making enough money to get through the winter. In the meantime, Marie was wondering how to find someone in Strasbourg who, for a certain sum of gold coins, would put an end to Rupert's life. She wasn't sure how to go about that, however, since she didn't want to lose her money again to someone who'd run off with the down payment.

Marie and Hiltrud didn't have to walk the final stretch to Strasbourg, as they were invited to join ferrymen whom Hiltrud knew to be honest. It was pleasant to sit on two shipping bales and watch as the horses, plodding along the towpath, pulled the ship upriver on a long rope. Carefully trimmed willows along the path shaded the animals from the burning summer sun, and Marie was grateful to Hiltrud for thinking to fill the jug at their previous stop with tart wine diluted with water.

Soon they saw the massive tower of the Strasbourg cathedral rising up over the flat meadowland along the river. Marie and Hiltrud said good-bye to the boatmen upon reaching the harbor, jumping into the outstretched arms of some cheering sailors on the shore. One wanted to drag Marie off into the nearby bushes, but his lust was greater than his purse, and so she slipped away from him, laughing.

The two women strolled around the harbor, watching the many small boats, high-walled barges, and the innumerable rafts that had been tied up at the wharf or had been pulled onto shore. Goods from all over the world were traded here: Marie saw Dutchmen in baggy trousers and striped shirts, their unruly hair tucked under dark felt caps; merchants from the Rhineland with tight-fitting stockings that shamelessly accentuated their masculinity; men from the Black Forest in dark overalls and broad-brimmed hats; and people in the traditional garb of the Upper Rhine area and Lake Constance. Only a few honorable women were visible, usually upper-class travelers, and a number of prostitutes eyed the newly arrived competitors with hostile gazes.

Ignoring their looks, Hiltrud led her friend easily through the streets. From a previous visit to the city, she knew about an inn that was avoided by respectable citizens but would accept anyone who paid in advance. Located some distance from the harbor along an old canal that had turned into a garbage-filled swamp, the inn was filthy but also the only place for miles around that would offer accommodations to wandering prostitutes.

Hiltrud opened the heavy oaken door that, if necessary, could be secured from the inside with several crossbeams. Anybody trying to get in here without the permission of the innkeeper would need a battering ram. There were only a few tiny windows carved into the massive walls, and the entryway was so dark that Marie could barely see her hand in front of her face. Only the cold seeping into her feet revealed to Marie that the floor was paved with stone.

They had barely gotten inside when a door was flung open and a man held out first a light, and then stuck his head out. He stared at them for a moment, then grinned, as if he were already counting the gold coins he could take from them.

"We need a place to stay for several days, just one room for the two of us," Marie told the man, who seemingly hadn't changed his shirt and apron since the previous autumn.

"Well of course," the innkeeper scoffed. "How are you going to pay? And don't go lifting your dresses."

Hiltrud threw back her head with a laugh. "My dear Martin, surely you don't think I'd let anybody like you touch me. I'd rather sleep outside by the canal, but our last customer was very generous." She showed him a large, sparkling silver coin.

The innkeeper's greedy eyes nearly popped out of his head "You must have been paid very well to offer such a splendid coin for a week's stay."

Hiltrud pouted. "Let's agree on two weeks, Martin. That's a handsome profit for you and no loss for us."

The man nodded hesitantly. "Very well, one room for two weeks, but no board."

Before Hiltrud could reply, Marie agreed, since she knew she wouldn't be able to eat a thing in this squalid house. She was already horrified at the idea of having to stay there for two weeks and was happy when Hiltrud suggested that they return to the harbor after a short inspection of the room under the gables that the innkeeper showed them.

"But you can't bring any men into my place, or it will cost you another silver coin," he called after them.

Hiltrud waved him off contemptuously and whispered to Marie that she couldn't bring her customers into this bug-infested hole, anyway. Marie nodded without replying, as she was holding a cloth with a sharp-smelling tincture up to her nose to mask the foul odors.

As they left, she stepped aside to avoid bumping into a man pacing in front of the inn, but he turned around and seized her by the arm.

"Marie! I'm so happy to have found you. When I saw you down at the harbor earlier, I almost didn't recognize you. I could hardly believe my eyes, for I never dared to hope I'd find you again so quickly, and today, of all days, on such an important day for me."

Puzzled, Marie stared at the man. For a brief moment she was afraid he might be one of Riedburg's mercenaries who had come for the stolen money. But this man's eager, watery eyes expressed a lust for something other than gold. His haggard face with its pointed nose and thin lips seemed familiar, but she just couldn't place him. Then, all at once, when he moved his chin and made that funny sound, she knew.

"Jodokus!"

It was the scribe from Arnstein, the monk who had run off after destroying the will. He looked very different from how she remembered him. Tight-fitting dark green stockings highlighted a bulging embroidered codpiece, which Marie assumed was filled with stuffing, judging from Hiltrud's accounts of the man's endowments. He didn't seem poor, as he wore a short, new-looking overcoat made of fawn-colored wool that had slit sleeves and a florid lining. Light brown hair with graying strands protruded from beneath his round, feathered hat. The difference between the respectable citizen standing before her and the haggard monk she knew in Arnstein was so great that Sir Dietmar's people could have walked right past the man without recognizing him.

279

Jodokus pulled her so close that his foul breath blew right into her face, and his stomach pressed tightly against hers. "You have not forgotten me, I see, my dear, as I also have not forgotten you. How often my loins have ached thinking of you. Finally my longing for you will be satisfied."

He doesn't think I'll go to bed with him, does he? Marie thought, horrified and remembering only too well his betrayal of Sir Dietmar and Lady Mechthild. She was about to hurl her contempt for him in his face, but she was suddenly struck by a thought that at first seemed so absurd she almost laughed out loud.

Jodokus must have been one of Rupert's accomplices, for who except the counselor and his noble half brother would have had any interest in destroying Sir Otmar's will in Arnstein Castle and stealing the copy from Saint Ottilien's monastery? If she ingratiated herself with the former monk now, maybe she could find a way to get her revenge on her enemies. So rather than rejecting Jodokus's advances, she giggled and allowed his hands to caress her breasts.

"You don't know how much I envied Sir Dietmar his enjoyment of your beauty and your body while I almost died of longing in my little room." He groaned lustfully, but a sneer flickered over his face, as if he were thinking of the dirty trick he'd played on his former master.

Thinking back on the former monk's treachery made Marie even more determined to spin her web around Jodokus until she'd learned all that he knew about Rupert's exploits and accomplices, though she shuddered at the thought of allowing such a filthy customer in her presence. In consolation, she swore that she'd make him pay every time he touched her, if not with money, then at least with information.

"You look so different than I remember you, Brother Jodokus," she answered, concealing her true feelings behind a syrupy smile.

Jodokus raised his hand to correct her; then he stroked her cheek. "I am no longer a monk and have cast off that name along with my cloak. Now I go by the name of Ewald von Marburg and am, if I may say so, a prosperous man. Soon I will be very wealthy, and I'll be able to give you anything you wish—clothes, jewelry, even your own house."

Coming from any other customer, Marie would have brushed off such words as nothing but idle boasting, but Jodokus's pride showed in his face, and it was clear that he meant what he said. Somehow, his betrayal of Sir Dietmar, along with any other tasks he had performed on Rupert's behalf, had turned the penniless monk into a prosperous citizen. Marie wondered if this traitorous monk was once again working on some other mischief for Rupert. If that were the case, she'd find out. Perhaps Rupert would make a mistake, or go too far for once, and a few well-chosen words said to the right person would be enough to destroy him.

With a renewed sense of hope, Marie allowed Jodokus to fondle her. Meanwhile, Hiltrud was waiting for her nearby and wondering about her friend's behavior. Marie had often told her how she much despised the treacherous monk, and now she was acting as if she had found a long-lost close friend with whom she couldn't wait to disappear behind the nearest bush. Hiltrud had to clear her throat a few times before Marie noticed her, signaling to Hiltrud to leave her alone. Annoyed, Hiltrud turned on her heels and walked away, resolving to get an explanation of Marie's behavior later that evening.

Jodokus wrapped his arm tightly around Marie and pointed toward the city. "I have a few free hours. Let's find a better use for them than standing around talking next to this stinking canal. My innkeeper will certainly not have any objection if I take you up to my room."

"I don't just go away with anyone, especially without being paid." Marie spoke in a coquettish tone, half-seductive and half-demanding, and Jodokus fell for it at once. "You will get more from me than just the few shillings you usually earn, my dearest. Much more! If you stay with me, you'll never have to go to bed with another man again, and you will wear the finest jewelry . . ."

"In bed?" Marie asked mockingly.

He seemed pleased by that idea. "Yes, there, too. But you'll have to be patient because it may take a while before the golden ducats start rolling into your lap. I'm having an important meeting this evening, however, that will make me a lot of money."

The thought flashed through Marie's mind that Jodokus was indeed planning another act of treachery. She let him take her by the hand, leading her back to the harbor where they stopped at a little house abutting the rough-hewn stones of the city walls right next to the gate tower. The woman who received them looked askance at Marie, but she didn't object. Jodokus had explained to Marie that his quarters were not officially an inn but belonged to a widow who rented her rooms, and sometimes her body, to paying guests.

As they climbed the narrow stairway inside the house, Jodokus turned to the widow. "Frau Grete, please bring a jug of wine and two cups to my room."

"And a bowl of water," Marie added quickly, since despite his new clothes, the monk stank just as much as he had before.

Nodding sullenly, the landlady disappeared into the kitchen. When Jodokus reached the top of the stairs, for a few moments he fumbled with the door, which had two locks on it. One was an ordinary door lock that Marie wouldn't have expected to see in a modest house like this. The other was a padlock with a chain passing through a hole in the bolt that could be opened only with a complicated-looking key. Marie watched Jodokus with curiosity and shook her head.

He smiled and gently ran his hand through her hair. "You're surprised? I can easily explain. Couriers and servants of wealthy merchants carrying large sums of money or important documents often stay at the widow Grete's house. They want to know their things are safe behind locked doors while they're here."

Marie nodded and looked at him wide-eyed; Jodokus smiled patronizingly at her apparent naïveté. Inwardly, however, she was trembling with excitement, for she was now firmly convinced the man was carrying important documents.

The room was half the size of the one that she and Hiltrud were sharing at the canal-side inn, and most of the space was taken up by a comfortable-looking bed. The only other furnishings were some sturdy wall pegs for hanging clothes and luggage and a stool at the head of the bed. A large gray cape seemed to be concealing something on the stool. Marie was dying to get her hands on the cloth to see what was underneath, but Jodokus forced her down onto the bed and seized her just as the landlady walked in.

Frau Grete grimaced. "If I'd known how badly you needed it, I'd have come to you last night."

Jodokus gruffly commanded her to put the wine and water down next to the stool and then to leave. As the landlady withdrew in a huff, Jodokus undressed so fast, he almost ripped his shirt and presented Marie with his erect rod, ready to do battle. Just as he was about to throw himself onto her, she raised her hand and pointed to the jug of wine. "Easy, my friend. Let's have a little drink first. Then you should trust me and do what I tell you."

"I must have you," Jodokus groaned in despair.

"If you are overexcited, you will cheat yourself out of this pleasure." Marie sat cross-legged on the bed as he sat staring at her pleadingly. Then she filled her glass and drank to his health. Pouring some of the wine into the water, she took a cloth from one of the coat pegs, dipped it in the wine, and began washing the monk from head to toe.

As Jodokus writhed in desire, Marie finally lay down, ready for him. He was anything but a skillful lover, fumbling around clumsily while Marie concealed her feelings behind a smile. After a short while he collapsed on top of her with a loud groan, and she fondled him and stretched as if in ecstasy.

"You are so different from before, Jo . . . , no, Herr Ewald. Now you really seem like a man of noble standing. How did you do that?" She sat up a bit and scratched his hairy back, all the while moving her hips back and forth invitingly.

A contented smile spread over his face. "With my head, my darling. The noblemen think they're so clever and always want to get their own way. They regard people like us as tools they can use however they want, casting us off like old shoes when they're done. But I'm smarter than they are, and I'll make Count Konrad and Rupert Splendidus sorry that they cheated me out of my due reward. After I get what I'm entitled to, I'll disappear with you forever. What do you think of Flanders? They say it's very beautiful there. But perhaps we'll leave the Reich and go to France or even England. There you could toss away these silly yellow ribbons so we can live before God and the world like a married couple."

Marie gazed at him in feigned admiration, pretending to be amazed that he could stand up to a nobleman like Count Konrad von Keilburg, but she was unable to learn anything more about Jodokus's connections to her former fiancé. The former monk made only a few vague references to Rupert, then deflected further questions, telling her only that he was going to meet Count Konrad's messenger that very evening to collect a significant sum of money.

Grinning maliciously, he started to laugh. "There is something I have that is very valuable to Count Konrad and his bastard brother, and it would be very bad for them if it fell into the wrong hands."

Spontaneously, Marie embraced him to hide her face in his shoulder and keep herself from crying out, stammering a few words of praise instead. She wanted whatever it was that Jodokus had, even if she had to drug him to get it, and she frantically wondered how she might outwit him. Her little bag full of herbs was back at the inn, but perhaps she could lure him there with promises of more pleasure in bed. At that moment, however, he seemed to have lost interest in her body. Springing out of bed, he jumped into his leggings with a bleating laugh and pulled on his shirt hastily, then triumphantly stretched his arms toward the ceiling.

"I know how to do it! The clever fellows I'm dealing with know all the tricks in the book, but I've figured out a way to pull the wool over their eyes. Marie, I'm going to give you a little package. You must take good care of it and not open it, do you hear? The landlady is dishonest, and I'm afraid that while I'm away negotiating with the messenger, one of Rupert's men will come here and steal the package. It would be disastrous for us both if he got his hands on it without paying my price, but neither the counselor nor his riffraff will guess I'm entrusting my valuable documents to a whore." Marie didn't share Jodokus's certainty, as she believed that the accomplices of the treacherous counselor would turn over every stone in Strasbourg and its surroundings to get their hands on the documents. But since she intended to steal whatever the insidious monk gave her, she didn't care. Wandering harlots came and went like the wind and rarely left any traces.

Jodokus pulled a package out from under his cloak. It was wrapped in an oilskin and secured with a seal. "Can you hide this under your dress when you leave?" She opened her mouth and eyes wide to seem eager and ready to help. "Yes, of course. I'll tie it securely to my undergarments, and no one will notice you gave me anything."

Jodokus bent over her, rubbing his nose on her breast, and unfastening his pants. "You're a bright girl, Marie. But now open the portals of your cathedral, as I'm overcome by my desire to pray there again."

XII.

In her room in the inn two hours later, Marie was sitting on one of the fresh, clean beds of reeds that Hiltrud had made for them, staring incredulously at the documents she had spread out before her. Either Jodokus had been in Rupert's service for a long time and was complicit in some of his scams, or he had stolen this bundle of papers, in which case Jodokus was even more cunning than she had suspected.

In the package, along with Otmar von Müringen's will that had been stolen from Saint Ottilien's monastery, were five other documents containing testamentary dispositions and transferences of property. Also included were documents in which Jodokus had recorded every one of Rupert's acts of trickery and deception in fine, neat handwriting, noting whether they were on behalf of his father, his brother, some high men in the church, or on the counselor's own behalf.

For the first time in her life, Marie was glad that her father had forced her to learn to read and write, just like a daughter from a Constance patrician family. Though she had since forgotten much of what she had learned, she remembered enough to decipher the gist of the notes Jodokus had written in Latin.

Jodokus must have been Rupert's confidant or possibly even one of his teachers, for he seemed to know all of the counselor's activities. In his writing, Marie discovered that her former fiancé had used forged documents to steal the property of Sir Dietmar's neighbors Gottfried von Dreieichen and Walter vom Felde.

Glancing at other entries, she saw her name and her father's. It felt strange to read a report about her own fate, and that person named Marie seemed like a stranger. Fortunately for her, and despite his accurate description, Jodokus hadn't made the connection between Master Matthis Schärer's daughter and Marie, the wandering harlot.

Jodokus described in detail what Rupert had done to appropriate her father's property. Apparently, the crime had been prepared even before the victims had been selected. The carriage driver Utz had scouted for suitable prey on behalf of Rupert Splendidus, recommending that the counselor ask Schärer for his daughter's hand in marriage. Utz knew that Linhard had been harshly rebuffed by her father for wanting to marry Marie, making it easier for him to convince Linhard to slander Marie and take part in the rape. Utz had also made the widow Euphemia his willing tool, only to kill her when she tried to blackmail Rupert. Marie shuddered at the depravity documented on the thinly shaven parchment as if it were a document from a demonic world in the distant past.

As darkness was falling, she was unable to read any more of the counselor's despicable deeds. In any case, she had spent too much time with the documents, since she had to be gone before Jodokus returned and demanded his package back. For a moment she considered running away immediately without waiting for Hiltrud, since her friend had not yet returned to the inn. Just in time, Marie remembered that Jodokus or Rupert's people would take out their anger on Hiltrud and probably kill her, and so she remained, even if the ground seemed to be burning under her feet.

The bells of the cathedral tower struck eight. In half an hour it would be dark, and Jodokus would meet with Rupert's go-between. Marie was tantalized at the thought of secretly observing the meeting. For a few breathless moments she fought against the rising tide of her curiosity, threatening to sweep away all reason. Then she yielded to the idea, gathering up the documents and wrapping them up again in the oilskin. Since she didn't want to leave the package at the inn, she put it in her shoulder bag, knotting the ends over her chest so it looked like she was carrying a child on her back, and left the house unobserved.

Before she had left him earlier, Jodokus had told her his meeting would take place near an especially large willow tree along the Ill River about a hundred paces from the harbor gate. Marie quickly spotted the tree and searched in the darkness for a person's vague outlines, creeping closer with care to avoid being seen. But her caution was unnecessary as no one was there, so she hid behind a bush by the shore and waited. Hours seemed to pass before a man exited the harbor gate. She recognized Jodokus from his walk; he was wrapped in his overcoat and appeared very nervous, repeatedly turning around as if afraid of his own shadow. Marie feared he'd look toward where she was hiding, but just then, someone came striding energetically toward the willow tree from the other direction. He was wearing a broad cloak and a wide-brimmed hat pulled down over his face, so she couldn't see who it was. She crouched down as he passed by and thanked God that a bank of fog was drifting by, hiding her from seeking eyes.

"Hello, Jodokus. We meet again." The man's threatening voice made the hair on the back of her neck stand on end. Suddenly, she pressed her hand over her mouth so she wouldn't cry out in fear or anger, for she had recognized the man. It was Utz, the wagon driver.

Jodokus seemed equally uncomfortable in his presence, for he stepped back and raised his arms defensively. "Do you have the money?"

"Yes, I have it with me, but first I want to see the goods."

Jodokus laughed nervously. "Do you think I would be so stupid as to bring the documents with me? As soon as you give me the money, we can go to the place where I've stored them, and I'll give them to you in the presence of witnesses."

"No, no, my dear renegade monk, I won't do that. You tricked us once, and I won't let you get away with it a second time. Do you think I don't know where the documents are that you stole for us? As of now you are expendable!"

"What?" Jodokus shouted, seized with panic. Turning, he tried to run, but Utz grabbed him by the neck. Throttling him so he couldn't cry out, Utz dragged the monk under the cover of the big willow tree only a few steps away from Marie, where he threw Jodokus to the ground and pressed his knee against his chest. It had become so foggy that Marie could only vaguely make out the men's shapes, and she had to listen carefully to figure out what was happening. Gasping for breath, Jodokus flailed wildly while the wagon driver mocked him.

"You're a fool trying to blackmail Master Rupert. Now you'll follow the greedy shoemaker's widow to hell!"

As he said *hell*, Marie heard the cracking of bones and then the murderer's heavy breathing followed by something large being dragged across the ground and hitting the water. Two heartbeats later, a dark shape that must have been Jodokus drifted by in the water.

On the shore, Utz shouted one last derisive farewell to the dead monk. "There's your reward, you ass! Now I'll go and get what belongs to us without paying a penny."

Terrified, Marie listened to the wagon driver chuckling to himself. "But first I'll enjoy a pleasant hour with the ever-available Frau Grete. Then I'll get the documents from Jodokus's room and take them to Rupert. He should give me few more guilders than usual." Marie then heard a metallic jangling, which she assumed came from Jodokus's room keys. Utz had evidently taken them from the man's body before throwing it in the water. Mumbling softly to himself, Utz passed so close to her that she held her breath, willing not even the smallest sound to reveal her hiding place.

Marie realized that when Utz went back to get the package from Jodokus's room, he would learn that the documents had disappeared and also that a woman had recently visited Jodokus there. Marie tried to guess how long it would take Utz to find her. One hour, maybe two? It wouldn't take longer than that. She had to leave the city as quickly as possible, and every fiber of her being was screaming out to not return to the inn. Knowing she couldn't abandon Hiltrud, she bit her finger to try to get over her fear.

Peering out, Marie listened as Utz left, whistling. It didn't seem to weigh on Utz's conscience at all that he had just killed a man. Marie briefly considered running back to town and reporting him as a murderer. But the word of a woman, especially a prostitute, carried almost no weight in court. Utz would simply laugh in her face and be happy she had spared him the effort of looking for her. Therefore she waited until she could be sure he had reached town; then she ran back to the inn as fast as she could in the ghostly light of the fog-enshrouded rising moon.

Luck was on her side, as she found the inn at once. Tiptoeing in through the front door, she could hear loud voices coming from the taproom. There was a quiet moment when only the rattling of dice in a leather cup could be heard, followed by cheers and an obscene curse. She sneaked past the taproom to her own room, where she found Hiltrud anxiously staring at the dwindling light of a small candle stump.

Smiling with relief, she looked at Marie. "Here you are, finally. I was afraid you'd absconded with the monk."

"Or the other way around," Marie replied. "All joking aside, we must leave at once. Our lives are in danger."

"Hiltrud gazed at her in astonishment. "What happened?"

"Jodokus was trying to blackmail Rupert, and Rupert sent Utz to kill him."

"The same Utz who raped you?" Hiltrud could see the sheer terror in Marie's face.

Marie tried to smile calmly but couldn't. "Yes, he's the one. It won't be long before he figures out I have exactly what he was trying to take from Jodokus, and then we'll be next."

Hiltrud shivered as if she were freezing. "Then let's leave. I'm only sorry we paid two weeks in advance for the room."

Marie demurred. "I'm not sorry enough to stay. I'd prefer a night out under the stars to this stinking hole."

"As I've said before, you're too fussy," Hiltrud joked as she quickly packed her belongings. Then she tied them all together in a bundle, which she hoisted over her shoulder. Before opening the door, she blew out the candle and put the stump in her pocket.

"After all, we paid for it," she said to Marie, who slipped silently past her and hurried down the stairs. To her relief, they left without being noticed, fleeing for the second time that year into the unknown.

PART FIVE
THE COUNCIL

I.

Marie sat on a log, drawing lines with her toes in the soft sand. She was bored, and so were the others. Hiltrud crouched in front of her tent, sewing with grim determination, and the two prostitutes they had joined after their abrupt departure from Strasbourg the previous year were sitting around with sullen faces, staring at the marketplace as if it were to blame for the lack of customers.

Helma, the woman from Saxony, was a pretty, young brunette with a round face and sparkling brown eyes. Nina, a southern woman with dark, curly hair and black eyes, was tiny, reaching just up to Marie's chin. Her exotic appearance and delicate figure with voluptuous curves attracted just as many men as Marie's angelic beauty. Here in Frundeck on the Neckar River, however, it seemed there were no well-to-do customers with full purses. If a man happened to approach, he usually shook his head regretfully on hearing the price, and continued on to the penny whores.

"No wealthy men, no merchants, not even moneyed workers with fur-trimmed coats are here at the market," Helma complained in her heavy Saxon dialect. "It's not possible that all the prosperous men have been swallowed up by the earth."

Hiltrud nodded grimly. "It wasn't like this at all last autumn in Kiebingen and Bempflingen. Back then, so many men were crowding into our tents that we had to turn most of them away. But now, in the spring, when we usually do our best business, there's nobody around who can afford us. If we'd known that, we'd have stayed in our comfortable winter quarters for a few more weeks." She conveniently forgot her complaints about the drafty cottage with its defective chimney and leaky roof.

"We could offer ourselves for half price," Nina suggested with her charming accent. "Otherwise, we'll go hungry." That was an exaggeration, as the Italian woman's purse was still full from the previous year. Nevertheless, she wasn't the only one to view this situation as alarming.

Marie was also worried. She had some savings from the year before, and also Siegward von Riedburg's purse brimming with golden guilders, but she was saving this money for her revenge and wasn't about to spend a single coin on daily living expenses.

Well aware of Marie's fortune but frustrated by her friend's unwillingness to listen to reason, Hiltrud had given up trying to give her advice. So when Marie commiserated with the others, expressing concern that she wouldn't even be able to afford a swineherd's cabin the next winter if things continued this way, Hiltrud gave her a derisive look. Then she glanced over at the penny whores' tents in the meadow across the way, where she saw more than a dozen men standing around, waiting.

"Those filthy women who ordinarily are no competition are earning more than us," she said in a tone suggesting she took that as a personal affront.

Helma undid her thick head of hair, then started to braid it up again.

"You're right. To stimulate some business, I think I'll offer myself for a shilling to the next man who comes along."

Marie raised her hand in warning. "I wouldn't do that. If we offer ourselves for less here, we'll have to do the same thing at the next market. Sooner or later we'll have as many fellows in our tents as they do over there."

Helma groaned. "But what should we do? Yesterday I had only one customer, and today not a one yet."

"The man over there looks like he could pay." Nina pointed toward a short, middle-aged man in ornate, fashionable clothing: tight red trousers with a blue-and-white striped codpiece, a white-and-green coat that just barely covered his waist, and a green felt hat with a red feather on top. The man had a rough-looking face, like that of a servant who had come upon money. Just then, he was walking past the tents of the penny whores, sizing some of them up, frowning, and shaking his head. Then, to the accompaniment of the rejected women's jeers, he headed toward Marie's group.

As he stood in front of them, his face brightened. "Well, I like you four. What do you think about earning some good money, eating well, and wearing the finest clothes?"

Hiltrud burst out laughing. "We think a lot of that. But we'd like to find out what the catch is first."

The man raised his hands in feigned horror. "No catch, for heaven's sake. My offer is sincere. If you're clever, you'll earn enough in one year to last you the rest of your life."

"Thanks, but we don't need to put ourselves in a brothel owner's hands. You scoundrels steal our money and shack us up with the kind of mangy old goats that no honest woman would touch even with a knight's iron glove."

Waving him off, Hiltrud turned her back on him.

He walked around her and grabbed her by the chin. "I can't let you get away with that, my darling. Do I look like a brothel owner? If you come with me, you'll work on your own and also receive a genuine golden guilder as an advance from the honorable council of the city of Constance."

Marie was startled to hear the name of her hometown, though at the same time she remembered that the planned council must have begun. Her first response was to leave immediately to ruin her former fiancé, but her fear of being recognized and whipped again was greater than her wish to watch Rupert being destroyed in person.

The man released his hold on Hiltrud and puffed up his chest. "I'm Jobst, the whore procurer, but I don't run a brothel. It's my job to find the prettiest courtesans near and far and to bring them to Constance so they can attend to our noble guests. The four of you meet my high expectations, and it would be a shame if you didn't come take a piece of the pie there."

Helma and Nina looked flattered, and the little Italian girl even cooed and asked if he'd like to step into her tent.

"If you'll come with me to Constance afterward, then gladly." Jobst rubbed a lock of her gleaming black hair between his fingers as if trying to decide whether the color was real. "You truly are a dainty morsel and could earn a lot of money in Constance—as could you all." His gaze drifted over Hiltrud and Helma, and came to rest on Marie.

"There's not much going on here," he said with a sweep of his arm. "Every respectable man with a few guilders in his pocket has left for Constance. The whole world is gathering there now: knights, counts, kings, but also high men in the church, scholars, merchants, city authorities, and representatives of the guilds. I'm telling you, you'd make a fortune there."

"Well, you four pretty ladies? How about it? Would you like to come with me and earn a gold guilder as an advance? I'll guarantee you'll make a lot of money."

"In truth, I suspect we'll be spreading our legs for a few lousy pennies from the riffraff that will be drawn into Constance in the wake of the noblemen. No, Jobst, I'll not fall for your slick words." Marie's sharp voice frightened the two women who didn't know her as well as Hiltrud did.

Annoyed, Jobst shook his head. "Good God, woman, you're as beautiful as an angel and will be able to attract the best of the noblemen in Constance."

"I hardly believe that a count or a prelate will come into the tent of a wandering harlot." Marie pursed her lips and stood up to leave, but Jobst blocked her way.

"For a reasonable price, I'll provide quarters for you and your friends, even though accommodations in Constance are so scarce that even noblemen are forced to sleep on straw in stables and many people have to stay on the other side of the lake."

But even that didn't convince Marie. "In a whorehouse, no doubt, whose owner pays you to find willing girls." As she was about to push him aside, he stomped his foot on the ground and shouted at her in irritation.

"Good God, woman, are you really so dense, or are you just pretending to be? I'll get a little house where you four can work independently. You won't owe me anything, because I'm paid a premium by the council for every courtesan I bring to them."

Hips swaying, Helma approached and took Marie by the shoulder. "I'm in favor of accepting this offer. Even if only half of what he's telling us is true, it's better than our current situation."

"I'm also in favor of going to Constance," Nina chimed in, clearly having already made up her mind. "A lot of my countrymen will be there, and I'll be able to speak my own language."

Hiltrud walked over to Marie and hugged her as she would a child, making it clear that she would stay with Marie even if the other women went.

Marie's head was spinning. How she would love to go to Constance! But she also remembered the verdict of a merciless judge.

"I don't like the idea," Marie said with a strained look. "A friend of mine was so badly beaten in Constance that she almost died, and I have other reasons to avoid the city."

Jobst roared with laughter. "Aha, I see. You've gotten into some trouble there. Don't worry, sweetheart. When you travel with me, you travel with the kaiser's protection. No one will dare lay a hand on you, and the bailiffs must allow you to move about the city freely."

The procurer winked suggestively at Marie and patted her cheek. "The kaiser has granted protection and free passage to all and declared a general peace in the Reich that will last from when the council starts until several weeks after it ends, since many noblemen gathering in Constance are engaged in feuds with one another. This peace applies not just to council attendees but to all those who contribute to its success. And a courtesan, it seems to me, contributes at least as much as a praying monk or a merchant selling food."

Perhaps the kaiser's safe-conduct issue really will keep officials away from me, Marie thought. But Rupert and his henchmen wouldn't pay it any mind, since the Rhine doesn't give its victims back and no one would think twice about a missing harlot. However, she knew that if fear kept her from going near Rupert, she'd never be able to wreak her revenge.

She also considered that she was still in possession of Sir Otmar's testament and Jodokus's other documents. In the hands of a banished prostitute, these documents were worthless, but she was sure that in the hands of the right person, Jodokus's notes and the documents could be the weapon that would finally destroy Count Konrad von Keilburg and Counselor Rupert Splendidus once and for all. But who was the right person? She realized that these documents would be worth more than gold to Dietmar von Arnstein and his wife. Sir Dietmar had been tricked by Rupert once already, however, and he would probably not prevail in his next exchange, either. But with the knight's help, perhaps she could find someone even more powerful to take action against Keilburg. Perhaps she herself would be able to find a high-placed enemy of the counselor who would use the documents in court to destroy her enemies. She'd have to keep her eyes and ears open and spread her legs for important people.

Taking a deep breath, Marie raised her head and replied. "Fine, Jobst. We'll come to Constance with you."

Helma and Nina cheered, and Hiltrud let out a deep sigh that didn't sound particularly relieved. The decision made, there was no going back, no matter what fate awaited Marie in Constance.

II.

It was early in the morning, and the lake was layered in a mist so dense that the island and its monastery were visible only in vague outlines. Fog billowed over the seawall and drifted like bizarre, deformed monsters through the still-deserted streets. Near the Saint Laurenz church, a young girl stepped through a doorway, looked around carefully, and ran down a narrow lane to Obermarkt Square. From there, she turned into the Ringgasse, which wound its way to a gate leading out of the city. Clad in a simple brown dress ordinarily worn only by maids, the girl had wrapped her upper body and head in a large threadbare shawl. Her solid cowhide shoes, however, were something a common maid could not afford.

She kept looking around anxiously, as if fearing discovery, and ducked into narrow side streets whenever she heard footsteps. But when she finally reached the Paradies Gate, she walked confidently toward the guard.

"You're up early, Miss Hedwig." The gatekeeper greeted her in a friendly voice, pointing at a small bunch of spring flowers in her hand. "You're probably heading to potter's field again, to your relatives' graves."

The girl nodded vigorously. "Indeed, Burkhard. Today is Annunciation Day, the day on which Marie was born and baptized, so I must pray for her and for the soul of her poor father."

The gatekeeper shook his head slowly. "There are some who don't approve of that."

"I know, but that won't keep me from going." Instinctively Hedwig looked back at the house that had once belonged to Matthis Schärer but where Rupert Splendidus now lived. The counselor was not pleased that she revered her two deceased relatives, but he couldn't forbid her from praying at her late uncle's grave. Her mother scolded Hedwig for being stubborn and admonished her to stop angering the gentleman, so Hedwig hadn't dared tell her she was going to visit the grave that morning. Though the counselor and a few others insisted that it was only a leprous beggar's grave, neither she nor her father believed that.

The gatekeeper opened a small door in the gate and wished her a good day. Since she heard someone else approaching, she darted through the opening without answering, and hurried on. Just behind her, a middle-aged abbot approached the Paradies Gate and motioned silently to the guard to open the door. Scowling, Burkhard took his time opening the lock and swinging the door back, as he didn't care for the fat abbot. The Benedictine arrogantly strode past him as if the gatekeeper were nothing more than an insect crawling around on the cobblestones in front of the gate. Burkhard wanted to call out to Hedwig and tell her to be careful, but when he peered through the gate, the girl had already disappeared into the fog. Burkhard was sure, however, that Abbot Hugo von Waldkron was also heading toward Brüel Field, the site of the Constance slaughterhouse, gallows, and potter's field.

Hedwig Flühi, Master Mombert's daughter, ran through the run-down area where beggars and drifters of Constance were taken to their eternal rest. Hurrying past unadorned mounds of dirt mostly covered with weeds, she stopped at a spot that looked quite different from the rest. When she had learned that her uncle was buried there, Hedwig had spread rich, dark soil over the grave and planted all kinds of flowers. Now she was delighted to find dozens of snowdrops blooming like bright shining stars as well as the first crocuses poking their green shoots out of the ground.

Stooping down, Hedwig smoothed over a rough patch where a dog had been digging, then looked sadly at the small new gravestone her father had put there recently. The first monument had been granite, but since the stone was smashed at least once a year, that became too expensive, and Mombert now had simple slabs of fired clay made as replacements. This marker was the fourth one since the dreadful events of the year 1410, and though no one knew who ruined the stones, Mombert and his daughter were convinced that Rupert Splendidus was the culprit. They knew that the counselor didn't want to be reminded how he had come by his wealth, but Hedwig, who hated him with every fiber of her being, swore to do everything she could so that he wouldn't forget.

She ran her hand lightly over the simple inscription on the stone that bore Matthis Schärer's name. Marie's name was also on the stone, though Master Matthis's daughter was not buried there. Hedwig's parents, like many others, didn't think that Marie could have survived very long after her unusually severe beating. Hedwig was still haunted by nightmares of Marie's whipping, for she had been wedged in between onlookers in the market square that day. Still, she couldn't accept that Marie had died from it, as she didn't believe God could be so unjust. Instead, she imagined her cousin living as a God-fearing hermit in some remote hideaway, where she'd be visited by forest animals that would come to her as they would to a saint.

Suddenly she heard the sound of crunching pebbles on the nearby path. As the steps quickly drew closer, she withdrew behind a withered bush and stared out into the fog. Upon seeing the fat monk, who in his flowing white cassock reminded her of a bloodthirsty ghost, she looked around for a way to escape.

Hugo von Waldkron was a guest in her enemy Rupert Splendidus's house. The cleric had been following her for several weeks, but she had always been able to elude him before. Jula, the daughter of a neighbor woman, worked as a maid for Rupert Splendidus, and she had warned Hedwig about Hugo. If this man wanted a woman, Jula said, he would take her by force, if necessary, since despite his huge potbelly, the abbot was reputed to have the strength of a bear.

Hedwig panicked. If he caught her, he would likely rob her of her virginity, and then she would suffer the same fate as Marie. It was unlikely anyone would hear her cries for help at this hour, and even if someone did show up unexpectedly, he would probably not be willing to confront such an influential man.

"Forgive me, Uncle Matthis and Marie, for not praying at your grave today."

The abbot turned around as if he had heard something, and Hedwig quickly threw her flowers on the grave and ran to the far end of the potter's field. Though the area was bounded by a thick hedge, there were a few gaps she could slip through. Hoping the abbot didn't see her, she stepped behind some bushes and crawled along the ground as she watched the abbot heading toward Matthis Schärer's grave. Someone must have told him that Hedwig usually visited the grave on Marie's name day and given him precise details as to her routine.

Hedwig watched as he turned and ran back to the entrance. Squeezing her way through the hedge, she quickly dashed away. Assuming that the abbot would keep an eye on the Paradies Gate for a while, she headed back home through the Scottish Gate instead.

Still afraid that the abbot might have followed her after all, she kept turning around, not noticing four men in colorful military garb headed her way. They were mercenaries, and like crowds of other similar men, they had nothing to do but hang out in Constance and neighboring areas, waiting for orders from their leaders. These four had left their quarters near the Scottish Gate and were on their way into the city. At the sight of a young woman, they cheered and came toward her.

Before Hedwig could react, one of the soldiers had pulled her to him and reached under the neckline of her dress. "Look what a fine little bird we've caught!"

"Let me go!" Hedwig hissed. "I'm not a whore!"

Though she tried to sound brave, she was completely terrified. In her fear of the lustful abbot, she had completely forgotten to watch out for the mercenaries who had descended on the city like a flock of locusts making life hard for everyone responsible for preserving public order, including local bailiffs, the council guards of Count Palatine Ludwig, and the kaiser. Too late, she realized that she should have taken a maid with her on her errand, as was proper for the virtuous daughter of a Constance citizen. On the other hand, these boors looked like they'd even assault Wina, who had become wrinkled and gray and didn't have a tooth left in her mouth.

The man who had grabbed Hedwig turned her around for the others to see. "Well, what do you say, comrades? This girl is a tastier morsel than the whore we shared last night."

One of his friends tore the shawl from her head and tugged at her long, golden blond braids. "Indeed she is. I can hardly wait. Will you let me go first this time, Krispin?"

The other laughed. "You can wait your turn. Naturally I'll take her first."

Hedwig had hoped the men were just teasing, but she now realized her dire situation and opened her mouth to scream. It was possible the pious brothers in the nearby Scottish monastery would hear her, or at least the tower guard, but the soldier pressed his hand over her mouth. "You won't deprive us of our fun!"

As he was dragging Hedwig into a wooded area at the edge of a pasture, an officer wearing the emblem of the palatine lion on his chest came walking up from the river. Struggling hard, the girl kicked her attacker, freeing herself long enough to let out a half-stifled scream.

The officer only looked briefly at the group, however, making a disgusted face when he saw the four men and the girl. Continuing on his way, he at first showed no interest in getting involved. Hedwig groaned, as the soldier pressed her body hard against his shoulder, bending her neck painfully. Gazing helplessly into the sunlight breaking through the fog, she didn't see that the officer had turned around and was now staring incredulously at her face and bright blond hair.

Stepping in front of the men, he unsheathed his sword with an angry curse and blocked the men's path. "Let the girl go, you scoundrels!"

"Why should we?" Krispin snapped at him. "This is our whore, so just mind your own business."

"I said let her go!" The officer took another step forward and smacked Krispin over the head with the flat blade of his sword. The mercenary dropped the girl and reached for his weapon, then noticed his opponent's coat of arms and paused. "Since when do you bloodhounds make a fuss over a prostitute?"

"I'm no prostitute, but the daughter of a Constance citizen," Hedwig shouted.

The officer seemed confused.

Krispin waved his hand dismissively and tried to seize Hedwig, who was crawling away from her tormenters. "Even if that's true, the daughters and wives of citizens also hop into bed with every fellow who can pay for it."

The officer put his sword to the man's chest. "If this were a matter of mutual agreement, then this would be none of my business, but the girl has clearly shown that she's not of the same mind." The officer's sword pushed deeper into the mercenary's leather doublet, and he seemed to be itching for a fight.

Putting his foot on Hedwig's dress to keep her from slipping away, Krispin looked at his comrades defiantly. "Are the four of us going to let ourselves be bullied by one little wimp?" Two of them shook their heads and drew their swords while the other raised his hands, protesting.

"Are you mad, Krispin? We can be hanged if we attack a vassal of the count palatine."

At that, the other two men placed their swords back in their sheaths, though their expressions showed how reluctant they were to yield to just one man. The officer's demeanor rattled them, however, for he seemed ready to take on all four of them.

Krispin stepped back from Hedwig. "Damn, a man should be allowed to fool around a little!" The look on his face as he walked away warned the officer not to meet up with him in a dark alley. The other three mercenaries followed their leader, grumbling.

Hedwig brushed the dirt from her dress and looked up at her rescuer curiously. He couldn't have been more than twenty-five years old, with an angular but friendly face and a prominent nose, and his bright blue eyes stared back at her with a mix of astonishment and doubt. Noticing his odd expression, Hedwig tried to remember her good manners.

"I thank you, sir. You have saved me from a very bad situation."

He reached out and carefully caressed her heavy braids. "It was dumb of you, girl, to be running around alone out here."

Hedwig lowered her head and stared helplessly at the tips of her shoes. "You are right, but I couldn't take the direct way back into town because the fat abbot was after me again. He followed me to my cousin's grave and would certainly have attacked me if I hadn't succeeded in outrunning him."

The man snorted irritably as he continued to gaze at Hedwig's face. "There's too much riffraff in this city. An abbot, you say?"

"Yes, Hugo von Waldkron, the abbot of the Waldkron monastery."

Hedwig saw that his mind was elsewhere. He passed a hand over his forehead while still holding one of her braids in the other. "You're really too young . . . No, you can't be Marie, but you look a lot like her."

Hedwig looked up, startled. "You know my cousin?"

The soldier gaped at her wide-eyed. "Marie Schärer is your cousin? Then you must be Master Mombert's little Hedwig."

"Yes, I'm Mombert Flühi's daughter." Hedwig was amazed that a total stranger knew her and her family. She was also ashamed, since the officer probably thought she was a woman of easy virtue.

"I was not just running around, but I wanted to go to Marie's grave in potter's field. Today is her birthday and name day."

The man's face fell. "Marie is dead? Oh my God!"

Hedwig raised her hands, uncertainly. "We don't know for sure. It's actually the grave of her father, who was buried secretly by our adversary. Ever since my father discovered that his brother-in-law was buried there, we have also been going to pray for the soul of my missing cousin."

The soldier's face turned so dark with fury that Hedwig became afraid. "Master Matthis is dead? That's certainly the fault of this scoundrel . . . When did he die?"

"We don't know the details. He disappeared right after Marie was driven from town. My father thinks he knows who is responsible. We can't say publicly, but . . ." Hedwig stopped short. She didn't know this man, but she did know that there were certain things she shouldn't say to strangers. At worst, the officer could be one of Master Rupert's confidants, and if the counselor heard what she was saying, things would go badly for her father.

"I'm talking too much," she said. "Please let me go, sir. They are probably already looking for me at home."

The man gave her his arm. "I'll take you back to your house, or other men might seek to take advantage of your situation."

"How do I know I can trust you?" Hedwig asked. The man laughed. "You're safe with me. After all, I used to wipe your nose when you were a child."

Hedwig placed her fists on her hips and glared at him. "You've been saying all along that you know me and my father, but you won't tell me who you are."

"I'm Michel, son of the taverner Guntram Adler on Katzgasse Lane."

Hedwig jutted out her lower lip. "That can't be true. The taverner on Katzgasse Lane is named Bruno Adler."

"That's my older brother. My father isn't alive any longer, either." Michel sighed as he said that, but he didn't feel particularly sad.

Hedwig squinted, trying to find any similarities between the slender, strong warrior standing before her and the stout taverner on Katzgasse Lane, but simply concluded that Michel was quite a bit better looking than his brother. Giving him her arm, she let him accompany her home.

III.

"Your wife wants to know if you have seen Hedwig, master."

Mombert Flühi pondered the question carefully, since the journeyman's voice was as anxious as if he were asking about his sister or even his bride. "No, Wilmar, I haven't seen my daughter today. I hope she hasn't slipped out of the house alone."

Hurrying over to a little bull's-eye window, Wilmar looked around outside. The window let just enough light into this part of the shop for them to be able to work without a torch. "She didn't take any of the maids along, for they're all with your wife. Good Lord, how can Hedwig be so reckless!"

Mombert Flühi could see how worried the young man was about his daughter and raised his hands in resignation. He wanted to tell Wilmar that a seventeen-year-old girl couldn't be locked in her room night and day, even in times like these. Wilmar had told him that the abbot of the Waldkron monastery had an eye on his daughter and was stalking her like an infatuated young man. But she wasn't even safe in her own home, and he couldn't do anything to stop the abbot any more than he could block the nobleman he was obliged to take into his own house on the city council's orders. Several times already, his noble guest, Philipp von Steinzell, had accosted Hedwig and tried to kiss her, although the one time Philipp had tried to pull her into his room, Wilmar was able to save her by telling the nobleman an inventive story about someone waiting for him in the street.

Grinding his teeth in angry frustration, Wilmar made a face, and Mombert Flühi assumed his journeyman was also thinking about these threats to Hedwig's honor. Both men wanted nothing more than to run up to the squire's room, pull him out into the hallway, and throw him down the stairs. Mombert swore he'd toss Philipp von Steinzell out the next time something happened, even if that caused problems for him with the city council that required citizens to provide quarters for the visiting noblemen and ecclesiastical higher-ups. He owed that much, at least, to his daughter and to ensure peace in his house. He resolved to file another complaint soon to the quartermaster of his district, and to pester that official until he got permission to evict the arrogant knight.

Wilmar looked at his master disapprovingly. "You shouldn't have allowed Hedwig to leave."

Mombert flared up. "What can I do? Tie her up? She probably went to the potter's field at the crack of dawn to pray for Marie, since this is Marie's name day. If I'd thought of that earlier, I would have gone along with her."

Wiping his brow, Mombert pushed aside the barrel he had been working on. "Just keep working, Wilmar. I'm going out for a little walk."

Wilmar sighed in relief, as he knew his master would be looking for Hedwig. He was returning to his tasks when the three apprentices entered one after another, late again but clearly happy to see that their master wasn't there. Wilmar pointed to the back of the shop. "Hurry up and get to work! The wood won't carve itself."

The previous day, the apprentices had been told to cut staves for the barrels, but they hadn't gotten as far along as Master Mombert had expected. Isidor and Adolar, the two younger apprentices, looked contrite and hurried to the back of the shop to pick up their tools. Just three years younger than Wilmar, the other apprentice, Melcher, stood in the doorway, a scornful look on his face.

"I have no intention of continuing to do such scutwork. If Master Mombert won't give me proper training in barrel making, my father will send me to a better master. Jörg Wölfling would be glad to take me on."

Wilmar frowned and stuck out his jaw. "If you don't like the work here, you should go somewhere else. But I doubt Master Jörg will give you anything different to do. With all the important people and their entourages in town, there's so much to be done that everyone has to work as hard as they can. Moaning and whining are things you can do at home."

Turning his back on the surly apprentice, Wilmar picked up the small boards that Adolar and Isidor had already split, put them on the workbench, and started cutting them down to size with a sharp drawknife.

Melcher stood in the doorway for a few minutes with clenched fists. Then he walked to the back of the shop, muttering to himself.

"I'll tell the master you're stalking Hedwig," he snarled at Wilmar as he walked by, quickly trying to feint an anticipated smack.

But the journeyman moved faster, slapping Melcher so hard that the sound could be heard all over the house. Isidor and Adolar looked at each other, grinning. They both agreed that Melcher had it coming to him, for as the oldest apprentice, he was always pushing them around and acting as if he were the master.

IV.

Mombert Flühi was about to turn the corner and head for the Paradies Gate when he heard his daughter's voice behind him.

"Father, where are you going?"

Despite his impressive girth, Mombert instantly wheeled around and saw his daughter heading up the lane on an officer's arm. He gasped with anger, as he never imagined his daughter would give all the women of Constance reason to gossip. If Hedwig earned herself a reputation as a girl who flirted with soldiers, she'd forfeit any chance of a good marriage.

"Where were you? Aren't you ashamed of yourself, strolling around with a total stranger, and a soldier at that?" he fumed.

Hedwig was startled by her father's sharp words, but her companion raised his hand reassuringly. "Good day, Master Mombert. I'm very glad to see you again."

Hedwig's father stared at the man and scratched the side of his head. "Do I know you?"

Michel took him by the shoulder, laughing.

"But Master Mombert, do you have such a poor memory? I'm Michel from Adler's Tavern on Katzgasse Lane who followed your niece and searched for her in vain." A shadow passed over his face.

Taking both of Michel's hands in his own, Mombert squeezed them tightly. "Where have you been all this time, boy? And what are you doing in the military? That's no place for a good lad like you."

Glancing around, Michel tried to temper the man's exuberance. "I think I should tell you over a cup of wine at your house, and not here on the street where people keep bumping into us."

Mombert slapped his forehead. "Right you are! Come along! I'm eager to hear what you've been up to in the last five years."

He took Michel by the arm, pulling him along. After a few steps, he turned to Hedwig. "It's wonderful that you recognized Michel and brought him home with you. He has changed so much, I would never have known him."

Hedwig lowered her head in shame. "I didn't recognize Michel, Father. I went to the cemetery to place flowers on Uncle Matthis's grave and pray for him and Marie. That portly abbot followed me there, and when I tried to flee, I ran right into the hands of four soldiers who wanted to hurt me. If Michel hadn't rescued me from those vile men, I would certainly already be dead."

Turning pale, Mombert grabbed Michel. "Is that true? Then, by God, you are a brave man, a hero, the kind we never see anymore."

Michel blushed, his cheeks getting pink. "That's more praise than I deserve, Mombert. The four ran away because of the coat of arms I'm wearing, not because of anything I did."

"The palatine lion!" Mombert exclaimed respectfully. "So now you're a soldier of the count palatine on the Rhine?"

Michel nodded proudly. "I'm one of the foot-soldier leaders summoned here to reinforce the council guards. Our ship docked yesterday in Gottlieben, where we'll be staying, but I wanted to see my hometown again before my duties begin, so I left before dawn to come here."

"Thanks be to God! I don't even want to think what might have happened to my Hedwig if you hadn't stepped in. She's my only child, you know." Master Mombert vowed to light a large wax candle to Saint Pelagius for sending the young warrior to help his daughter at just the right time.

After a short walk, they reached Hundsgasse Lane, where Master Mombert's shop was located. Michel knew the place well as he used to deliver beer to him frequently. Back then, the cooper's house was equally as splendid as Matthis Schärer's home. Now, he noticed that time had not been kind to the buildings, and they were showing their age. Though all of the finished barrels in the yard and the piles of wood in an open shed showed that there was a lot of work being done, Master Mombert seemed less prosperous than before.

His hospitality, however, was still bountiful. Opening the front door, Mombert called to his wife, Frieda, and introduced her to their unexpected guest. She initially frowned when she saw the young palatine officer's martial attire, but her expression changed in a flash after she learned that Michel had saved her daughter from great danger. Before attending to their guest, however, she gave her daughter a stern lecture.

"I hope this incident will be a lesson to you," she concluded. "Though the great demand for barrels keeps your father busy with work, I'd rather have the noblemen hold their council somewhere else."

Mombert raised his hand, trying to placate her. "You mustn't think of it that way, woman. It's a great honor that Kaiser Sigismund chose Constance as the place for the council."

His wife snorted scornfully. "It will really be a great honor when in a few months all of the maids are running around with big bellies after selling their virtue to a soldier or prelate for half a penny."

"It's not going to be that bad," said Mombert, trying to calm her down. "There are enough women of easy virtue here to serve every guest. In fact, the most beautiful harlots have been brought to Constance from all over the Reich for the noblemen. No local girl or woman will have to worry about her virtue."

"Indeed? And what almost happened to Hedwig?" Frieda nagged.

"There are bad people everywhere, even here in Constance. Just remember what happened to poor Marie, and we still don't know what happened to her after she was banished." Mombert's statement silenced his wife and caused Michel's face to darken. Frieda hurried into the kitchen to get wine, sausage, and bread, and Hedwig followed her to help, not wanting to give her mother any more reason to scold her. Leading Michel into the sitting room, Mombert offered him the place at the head of the table usually only occupied by the master of the house.

"My wife will be bringing us a bit of wine and something to eat in a moment, and then you can tell me what you've been up to."

Michel waved dismissively. "My life has not been very exciting. I followed Marie as far as the Rhine without finding her. Since I didn't want to return to my father, I signed up on a ship sailing down the Rhine. When we reached the mouth of the Neckar River, two ships behind us collided. They were lucky, as neither boat sank, but a boy standing on one of the ship's decks fell into the water. The current carried him toward our boat, so I was able to grab hold of him and pull him out without suspecting that he'd be literally worth his weight in gold."

Michel took a drink of wine and shook his head, laughing, as if he still couldn't grasp his good fortune. "The boy turned out to be the count palatine's nephew. Ludwig thanked me profusely and gave me more gold than I had ever seen at once in my life. After the incident, the captain of the guards in the harbor where we had docked invited me for a drink and listened to my story. Of course I told him about Marie, and he suggested I become a soldier. He thought I would do better in the world as a servant of the count palatine than as a boatman who just travels up and down the Rhine."

"And did you accept?" Mombert asked curiously.

"I was so drunk, I still don't know what I told him," Michel admitted. "The next morning when I woke up, I was surprised to find myself on the count's own ship. But everything worked out in the end."

"Have you been made a knight?" Mombert asked excitedly. Many men of high standing in Constance wanted nothing more than to be granted knighthood, but only a few were given this honor.

"No, I haven't made it that far yet. But I have become captain of a band of foot soldiers, and if my luck holds out and my superior remains favorably disposed, I may one day become a castellan, or captain of a castle."

Michel sounded so self-confident and proud that Mombert became a bit envious. This boy who was so scrawny only a few years ago, who was only the younger son of a simple taverner, had seized an opportunity and risen to an officer's rank of one of the most respected men in the Reich. The cooper was only sorry Marie wasn't there to witness it, since he knew she would have been thrilled for her childhood friend. Seeing Marie's bloody and beaten body before his eyes once again, he struggled to hold back his tears.

For a while the conversation wandered, Michel telling more about his time as a vassal of the count palatine and Mombert talking about all the things that had happened in Constance. Michel's face darkened when he heard about the suspicious circumstances under which Matthis had died, along with details of how Counselor Rupert had managed to seize all of Schärer's property without question and almost ruin Mombert. Since Michel wasn't in a position to help his host, however, Mombert changed the topic and spoke of the council that was currently the object of so many heated discussions in the Reich.

"I'm glad you're one of the leaders of the council guards. With so many strangers here, it's good to have a local person to maintain order."

Michel turned the wine cup around in his hand and seemed to be deciding how to reply. "Well, my people are not exactly council guards; nor am I."

Mombert looked at him in surprise. "But didn't you say . . ."

"Yes, I was ordered to come here, but it wasn't to parade through the streets in full uniform, saving young women from drunken mercenaries or lecherous monks. Our task is different."

"What is it?" Mombert didn't realize that his guest felt uneasy speaking about it.

Michel realized he had to be careful what he said if he didn't want to start spreading rumors. "Do you know Master Jan Hus?"

Mombert nodded excitedly. "Of course! He's a good, God-fearing man. I heard him preach once, and he says exactly what ordinary citizens are thinking."

"You shouldn't announce that so loudly around here. Master Hus has made himself unpopular with some of the noblemen. My soldiers and I are here to stop him from leaving Constance as surreptitiously as Pope John did."

"Has word already gotten around that the only pope following the orders of the kaiser has secretly fled?"

Michel smiled softly. "The count palatine learns everything that happens not only in Constance but also in the entire bishopric, or else he wouldn't be able to fulfill his responsibilities to the kaiser. The people around the kaiser suspected that John would attempt to flee after he had been urged to resign. Once a person is at the very top, it's not easy for him to relinquish his post."

Mombert cast a sly glance at Michel. "Are you one of those trying to bring Pope John back?"

"In that case I wouldn't be here. No, the kaiser sent out his own people, and I don't think it will take them long to capture him. What the nobles are more concerned about now is what to do with Friedrich von Habsburg, the Tyrolean duke who helped John flee. I've heard rumors that the kaiser will declare him an outlaw. Then the man will have truly earned the nickname Friedel with the Empty Pocket."

Grinning broadly, Mombert snapped his fingers. "That would be fine with me, as then we'd be rid of a troublesome tenant. Philipp von Steinzell is a vassal of Friedrich's. If the duke is banned from the Reich, then Steinzell will have to leave Constance as well."

Michel frowned in surprise at his host's vexed tone. He was about to ask more about Philipp von Steinzell when they suddenly heard a commotion in front of the house followed by suppressed curses and a woman's shrill scream.

Michel jumped up, but Mombert, despite his corpulence, reached the door first and stormed out. On the stairway stood a young man in a nobleman's colorful clothing, holding a struggling Hedwig in his arms. The girl had thrown a barrel down the steps at him and bitten his hand, as blood was visible on the fingers he'd placed over her mouth. Evidently Philipp von Steinzell had been lying in wait for Hedwig in order to drag her into his room. "You bastard, I'll bash your skull in!" Mombert roared so loudly that he was heard out on the street.

The threat seemed to amuse the squire. "Well, come on then, if you dare. I'll give you the worst beating of your life."

"I don't have to tolerate this in my own home!" Mombert shouted, frothing at the mouth, but he stepped back when the man raised a hand to strike him. Mombert knew he was no match for the seasoned fighter and therefore just continued to yell. "Let my daughter go, you scoundrel, then pack your things and get out. I don't want to see you in my house again."

The squire just laughed, but realizing that the cooper's shouts would bring half the city running to his door, he let the girl go. Hedwig barely managed to hold on to the railing to avoid a fall, then got her footing again and rushed past her father into the house. Clenching his jaw, Philipp von Steinzell stared furiously at them and rubbed his bloodied left hand. For a moment it seemed he was about to give Mombert a good thrashing as punishment for his interference.

Standing at the door up to that point, Michel now stepped out into the hallway, ready to assist the cooper. In the room's dim light, Philipp could only see a man's contours and the shape of his long sword. He immediately stepped back, turned with a half-angry, half-disappointed snort, and went up the stairs. At the top of the staircase he looked down contemptuously at Mombert.

"Our business isn't finished yet. You offered a room to me and my servant for as long as the council lasts, and I am going to make use of it."

The look on his face showed that he hadn't given up.

Turning red with rage, Mombert rashly went to follow his tormenter up the stairs and start a fight, but at that moment his eldest apprentice appeared from his hiding place in the hallway, staring at his master. Mombert hadn't heard a door creaking open, so he knew that Melcher must have been concealed there when the knight attacked Hedwig. Now the cooper's anger was directed at the youth.

"What are you doing here, you lazy fool?" he shouted, followed by a string of various other insults.

"Wilmar sent me to ask when you'll be coming to work," he sneered, laughing at his master. "We have a lot to do."

Mombert stepped toward the boy, his hand raised as if to strike, but then stopped and waved Melcher off with irritation.

"I don't owe either you or Wilmar an explanation. I have a guest at the moment—tell him that." Turning away brusquely, Mombert took Michel by the shoulders, urging him back into the sitting room.

Melcher stared at the sitting room door for a while. Then he peered up the stairs, where Philipp's curses could still be heard through his closed door. He next ran to the workshop door and listened there, trying to discern if anyone inside had noticed the activity in the hallway. Hearing only the usual sounds of men working, he tiptoed back again toward the sitting room, putting his ear against the door. Disappointedly turning away, he slipped out the front door, checking cautiously once outside, then ran down the lane.

A few minutes later, he arrived at a tavern near the harbor that was already busy despite the early hour. Positioning himself by the front door, he looked around, then was suddenly seized by a powerful hand and dragged into an empty adjacent room.

"Here you are finally! I've been waiting for you since yesterday. Tell me what's going on in Flühi's house? Is there any news?" Utz had been idly sitting in the tavern at a time when every other wagon driver was earning double pay trying to carry all the guests in and around Constance.

Standing on tiptoe, the boy whispered in Utz's ear. "There was another confrontation between the master and the squire, and Flühi shouted so loudly that people living three houses away could hear. He threatened to bash in the squire's skull if he touched Hedwig again."

"And you can testify to that." It sounded like an order.

Melcher nodded excitedly. "I can swear it!"

"Not before I tell you to. I'm warning you. Don't say another word of this to anyone, and do what I say."

"Of course, Utz, I understand."

The wagon driver tousled the boy's hair. "If you listen to me, you'll make out all right, Melcher."

"But you'll keep your promise to me, won't you? Becoming a nobleman's vassal is quite different from trimming boards and making barrel staves for Master Mombert."

"Of course," Utz replied with a laugh. "When this is all over and you've done everything I've told you, I'll take you to a nobleman who'll accept you into his service. We've already agreed to that. Then you'll wear fancy clothes like the officers you idolize so much. But now you must go! I don't want them to notice you missing."

Melcher ran off, beaming, and Utz watched until the boy had vanished among the crowd in the narrow street. Then grinning with satisfaction, the carriage driver returned to his table to finish his wine. A short time later, he ambled through the little streets, stopping in front of the cathedral where the upcoming council was going to meet.

High dignitaries were standing around the church square, engaged in animated discussions. Armed guards attempted to keep an eye on their lords and at the same time drive away street vendors who were crowding in too closely in order to sell their food and sweets.

Utz strolled through the throng like a casual spectator, deftly stepping out of the way of the soldiers, until he reached the upper church courtyard where a group of canons was engaged in a lively conversation. While keeping an eye on the North Gate, Utz pretended to be interested in the discussion, which centered around the pope's secret departure a few days earlier. As soon as he saw the man he'd been waiting for exit the church, wearing a scholar's flowing robe, the wagon driver moved away from the group, crossing paths with him as if by accident.

"The case involving Steinzell and Mombert Flühi can begin in a few days," he said softly as he passed.

Counselor Rupert Splendidus bowed his head without glancing at the wagon driver, then turned to look at the abbot of the Waldkron monastery who was just leaving the cathedral behind him.

"Shall we walk home together, Herr Hugo? Along the way you could tell me how your hunting party went this morning."

Hugo von Waldkron grimaced. Rupert responded to the silent show of emotion with a malicious smile, put his arm around the cleric's shoulder, and pulled him closer, as if to support him.

V.

Looking down from on top of Mount Lichten near Meersburg, Marie saw the blue waters of Lake Constance lying before her again for the first time in years, and a shiver ran down her spine.

In the clear air of that beautiful spring day, she was just able to make out the huge main tower of the Constance cathedral to the south with its golden weathercock perched on the roof. That rooster was the last thing she had seen when she had left the city, and now she imagined it letting out a mighty crow heard throughout town when she returned, announcing that she had come back to seek vengeance.

She quickly shook off this thought. If she wanted to stay alive and plot her revenge, she couldn't strut about like a mighty gentleman loudly demanding his due, but would instead have to be as quiet and inconspicuous as a little mouse. She could only succeed if no one in town recognized her and started gossiping.

Except for Hiltrud, none of the other traveling harlots knew her story; nor did the procurer, Jobst. In his group, there were sixteen courtesans, as Jobst called them in his flattering way. Only a few of them were especially beautiful, but they all had pleasant faces and good figures, and there were no penny whores among them.

These women all came of their own accord, drawn to the especially large gathering of soldiers, servants, and monks like bees to honey. Some of these women helped fill the better municipal bordellos where council members would seek to unwind after their long and difficult negotiations, and some, like Marie and Hiltrud, wanted to work independently.

Jobst had rented a wagon so none of the women would have to walk and none would get sick. The carriage could be closed on all sides in case of bad weather, but at that moment, the canvas was tied up so the women could view the countryside and, as Marie chuckled to herself, so that other travelers could inspect them. Sitting up front on a board fastened to the wagon sides, Jobst had been entertaining the women with stories about the area. Now he looked down on the tired group and pointed at the lake. "Your lovely free time is coming to an end. By this evening we'll be in Constance, and then you can start working."

The women looked relieved, as they were exhausted and looked forward to leaving the bouncing vehicle. Kordula, the oldest woman, said with a groan, "It's high time, Jobst. My ass is beaten up with all of the bumps."

"But not the way you're accustomed to," Helma joked, adjusting the soft part of her pack as a cushion against the potholes.

The others had folded up their blankets and laid them out on the bare wood, but that didn't help much. The wagon was sturdy, built to carry barrels and other heavy merchandise, and it wasn't well suited for women's tender backsides. The procurer was assailed by complaints from all sides.

Jobst, offended, raised his eyebrows and ordered the servant walking alongside to stop the two horses. "If you're so uncomfortable with the ride, then get out. You can go the rest of the way to the shore on foot."

He jumped over the side of the wagon and bowed slightly. Marie stood up first. Tossing her blanket over her shoulder, she picked up her bundle and let Jobst help her down. Hiltrud placed her hand on Marie's shoulder and also jumped to the ground, then nudged her friend to the side for a quick chat. The contact made Marie's back start to itch again, and she scratched vigorously.

"What's the matter? You haven't caught some disease, have you?" Hiltrud asked anxiously.

Marie rolled her shoulders, trying to relieve the tension. "It feels as if the scars on my back are still fresh."

"We shouldn't have come here." Hiltrud lowered her voice so that no one else could hear.

Marie shook her head. "No, it was the right decision. I must finally come to terms with my past."

Hiltrud waved her right arm dismissively. "Forget what happened. Just try to earn as much money as you can in Constance, and afterward, perhaps you can settle down somewhere else with your savings and start a new life."

"You think we should start a new life afterward? I have nothing against that, but no city would give citizenship to two women with dubious backgrounds unless we're rich enough to buy ourselves the mayor's sons as husbands."

Hiltrud knew Marie was right and that she was just dreaming. Just the same, she started to laugh. "Who knows? Maybe we'll actually make that much. According to Jobst, the attendees are very generous."

"Let's hope so," Kordula said, walking toward Marie and Hiltrud when she heard what they'd just said. "It wouldn't be a bad idea for us to get out of this business after the council. After all, we're still young enough to have children, but in a few years we'll just be a bunch of old hags."

Marie made a face when she heard that. Who would marry a prostitute except for perhaps a knacker, a gravedigger, or an executioner?—men that not even a maid would want, to say nothing of a respectable lady. And even these men would make demands, if not for looks, then at least for money. Shaking her head pensively, Marie stomped away in the direction Jobst was pointing.

Hiltrud and Kordula were close behind while Helma and Nina stayed with the procurer, fawning over him. Jobst had persuaded those two to stay in one of the city bordellos, and had also described life there in glowing terms to Marie and Hiltrud. But they had rebuffed him because they, like Kordula, wanted to be their own bosses and not have to hand over a large portion of their hard-earned money in exchange for a leaky roof and bad food. At some point Jobst had given up and promised them a modest house by the brick pits; although, his rate was exorbitant and he wanted the first three months' rent paid in advance.

Marie knew the part of town where the brick pits were located. Five years before, that area had been undeveloped wetland along the Rhine where poor townspeople went to harvest grain for their goats. Based on that, Marie knew their housing would probably be little more than a stable. But she wasn't alarmed: she and Hiltrud had to fix up their winter quarters every year anyway to make them livable, and Kordula had already offered to lend a hand with the work and to share in the expenses. Though the two friends hadn't yet decided whether or not to let Kordula join them, Marie liked the idea. Kordula reminded Marie of Gerlind when she first met her, even though the broad-hipped woman was younger than Gerlind had been at that time.

Marie decided not to worry about the future for a while and instead concentrated on placing her feet on the stony path, covered with giant tree roots winding down to the lake. Though it was only March, the sun burned down from a cloudless sky, and the women were happy to be walking in the shade. Despite the afternoon's warmth, the morning had been bitterly cold, and most of them still wore their woolen jackets or two layers of dresses, making them all glow damply. The little streams of sweat that ran down Marie's back irritated her scars even more.

Hiltrud noticed her rolling her shoulders in discomfort, and scratched Marie's back with her fingers. Marie turned to thank her friend and noticed the wagon driver circling the horses behind them in order to drive back. Seeing with a start that the man looked a little like Utz, probably due to his clothing, Marie realized how lucky she'd been up till then, as Jobst could have met her tormenters when he rented the wagon. She hoped that Utz would be so busy with the council that there'd be little danger of her meeting him by chance in Constance.

Leaving the forest, Marie had a clear view over the lake. At the foot of the slope, a large barge already fully loaded with sacks and boxes was tied to a rickety-looking pier extending over the water. The first passengers pressed forward to board, but the boat seemed much too small to accommodate both the prostitutes and a group of scholars also waiting for transport, as well as a man on a mule now approaching on the shore road from Uhldingen. Even from a distance it was easy to see that he was a cleric, and when he got closer, his badge showed he was the abbot of a Benedictine monastery. As he rode past, the arrogant look on his chubby face and the way he pulled his robe and overcoat to him tightly in order to avoid contact with the women made a mockery of the concept of Christian humility.

Riding onto the pier, the abbot stopped by the boat, and two boatmen helped him out of the saddle. One of the boatmen gave him his arm to help him climb over the side while the second led the mule to some buildings on a forested knoll back on shore.

"Hey, you there! Hurry up and get in! I want to get to Constance before nightfall," the boatman shouted at the whores and the learned gentlemen. The men crowded together in front, pushing Helma and Nina roughly aside.

Hiltrud and Marie climbed aboard, but the boat was so crowded, they had to clamber on top of the boxes where Marie wound up sitting next to the abbot. Snorting with contempt, he acted as if she repulsed him, but Marie noticed him casting furtive glances her way. Suddenly, he smacked his lips and reached for her, trying to put his hands down her dress. She quickly drew back as far as she could, turned her back to him, and pulled her shawl over her head to keep him from touching her hair. Kordula, who sat between her and Hiltrud, nudged her with a slightly malicious grin.

"The man sitting next to you is Hugo, the abbot of the Waldkron monastery. I'm surprised he's staring at you like that, since he's got a reputation for chasing young virgins and requesting prostitutes who look like very young girls."

"Whereas I don't look either young or innocent," Marie joked.

"I didn't mean it that way. I'm just wondering why he's suddenly taking an interest in a grown woman . . ." Kordula pressed her right index finger against her nose, deep in thought. "Last time I saw him, he kept a girl who was as blond as you are and had a Madonna-like face just like yours. Maybe you've picked up a loyal customer."

Marie shrugged. "If he pays well, he can have me."

Leaning forward, Kordula lowered her voice even more. "Be careful. The abbot is one of those repulsive men who like to hurt women. The young girl I just mentioned used to sob as she told me things . . ." The rest remained unsaid as one of the boatmen cast off the lines and the ship began to toss alarmingly. Kordula screamed and grabbed hold of the bundle she was sitting on.

The boatman used a long pole to shove off from the shore and headed out into open water while his two assistants raised the sail. The sail billowed out as the wind caught it, and the captain put down the pole to reach for the rudder. A breeze from the north drove the heavy boat out onto the lake.

When Marie was younger, her father often took her to Meersburg on the river, so she was familiar with this type of travel, and the rocking of the boat didn't bother her. Hiltrud was also unruffled, but Kordula stared anxiously at the receding coastline. Once she had calmed down and resumed talking, she'd forgotten the abbot, and the only thing that interested her was what might be awaiting them in Constance.

Marie was so tense with anticipation that she only added a few mumbled words to the conversation. For years she'd been upset whenever she heard someone mention her hometown, but now she was dying to be there again. The boat rounded the peninsula, heading for the international merchant's pier next to the warehouse. Crowds of people packed the shore in front of the tall buildings, and Marie panicked, assuming she'd be recognized at once and turned over to the guards. To keep her fear in check, she silently repeated Jobst's assurance that all invited visitors, including harlots, were protected by the kaiser's decree and could not be bothered.

When the boat docked, Abbot Hugo pushed to the front of the line and reached out for the boatmen helping passengers disembark. They struggled to lift him over the side, holding on to him until he was safe on dry land. Their hope for a tip was in vain, however, as the abbot pulled his cloak tightly closed, walking right past their outstretched hands without giving them a second look as he pressed his huge body through the crowd.

Marie watched as the abbot headed toward a man dressed in academic robes made of good, fur-trimmed cloth and a fashionable cap, indicating that the wearer, unlike most of his scholarly colleagues, was a man of means. Though his robe concealed his body, he seemed familiar. When he turned to speak to the abbot, she recognized his face, and her heart skipped a beat. It was Counselor Rupert. Greeting the abbot with obvious pleasure, Rupert put his arm around him.

Trembling with anxiety, Marie was simultaneously sweating and freezing even though the weather was pleasantly warm, and she wanted to hide under the cargo until everyone had left. As the boatman drove the passengers off the boat like a herd of sheep, she clung to Hiltrud's skirt, trying to disappear behind her statuesque friend.

Hiltrud looked quizzically at Marie and noticed her panicky expression. Though she initially couldn't imagine what might have frightened her friend so much, she swiftly caught on. "That fellow over there who looks like a vulture . . . Is he your former fiancé?"

Marie just nodded silently, since she had lost her voice. But then her fear suddenly gave way to overwhelming hatred, hitting her as hard as Hunold's whips had long ago. At that moment she wanted nothing more than to attack the man responsible for all her misfortunes, flinging her anger and bitterness back in his face and letting everyone know what a scoundrel he was. She quickly came to her senses, however, as she knew that no one would believe a prostitute.

As Rupert and the abbot disappeared toward the fish market, Marie breathed a sigh of relief and followed Hiltrud's lead as she hopped off the boat and back onto dry land.

Jobst was gathering together his small group of harlots, and he waved at the two others to join them. A small crowd of men surrounded the women, commenting on their appearances and shouting obscenities. One of the men even jokingly asked Nina to show her breasts and raise her skirt so he could see if it was worth his time to come and visit her. Such behavior would have been deemed offensive in Constance five years ago, and the perpetrator might have even been put in the stocks, but apparently the city council had looked the other way as moral standards slipped.

Marie attempted to shake off her fear at seeing Rupert by assessing the men to find someone who might prove a good customer. But the only one who looked like he might have more than six shillings in his purse seemed repulsive, though he didn't really look dirty.

Instead, he was a strong-looking middle-aged man with the face of a peasant but dressed like a courtier in fashionable, tight green trousers, a richly embroidered fur-trimmed jacket, and a round fur-lined cap. His right eyelid hung down, but he was carefully examining the arriving harlots with his left eye as if they were mares at a horse market. He smacked his lips when he saw Nina, but when he caught sight of Marie, the lecherous look on his face became downright possessive. Marie turned her shoulder to show she was not interested, but out of the corner of her eye she could see he was looking her over as if she were stark naked. Knowing that the man would be among her first customers, she could only hope that he would either be turned away by her prices or that he'd be a pleasant lover despite his coarse appearance and arrogant behavior.

The man eagerly approached her, rudely shoving aside the two young men who had stepped in front of him. Just then, a heavily made-up black-haired woman wearing a flamboyant hat appeared behind him and tapped him on the shoulder. Turning around, he stepped back with a polite but somewhat derisive expression. He looked angry at being disturbed, which made the woman erupt in such hearty laughter that her quivering breasts looked like they were going to burst through the indecently low neckline of her dress. As the woman walked up to Jobst and greeted him with a casual wave, Marie couldn't help noticing the bright yellow ribbon knotted around her belt.

"I'm Madeleine from Angers, my dears," she said, "and I welcome you to Constance. My friends and I have been eagerly anticipating your visit. There are so many powerful men gathered together here that we can hardly handle the business. But though we are happy to get reinforcements, we don't want you to drive down our prices. Some people think we're too expensive"—she cast a derisive glance at the man with the drooping eyelid—"but the demand determines the price. Along with an impressive number of worldly nobles, many monks and prelates are staying in the city now, and they all seem eager to enjoy our services."

Marie and her companions were taken aback at the prostitute's friendly greeting, but the dark circles under her eyes implied that she'd used her bed for sleeping only rarely over the previous weeks, which was no surprise given the prices she mentioned. The women squealed gleefully and rubbed their hands together in excitement when they heard the prices they could ask.

"I'm anxious to find out what a loaf of bread or a mug of wine costs," Marie could hear Hiltrud mumbling beside her, and she agreed. With so many people here, supplies had to be brought in from far away, and that drove prices up. But if the customers would pay as much as Madeleine had said, they would earn good money anyway. Perhaps most startling to Marie, however, was that Madeleine's dress had no yellow ribbons. Only a thin yellow braid decorating her neckline and the small bit of cloth tied around her belt indicated her profession.

Marie turned away from the woman. It was part of a harlot's job to undress for a well-paying customer, but she couldn't bring herself to run around with almost completely exposed breasts.

Meanwhile, Jobst paid no attention to Madeleine, but instead distributed the women among the local brothel owners, doing his best to placate the squabbling men and keep them from fighting over the women. Nina and Helma were taken by a townsperson

Marie recognized. She didn't know his name, as he hadn't frequented her father's house, but she'd seen him address her father in an almost-servile manner when they'd met on the street.

The brothel owner who had already acquired Nina and Helma seized Marie by the arm possessively and snapped at Jobst. "What about these last three women?"

Jobst made a sour face. "They want to work on their own."

Hiltrud, Kordula, and Marie were in fact the only ones left. Annoyed, Marie shook herself out of the brothel owner's grip and tapped Jobst on the shoulder. She could tell that he still hoped to persuade them to join a bordello, as he stood to receive money not only from the bordello owners but also a bounty from the city council. Marie had often heard from women working in the bordellos that they had to stay and repay the bordello's investment in them as well as the cost for a bed and other expenses.

"How about our little house?" she asked Jobst for the second time.

"You won't have any luck with that," the bordello owner called out. "Here in Constance there isn't enough room anymore to house a cat, much less three whores."

Kordula placed her hands on her hips and looked at Jobst threateningly. "You'd better get the house for us. After all, you've already received your broker's commission and three months' advance rent."

"The guy cheated you, girls. Have him give you back the money and come with me." The bordello owner harangued Kordula and Hiltrud, but the two weren't listening. Instead, they looked questioningly at Marie, since most of the money was hers. She laid her hand on Jobst's shoulder. "The house you rented for us is over by Saint Peter's, isn't it?"

Jobst nodded grimly. "Yes, but who knows if it's still available."

"Then you'll have to throw out the people who've already moved in," she replied with a menacing smile.

To Marie's surprise, the nobleman with the drooping eyelid came to their defense. "If that's what you promised these women and took money for it, then you've got to turn the house over to them."

Marie sighed softly. She'd probably have to sleep with this man, no matter what he paid. When Madeleine also spoke up for them, Jobst hung his head and gave in.

"Very well! Come along then, for God's sake." Irritated, he started walking away. The three harlots, along with Madeleine and the nobleman, all followed close behind.

Passing by the bridge that led over to the island monastery, Marie felt a knot in her stomach. Five years ago, she had stood there before a judge, listening in disbelief as her fiancé brought false charges against her. For a moment she considered simply hiring someone to murder Rupert. Then she wouldn't have to be there herself, and she could leave the city just as inconspicuously as she had come. But then all of her efforts and the risks she had taken to get Jodokus's documents would be in vain. Since they had almost arrived at their rental house, she decided to put off any decisions until later.

The building was no larger than a farmer's cottage, but a gable window suggested the attic might be also livable. Like some of the nearby houses, it must have been built within the last five years, but it already seemed shabby and neglected. Its windows were so small, you could barely put your head out of them, and their pigs' bladder coverings were full of holes. The thatched roof still appeared in good shape, though, and the door was solid enough to offer some degree of protection against intruders.

Standing in the doorway, Marie glanced at the view across the road. The former goat pasture was now covered with tents, primitive huts, and houses, some still under construction; beyond that she could see the brick tower farther down the Rhine. Her heart began to race at the sight, and she realized that every time she stepped out that door she would be reminded of the day her life had been destroyed. She almost wanted to change her mind and ask Jobst for a bordello room, but then she scolded herself for being so foolish. The sight of that massive tower was no worse than the yellow ribbons on her dress that reminded her daily of her disgrace and the humiliation and pain that followed. She looked over toward Saint Peter's as if the church could give her the strength, reason, and inner peace that she would need in the coming days.

Upon entering the house, Marie saw that some fifteen monks were sharing the two ground-floor rooms, while a knight and his two servants were using the small attic space. Hiltrud peeked into one of rooms and shuddered. Clearly, the monks who had been living there were more concerned about caring for their souls than for their surroundings.

When Jobst told them all to leave, they cursed and threatened to hurt him. Before the quarrel could escalate further, the droopy-eyed nobleman intervened and gruffly told the knight to look for another place to stay. To Marie's amazement, the knight immediately complied.

While the lower-ranked monks and the knight's servants carried out their belongings, the knight and the higher-ranking brothers clearly intended to have the three women sweeten their departure. The knight expressed specific interest in Marie, but the nobleman wrapped his arm around her, pulled her to him, and glared at his rival with one open eye. Sighing, the knight shrugged his shoulders and turned to Kordula, who gave Madeleine a questioning glance, since she didn't know what to do.

The spokeswoman for the harlots nodded. "Since the gentlemen were so obliging, you should show them your gratitude. That holds true for you, as well, Marie. After all, Wolkenstein came to the aid of you and your companions."

The name Wolkenstein didn't mean anything to Marie, but the knight told her she was fortunate to have met such an excellent man. According to him, Wolkenstein was a favored liegeman of the kaiser as well as a renowned singer and poet, and she had to thank God for becoming acquainted with such a famous man.

Interrupting the knight with a few kind words, Marie thought that she'd thank God if Wolkenstein didn't turn out to be a crude bungler in bed. As Hiltrud and Kordula disappeared with their customers into the rooms on the ground floor, one of which also served as a kitchen, Marie led Wolkenstein up a ladder to the loft. The room was so small that only one person at a time could stand upright, and the filthy gable window barely let in any outside light. In the near darkness, Marie could only feel and smell the old straw sacks covering the floor.

None of that seemed to bother Oswald von Wolkenstein as his hands glided smoothly over her body and he removed her dress with experienced movements. He tore off the oilskin covering the window and laid Marie down so that the sunlight played over her head and breasts. Then he sat down beside her, raising his hanging eyelid with his fingers so he could admire her with both eyes.

"You are beautiful, woman. I don't think there's a single harlot in Constance who surpasses you in beauty. If I were a rich man, I'd put you up in my house and make you my mistress."

Marie stroked the gold embroidery on his jacket. "You have beautiful clothing for a poor man."

"Anyone who wants to amount to something at the kaiser's court can't cut corners on his clothing," Wolkenstein answered, laughing.

Pulling off his jacket and opening his shirt, he moved closer in order to fondle her. He ran his fingers along the contours of her body and began reciting short, tender verses praising her curving hips, firm rosy-tipped breasts, and the small, blond, curly triangle between her thighs. It seemed he was almost more enraptured by his own words than by the anticipation of possessing her. Finally, he undressed completely, then lay down on top of her slowly and with visible pleasure. When he was finished, he didn't stand up right away but remained lying there, pressed tightly against her while whispering precious verses about love in her ear.

In general, prostitutes weren't especially fond of men who clung to them like leeches after the act was finished, as it hindered potential earnings. But Marie wasn't interested just then in finding any more customers and instead enjoyed the verses praising her beauty. She wondered if married men used similar words to thank their wives for their nocturnal bliss.

VI.

Within two days, the women's busy hands transformed the little house into a comfortable home. Removing the filth and old reeds by the shovelful and burning the old straw sacks, they scoured the wood floor with soap and pumice until it gleamed.

After purchasing simple but solid bed frames, the women laid linen sacks filled with straw over them. Three chests with locks, a table, three stools, and new kitchen and dining utensils completed the household furnishings. Lastly, they decorated the walls with woolen hangings and spread fresh reeds mixed with fragrant flower petals and herbs on the floor. When they were finished, they looked at one another with satisfaction, congratulating themselves on their new home.

Marie sank down onto Kordula's bed. "Even the noblest gentlemen will feel so at home here that he'll want to come again."

Kordula's shoulders sank. "They'll have to. I'll no doubt have to double Madeleine's prices because of all the money I owe you."

Laughing dismissively, Marie waved her hand. "We could hardly have let you sleep on the floor."

Hiltrud understood Kordula better than Marie did. "We've already discussed it. You would have paid a higher fee to a bordello owner and couldn't make nearly as much money as you can working on your own. So you'll pay us back soon. Now, hear that? There's a customer at the door again."

To Kordula's great disappointment, the visitor was Oswald von Wolkenstein, who immediately led Marie to her attic room, paying her price with a sigh. Once again, he remained lying beside her after he was pleasured, reciting verses that caricatured Constance high society as well as council participants. He seemed happy to have found an attentive audience for his sarcasm, for many a harmless verse had offended listeners in the Imperial Court.

Shamelessly encouraging him, Marie listened to him and let him play with her body, as she thought she might be able to use what he knew. Indeed, he seemed to know everything and everyone, and she quickly learned many council participants' names and political opinions, as well as the fact that the knight Dietmar von Arnstein and his wife were expected soon.

A number of other highly ranked people also hadn't arrived yet, including those coming from Spain. Apparently, Wolkenstein was infuriated because nobles on the Iberian Peninsula refused to recognize the council's right to pass judgment on Pope Benedict XIII, whom they supported. If Kaiser Sigismund failed to win the support of the Spaniards, there would be a division in Christianity. Marie wasn't especially interested in the outcome of the kaiser's plans, but she proved such good company that Oswald von Wolkenstein called on her every day.

Finally, Oswald told her he had to leave Constance the next day, as the kaiser had given him the honorable task of traveling to Spain and Portugal with messages for those rulers. He said a mournful good-bye to Marie, but she was glad because he was becoming tiresome. Bidding him farewell like a tender, loving mistress, she uttered a big sigh of relief only after he'd left the house.

The following morning, Marie decided to visit the quarter where her father's house stood. Fearful of being recognized, she had avoided going into the city before then except for trips to the market. Even when she had met people she knew in the marketplace, no one had given her a second glance, as if her yellow ribbons had cast a magical cloak of invisibility over her. Just the same, she tucked her hair under a scarf before entering the narrow street leading from the Ziegelgraben to the cathedral.

Despite the early-morning hour, large groups of mercenaries and other loiterers were hanging around. Though some yelled obscenities at Marie from a distance, not even the drunks got too close. The yellow ribbons afforded her a degree of protection that honorable women and girls did not have, since a man who pestered or molested a harlot would find the doors and tents of all the other prostitutes closed to him. Even though the harlots came from different countries and were often fierce competitors, here in Constance, they stuck together.

As Marie strolled down the lane where she had once lived, she almost walked right by her family's home. Totally rebuilt with a pretentious façade, where there used to be a courtyard with sheds and outbuildings, the new structure several stories tall that Rupert had erected didn't seem quite finished. Nevertheless, servants were entering and leaving the building, and armed guards stood at the entrance. She guessed that was the building where Wolkenstein had told her that Rupert was housing his half brother, Konrad von Keilburg, as well as other high-ranking dignitaries and their retinues.

Not wanting to attract attention, Marie quickly moved on, struggling with tears at the sight of the house. Up until then, she at least had her memory of home, a place to which she could return in her daydreams, and now this, too, was taken from her. She squared her shoulders and was upset at herself for even coming.

Suddenly, Mombert Flühi's house appeared in front of her, and she realized she'd instinctively taken the turn into Hundsgasse Lane where she'd often gone as a child to visit her uncle and play with little Hedwig. She wondered how they were and for a moment considered going up to the front door. Then she laughed at herself. The door would probably be opened by a servant or her uncle's wife who would stare at her yellow ribbons, then curse her and send her on her way before she could defend herself. Her eyes welled up with tears again, and she was annoyed at her self-pity.

She fled quickly to the next lane, not paying attention to where she was going. Bumping into a man, she tripped and would have fallen if he hadn't caught her and pulled her up onto her feet.

Before her stood a man in a palatine guard's uniform. Startled, Marie knew it was best not to tangle with council guards. "Pardon me, sir. It was unintentional," she cried, reaching for the scarf that had slipped off her head.

Waving her off with a friendly smile, he was about to keep walking, but then grasped her arm, pushed her scarf back again, and looked at her closely. His eyes widened with surprise. "Marie? By all the saints, I thought you were dead!"

Marie looked at him and swallowed hard. Though he had changed a lot in the last five years, she recognized him at once." Michel? Oh my God!"

She was so ashamed to be facing her childhood friend dressed as a disgraced prostitute that she wanted nothing more than to be swallowed up by the earth. She tried to pull away and run off, but he took her in both arms, drew her to him, and spun her around, laughing.

"Marie, what a joy to see you. I was so worried about you. My God, how happy Mombert is going to be. Come, we'll go and see him right away."

Putting her down, he tugged at her hands, but she struggled to break away, shaking her head violently. "No! My uncle doesn't need to know I'm still alive, and you should forget me as well. The Marie you knew is dead."

Michel stared at her, baffled. "What do you mean? Why would you say such a thing?"

"Just look at me!" she hissed, holding one of her yellow ribbons under his nose. "This is the reason, don't you understand?"

"That won't bother your uncle. He'll be happy you're still alive and will surely want to help you."

"No thanks, I don't need any help. After all, I've been banned from Constance for life and only allowed to enter the city as a whore invited to serve the noble gentlemen." Marie took a deep breath and glared at Michel, ready for a fight. "Do you think I'd want to have people pointing their fingers at me and saying they'd always known I was nothing but scum?"

Michel thought it over, shaking his head and stroking her cheek to comfort her. "But it wasn't because of something you did."

"But that isn't what it says in the Constance court records. People here think I'm a hussy who'd bed anyone, even the murderer Utz." That last part had slipped out unbidden.

Michel squinted. "Utz, the wagon driver, a murderer?" It sounded a bit like a reproach, as if he didn't quite believe her, as if he thought she was just trying to say the worst thing she could about the man who'd accused her.

When a passerby stared at them, he took her by the shoulders and pushed her against a wall as if he were flirting with her. "Don't you have a little room where we can make ourselves comfortable?"

"Where you can bed me, you mean," Marie shot back. "You can put that out of your mind right now."

Michel held her at arm's length. "I don't think I should. You're really the prettiest girl I've ever seen."

"I don't just sleep with anyone!" Marie tried to pull away from him, but Michel wouldn't let go."

"Don't act like that," he replied, with a broad smile. "Can't you see that people are staring at us? Take me to your room, or I'll go straight to Mombert and tell him about our meeting."

Marie turned up her nose and stuck out her chin, trying to look as disdainful as possible. "How disgusting! You've turned into a wretched extortionist, running around in an officer's uniform of the palatine guards! Very well, you can come along with me, but a block of wood would show you more tenderness than I will."

Michel gave her a gentle slap across her rear. "I don't believe that. I'm usually said to be a good lover."

Since he wouldn't release her, Marie led him to the house in the Ziegelgraben. Looking it over, he glanced into the downstairs room, then let Marie lead him up to her loft. After examining the furnishings, he nodded with satisfaction. "I like it here. I think I'll stop by often."

"Just who do you think you are? You won't be welcome here." Marie wanted to throw him out, but his threat to tell her uncle held her back.

Inwardly she was writhing in frustration. Didn't Michel understand she'd left her past behind and that his presence now only ripped open the wounds in her soul? Did he just want to demonstrate how he was now of higher social standing, and that she was just something he could buy? She couldn't possibly have offended him that much before.

Growing up, she'd really liked Michel and remembered how sad she'd been when her father forbade her to wander with him through the fields. Wina had kept her in the house for weeks afterward, telling her that being seen with such a boy would damage her reputation and harm her marriage prospects. She'd never been able to tell him why she hadn't played with him again, and now it was too late.

She'd have to shake him off soon, since it was imperative that neither he nor her relatives stand in the way of her revenge. She briefly wondered if he could find her a hired assassin, but one look at his face made her reject that thought. Michel was still the same honorable lad as before, and if she let him in on her plans, he might stand in her way and try to protect her from herself.

Without hesitating, she pulled her dress over her head and lay down on the bed. "Hurry up. I don't have forever."

Michel had actually only wanted to talk with Marie and learn what had happened in the last five years, but he couldn't resist her nakedness, undressing and lying down alongside her. To his disappointment, she withdrew from his tender touch like a snail into its shell, clenching her fists. Annoyed, he knew that she had certainly slept with more men than there were in the entire army of palatine guards. Why was she so unwilling to sleep with him?

As a teenager, he had dreamed of her at night and was willing to do whatever it took to make her his wife. But she was the daughter of an important Constance businessman, and he didn't stand a chance. After her banishment, he had hoped to make his dream a reality, and he looked for her wherever he went. But after searching for three years, he had gotten discouraged and finally gave up, rarely thinking of her anymore. It wasn't until he met Hedwig that he remembered her, and now she was lying under him, available at long last as his heart desired. Nevertheless—or perhaps for just that reason—he didn't enjoy himself.

Since she completely ignored him, he slid down from her almost before he had finished. She seemed to expect him to get up, dress, and go, but he wasn't about to do her that favor.

He lay down next to her, pulling her close to feel the warmth of her body.

"That wasn't nice of you, Marie. After all, we're old friends."

"I kept still, as is proper for a whore. What more do you want?"

Michel realized he hadn't gone about this correctly. He should have first earned her affection, building on their former friendship, before sleeping with her. But instead, it had seemed like he had simply been motivated by desire, like any other paying customer. He was determined to redeem himself, and he started by complimenting her.

"You're even more beautiful than I remember. Your cousin Hedwig bears a resemblance, but she can't hold a candle to you."

Shrugging, Marie rolled her eyes at his cheap flattery. "You can't compare a whore with a decent daughter of the middle class. A moral young woman's purity and innocence are what give her true charm."

Michel sat up, looked at Marie's Madonna-like face, and shook with laughter. "Tell me, when's the last time you looked at yourself in the mirror? Most middle-class girls would envy you for your appearance. By God, you are the very embodiment of virginity! And you, as much as anyone, would have to know that most men are not interested in moral and—please excuse me for saying so—boring women."

"They are for their conjugal bed, because they have people like me for their pleasure."

Putting his hand on her shoulder, Michel became serious. "Could we please talk to each other like reasonable people? I'd really like to know what actually happened. Mombert suggested that you had been horribly wronged, but he avoided my questions when I asked, just saying we should leave the dead in peace. I think he was afraid I would cause him more difficulties. All I know is that you were whipped in the market square and driven out of town. I left Constance that same day to try to save you. Don't you think I have a right to know the truth?"

For a minute, Marie wondered if she should tell him everything. It would be nice to confide in an old friend who might empathize more than Hiltrud, who saw everything from the pessimistic viewpoint of someone sold into prostitution as a child. Then Marie remembered how he had coerced her in order to sleep with her, and she shook her head.

"It's not my fault that you panicked and came running after me. Go to hell, boy, and leave me alone."

"You're still the same stubborn girl you were as a child, when you stopped talking to me because I wouldn't pick cherries from trees that didn't belong to us. Don't you understand that I only mean well?"

Marie bared her teeth. "If you mean well, give me the eight shillings that my other clients think I'm worth."

Moving away from her, Michel stood up and reached for his clothing. "I had hoped to find an old friend but met only a greedy harlot." No sooner were the words out of his mouth than he regretted them.

Sitting cross-legged on the bed, Marie held out her hand. Desperately wanting to punish her for her scornful look, but at the same time wishing only to kneel down in front of her and ask for forgiveness, he did exactly the wrong thing again. Untying his purse, he took out eight shillings and threw them on the bed. "Here's your pay, even though you weren't worth that much."

Marie picked up his helmet and hurled it at him. Catching it before it could do any harm to him or anything else, he grabbed the rest of his uniform and fled naked down the ladder, carrying all his things.

Fortunately for him, Marie remained sitting on her bed, but a string of curses followed him as he dressed and left the house. She felt nothing but contempt for the man who ran from her like a scared rabbit, but she wept bitterly over the loss of a childhood friend who had comforted her when she was sad and been her knight in shining armor on their innocent expeditions together.

VII.

For the next two days, Marie looked like she was a million miles away, and her friends had to repeat their questions several times before she would answer. She was friendlier than usual with her clients, however, and had plenty of business, which also helped her housemates. Though everything seemed fine on the face of it, Hiltrud noticed that even the lure of finding fried sausages wasn't enough to persuade Marie to go into town. Hiltrud wondered what might have happened, as Marie always enjoyed strolling through the market and had plenty of money to spend on good food. But Hiltrud was familiar with Marie's grim expressions, and she avoided asking her friend too many questions. Hiltrud could only hope that her mood would slowly improve. So far, not even visits from other harlots seemed to tear Marie away from her secret worries.

Their most frequent visitor was Madeleine, who would pop in for a chat, passing along the latest gossip. Usually complaining about their bordello owner, Nina and Helma also stopped by often. They earned plenty of money, but the owner took most of their pay for room and board, and they said how much they wished they had moved into the little house with Hiltrud, Marie, and Kordula. Though the rent on the cottage was high, it would be a lot better than their current situation, where the owner was starting to rudely demand that the women pay him three additional shillings if they turned away a customer.

Though Marie suspected the two women were exaggerating their claims, Madeleine told her that the women's complaints were justified. As an official nobleman's mistress, the French woman lived in a room he had rented for her in a Constance home, but she had no intention of staying faithful to her patron, working by the hour in a bordello and sharing a room there with two other women who likewise had steady lovers.

On this particular afternoon, a few other prostitutes were visiting the little house. Marie was warning Madeleine that her double life could end badly depending on a deceived nobleman's temperament, but Madeleine just laughed. "Bah, why should I sit around and wait until he deigns to come to me? I'm too good for that. Moreover, my lord does not make love in the usual way." Puckering her lips, she winked conspiratorially at the other women.

Noticing the frown on Marie's face, Madeleine told her she was being a prude, and then talked at great length about the sexual preferences of all the other noblemen whose mistress she had been. It did seem, however, that her present suitor kept her not so much because she was willing to do anything he asked, but rather so he could converse with her in their shared native language. In any event, he was very generous, providing Madeleine with clothing and jewelry that only rich burghers and noblewomen could afford.

Kordula sighed longingly. "I'd be happy just to have a nobleman who would regularly keep me for an entire evening. That wouldn't be so demanding, and he might even give me a gift every so often."

Nodding, Helma agreed. "I'd like that, too. But we should be happy we still have any customers at all. Many noblemen, especially the clergy, don't bother with us but just chase after local middle-class girls."

"The monks and priests constantly talk about the dangers of fornication and lust, but it's them, of all people, who prey on innocent girls." Madeleine sounded irate, and two other prostitutes chimed in.

"It's not just the middle-class girls who keep the men away from us," the older of them said. "Many local maids would rather lie under horny old goats than do their housework, spreading their legs for two or three Hallers and ruining our prices."

"What can you do about it? The men don't have as much money to throw around as they did in their first few weeks here." Hiltrud shrugged dismissively but couldn't completely hide her worry. "But you're right. Recently the so-called honorable women have been behaving even worse than the penny whores. If this continues, Constance will just be one big brothel by the council's end, and we'll go hungry because local women and maids will have taken our customers away."

The younger prostitute nodded. "I also wonder what's going to happen when the council is over. When all the wanton maids are driven out of town and have to sell themselves at fairs outside town, there'll be more whores than customers there as well."

Kordula stood up and spat angrily into the fire. "To hell with all these honorable women who think they're so much better than us but sleep with every man who so much as looks their way. Now, ladies, it's time to go to work again."

After the women had left, Marie stood in the doorway thinking, to the approval of some lecherous onlookers. Though the other prostitutes' frequent visits were sometimes annoying, it was through those visits that Marie learned what was happening in the city.

In the brothels, every conversation was overheard, but in Marie's nest, as she called the little house, women could swap information about money-grubbing bordello owners and merchants who drove their prices sky-high, exchanging advice on how to deal with them.

Conversations like these always reminded Marie of Hiltrud's sage words—that prostitutes might be weak, but they weren't defenseless. Many a brothel owner was surprised when his girls quietly moved on to other bordellos, and some merchants lost prostitutes' business when former customers switched to their toughest competitors.

As a result, even though Marie was humble and didn't crave attention, her thorough knowledge of the city and its inhabitants made her a much sought-after adviser for the others. In addition, as Marie became more popular with customers, she felt besieged and had to turn some clients away—an insignificant loss, however, as the other whores thanked her with small amounts of money. Hiltrud joked that Marie would soon be earning more money from other women than from her customers, and Marie laughed, but it set her to thinking.

Meanwhile, in her digging for information about Counselor Rupert, Marie had learned that the repugnant abbot she met on the boat to Constance had since molested a girl who looked just like her. Gradually, she figured out it had to be her cousin Hedwig. Unfortunately, the young girl was also being pursued by another undesirable man, the young nobleman Steinzell, whom Marie remembered from Arnstein.

She considered visiting her uncle and pleading with him to take her cousin away from Constance, but Marie knew that would put her in too precarious a position. Soon word would get out that she was still alive, and Rupert would be one of the first to find out, since he had spun his web throughout the city. Then the counselor or Utz would discover that she was the harlot to whom Jodokus had given his documents—and her fate would be sealed.

Irritated by her cowardice and indecision, she still hadn't taken action against her enemy. When she had been wandering far away from her hometown, she'd considered numerous plans, but here in

Constance, none of them seemed practical. Thus she went about her daily activities, hoping fate would give her the means to fashion a noose with which to hang her former fiancé.

It was now four mornings after her meeting with Michel, and Marie's nest was quiet. She'd just finished a conversation with two young, still-inexperienced prostitutes who had come to her with some medical concerns, and Marie was brooding in the doorway and watching people go by. Suddenly she froze, spotting a man turning the corner. He was decked out in full armor and a helmet as if on his way to a military parade. Immediately recognizing him, she didn't even have to see the coat of arms with the two palatine lions on his chest. Catching her eye, he waved cheerfully and was soon standing in front of her.

"Hello, Marie! Nice to see you. I need a little tussle between the sheets. Wasn't your price eight shillings? Here they are, along with a couple extra, so that you'll make it especially nice for me this time."

He sounded so bright and sunny that Marie wanted to slap him in the face. Folding her arms across her chest and jutting her chin forward, she replied coldly, "Sorry, I don't just let everyone into my bed."

Hiltrud stuck her head out the door. "Marie, what are you saying? The gentleman is a captain of the guards, and it's not smart to quarrel with these people."

"Do you hear that, girl?" Michel said, laughing. "You won't be sorry, as I pay good money."

She wanted to scratch his eyes out, heap scorn on him, and send him packing, but she also had to be considerate of Hiltrud and Kordula. There was always the risk that he'd send his soldiers to their house if she made him too mad, and nobody would come to their aid if his men went on a rampage there.

"Very well, come along upstairs with me," she said in an unfriendly tone, and began climbing up the ladder in front of him.

He followed her so closely, she could feel his chest pressing up against her. Once upstairs, he took his time undressing, putting his things down out of her reach with a provocative smile. She lay down naked on top of the bed and acted completely disinterested in what he was going to do next.

Leaning over her, Michel tried to force her to look at him, but she turned away with such an indifferent expression that he was annoyed at himself for returning. He should have known better, as she had clearly indicated the first time how much she despised him. At that time he had left with the firm intention of never seeing her again, but his later visits to Mombert Flühi had changed his mind.

He had dined with the cooper several times now, flirting with Hedwig in hopes she could help him forget Marie. But every movement she made, every facial expression she had, and every word she spoke made him realize how much more beautiful, intelligent, and desirable her cousin was. That morning he hadn't been able to stand it anymore and set out on his way to the Ziegelgraben. Dressing up in his finery, he wanted to impress her and show her how important he had become. "Look at me," he wanted to say. "Even a knight is hardly better than I am." But she wouldn't even glance his way.

As he sighed with resignation, his eyes wandered admiringly over her flawless body. He had to figure out how to win her back. Staring at the ceiling of the narrow but nicely decorated attic room, he suddenly had an idea.

"What would you say, Marie, if I made you my mistress and rented a larger room for you where we both could live? Then you'd finally have peace and quiet from the filthy old goats that come beating at your door."

"I hardly believe you have enough money to support me. I'm a very expensive whore." She tried to sound facetious. She was in fact furious, assuming that because she had rejected him, he now wanted to humiliate her by buying her outright and keeping her for himself.

"I'm not a poor man," Michel assured her with naive pride.

"You'd have to spend more than twice what I earn in a day, plus pay for my clothes and the laundry. Not even a knight with a hundred bonded servants can afford that."

Michel lay down alongside her and placed his right hand gently on her belly. "You don't seem to know how much a captain of the guards makes. I've lived very modestly and have put together a small fortune."

"As anyone can see looking at your splendid armor and clothing," she replied in a mocking tone.

"So you like me." Michel grinned, pleased with himself, which irritated Marie even more.

Trying to stay calm, she admitted to herself that it was indeed tempting to be at the service of only one man even if it did mean being his servant and his bedmate. But she didn't want to give this brash taverner's son the chance to puff out his chest every day, reminding her of her fall into disgrace and his own rise up the social ladder. "You're the last man in the world I'd give myself to," she wanted to shout in his face. Yet she couldn't risk antagonizing him, so instead, she tilted her head to the side and looked at him , raising an eyebrow.

"What does it mean to like you? Every rooster looks splendid in its bright feathers, but only after it's been plucked can you can see whether it's suitable for frying or only fit to make soup."

Michel burst out laughing. "What has become of the shy little Marie Schärer that I used to know? Your tongue has become as sharp as a sword."

"Through no fault of my own." With those few words, Michel suddenly understood much more about Marie's true feelings, and it was clear to him that he'd have to be very patient to win her over.

Sooner or later she'd realize that he wasn't just another customer but that he wanted to be her confidant and friend. But how, he wondered, could he prove to her that he didn't look at her simply as a body to be paid for, used, and forgotten, but rather as a woman worthy of being cherished?

VIII.

Mombert Flühi's journeyman Wilmar was once again at odds with God and the world. As if there weren't already enough problems with Abbot Hugo and Philipp von Steinzell, now fate had also washed this palatine captain onto Constance shores. Though Hedwig carefully avoided the two others, she was clearly pleased to welcome Michel Adler into the house.

Intimidated by the officer's presence, he was quite aware that Michel impressed Hedwig. This aggravated Wilmar to no end, as he loved the girl and hoped that she would someday return his affections.

As the third son of a Meersburg master cooper, Wilmar could become a master himself only if he married another master's daughter, since then his father-in-law would customarily help advance his career. Before the council meeting had overshadowed everything else in the city, Hedwig had shown a modest interest in him, and he had fallen passionately in love with her.

Now, however, Mombert and his daughter had quite different concerns and hardly paid any attention to Wilmar. Brooding so deeply he forgot to pay attention to his work, Wilmar suddenly saw that he'd ruined a stave he was about to insert into a barrel. He blamed that on Michel as well. Throwing the remains into the scrap pile, he went to pick up another stave. As he did so, he glanced at the apprentices and noticed that once again, Melcher was missing. Wilmar resolved to speak with his master about that rebellious youth who constantly skipped work, setting a bad example for the younger workers. While Wilmar was still wondering where Melcher might be, the door opened and the master entered.

Mombert noticed at once that the apprentice was missing. "Wilmar, where is Melcher?"

His barking made Wilmar cringe. "I don't know. Perhaps he's gone to the outhouse."

The two younger apprentices looked at each other, grinning. They were pleased to see the master so angry at Melcher, because if what Melcher told them was true, he wouldn't be coming back any time soon. Bragging to them that he had friends who offered him more money than what his father had paid for his apprentice fees, Melcher no longer took his cooper training seriously and mocked the younger ones for their willingness to learn.

Mombert glared at Wilmar. "So, you don't know? It's your job to keep an eye on the apprentices. If you let them fool around like this, I'll have to look for another journeyman."

Shocked, Wilmar jumped up. "I'll go get Melcher right away and bring him back, master."

Mombert shoved him back onto his seat. "So then two pair of hands will be missing, even though we have so much work we don't know what to do? No, you'll work longer in the shop tonight to make up for what Melcher skipped out on. Then when he returns, I'll give him a good thrashing." As he said this, Mombert placed his foot down on a large barrel and inserted the last few staves.

Meanwhile, Melcher was strolling through back streets and eating some cake. Looking around, he spotted Utz standing beneath a wine pavilion, and he grinned complacently.

The wagon driver stood up and approached him, cup in hand. "Greetings, Melcher. I expected to see you sooner."

"I couldn't get away from the shop as quickly as I wanted," the boy lied.

Utz smirked at the sight of the half-eaten piece of cake in Melcher's sticky hands. "If you loll around like this when you work for a nobleman, he'll kick you out soon enough. Maybe I should look for another helper."

Melcher quickly gulped down the last bite of cake and wiped his hands on the seat of his pants. Putting his arm around Melcher's shoulder, Utz leaned down to him. "Did Steinzell go to see his friends?"

"Yes, and he told his servant he wouldn't be back before nightfall. Knowing him, he won't return until midnight."

"Good. Then we'll do it tonight. Do you know your part?"

Melcher gazed admiringly at the wagon driver. "Oh yes. I'll do everything exactly as you said."

"I know you will." Utz grinned, patted the youth on the cheek, and handed him the half-full cup of wine. "Come, lad, and drink. You richly deserve it."

IX.

While Melcher was drinking the rest of Utz's wine, Philipp von Steinzell was also tightly holding a cup. Sitting in the lodging occupied by the knight Leonhard von Sterzen, he was listening to the men who were trying to draw up a peace agreement between their feudal lord Friedrich von Habsburg and Kaiser Sigismund. Philip was bored by all the political talk. These meetings were only bearable for him because Sterzen's tavern served an excellent wine. Philipp emptied his cup and waved a servant over to fill it again.

Talks continued far into the night, and Philipp von Steinzell drank many more mugs of wine so that he could endure the discussions. When the men finally got up to leave, Philipp was so drunk, he could barely stand. Only his strong will drove him, limping, toward the door, where a servant handed him a torch to light his way home. The cold air pierced his coat and his legs nearly gave way under him, but the habits of many nights of carousing kept him going and led him to the cooper's house.

Finding the door to the courtyard ajar, the young nobleman staggered in contentedly, threw the torch in a corner, and emptied his bladder of some of the wine against the wall of the house. The apprentice Melcher seemed to have expected him, for he carefully opened the front door and, holding a hooded lantern, lit his path inside. As Philipp staggered toward him, the boy placed the hood back over the lantern. Philipp could sense a shadowy figure next to him, but before he could react, a hand clamped over his mouth, muffling his cry. At the same time, something bored into his chest, and a searing pain shot through his alcohol-clouded consciousness. Then he expired like a snuffed-out candle.

"The fellow won't bother you again," Utz whispered to Melcher. "Now hurry, close the door, and put the hood back over the lantern so we can carry him into the house."

In the slit of light that the lantern cast over the corpse, Utz checked where he had stabbed the man. "Right in the heart. Nobody could do better."

Wrapping the young nobleman in a blanket he'd brought along, Utz grabbed him under the shoulders and lifted him up. Melcher held the lantern handle between his teeth and carried the dead man's legs. After Utz had removed a few bloody drips from the ground, they dragged the body into the house. It would have been impossible to carry Steinzell up to his room, since the creaking stairs would have awakened the people sleeping in the house, so Utz laid the nobleman on the bottom step, removed the blanket, and pulled the dagger out of the wound. A torrent of blood shot out and ran across the floor. Utz nodded contentedly, as now it looked like the nobleman had been stabbed at the foot of the stairs.

He stretched out his hand. "Where's Flühi's knife?"

Melcher tugged a thin, well-sharpened knife with a large handle from his belt. "It wasn't easy to snatch it without being noticed," he said, hoping for a compliment.

Utz patted him on the shoulder, then thrust Master Mombert's knife into the corpse's wound. "Done. After I leave, close the doors in the courtyard and at the front of the house behind me, and go lie down in bed. When the guards come to question you, say you were sleeping all night and didn't hear a thing. Do you understand?"

When the apprentice didn't respond quickly enough, Utz pointed at the dead man. "Take a good look at him, Melcher. If you don't do exactly what I say, you'll soon look just like him."

Melcher understood that the wagon driver was deadly serious, and he was afraid for the first time. Though trembling, he still wasn't ready to let himself be intimidated. "You promised to find me a job with a nobleman. When will that be?"

Utz placed his hand on the apprentice's shoulder. "Tomorrow. After the murder has been discovered and Master Mombert is sitting in jail, go to the harbor and get on board Captain Hartbrecht's boat. He will take you to Lindau and hand you over to the caretaker of your new master."

Hearing a noise on the floor above them, Utz quickly blew out Melcher's lantern so that both of them were standing in the dark. Then he grabbed the boy and took him to the front door. "Be careful, and remember what I've told you," Utz warned the apprentice. Then he slipped silently away into the darkness.

X.

The corpse wasn't found until the next morning. Mombert Flühi stumbled over the body at daybreak, initially thinking that Philipp von Steinzell had fallen asleep drunk at the foot of the stairway. Just as he was about to call the young nobleman's servant, he discovered a dark spot on the floor, then saw the knife handle lodged in Philipp's chest. In his agitation, he didn't notice that the knife was his, but instead stepped back and shouted helplessly.

"Jesus, Mary, and Joseph, what a tragedy!"

His wife stuck her head out of the bedroom. "What's the trouble, Mombert?"

"It's the young nobleman Steinzell. He's dead." Mombert stepped aside so his wife could examine the body." There's a knife in his chest. Call Wilmar and tell him to run to the governor and report the crime."

Frieda Flühi nodded and rushed off in her huge, flowing nightshirt, speaking to the journeyman in her shrill voice. Moments later, Wilmar came dashing around the corner, staring at the dead man while he stuffed his shirt into his trousers.

"Is he really dead?" He didn't exactly sound sorry.

Mombert told him to hurry and at the same time wondered if he should move the corpse aside so the stairway was clear. But then he decided that the governor would want to see where the nobleman had died, and the master left everything untouched.

The sun was already rising when Wilmar returned with a representative of the royal governor. The man bowed slightly so as not to hit his helmet against the top of the doorway and walked over to Master Mombert.

"What's all that nonsense the boy is telling me about a murder?"

"The body is here." Mombert stepped aside and pointed at Philipp.

The man looked into the corpse's face. "Good God, that is indeed young Steinzell. Master Mombert, this is a serious matter. Do you know how it happened?"

Mombert shook his head, not knowing what to make of it. "I can only imagine that Philipp got into an argument with someone who stabbed him to death. He was probably going up to his room but collapsed here on the stairs."

As the cooper was explaining his assumptions, the official leaned down to examine the nobleman. "With a stab wound like this, the man wouldn't have gotten more than a few steps. The knife went straight into his heart, so he must have been stabbed right here."

"Impossible," Master Mombert exclaimed. "If there had been a fight in the hallway, my wife and I would have heard it. In addition, the murderer would not have been able to lock the door from the inside."

"Unless he stayed in the house," the official declared in a sinister voice.

Irritated, Mombert shook his fist. "That's ridiculous. Neither my assistants nor my apprentices would have been able to dispatch this man—he's as strong as an ox. And his own servant certainly didn't kill him."

"I didn't say that." Turning to Mombert, the official looked at him darkly. "You must admit there is something very strange here—a dead man who must have been murdered by someone still in the house this morning, as the door was locked."

"That would mean the murderer is still here." Mombert spun around to warn his wife and daughter to be careful. Just then, the door opened to the little cubicle where his oldest apprentice slept, and Melcher stepped out. He yawned several times, then saw the bailiff and stepped closer.

"What's happened here . . . ?" he asked, pointing to the corpse. "Master Mombert, isn't that your knife?"

Mombert Flühi stared wide-eyed at the weapon sticking out of the wound. It was in fact his knife with a staghorn handle set in silver.

"Is that right?" the official asked in a severe voice.

Mombert raised his arms helplessly. "Yes, that's the knife I use at dinner. It's normally kept on the board next to the kitchen door with the other silverware. The murderer must have taken it from there and used it in the crime."

The bailiff seemed to have reached the obvious conclusion, sneering as he stared at Mombert. "That's just as improbable as your nonsense about the nobleman being stabbed on the street, then being dragged to the house, since there isn't a drop of blood between here and there. Yet he bled like a stuck pig on the stairwell. And, yes, I forgot, before he died, he must have carefully locked the door."

Mombert spun around in shock. "You don't mean to imply I stabbed Philipp von Steinzell, do you?"

The official folded his arms. "Doesn't that seem like a logical determination? Plus, I've heard that you've cursed the nobleman and threatened him."

"Yes, I've had a few angry words with him because he wouldn't leave my daughter, Hedwig, alone," Mombert admitted reluctantly.

The official pointed to the knife in the victim's chest. "Last night it went beyond mere threats."

"By God, it wasn't me. I swear by all the saints." Mombert stepped back, horrified, and reached for his wife.

"It can't be true," she shouted at the bailiff. "My husband was lying next to me all night."

"And he didn't get up once to go to the outhouse? And you didn't close your eyes once all night? Go tell your lies to someone else, woman. As for you, Mombert Flühi, admit you stabbed the nobleman to protect your daughter from him, or you'll make things even harder for yourself. If the judge is lenient, he won't break you on the wheel while you're still alive, but he'll instead have you strangled first so you won't feel any pain."

Mombert Flühi panicked. "By God and all the saints, I swear I didn't kill him!"

"If you want to deny it, I can't stop you, but you'll have to confess everything when they torture you."

The official summoned his assistants and tried to grab Master Mombert, who let out a shriek and ran into the shop. Two more men had come in through the back door, and they seized him there.

"Now you've practically confirmed your guilt." It was clear that the official was happy to have solved the case so quickly. While the guards tied Mombert's hands behind his back and led him across the front yard and out onto the street like a calf on its way to slaughter, the cooper kept cursing, praying, and swearing his innocence. The official turned to Frieda Flühi again.

"I'll have the corpse picked up right away. In the meantime, you can pack up some things for your husband."

The official's words reminded Mombert that he was wearing nothing but his nightshirt. The shame of being led like that through the streets made him burst into tears.

XI.

After the official left, a deathly stillness pervaded the house. Frieda Flühi could barely stand up and had to lean against the wall. Hedwig, who had been hiding with Wina, came out of her room to ask what had happened. Frieda's voice failed her, and Wilmar told the girl about her father's arrest.

"Father never would have killed the nobleman," Hedwig whispered tearfully.

"Of course it wasn't him. I would have noticed if he got out of bed." Frieda was sobbing so hard that it was almost impossible to understand her. She clung to her daughter, wailing, and Wina wrung her hands, lamenting the ill fortune now visited also on Matthis Schärer's brother-in-law. Wilmar suddenly remembered the nobleman's servant and hoped he could blame him for the murder, but when he went upstairs and opened the door to the man's room, he found him lying on his straw sack and snoring. He had no blood on his hands, and his sour breath revealed that he had helped himself to his master's wine closet the day before. Wilmar was convinced the man couldn't be the killer, either.

Downstairs, a group of armed mercenaries appeared, and their leader, a brawny fellow wearing a brightly checkered outfit, stared brazenly at the mistress of the house.

"I'm looking for Frieda, Mombert's wife, and Hedwig, their daughter," he declared harshly.

"I am Frieda Flühi, and this is my daughter, Hedwig." She looked at the man, puzzled.

"Along with Mombert Flühi, you are both accused of the murder of the honorable nobleman Philipp von Steinzell, and I have been ordered to take you into custody."

Hedwig screamed and tried to hide behind her mother, but Frieda Flühi, as pale as chalk, leaned against the wall. "This has to be a bad joke."

Instead of answering, the leader beckoned to one of his men, who bound her hands and wrapped a robe around her waist with practiced moves.

"Where are you taking us?" Frieda asked.

"To the tower, as the dungeon is already full," the man quickly informed her.

Hedwig turned ashen and stared at her mother anxiously, but Frieda looked back with resignation. Frieda addressed the leader again.

"Couldn't you have given us some time to get dressed? Or do you mean to drag us through the streets in our nightgowns?"

The man looked as though he would just as soon take them naked, but he finally allowed Wina to wrap coats around the two women's shoulders. Then his servants shoved the mother and daughter out toward the street, leading them past a crowd of onlookers already gathered in front of the house.

The apprentices and maids had all run off right after their master was arrested, so only Wilmar and Wina remained behind. He found it impossible to talk to the old lady—she whined and prayed as if expecting heaven to open up and the Last Judgment to sweep down over the earth. Wandering helplessly through the shop, the journeyman was unable to process what had just happened. Could kind, gentle Hedwig really have conspired to murder Philipp? No, he knew with certainty that neither she nor her parents were capable of that.

At first, Wilmar was convinced it would all turn out to be a mistake, and he expected to see Mombert Flühi and the two women come back at any moment. While he waited, he sat down in the shop and, out of habit, started to make another barrel.

Then a thought occurred to him, making him break out in a cold sweat. Would the bailiffs view him as a coconspirator and come back to arrest him, too? As all citizens well knew, anyone caught in the wheels of justice could hardly expect mercy. Kicking the barrel hoop away, he streaked out of the house in a panic and didn't stop running until he saw the Augustine Gate in front of him. There, he leaned against a wall and tried to decide what to do.

In his mind, he could picture Hedwig, bound and sitting in the damp, dark dungeon of the tower, unable even to dry her own tears. He felt like a coward and a traitor. He loved Hedwig more than anything in the world, and yet he hadn't lifted a finger to help her.

A while back, his master had emotionally recounted how Marie, his niece, had likewise been locked in the tower five years before. The day after her arrest, the girl had sworn by the Virgin Mary she had been violated by three men during the night. Except for Master Mombert, no one had believed her, however, and so she was whipped and driven out of town. Upon first hearing the story, Wilmar couldn't imagine that a city bailiff would have anything to do with such a vile scheme, but now he was tormented by the possibility that Hedwig could be similarly attacked—and he didn't think that the men who had led Hedwig and her mother away looked any more trustworthy than the mercenary rabble roaming about the town and pestering women.

Wilmar wanted nothing more than to run through the Augustine Gate and keep going until he got to his father's house, where he could close the door behind him on all this. But he gave a contemptuous snort for his own faintheartedness, then started walking back through the city, unsure of what to do. If he wanted to help Hedwig, he'd have to think of something soon, but his head was as dry as an old wineskin.

XII.

After Rupert Splendidus checked to make sure that no one had entered the hallway and could overhear him, he closed the door and walked to the table where Konrad von Keilburg, his half brother, was having breakfast. Konrad was unrestrained in his love of good food and drink and as a young man had impressed his peers with his size and strength. Now that he was thirty-five years of age, however, his eyes had almost vanished behind huge fleshy folds, and his stomach bulged out so far, he could no longer see his feet. It was uncertain whether he could still swing a sword or carry a shield, and there wasn't a horse anywhere able to carry him. Rupert was careful not to underestimate his half brother, however. When Konrad became enraged, he was like an angry bear that wouldn't let go until his opponent lay dead at his feet.

Rupert greeted his brother with a friendly smile in which only an attentive observer could have detected a hint of mockery and condescension. "You can take special pleasure in your food today, for young Steinzell is dead and the cooper Mombert was accused of his murder."

Plunking his mug down on the table, Konrad laughed so hard that the seams of his jerkin threatened to burst. "No doubt another one of your little tricks, eh? You get the man out of the way for me and give Waldkron the girl that's he's been chasing. Good! Then that abbot can finally cease his lovesick whining. That is, if you really can manage to reduce this cooper's daughter to bondage. What do you think Waldkron will do to you if his little darling winds up on the scaffold? I'm just wondering if you'll take it too far someday and fall victim to one of your own schemes."

Rupert clenched his fists but otherwise managed to conceal the hatred raging inside him. Unlike their father, Heinrich, who had treated Rupert like a vassal but had respected him for his services, Konrad despised Rupert and mocked him every time they met.

"He won't do anything, because everything I do is successful. When Mombert Flühi is broken on the wheel, his daughter will be in the abbot's bed."

Konrad von Keilburg snorted. "I hope that's not just idle talk. Instead of worrying about this silly abbot, you should see to it that I get my hands on Degenhard von Steinzell. The simplest thing to do, of course, would be for me to split Degenhard's head open and seize his land."

"It will be a lot easier than that, dear brother. Now that Philipp is dead, Degenhard's daughter, Roswitha, is Degenhard's only heir. Have her married off to one of your vassals, and her father's possessions will fall into your lap like ripened fruit."

"Yes, I'll give the order today for the abduction of Roswitha von Steinzell. I only have to decide who should marry her." For a moment, Keilburg forgot the pork loin on his plate and thought hard.

The counselor knew that his brother would neither tolerate any opposition nor hesitate to mercilessly beat anyone who didn't agree with him, and he would therefore have to proceed as diplomatically as possible.

"I don't think that's a good idea. People might suspect you were behind the death of young Steinzell, and there are plenty of people close to the kaiser who are just waiting for a chance to throw a noose around your neck. Wait until the alleged murderer of the nobleman has been condemned and executed. Then people will think you took advantage of a good opportunity when you take Steinzell's daughter."

"But what if this bastard Degenhard marries her off first? Then I'll look foolish."

"It's possible he'll betroth her, but the wedding certainly wouldn't take place before the mourning period is over, and it would be easy to prevent. I don't think anyone will take the girl if someone else has already made her pregnant."

Roaring with mirth, Konrad looked at his brother with a mischievous grin. "Would you like to take that on yourself? For all I care, you can have Roswitha. Since you managed to get our old man to recognize you as a legitimate son before he died, you are her equal. Sir Rupert von Steinzell! Don't you like the sound of that?"

Rupert's smile broadened, and a strange glaze came over his eyes. "No, no. You can give Roswitha to one of your men. I prefer to live in the city and have no desire to live in a drafty castle at the edge of the Black Forest."

"As you will." Konrad von Keilburg's suggestion was not completely serious, and he was relieved when Rupert dismissed it. Rupert was useful to his brother as a dishonest counselor, but as a knight in a distant castle he would be an unwelcome competitor with plans only to expand his fiefdom. "In any case, I'm happy that the Tyrolean duke Friedrich has been declared an outlaw by the kaiser, as now his lands in the Black Forest and on the Rhine are free for anyone to attack. I think I'll be the first to take some of it."

"I'd advise you to exercise a bit of patience and not do anything rash that you will come to regret."

Konrad pounded his fist on the table so hard that his plate flew up and gravy splattered across the inlaid woodwork. "You're a damned coward, Rupert. If you want something, you've got to act."

Mulling over his brother's words, Rupert shook his head. "But you have to wait for the right moment, dear brother. Today the kaiser is angry at Duke Friedrich, but tomorrow things could change. The Habsburger has many friends and allies who will stand up for him, and Kaiser Sigismund can't afford to anger them all. He has to think about Albrecht von Österreich, the Tyrolean's cousin. I'm sure that Friedrich will cancel his decree in the next two months. All the duke will have to do then will be to promise not to recognize any pope not selected by the kaiser. If you start a war now over the Rhinelands, we'll soon have to face not just the duke, but his relatives and allies. You must be content with luring away some of his vassals and getting control of their castles, and as long as you do this legally, Friedrich can't do anything about it."

Konrad's expression darkened again. "Stop showing off how clever you are. In truth, you are as devious as a scorpion and as gutless as a rat. If you didn't have unprincipled scum to wield your daggers for you, you'd never have attempted your little trick with Philipp, as you don't have the courage to actually face your victims. It's clear that your mother was a worthless serf that people used and then forgot."

Count Konrad waited to see if Rupert would lash out at him. He would have liked nothing more than to slash him across his smooth face.

The counselor could see the malevolence in Konrad's eyes, and he withdrew to the door. "I'll leave you to your pork roast, brother, as I have some things to do." Bowing stiffly in farewell, he stepped out into the hallway.

Rupert was furious at his half brother's arrogance and crassness, but he was also amused. The man was much too gullible. Their father would have been amazed at the document by which he supposedly recognized his bastard son. After his death, all Rupert needed was a sheet of parchment, a clever hand, and the quickly copied seal of the old count in order to gain legitimate standing. Caught by surprise, Konrad had cursed at him, but he hadn't doubted the authenticity of the document.

To Rupert's relief, Konrad had not understood that with that document, the counselor had become his lawful heir; nor did he suspect the goal that Rupert had set for himself, or he would have killed him right there on the spot. That aim was nothing less than seizing his brother's castle and acquiring the title of count for himself. Rupert smiled. Judging from the way his brother behaved, Rupert would soon reach his goal.

His pleasant musing was interrupted by a violent pounding on the door he had installed at the bottom of the stairway to detract eavesdroppers and unwanted disturbances. Opening the door, he found himself staring at Abbot Hugo, whose face was purple with excitement.

"I must speak with you."

"Please come in," replied Rupert with an open, warm smile that he had rehearsed with great effort. Though it looked convincing, it was nothing but a practiced façade, like the one he used to destroy his opponents in court.

Hugo von Waldkron nervously followed the counselor into his office. "The cooper murdered Steinzell, just as you said he would. What about the girl?"

"As soon as Mombert Flühi is convicted, his daughter will be declared a serf and handed over to you."

"That could take months because of the case with Master Hus, but you promised to get me Mombert's daughter as soon as possible."

"I'll make sure the trial is quick, but if we don't do everything in an orderly fashion, we'll both have trouble. Until her father is declared guilty, the girl is considered a citizen of the city, and the council would put you on trial if you touched her."

The abbot seized Rupert and shook him. "I must have Hedwig at once. Do you think I rented the house in Maurach just to dream about her there? I'm dying of passion."

"If you're in dire straits, go find a maid or a whore, but don't bother me and my plans with your impatience. What does it matter if you have to wait for the girl another week or two? Before long, you can do with her as you wish, but for now, leave me alone. I'm busy." Rupert removed the abbot's hand from his jerkin, opened the door, and pointed down the stairs.

With a strained expression, Hugo von Waldkron descended the staircase, but then suddenly stopped by the front door. Smirking evilly, he ran across the courtyard to the inn, his robe fluttering around him. Entering his room, he closed the door behind him, rummaged about in his chest, and pulled out a long, carved wooden box. The table was soon covered with finely shaven leaves of parchment, a pen case, an inkpot, sealing wax, and various stamps. Picking up a leaf and smoothing it out, Hugo began to write. He poured fine sand over the parchment to dry the ink and dripped wax along the leaf's lower edge. Then he picked up one of the stamps, examined it carefully, and pressed it gently on the still-oozing wax. When he removed the stamp, he could see the imprint, *the Free Imperial City of Constance.*

Proofreading his document, he cursed Rupert for being such a fool. Why should he wait for the girl? This wasn't the first document he had falsified. Indeed, a large portion of his abbey's wealth had been acquired this way. The heirs of dead noblemen rarely questioned a transfer of property or villages as the price for heavenly salvation, and when they did, the courts quickly stepped in and

379

set them straight. The abbot assumed that Rupert must have also gained some of his success this way; after all, the counselor had once been his student and had helped Hugo alter the old abbot's testament in his favor.

Feeling like he was always a few steps ahead of everyone else, including his talented pupil, Rupert, the abbot rolled up the parchment, put it in a case, and left the room. His servant was sitting downstairs in the kitchen, flirting with one of Rupert's maids. The women were attractive enough, and as the abbot had learned from experience, not averse to being at their lord's service, but the thought of Hedwig stifled any longing he might have felt for these willing maids. Hedwig wasn't a great beauty like the blond harlot he had seen on one of his ferry trips. But whores were too fresh for him, and they didn't give themselves to him the way he wished, nor did they have the veneer of innocence he loved so much that made Hedwig Flühi stand out so clearly from all the other women in the city.

Becoming impatient, he heard his servant's voice in the kitchen and shouted, "Selmo, can't you see I need you?"

The man immediately jumped up and hurried toward him. Even though he wasn't a monk, he wore the robe of a Benedictine brother as his abbot ordered. Because of his dress, people treated him with greater respect and rarely asked questions when he was on an errand for his master.

"I'm going over to Maurach for a little while," the abbot declared after they'd left the house. "Follow me to the harbor, then go to Saint Peter's and pray there until it is dark. I don't want anyone to see you in the city before that. At nightfall, go to the tower, show the watchman there the document I'll give you, and have him hand the cooper's daughter over to you. But for God's sake don't forget to keep the document and bring it back with you."

The servant smiled knowingly. "Yes, master, I know. It's not the first time I've carried out an assignment for you. Shall I follow you with the girl or take her to Counselor Rupert's house?"

"Naturally you will bring the girl directly to me. And unless you want to feel my wrath, keep your hands off her."

"Oh, of course, master! I would never touch a woman intended for you," Selmo replied, not altogether truthfully. "But when you are through with her, can you pass her along to me?"

"Of course! After I tire of her, you can have her, but I think you'll have to be patient for a while."

Chuckling, the servant trotted off behind his master until they reached the harbor. Pointing to a small boat moored off to one side, the abbot looked at Selmo.

"The boat's owner has no objection to traveling across the lake at night and won't ask any prying questions. He'll be waiting for you at nightfall."

"Why don't you take the girl with you now?"

The abbot smacked him on the chest. "Don't pretend to be dumber than you are. The busybodies in the bars would start wagging their tongues if I took a young girl on a ship in broad daylight. At night all cats are gray, and if you pull your hood over your robe, nobody will recognize you. Oh, I almost forgot. Here's a bottle of poppy juice. Give it to the girl so she doesn't make a fuss. And just to be safe, take another monk's robe from the church to hide her from prying eyes."

Taking the bottle and document roll from the abbot, Selmo walked slowly toward Saint Peter's, as if lost in thought. Hugo von Waldkron, for his part, got on a boat bound for Meersburg, which was near the rented house in Maurach. A short time later, he was sitting with other passengers on a large crate, smiling gently, as was appropriate for a true servant of Christ.

XIII.

In the course of his aimless wanderings, Wilmar happened upon Hugo von Waldkron and his companion, and noticed that the abbot's strained expression of late had been replaced by a smug grin. Though he couldn't understand the men's whispered conversation, the abbot's gestures toward the tower were unmistakable. The journeyman's concerns for Hedwig grew when he noticed the abbot surreptitiously handing over parchment rolls and a small bottle to his servant. With a smirk, Selmo watched his master leave on the boat, repeatedly checking under his robe to make sure the parchment roll was still there.

Before setting out, the abbot's boat had to wait for a boat bound for Lindau to pass. Glancing at the second boat, Wilmar saw Melcher standing at the stern, staring at the city. Briefly wondering how Melcher had found enough money for the rather expensive trip, Wilmar noticed Selmo leaving, and he followed him without giving Melcher a second thought.

The servant looked up at the tower as he passed, and Wilmar was convinced that some vile deed would be carried out that day and that the victim would be Hedwig. There were few secrets in a city like Constance, and since it was common knowledge that Hugo von Waldkron had rented a house in a secluded part of Maurach, Wilmar drew the right conclusion.

In despair, he considered his options for freeing Hedwig from the clutches of the notorious abbot. If only he had the strength of the mythical Hercules, he could have torn down the tower and carried her away. But he was just a poor journeyman who'd lost his master, and he would be lucky if another cooper would even take him in after what had happened. Overwhelmed by both his and Hedwig's misfortune, and blinded by tears, he staggered on through the city.

Arriving at the Scotch Gate, he bumped into a group of palatine foot soldiers. Wilmar stood there, breathing heavily. Snapping him back to the present, away from the question of whether to end his miserable existence at once or kill the abbot first, he stared at the departing soldiers and couldn't help thinking of the dashing young captain who'd been his master's guest. Perhaps Michel could help save Hedwig, but if he did, then her heart and gratitude would belong to him.

Struggling with his emotions, Wilmar finally lowered his head in shame for even considering his own feelings above the welfare of the girl he loved. If he wanted to continue living and hold his head high, he'd have to do everything possible to help Hedwig, even if it meant pasting a fake smile on his face and having to watch, brokenhearted, as she found her happiness with another man.

"Please, sir, can you tell me where I can find your captain, Michel?"

"Either at the beautiful harlot's place on the Ziegelgraben or in Adler's Tavern on Katzgasse." Scratching his head, he mulled it over. "I think he was headed for the tavern."

"Thank you, sir." Bowing briefly, Wilmar ran as fast as he could to the Katzgasse. It was nearly noon, and the tavern was so full that people were standing outside having their soup and bread by the front door, mugs of wine set at their feet. Wilmar pushed his way through the packed crowd in the tavern and found the captain in a niche in a far corner, much to his relief. Shifting his feet restlessly, the journeyman cleared his throat. Since the captain still didn't look up from his empty mug, Wilmar took a deep breath and tapped him on the shoulder.

Michel hadn't noticed Wilmar until that moment, as he was deep in thought about Marie. She wouldn't respond to his questions when he visited, and she stayed disappointingly silent and detached in bed. Michel couldn't figure out whether he was more annoyed at Marie, or at himself for throwing good money out the window for a few disappointing minutes with her. So when Wilmar touched his shoulder, Michel flared with rage and instinctively reached for his sword.

"What do you want, boy?"

"I must speak with you urgently, Captain. Privately." He sounded so serious and desperate that Michel reluctantly nodded.

"Did Mombert send you?"

"No, but it concerns my master and his daughter." Wilmar turned around, searching for a place he and Michel could talk without a dozen curious people listening in. Understanding at once, Michel took his mug in one hand and Wilmar by the other, then led him to the foot of the stairs.

"We'll go up to my old room. My brother has lodgers there, but they are away at the moment. I only hope for your sake that you have something important to tell me."

Wilmar nodded excitedly, and once they got upstairs, he gave Michel a brief account of recent events.

The captain cursed. "They say Mombert Flühi killed the Steinzell nobleman? I can't believe that."

"Master Mombert certainly didn't do it. He shouts a lot, but he's never hurt anyone."

"I believe you. Had he done it, Mombert wouldn't have been so foolish as to call the governor while the corpse was still lying there with Mombert's own knife stuck in his chest. Anyway, he'd never have been driven to attack Steinzell unless the nobleman had tried to violate Hedwig, and that wouldn't have happened without a lot of noise and shouting."

"I didn't hear anything, even though I sleep in a room right next to the shop where every word can be heard from the hallway. But the murder must have taken place in the hallway, as both the front door and the door to the courtyard had been locked from the inside."

"That doesn't make sense." Eyes closed, Michel appeared to be concentrating.

Wilmar tried to remember everything that had happened that morning. "I think Philipp von Steinzell was murdered somewhere else and secretly brought into Master Mombert's house."

"Then someone in the house must have opened the door for the murderer and bolted the door again after he left. That's not very likely."

Wilmar snorted and suddenly looked up. "Melcher could have done it! He pointed to the body as calmly as if he'd seen it all before, and he was the one who called attention to Master Mombert's knife. Perhaps he let the murderer into the house out of revenge, since the master had recently whipped him for loitering around town instead of working. It's also suspicious that he's recently had a lot of money, which he claimed friends had given him. Maybe someone paid him to spy on the master or the nobleman. Just now I was down at the harbor and saw Melcher getting on a ship sailing for Lindau, and I wondered where he got the money for that trip."

"No judge in the world would accept that as proof. Perhaps he earned the money in town. If an apprentice wants get back at his master, he puts a mouse in his wife's bread dough—he doesn't help murder him. Unless . . ." Michel fell silent, staring through the little window out into the street. "Unless the act was carried out by someone who wanted to get rid of Steinzell and used Melcher as an accomplice. But who could be interested in killing an almost-unknown nobleman?"

Wilmar fidgeted nervously in his chair, eager to share his theory. "Abbot Hugo von Waldkron! He was chasing after Hedwig like the devil and viewed Squire Philipp as a rival. Now that he's gotten rid of him and pinned the murder on Mombert, no one is there to stand in his way. He had Hedwig taken to the tower, and I'm worried that Hedwig might now meet with the same fate as her cousin Marie . . ."

Upon hearing Marie's name, Michel interrupted. "What happened to Marie in the tower?"

Wilmar stared at him in surprise. "Didn't Master Mombert tell you? Marie had accused three men of robbing her of her virginity in the tower the night she was arrested. The judge didn't believe her and condemned her to additional whipping for slander."

Michel felt as if he'd been punched in the gut. "Marie was raped? I never knew that. Wait . . . Let me think."

It's no wonder that Marie doesn't enjoy sleeping with me, Michel realized, suddenly filled with shame. What an idiot I've been.

"Who were the men?" he asked in a voice that shocked Wilmar.

"Hunold, the city bailiff; the wagon driver, Utz; and Linhard Merk, who now calls himself Brother Josephus and lives in the monastery of the Barefoot Friars." he replied.

"My God, how Marie must have suffered!" Michel jumped up, pacing and gesticulating as if he wanted to catch and throttle her attackers at once.

Wilmar tugged at his sleeve. "This is not about Marie, Captain, but Hedwig. If we do nothing, she'll also fall victim to these vile men, and what I've heard about Waldkron makes me fear the worst. Earlier tonight, he hopped on a boat to Meersburg, and I'm sure that from there, he'll go to his house in Maurach. I'm convinced Selmo will take Hedwig out of the tower and bring her to him, where the abbot will use her and torture her. We must free her!"

Michel laughed bitterly. "How do you think we'll do that? I don't have the power to release Hedwig."

Wilmar buried his face in his hands. "Then Hedwig will suffer the fate of her cousin. If she even survives what Waldkron will do to her, that is. She's so tender and fragile . . ."

Seizing the boy by the shoulders, Michel pulled him up. "Stop moaning and take heart. Before a fellow like Abbot Hugo can get his hands on the girl, I swear he'll have to get past my drawn sword."

For a moment, Michel considered telling Marie about the matter. Perhaps she would be more inclined to accept him if she found out that he was going to help her cousin, but then he decided she'd more likely call him a braggart and slam the door in his face. No, first he would have to free Hedwig. A deed like that would earn her gratitude and finally bring the two of them closer. Once again, he asked Wilmar to describe what he had seen in Mombert's house and then later in the harbor.

XIV.

Darkness descended over the city as Michel and Wilmar set out for the city tower. The city gates had been closed for hours, and it normally wouldn't have been possible to smuggle a girl out of Constance, but because of the council, the watchmen let people pass through at any hour.

Michel still wondered if Wilmar had made up his accusations against the abbot out of pure jealousy, but he couldn't reject the slight possibility that the young apprentice might be completely correct in his assumptions. In any case, it was unlikely that the abbot would have the girl abducted in broad daylight in front of dozens of witnesses, so Michel waited in the tavern with Wilmar until sundown, when the streets began to empty out. All of Michel's doubts were dispelled, however, when he caught sight of a man in a white cowl walking briskly toward the tower. In a hushed voice, Wilman identified the man as Selmo.

Holding a hooded lantern so that the light fell only on the pavement ahead of him, the man was carrying a coat over his arm and heading directly for the tower entrance. He pounded on the door, and waited until the eye-level shutter was pushed aside.

"Who's there?" someone asked in a gruff voice.

"Open the door in the name of the Council of Constance!" Selmo held Abbot Hugo's document up to the shutter so that the watchman could see the seal, and was happy soon afterward to hear the bolt being pushed back. The door opened a crack, and he slipped inside. "I am here to fetch the prisoner Hedwig Flühi," he declared in a harsh tone.

Confused, the guard passed his hand over his bare head. "So late at night?"

Selmo replied in a haughty tone, attempting to intimidate the man. "These are my orders."

"Very well, then. I'll go get her." The watchman shuffled away, returning shortly with Hedwig. The girl's face was swollen and tear-stained, but there was a look of hope in her eyes.

"Am I being released?" she asked Selmo.

Selmo gave her the same beneficent smile he had learned from his master. "That will be decided when we get to where I'm taking you."

Taking that as confirmation, she suddenly seemed ashamed of having thought first of herself, and she quickly asked what would happen to her parents.

"That's entirely up to you. If you are sensible and behave, and do what you are told, your mother will be released soon and your father treated mercifully. You can help convince the judge of your father's innocence."

Hedwig folded her hands, promising to be obedient and do everything she could to help her parents. Suppressing a grin of satisfaction, Selmo tried to maintain his suave demeanor. His master would be happy, because now he'd acquire a willing lover. But since women were unpredictable and he didn't want to take any chances, he filled a cup from the guard's table with the bottle of poppy juice and handed it to her.

"Drink this. It will be good for you."

Hedwig stared in disgust at the filthy cup. "What is it?"

"Medicine. It will keep you from getting sick from the tower's filth. If you drink it, I'll see to it that your father and mother also get some."

Nodding vigorously, Hedwig emptied the cup even though the bitter liquid made her shudder. Selmo put the empty bottle back in his pocket and placed the other cloak around Hedwig's shoulders.

"Let us out," he ordered.

The guard grumbled, but he took the key, shuffled to the door, and opened it.

As Selmo pushed Hedwig out into the street, he heard the gate closing again behind him and chuckled. The bailiff wouldn't realize until the next morning that he'd handed over the prisoner without keeping a copy of the command to show his superiors.

Draping his arm around Hedwig's shoulders, Selmo pulled her toward him as if trying to keep her from stumbling on the holes in the pavement. Through the cloak's heavy material, he could feel her trembling, and he had to suppress his lustful desires. Hearing a noise, he jumped, but before he could turn around, something hit him on the head, and he fell unconscious to the ground.

Unlike Selmo, Hedwig had seen an arm and a sword appearing out of the darkness and watched as the sword's pommel struck her escort. At the same time, someone seized her from behind, stifling her cries.

"Please be quiet, Hedwig. Captain Michel and I have come to set you free."

"Free? But why? I'm going to be released." Hedwig tried to turn around to Wilmar, but then the ground started to buckle under her feet, and she fainted.

Catching her before she fell, Wilmar lifted her back onto her feet and searched for the captain, who had pulled Selmo into a dark alley by the tower and was searching him. Upon finding the parchment roll, he quickly glanced at the contents by the light of Selmo's lantern and stuffed it into his jerkin with an angry snort.

Wilmar ran over to him, pointing with his chin at Hedwig lying in his arms. "She suddenly passed out and isn't moving. I'm afraid her heart has stopped."

Michel placed his hand on Hedwig's throat and could feel her weak pulse. "Don't worry, she's alive. I think the fellow sedated her. Well then, we've done him a favor by taking the girl off his hands, as he would have had to drag her all by himself across the city." His tone revealed his relief at their quick success. "Come, give me the girl and take the lantern. We have to carry her someplace safe before the fellow back there wakes up."

Wilmar didn't want to let go of Hedwig, but he could see that the strapping young captain was better able to carry her. Not until that moment, however, did it occur to him that he hadn't given any thought about what to do once she was free, and he gasped. "We've got to hide her someplace where neither the abbot nor the bailiffs will find her."

"I know a place where nobody will come looking for her. We'll take Hedwig to a whore I know well. She'll take her in and care for her."

"To a whore?" Wilmar asked indignantly. He wanted to explain to Michel that a brothel wasn't a suitable place for an innocent virgin like Hedwig, but he realized this wasn't the right time to discuss the matter. Clenching his teeth, he hurried to keep up with the captain's long strides while lighting their way. After a short time they turned into Ziegelgraben Lane, and Michel beckoned to him to stop at one of the small houses.

"Here it is. Go to Zolfinger monastery and throw the lantern in a ditch. Then come back."

Wilmar watched as Michel knocked on the door; then he went quickly so that the captain wouldn't be left alone too long with Hedwig.

XV.

Marie, Hiltrud, and Kordula were sitting in the kitchen. They had just said farewell to their last customers of the day and now were relaxing and enjoying some white bread they'd dunked in warm, mulled wine—a delicacy they'd never before been able to afford. While Hiltrud and Kordula talked about the quirks of a few regular customers, Marie sat brooding in a corner by herself as usual.

Suddenly there was a knock on the door. "Who could that be so late at night?" Kordula jumped up to see, but Marie took her by the wrist, holding her back.

"It's past business hours. Anyone showing up now probably has nothing good in mind." Marie couldn't explain to her that she lived in fear of being recognized and was afraid that a murderer sent by Rupert might be standing at the door.

The knocking got louder.

Hiltrud looked up. "We should at least have a look. Perhaps Madeleine or one of our other friends is in trouble."

Without waiting for Marie's reply, she stood up, reached for a butcher's knife that doubled as a weapon, and stepped out into the hallway.

"Who's there?" she asked loudly enough to be heard outside.

"It's me, Michel."

Without further hesitation, Hiltrud pushed back the bolt. In the light coming from the kitchen, she could see the heavy burden in Michel's arms and quickly put the knife down.

"Who is this you're bringing into our house?"

"Close the door and put up the shutters. No one must see us," Michel said.

Hiltrud had no idea what was going on but quickly closed the door behind Michel and pointed toward the kitchen. "Marie's in there."

Upon hearing his voice, Marie stood up to give him a good piece of her mind, but instead saw the girl and swallowed hard.

"But that's Hedwig! What are you doing with her?" It sounded as if she suspected Michel of having kidnapped her.

Michel was not in a congenial mood and updated her on the day's happenings.

"My uncle arrested?" Marie bit her finger and took a deep breath. Even as her expression became suddenly furious, a mocking grin spread over her face. "This will be Rupert's last shameful act."

Michel looked at her blankly. "Counselor Rupert Splendidus, the man who wanted to marry you? What do you think he has to do with Hedwig? Wilmar is certain that Abbot Hugo von Waldkron is behind all this."

"Who's Wilmar?"

"Your uncle's journeyman. He told me about Mombert's arrest and how they were going to give Hedwig to the abbot as his lover. Wilmar will be coming back in a moment, but right now I'd like to put your cousin down somewhere. She's starting to get heavy."

"Come, we'll take her upstairs to my room. Hiltrud, can you help us?" Marie climbed up the ladder while her friend took the unconscious girl from Michel and handed her to Marie. Together they hauled her upstairs and laid her on Marie's bed. Michel followed with a lantern that Hiltrud had given him but had to stop at the entrance as the space above was too small for all of them.

Mombert's daughter was as pale as a ghost, and the only way they could tell she was still alive was the slight but steady rise and fall of her chest.

"I'm afraid that Hedwig was given something by the fellow we took her from in order to get her out of the city without attracting attention. She fainted on us in the street." Michel looked at the girl anxiously.

Hiltrud bent down over the girl and smelled her breath. "She drank poppy juice, and quite a bit of it, apparently. Believe me, she won't wake up until tomorrow afternoon."

"I hope she survives." Marie gazed at her cousin with concern. Poppy juice was generally used as a soporific, but drinking too much could kill a person.

Hiltrud felt Hedwig's pulse and shook her head, "I don't think she's in danger. The girl is obviously strong and healthy."

Before Marie could reply, someone else knocked on the front door. "That must be Wilmar," Michel said.

"I'll open the door." Hiltrud squeezed by him out of the room, and climbed down.

Michel took Marie by the arm. "Can you trust the two other women? No one must know who freed Hedwig and where she is hiding."

Marie immediately pulled free from his grip, but she gave him a friendly look. "Hiltrud saved my life and has been a loyal friend to me, and Kordula will not betray us, either, especially to men who stalk innocent girls and thus rob us of a living."

"Then it's all right." Putting his head out the door, Michel saw Wilmar standing below in the hallway alongside Hiltrud, who was examining him in the light of a burning wood chip. The journeyman stared back at Hiltrud, who was quite a bit taller than he was, as if he feared she would eat him alive.

Michel motioned for the two to join them in the attic. "Bring the third woman along as well. We have to talk about what to do next, but we mustn't risk being overheard by a random passerby standing outside the window."

Wilmar raced up the ladder as if fleeing from a venomous snake. Hiltrud and Kordula followed him, smiling. They were amused by this boy who had tucked himself into the farthest corner of the attic, his legs pulled up tight and his arms wrapped around himself so as not to touch the women next to him. But due to the tight quarters, the others also had to hunker down on their hands and knees, keeping their heads down. Marie pushed Hedwig up against the wall, sat down on her bed, and from that vantage point looked down at the others. Michel seized the chance to lean against her legs.

With everyone looking at him expectantly, Michel retold what had happened and why he'd brought Hedwig there. "What Wilmar and I did," he concluded, "surely won't please the officials here in Constance, so please don't mention this to anyone and keep the girl hidden from prying eyes."

Kordula clicked her tongue and shook her head emphatically. "Out of the question. If Marie hides the girl here, she can't work anymore."

Raising her hands in assurance, Marie nodded. "But we can do it! When Hedwig is back on her feet, she'll just hide when my customers are here."

She pointed to the ceiling boards. If two were removed, it was possible to stand on top of Marie's trunk and hoist oneself into a small partitioned area under the gables. It was as small as a coffin, and the construction seemed a bit shaky, but it would suffice for a slender girl like Hedwig.

Wilmar protested vehemently. "No! No, that's out of the question. From up there Hedwig will hear everything that happens here and will lose the innocence of her soul. After all, she is a pious virgin."

Marie gave him such a withering look that he froze. "Would you prefer her to lose her innocence by force under the most repulsive conditions?"

Placing his hand on Marie's knee, Michel smiled gently. "Wilmar loves Hedwig and wants to protect her. I don't like that you're still receiving customers, either."

"Marie has to keep working, or people will start talking," Hiltrud replied quickly, for she could see that Marie was itching to lash out at her loyal admirer. "People would wonder why she stopped taking people into her room."

Taking a deep breath, Marie held her tongue. "Hiltrud's right. We have to continue as before." Before Michel could object, she turned to Wilmar and asked him to tell her everything that had happened before and after the murder. When he described how they found the dead nobleman, Marie winced. Philipp von Steinzell deserved his inglorious end, but she only wished the grim reaper had chosen to take him somewhere else.

When Wilmar concluded, Marie shook her head. "Why are you so sure the abbot of the Waldkron monastery is responsible?"

"Because this is the way he could get Hedwig for himself."

"Why would he murder a man in order to abduct someone else?" Marie objected. "He could just as easily have lain in wait for her on her way to morning Mass. Do you have any reason to believe that the abbot and the nobleman were sworn enemies?"

Wilmar admitted he didn't.

Marie put her head in her hands. Michel played absentmindedly with her braids while looking at her expectantly, but she was not yet ready to mention her suspicions. While staying at Arnstein

Castle, she had learned that Konrad von Keilburg had plans to seize castles and lands in the murdered nobleman's homeland. With his death, the Keilburgs came one step closer to getting their hands on Steinzell's property. Also, Mombert's arrest not only helped Abbot Hugo get his hands on Hedwig, but it would also make Rupert happy by ridding him of her uncle—whether as revenge for past events, or seeing him as a possible threat for the future.

Additionally, Marie knew that both Konrad von Keilburg and the abbot had been guests of her former fiancé, and that Rupert had no reservations about ordering someone's death. Perhaps, she thought, Utz had now committed one murder too many at the request of his master, Rupert. She smiled reassuringly at Wilmar, who had fallen silent again. "You're convinced that Melcher let the murderer into the house?"

"He's the only one who could have given him the master's knife. How would a stranger know where he kept it?"

"Then we've got to get to Melcher before somebody kills him. He's an undesirable witness." She placed her hand on Michel's shoulder with pleading eyes.

The captain looked doubtful. "I have my orders and can't leave Constance."

"I could look for him," Wilmar exclaimed. "If I take the first ship leaving for Lindau tomorrow, Melcher will only be one day ahead of me, and I should be able to catch up with him." Pausing, he bowed his head in embarrassment. "But I don't have any money for that."

"That's the least of our problems." Michel untied his purse from his belt and tossed it to Wilmar. "That should be enough. It's unlikely the fellow will flee to Bohemia or Hungary."

"I can also contribute a few coins," Marie added.

Michel caressed her knee. "That's kind of you. I'll also send two of my most trusted men on the hunt, as it's unlikely Melcher will return voluntarily."

"But that won't be enough. We need high-ranking allies to help us confront our enemies. If only the Arnsteins were in Constance!" Marie stared dejectedly at Michel.

Raising his head, he looked up. "Do you mean the knight Dietmar von Arnstein? He arrived the day before yesterday."

Marie licked her lips. "Do you know where he's staying?"

"Of course. Everyone's talking about the knight. They think it's funny he brought his wife along, since there are so many courtesans in Constance that a man could take a different one every day for three years and still not have had them all."

Marie shook her head so indignantly that her braids swatted Michel in the face. "What nonsense! Dietmar von Arnstein knows how lucky he is to have his wife, and I'm glad Lady Mechthild has come along. That will make things easier."

Rupert couldn't dupe the mistress of Arnstein Castle quite so easily, Marie thought with satisfaction, and resolved to visit the lady the very next morning.

XVI.

Along with their vassals and allies, the Arnsteins were staying at the inn with the sign of the fish. If it had been up to Marie, she would have visited the inn right after sunrise. But Hiltrud convinced her to stay long enough to be there when Hedwig woke up; otherwise the girl might misunderstand the situation and scream loudly enough to bring all the neighbors running.

Marie was sitting cross-legged on the bed next to Hiltrud, sewing a new dress and occasionally checking on her cousin. Since Marie couldn't take customers for Hedwig's sake, Michel came back early that morning and loudly declared at the front door that he was taking Marie for the entire day, so others either had to leave or take Hiltrud or Kordula instead.

Michel was now perched at Marie's feet, obediently handing her thread and shears or getting her something to drink when she became thirsty. Instead of keeping quiet about her past as she had on his earlier visits, she was answering his questions about her five years on the road. Though she maintained a jovial tone, Michel could sense the horror and torment of the humiliation she had gone through so clearly that the hair on his arms stood on end, and a few times he even felt ashamed of being a man. When Marie told him about the cruelty of the Riedburg mercenaries, he thanked God that Siegward had perished so quickly afterward. Otherwise Michel would have tried to personally send him off to hell as a gift for Satan.

A mournful sound and a slight trembling around Hedwig's lips put an end to the conversation. Marie and Michel bent down over the girl and waited anxiously. It wasn't long before Hedwig opened her eyes, staring in confusion at the unfamiliar surroundings.

She sat partway up, then sank back down again with a loud cry of pain. "Oh God, my head hurts so much, and I feel sick to my stomach."

Then she recognized Michel and Marie nodding at her cheerfully, and she stared at them wide-eyed. "Marie? Am I in heaven? When did I die?"

Marie laughed and patted her cousin on the cheek. "You're not dead, and neither am I."

With Michel's help, the young girl pulled herself up, smiling at him gratefully as he tucked a pillow behind her back. Then she took her head in her hands as if hoping to gather her thoughts. "What happened? How did I get here? A man came a little while ago and told me I'd be set free."

Michel stroked her hair, trying to calm her. "He was lying. That fiend was taking you to Abbot Hugo."

Hedwig let out a wail. "Good Lord, he was the abbot's servant? How could I have been so stupid!"

Tenderly stroking her cousin's forehead, Marie handed her a cup of diluted wine. "You were too upset, and even if you had figured out what was happening, it wouldn't have done you any good. Selmo would have just forced you to drink the potion in order to break your resistance and take you to his master."

Hedwig stared at her cousin incredulously. "But how could he just come and pick me up as if I were a bolt of cloth that his master had purchased?"

"Unfortunately, it was almost that easy." Marie handed Hedwig the roll of parchment that Michel had taken from Selmo. "As you can see, Alban Pfefferhart, the city councilman and assessor, signed the order for you to be handed over."

"Pfefferhart? I can't believe that. Herr Alban is an honorable man." Hedwig shook her head in surprise, but the signature on the document seemed genuine.

Marie let out a cynical laugh. "Not every person is who you think. It's possible Hugo von Waldkron knows things that Alban Pfefferhart wants to hide from others. But don't worry. I won't allow those wretches to exploit your situation the way they did mine."

The wine put a little color back into Hedwig's face and seemed to revive her spirits. "Why didn't you try to get in touch with us for all those years? We thought you were dead."

"I don't think I should tell you what I've been up to for the last few years," Marie replied sharply, twisting so that Hedwig could see the yellow ribbons on her skirt.

Hedwig understood and lowered her head in shame. "I'm so sorry."

"Don't be silly—it's not your fault. On the contrary, I think you're a victim of the same scoundrel. But this time I'm going to cut the ground out from under him and his accomplices."

Hedwig grimaced at her cousin's harsh tone even as she remembered what the man had done the night before to gain her confidence. "What happened to my parents? The abbot's assistant said my mother would be set free and my father would also be treated mercifully. Was that also a lie?"

"Yes, unfortunately. As an alleged murderer of a nobleman, your father is due to be tortured and will probably meet a dreadful end. But things haven't gotten that far yet. We have proof that someone else killed the nobleman." Marie's smile was so malicious that Hedwig drew back in shock.

"Wilmar believes your apprentice Melcher had something to do with it. If we can find him, we can prove your father's innocence." Michel sounded more confident than he really was.

Marie snorted in contempt. "If we don't have the backing of any authorities, no one will pay attention to what the boy says. Now, I'm going to try and find us some powerful allies."

She left the room, then paused halfway down the ladder and turned to her cousin. "Michel will tell you what to do from now on. Please listen to him, because if the bailiffs find you, they'll immediately hand you over to Abbot Hugo."

Nodding obediently, Hedwig promised to respect whatever Michel told her. With a doubtful sigh, Marie left the house and swiftly ran through the city.

When she reached the inn where the Arnsteins were staying, she hesitated, wondering if she was doing the right thing. Perhaps she should have brought Otmar von Mühringen's testament with her as proof, but the caution she had learned in her hard years as a wandering harlot held her back. Constance was swarming with robbers, so she decided to wait and have Giso, Sir Dietmar's castellan, pick up the document later.

Pulling herself together, she walked up to the building marked by the relief of a huge, ornately designed cast-iron fish, and knocked on the door.

A maid opened the door, then started to close it again when she saw Marie's yellow ribbons.

Marie stuck her foot in the opening. "I'm looking for the knight Dietmar von Arnstein or Lady Mechthild."

Since the maid showed no signs of stepping aside, Marie tried something else. "I'm not leaving until you've announced me to your lord and lady. Tell them Marie, who spent the winter before last at their castle, would like to speak with them."

The servant girl wavered at Marie's serious tone. "Very well, then, I'll ask her lady-in-waiting if I can let you in. But first take your foot out of the door."

The maid shut the door, but only slid the bolt halfway before she hurried away. Less than a minute later the door opened again. "Marie! Indeed, it's you!"

"Guda! How glad I am to see you." Marie was so happy, she wanted to hug Mechthild's lady-in-waiting, but restrained herself and gave a slight curtsy.

"Come in," Guda said, "and let me have a look at you. You look well. It seems things have not gone badly for you since you left Arnstein."

Marie smiled at her upbeat tone, realizing that Guda had no idea what the life of a wandering prostitute was like. Happy to have been received so warmly, Marie asked Guda about the lady.

Guda beamed with joy. "Lady Mechthild is well and so is her darling boy. He's growing up and won't be an only child much longer."

Marie looked at Guda with interest. "Lady Mechthild is pregnant again?"

"Yes, but it doesn't show yet. This time she won't call upon you, however, as Sir Dietmar won't even consider having a temporary lover again."

It sounded like a warning, but Marie silently chuckled. She assumed that meant Lady Mechthild found it dangerous to let her husband get used to the company of attractive courtesans. Now that she'd had the longed-for heir, the lady's position at Arnstein was so secure that she could afford to keep other women out of her husband's bed.

Guda led Marie into a small but elaborately furnished room, richly covered with pinewood paneling and with floors of inlaid oak. Lady Mechthild's traveling chest stood along one wall, and next to it was the cradle in which the Arnstein heir was sleeping, watched over by a servant girl. Enough soft light fell into the room through the bull's-eye windows that Lady Mechthild, sitting on a chair and sewing next to the hearth, could easily thread her needle. Sir Dietmar was sitting next to her, alternating his attention between his son and his wife.

Lady Mechthild looked up when Marie entered. "Greetings, Marie. This is certainly a surprise."

Though her words were friendly, Marie detected some hostility, and Sir Dietmar was clearly uncomfortable. Apparently he didn't want to think back on his time with her.

Marie was annoyed at their cool reception, especially since she was there to help the knight and his wife retrieve their lost inheritance. She didn't speak of it at once, however, but first said a few polite words of greeting, admiring the baby in order to flatter the parents.

"What brought you to Constance?" Lady Mechthild finally asked.

Clearly, the lady wondered why the young woman had risked coming to her hometown again despite all that had happened. Marie couldn't help but feel the wide gulf separating a noble lady and a despised harlot here. It was quite different than it had been in the castle, where Marie had been one of the lady's closest servants.

"Since the nobility are all gathered in Constance, there was no way for me to make a living anywhere else. I had to come here, and to tell the truth, I also hoped you would be here."

Lady Mechthild raised an eyebrow. "You wanted to see us? You've probably heard that I'm pregnant again and wish to offer your services, but this time we don't need them." Her face looked so forbidding that it appeared she wanted to throw Marie onto the street then and there.

"No, it's something else," Marie replied hastily. "I have . . ."

She paused, realizing that she'd almost revealed that she had possession of Sir Otmar's lost testament, and she wasn't ready to talk about that yet.

Instead, she asked, "Have you heard that Squire Philipp was murdered?"

Sir Dietmar grumbled yes, and Lady Mechthild nodded.

"My uncle stands under suspicion," Marie continued. "But he didn't do it, and I'm going to prove it, but I will need allies to whom the officials and the judge will listen."

Lady Mechthild stared at Marie with contempt. "You've come to the wrong place. First of all, the proof against him is so overwhelming that it can't have been anyone else, and second, we don't want to incur the wrath of Degenhard von Steinzell by supporting his son's murderer."

"Uncle Mombert did not kill Philipp. This is another one of Counselor Rupert Splendidus's vile tricks, and I know he's an enemy you share with the entire Steinzell clan." Though her voice sounded as vehement as the noble lady's, she didn't succeed in convincing her.

"I think you're still hoping to provoke us into a fight with Count Konrad von Keilburg and his half brother Rupert in order to take your revenge, but I'm not willing to spill a drop of my people's blood for a whore. The situation seems favorable for us now, as Sir Degenhard will think carefully about who his friends are now that the Habsburger has been declared an outlaw, and I'm certain he will join forces with my husband."

"Good Lord, I'm not asking you to do anything improper. It's a simple issue of justice." Marie was having trouble masking her growing anger. "In addition, I haven't come empty-handed. I know who has your uncle Otmar von Mühringen's lost testament, and I can get it for you."

Lady Mechthild clearly didn't believe Marie, but Sir Dietmar seemed interested and gave her a piercing stare. "Is that possible?"

Since Marie didn't want to give them the testament before getting a promise of support for herself and her uncle, she racked her brain trying to figure out what to do next. Then an idea occurred to her. "I don't know if you noticed, but Jodokus was very much taken with me at Arnstein Castle."

"I know he made lewd advances, but that fortunately you always turned him down." It was obvious that Lady Mechthild didn't want to talk about it.

Marie couldn't worry about the lady's feelings if she wanted any chance at success. "I've learned from other whores that Jodokus is still looking for me. He's taken another name and is apparently quite rich, but his description is unmistakable. Recently he boasted to one of my friends that he had some documents that would soon make him even richer, and I think that it must be the stolen testament with which he plans to blackmail Counselor Rupert. If you help me, I'll go to the monk and take it."

Rubbing his clean-shaven chin, Dietmar looked at his wife pensively. "Maybe we should take her offer, my love. If we have the testament, Konrad von Keilburg will have to give up Mühringen, and our son's inheritance will almost double."

Lady Mechthild waved her hand through the air as if trying to chase away flies. "Oh, these are just the figments of a fallen woman's imagination. Sir Otmar's testament was destroyed long ago, and even if she managed to find Jodokus, the word of a runaway monk wouldn't be worth any more in court than that of a harlot."

Marie could feel the ground slipping out from beneath her feet. If the Arnsteins didn't help her, nobody would listen to her. At the same time, she felt a fierce anger welling up inside her. "This isn't a fantasy, Lady Mechthild. I can and will get the testament for you."

"Promises are easy to give but hard to keep. Do you really think I would make an enemy of Sir Degenhard based on your word? It would be best if you left now before I regret having let you in."

Her words sounded so final that Marie didn't even try to change her mind. She glanced questioningly at Sir Dietmar, but he just shook his head regretfully and seemed resigned to the loss of Mühringen. For the first time, Marie found it disturbing that Lady Mechthild called the shots in her marriage while Sir Dietmar went along with whatever she said, and she stormed out of the room without regard to their high rank. Guda, who was looking forward to chatting a bit with Marie, recoiled at the sight of her enraged face as she left.

XVII.

Marie had been counting on the Arnsteins' help, and now everything was in shambles. The trial against Uncle Mombert would begin in a few days, and her stomach turned at the very thought of his upcoming torture and public execution. Tears of anger and despair welled up, blinding her, and she felt like a failure. She stumbled into a passerby who then pushed her so hard that she bumped into a horse that reared up, whinnying, and tried to kick her with its front hooves. As she tried to get out of the way, one of the hooves hit her on the shoulder, knocking her to the street amidst the laughter of bystanders. For a moment it appeared the horse would trample her to death, but the rider got control of the animal just in time.

Standing up, she found herself looking into a laughing face framed by a well-groomed blond beard. The man, wearing a jerkin embroidered in gold and silver and emblazoned with the Württemberg coat of arms, leaned over to give her a hand.

"I'll be damned if you're not the pretty courtesan from Arnstein Castle!" Count Eberhard gazed at her shapely figure as if he wanted to pull her to him right there. "Are you coming with me?" It sounded like an order.

Marie nodded in confusion, her mind doing cartwheels. Eberhard von Württemberg was no friend of the Keilburgs and would be a much more powerful ally than the Arnsteins. She swore to herself she'd make the count her ally, even if she had to satisfy his every desire.

PART SIX
The revolt of the courtesans

I.

The little house on the Ziegelgraben was so full of prostitutes that not even a mouse could have squeezed in. Crowded into both rooms on the first floor, a few women had climbed up to Marie's room and were peering out through the doorway to hear what was being said below. Nevertheless, the house could accommodate fewer than half of the courtesans who showed up, so Madeleine had to open the windows and doors so the people standing outside could hear as well. She herself took a seat atop the reed-covered stove in Hiltrud's room.

Marie estimated there were almost a hundred women there. In relation to the total number of courtesans working in Constance, that wasn't very many, but Marie knew that most of the women there were also acting as representatives on behalf of their friends. In any case, they were all there to vent their unhappiness at the conditions in the city. Madeleine listened to each woman's complaint and kept checking the veracity of each point with the others.

When everyone had spoken, Madeleine raised her hand. "So we're in agreement that this can't go on?"

One woman, a recent arrival to town who had come to the meeting more out of curiosity than with a specific complaint, shook her head. "What do you mean, we agree? I haven't noticed any of these problems. What's so wrong with a handful of local maids earning a few pennies on the side? My room wasn't empty today, nor was it yesterday. This whining is a pure waste of time. If I'd stayed home, I could have served a half-dozen customers by now."

Other courtesans reacted angrily, cursing the new arrival. Madeleine asked them all to be silent and looked at the woman, shaking her head. "It seems you haven't been listening. We're not talking about two or three maids. Instead, most of the female servants and many poorer housewives are offering themselves to soldiers and barefoot monks for a few pennies. Even some women in the middle class and their daughters don't mind servicing knights and clerics for cash. The penny whores in the meadows have the most to lose from this unfair competition, but these so-called honorable women rob us of some of our money, too, and force prices down. What man would be ready to pay a courtesan her proper wage if he could get what he wants in a dark corner for less?"

Kordula pushed her way through the crowd to where the new arrival was standing. "Most important, I don't see why we have to wear yellow ribbons, or why we'll be forced to leave Constance right after the council, while these loose local women can stay and play the part of good middle-class housewives after we are gone. Even worse, if all hell breaks loose and these moneygrubbing local women have to suffer our fate, there'll be so many more prostitutes that most of us will starve."

Helma clapped her hands to get everyone's attention. "This isn't just about middle-class women and maids selling their bodies. By now, most men believe that every woman and every girl in Constance is just a cheap commodity whose refusal of sex will only drive the price up. Yesterday another young woman was dragged into the bushes by a few men and raped, and by the time the bailiffs arrived, the bastards were long gone."

"And do you remember what happened three days ago?" another woman called through the window. "A nobleman kidnapped a young girl on her way to church, took her to Überlingen, and is still holding her captive there. This isn't the first time something like that has happened. Haven't you heard how the cooper's daughter was abducted from the tower and since then has been missing without a trace?"

Like most of the women, Marie nodded, but it was hard for her to feign anger. A few days had passed since Hedwig was rescued, but it was still one of the most common conversational topics at the taverns and marketplace. People wondered why the officials hadn't taken any action or made a more thorough search for the girl and her rescuers. According to Michel, even Hugo von Waldkron, who was still living with Rupert, had not tried to find Hedwig. Marie suspected that the city councilman Alban Pfefferhart had stopped the abbot in order to conceal his part in the evil plot.

For Hedwig's sake, Marie hoped the meeting would soon end, as the girl had been in her tiny hiding place in the attic for hours with hardly enough room to turn around. It had to be stiflingly hot up there, since Marie was sweating from every pore in spite of the open windows.

Another woman's voice was so loud, it made Marie jump. "I'm for sending a mission to the kaiser's governor to explain the situation and ask for help. He'll have to realize that middle-class housewives should not be competing with us whores."

Madeleine waved her off. "I've already spoken with the governor when he was a guest of my bishop. He didn't really listen and afterward even made fun of me."

"Then we simply have to force the man to take us seriously," a woman called out from Kordula's room.

Hiltrud, who had remained silent to that point, laughed bitterly. "Force the governor to do something? Only the kaiser can do that, and for people like us, the kaiser is so far removed, he might as well be on the moon."

"We've got to think of something." Madeleine put a hand to her cheek, thinking hard.

The prostitutes stared at the French woman expectantly, and Marie, too, was wondering what the woman might suggest. If they wanted the governor to listen seriously to their problems, they needed a really spectacular way to get his attention.

Hiltrud tapped Marie on the shoulder. "The clock at Saint Peter's just struck three. Weren't you supposed to meet Count Eberhard von Württemberg now?"

Horrified, Marie stared at Hiltrud. "My God, I completely forgot." Squeezing her way into the hallway, she chased away two women standing on the ladder and climbed into her room. She'd promised to bring the count the last of Jodokus's documents that day, as she'd already smuggled the rest to him under her skirt, piece by piece. Now she was curious to learn how he planned to use the information against Keilburg and his scheming half brother.

When she got to her room, the women moved back enough for her to open the chest and take out the package for Count von Württemberg. Craning their necks, they turned away in disappointment when all they saw were clothes and some household goods. Wanting to keep her money safely out of the house, since the council had attracted many thieves and burglars to town, she had asked Michel to deposit her savings with a trustworthy banker. She didn't feel quite right doing that, for it meant putting herself at her childhood friend's mercy, but he was the only man whom she could halfway trust.

As Marie climbed down the ladder, one of the women asked enviously, "Are you going to see your good-looking lover again?" Since Marie had no desire to tell anyone where she was headed, she just nodded. Downstairs, the women cleared a path for her, grumbling at her early departure because she was just as esteemed by most of them as Madeleine and equally valued as a confidante and adviser.

Dismissing their questions and shouts with an apologetic smile, Marie hurried off. Michel joined her at the next corner, looking grim, and once again she was irritated by his uninvited presence. She felt as if she were being kept under surveillance. "Why pull such a face?" she asked.

Michel looked piqued. "How can I be happy when I'm always worried about you? You run around totally unconcerned for your own safety. But our enemies aren't asleep. Selmo's been lurking around, looking for the people who stole the girl from him. Warn Hedwig to stay out of sight, and especially to keep away from the harlots hanging around your house. Most of them would probably be glad to turn her over to Abbot Hugo—and you to your former fiancé—for a few pieces of silver."

Marie looked at him in surprise and smiled apologetically. Had she been so careless, or was Michel just imagining things? In any case, she appreciated his concern and resolved to be welcoming in bed the next time.

But today she had no time for him, as Count Eberhard von Württemberg was a very demanding lover and probably wouldn't let her leave until evening. As he paid her generously every time she visited him, she'd be able to get through the coming winter very comfortably with his money. At least this year she didn't need to worry about shelter, as the council would continue through the cold winter months, and she'd even make more in the winter than in the other seasons, for the chilly weather would drive the noblemen into the warm beds of the courtesans and willing middle-class women.

The moral conditions of the city and its double standards angered Marie—not out of fear of losing business but instead due more to local women's nonchalant attitudes and their husbands' support in tossing aside all sense of decency. Marie was not the only innocent woman to be unjustly accused, and even the prostitutes who had been punished according to the law hadn't usually been as promiscuous as the honorable ladies in the city who always gathered up their skirts whenever they encountered a courtesan.

Michel tugged at her sleeve. "You don't seem to be in a very good mood yourself."

Marie shrugged. "I have some things on my mind, most of them not especially pleasant. Have you found a way to smuggle Hedwig out of the city yet? She'll get sick if she has to remain in her narrow, hot hiding place."

Regretfully, Michel spread out his arms. "It wouldn't be hard to smuggle her out, but I don't know where we can take her. As an unmarried woman, she'll be considered wanton and treated accordingly. And if we put her in a nunnery, Abbot Hugo would find out."

Marie pressed her lips together. It appeared that they couldn't take her cousin somewhere safe as long as Mombert was imprisoned and awaiting trial, which was one of the reasons she'd be doing everything she could to please Eberhard von Württemberg. The count was currently the only person on earth who was not only willing but also able to help her and her relatives.

To Michel's chagrin, they arrived all too quickly at the house where the count and his retinue were staying. Townspeople gossiped that the count had threatened the former residents into moving away while the council was in session, although Marie knew that the owner of the house had probably just succumbed to the rich count's offer of a purse full of Württemberg guilders. The count was so pleased that the rumor was going around, however, that he even allowed his own people to spread it.

By Constance standards, it was an imposing building with a ground floor made of large blocks of hewn stone, two projecting half-timbered stories covered with elaborately worked carvings, and an unusually large attic. Unlike the yellowish bull's-eye glass windows produced locally, these windows were made of an imported Murano glass that was so transparent as to be almost invisible. If the residents wanted to see who was passing by on the street, they didn't have to open the windows, Marie mused as she walked up to the carved wood door, knocked, and was let in by a servant.

Without taking his eyes off the house, Michel gulped down the mug of wine he had purchased from a traveling merchant. Though he knew that she would ordinarily have received at least half a dozen customers over the course of the day if she had been at home, it still bothered him that she offered herself so willingly to the infamous womanizer. Michel leaned against a wall, staring intently at the brick walls of the count's residence.

Eberhard received Marie in his bedroom. The curtains of his four-poster bed were pulled back, revealing the elaborately carved, cherrywood bedposts. The red silk bedcovers bore his coat of arms, and that same leaping stag also adorned all the wall hangings and curtains in the room. The largest tapestry symbolically depicted a huge sixteen-point stag hurling a careless hunter to the ground. Württemberg was no beast of prey threatening others, but rather he stood ready to defend himself against any attacker.

Though the count didn't exactly look like a nobleman in his underwear and open shirt, Marie curtsied when she entered. "I brought along the other documents, my lord," she said, handing him the bundle.

Count Eberhard looked briefly at the little package before setting it down dismissively on a tabletop inlaid with the Württemberg stag. His gaze wandered longingly across her anxious face, paused for a moment on the two well-formed little hills beneath her blouse, and seemed then to cut through the material of her skirt. Knowing that all he could think of now was a little tussle in bed, she opened her blouse and pulled it over her head as the bulge in Count

Eberhard's trousers swelled and he started breathing harder, passing his tongue over his lips.

Marie had learned more about how to increase a man's passion until he could hardly bear it, and her charms were sufficient to almost drive the Württemberg count to madness. As she continued undressing, unconsciously moving in a sort of mysterious dance, the count could no longer restrain himself. He jumped up, seized her, and threw her on the bed, and before she could catch her breath, he had penetrated her impetuously.

II.

Some time had passed, and Eberhard von Württemberg was sitting naked and visibly exhausted on the edge of the bed, leafing through Marie's documents. His bearing suggested he was just waiting for his virility to be rekindled, but his eyes shone with great interest in the documents' contents.

"These documents are as good as the last ones you brought me. By rights, and by law, they should be more than enough to deprive Keilburg of his property and life, and send his bastard half brother to the gallows."

Marie's sensed a tone of resignation in his voice, and she recoiled. "Does that mean you aren't going to bring charges against him?"

"Be patient, my child. I said if it were a matter of rights and law, everything would be very simple, but Keilburg and his bastard brother have too often distorted truth into deception and lies, using sworn statements to their advantage by twisting them around to mean the opposite."

Motioning to Marie to pour him a cup of wine, the count became engrossed again in the documents. "These papers are too valuable to give to a court. In my possession they're secure, but I don't know what would happen if they fell into someone else's hands. As you're well aware, they can quickly disappear or be destroyed. Not every judge is immune to bribery, and our proof could easily wind up in the fire or even in the hands of our opponents."

"But what else could you do with the documents?" Marie made no effort to conceal her fear and disappointment.

Eberhard von Württemberg tossed the parchment scrolls on the table and turned to her. "I'll prepare myself for a feud against the Keilburgs and declare war. If the kaiser and the other princes call me to account, I'll show them your documents to finish the Keilburgs off, but otherwise, I won't use this proof until Konrad von Keilburg has been vanquished and his brother has been unmasked as a liar and perjurer."

And win rich lands and mighty castles for you, Marie thought, reading the count's mind. But even if Rupert should someday get caught in one of his own traps, that wouldn't help her or her uncle Mombert. When she said this to Count Eberhard, her voice had an edge that no one else of lesser standing would have dared use to address him.

"If I had the power, I'd free your uncle from the tower with my soldiers," he replied with a tinge of guilt. "But I haven't been sitting on my hands. I've presented the case to the kaiser, since the murdered man was a council guest. That means the Imperial Court will pass judgment rather than the city authorities or the bishop's court."

"But he's still sitting in the dungeon, accused of murder, even though he's innocent."

The count raised his hands in feigned despair. "Dear girl, even you must recognize that not everything is as simple as you would like it to be. It wasn't easy for me to stop them from killing your uncle. Influential friends of the Keilburg count urged sentencing of your uncle as soon as possible, and Habsburg's vassals were furious that Mombert still hadn't been broken on the wheel. Fortunately, a peace treaty between their feudal lord and the kaiser was more important to them than his execution, so they agreed when I persuaded the kaiser to take the case on personally."

Marie pursed her lips with contempt. "These are only ruses that will lead to nothing."

"Only because of this ruse, as you call it, is your uncle alive at all. If we could get our hands on his apprentice, however, we could expose the true murderer and stop Keilburg in his tracks."

Marie lowered her head in sadness. Michel's men had long ago come back empty-handed, and only Wilmar was searching for Melcher. The apprentice seemed to have vanished from the face of the earth, she admitted to the count.

Eberhard had expected nothing else. "In my opinion, the fellow drowned long ago and is at the bottom of the lake."

Marie buried her face in her hands. "For God's sake, no! Melcher is the only witness who can prove my uncle's innocence."

"Then let's hope he's still alive and that Wilmar finds him." His voice didn't sound too hopeful, but he placed his arm around her shoulder to console her. "Your uncle's trial isn't doomed. Someone just has to explain to the kaiser that Philipp wanted to attack Flühi's daughter, and that in itself will make it possible for your uncle to be pardoned. But we do need a defender with a good reputation, and I'm not generally regarded as a paragon of virtue."

Count Eberhard laughed at his own words. "It's not easy living with Kaiser Sigismund, Marie. The electors have made him both kaiser of the Holy Roman Empire and king of Germany, and thus the most powerful man in Christendom. But he doesn't have the intellect that this office requires. He's petty, easily offended, and unnecessarily gruff. Once he's gotten something into his head, he'll have his way and tolerate no disagreement. Don't you remember how he declared Friedrich von Habsburg an outlaw because he helped Pope John to flee from Constance?"

423

The pope was captured again, and thus the kaiser no longer has any reason to quarrel with the Habsburgs. Sigismund only focuses on what interests him at the moment and in doing so forgets everything else."

Eberhard continued to recount the kaiser's intrigues, then paused, looking at Marie. "Are you even listening to me, girl? I said that from now on you have to avoid talking about the philosopher from Bohemia, Jan Hus, or praising him for being an upright man. His sermons have angered Sigismund, and the kaiser's punishments usually affect not just those who attract his anger but also the people who side with them."

"What can happen? Master Hus came to the council at the kaiser's invitation and with a guarantee of safe conduct."

"Safe-conduct letters from the kaiser are no longer what they used to be," the Württemberger said derisively.

Marie took the words personally. If the safe-conduct guarantee was no longer valid, then she, too, was in danger. She suddenly felt like a leaf in a storm, and that her hopes of saving her uncle's life were futile. The court's documents specified her punishment if she returned to the city, and her plan to destroy Rupert by legal means seemed even to her to be presumptuous. Not even the count, one of the mightiest men in the Reich, had enough influence to free Mombert Flühi or unmask Rupert Splendidus, for he, too, ran the risk of being caught up in the finely woven net that the Keilburg bastard had so cleverly woven.

She was in despair. For a moment, she wondered whether to take her documents to the kaiser herself. But just as quickly, she dismissed the idea, since for a woman like her it would be impossible to get anywhere near the kaiser, and even if she could, he would just give the material to one of the city judges who frequently invited her former fiancé to their homes.

Longing to revive her old plan of hiring an assassin to kill Rupert, she realized that his death wouldn't save her uncle. No matter how she looked at it, she was dependent on Eberhard and had to hope he didn't just pursue his own interests and cast hers aside as a distraction.

Count Eberhard looked at Marie and sighed. She would hate him if he couldn't stop her uncle from being executed for the murder of Squire Philipp. But if he didn't want to endanger his own plans, he couldn't do much for her uncle, whose fate was probably sealed even if the apprentice reappeared and testified in favor of his master.

He couldn't say that to Marie, however, as he still hoped to at least help her get revenge on her former fiancé. Plus, he wanted to keep her as long as he could, as it wasn't every day he found such a beautiful and willing bedmate. He was shocked to realize she had become more for him than a random mistress. That might be because she'd given him an effective weapon to use against Keilburg, but also, up until then, no woman had ever dared to speak with him so frankly, and none had put so much faith in him as she had.

Musing about his pleasant feelings for Marie, Eberhard walked over to the window and saw, leaning against a wall on the other side of the street, a young officer whom he'd noticed hanging around before. The man, dressed as a palatine guard, was furiously staring at the house as if he wanted to set it on fire. Eberhard turned to Marie and beckoned her over.

"Do you see that fellow? Could he be a Keilburg spy?"

Marie demurred with a laugh. "A Keilburg spy? No, my lord, that's none other than Michel Adler. He's an old childhood friend currently in the service of the elector palatine."

"So that's who it is. Well, he looks like someone I wouldn't want to meet in a dark alley." Count Eberhard looked at Marie incredulously, then burst into laughter. "A childhood friend, you say? It seems there's more to it than that. That fellow looks like a jealous lover."

Marie joined in his laughter. "Michel jealous? He knows I'm just here on business and never gets angry about my customers."

"Then he seems to be making an exception with me. Perhaps I should feel honored." Looking at her intently, he realized she could indeed arouse strong feelings in a man, and he reached out and pulled her to him.

"Come to bed. I must leave soon and would like to do so feeling good."

Marie obeyed his order. Trying to be as tempting and seductive as possible, she turned her thoughts to how she could convince him to actually stand up for Mombert and his wife.

III.

"There you are, finally." Michel moved away from the wall he'd been leaning on for more than three hours and walked toward Marie.

He looked as if he were struggling to control himself, and Marie became irritated, remembering Eberhard's words. Who did Michel think he was? She was no one's possession, and if he was going to behave like a jealous lover, they would have to part ways. She could forget her past when she was with strangers, but his very presence was a reminder of his rise to prominence and her fall. On the other hand, she'd find it hard to do without him, because he helped her whenever he could, and his regular visits gave her little house and its inhabitants some degree of protection from unhappy customers and envious bordello owners.

Smiling stiffly, she looked at him. "Count Eberhard von Württemberg is a demanding man, and I must keep him happy so that he helps me get my revenge or at the very least protects me from my enemies. The kaiser's safe-conduct guarantee may apply to harlots, but Rupert won't let that stop him from having me thrown in the pillory or drowned in the lake."

Michel tried not to let her aggressive tone get to him. "I know, but just the same, I don't like that you've surrendered to the count unconditionally. He's no better than the other nobles. He'll help you only if he sees some advantage to himself, but if he changes his mind, he'll drop you like a clump of dirt."

"Thank you for reminding me again what I am worth," Marie hissed at him, and broke down in tears.

She didn't want to fight with Michel. Nevertheless, he'd inadvertently reminded her once again what a dirty profession she had. Constance was a good place, where prostitutes were treated almost like honorable women. Unlike people in other cities, locals here didn't spit at the sight of them when they walked through the streets, or stop them if they weren't wearing their yellow ribbons.

Here, they were even allowed into church. Since praying at Arnstein Castle, Marie had never again really been devout, but had instead often doubted her faith. Now, however, she felt the need to place her worries at the feet of the Holy Virgin and ask for her help. As a young girl, she'd often attended Mass at the cathedral in Constance, and now she saw the cathedral tower rising above the nearby houses. Hastening her steps, she turned into the lane leading to the main entrance.

Michel followed her angrily. "Where are you going now? That's not the way to your house."

"I'm going to the cathedral to pray." Ignoring Michel at her side, she simply hurried on. Catching her breath at the church door, she quickly slipped inside. The interior was dimly bathed in a cool light, just enough for her to make out the mighty columns and the walls of the nave. Under the high stained-glass windows, the burning candles on the three altars seemed like islands of refuge surrounded by the colorful paintings and statues of the saints.

Circling the main altar, Marie approached the Pietà, with Mary holding Christ in her lap after he had been taken down from the cross. An inconspicuous statue represented Mary Magdalene, appearing so small that it quite literally stood in the shadow of the Mother of God.

Marie wondered why a prostitute had played such an important role in Jesus's life. She assumed that it was because the Son of God had always administered to the needs of the despised and oppressed. But Abbot Hugo von Waldkron and the bloated clerics didn't want to be reminded of that. Silencing her rebellious thoughts, she tried to remember the appropriate prayer.

Michel stood next to a side pillar, keeping an eye on the nave. Watching Marie kneel at the altar, light illuminating her blond hair like a halo, he briefly considered taking her along on a military campaign as his mistress. Constrained in this overcrowded city, he reacted to Marie's moods much too sharply.

Roused from his thoughts, he saw someone enter through a side door. Michel looked at the new arrival, then shrugged with relief. It was only a haggard Franciscan monk probably from the nearby Barefoot Monks monastery, shuffling toward the Altar of Our Lady. His face was emaciated from fasting, and Michel smelled the sweet odor of blood. The monk must have chastised himself just a few minutes ago. Now he fell to the ground in front of the Pietà, disrupting Marie's muted prayers.

Moving two paces to the side, Marie was about to say a final prayer when the monk stared at her, raising his arms in a defensive gesture. His face contorted suddenly. "Be gone from me, evil spirit, and torment me no longer in this holy place."

Marie gaped at the monk, bewildered. Rising to his feet, he made a sign to ward off demons, and only now did she recognize him by his pale eyes.

"Linhard! You miserable traitor!" Her voice was so full of hatred that the man collapsed and crept along the floor toward the altar.

Suddenly realizing she wasn't a ghost, he turned whiter than anyone Marie had ever seen. "Who calls me by this name that I have long buried and forgotten? Is it you? Are you really Marie Schärer, the daughter of Master Matthis?"

Marie looked down at the man, wanting nothing more than to crush him underfoot like a worm and hurl her boundless contempt into his face. Just in time, she saw the danger she was in. If Linhard told the wrong people about their meeting, her life wouldn't be worth a penny. With all the self-control she'd learned in her hard life as a harlot, she forced herself to put on a friendly face.

"I don't know what you want from me, Venerable Brother. My name is Berta, and I have never seen you before."

She crossed herself, murmuring a hasty amen and curtsying one last time before the Mother of God, then headed toward the door. She almost had to force herself not to look back, for she had the feeling that Linhard's eyes were boring into her like two burning coals. Briefly, she turned around at the front door, pretending she was only waving to Michel. Linhard was standing with his back to the altar, reaching out to her with one hand. When he saw that she was motioning to a man, he crossed himself and threw himself on the ground again before the Holy Virgin.

Michel looked at Marie questioningly as they left the church. When he noticed that she was trembling, he put his arm around her and held her tight. "What happened in there?"

Her teeth were chattering so hard she could hardly speak. "The monk! It . . . was Linhard! He recognized me!"

Seeing the horror in her eyes, Michel knew that she was reliving her tormented memories, but all he could do was to hold on to her and lead her through the streets as if she were ill. He wished he could send her out of town, for she wasn't safe there anymore. He also considered lying in wait for Linhard in a dark alley and breaking his neck. But neither solution pleased him. Since he couldn't leave Constance himself, if she went away, she would have to once again become a wandering harlot with no one at her side. And even though Linhard was truly a repulsive scoundrel, Michel wasn't the kind of person who could kill a man in cold blood.

He leaned down to Marie and kissed her on the neck. "Keep your head up, girl. I'll take you home now so you can lie down. Then I'll bring you a little wine. A good sleep will help you get over your shock. I don't think the monk will go to Master Rupert right away and tell him of your meeting."

His caution belied his words, however. Looking around constantly, every time he thought he saw someone heading toward them in the Barefoot Monks' cowl, he changed direction.

Arriving at the little house on Ziegelgraben, they found Hiltrud and Kordula engaged in a heated discussion with Helma and Nina. The Italian woman had a black eye and a deep, bleeding cut on her forehead that Hiltrud was blotting. Though Marie was still absorbed with thoughts of her unexpected meeting, she immediately turned to Nina.

"What happened to you? Did a customer beat you up like that?"

Helma answered for her, shaking her head. "No, it was our brothel owner. He was annoyed she was at the meeting here today and therefore couldn't take any customers. At first he just screamed at her, but when Nina stood up to him, he hit her. We won't go back to that brute. Can we perhaps stay with you? I know it's pretty crowded, but Nina and I really don't take up much room."

Startled, Marie and Hiltrud looked at each other. As it was, it hadn't been easy to hide Hedwig from strangers, but if Helma and Nina joined them as well, they'd have to let them in on the secret, and that seemed too dangerous. As Marie was trying to figure out how to turn away her friends without insulting them or sending them back to their brothel, Michel cleared his throat and tapped Helma on the shoulder.

"There's not enough room here for the five of you, but I think I can help. My brother Bruno is planning on setting up a brothel in part of his house, and the two of you could stay with him. If he knows I'll protect you, he'll treat you well and not cheat you. Moreover, I have good friends who would be glad to get some advice on where to find some nice girls. What do you think?"

"Maybe you can be first on their list of customers." Marie was surprised by her angry reaction, but Michel roared with laughter.

"But, Marie, that would hurt your reputation. The whole city knows you're the only harlot for me." Marie grimaced, but Hiltrud started to giggle and finally burst out laughing. Nina and Helma also tried to hide their amusement, but their shoulders were twitching. The loyalty with which Michel clung to Marie, even though she treated him so badly, was a popular topic of conversation among Constance prostitutes.

Helma took a deep breath, tugging playfully on the buckles of Michel's breastplate.

"Your suggestion isn't bad at all, soldier. Will you vouch for your brother?"

"I believe I can." Just a few years before, Bruno had slapped his younger brother every time he talked back. Now his brother bowed and scraped to Michel as soon as he entered the Adler Tavern, anticipating his every wish. "Let's go right away. And Nina, if your bordello owner comes and demands you back, Bruno will know how to answer him. If Rubli still gives you trouble, I'll send my soldiers to his bordello to rough up the place."

Michel's laughter took some of the effect of the threat away.

All the same, the two young women were relieved, as they knew from experience how nasty a bordello owner could be when he lost his source of income. Saying good-bye to their friends, they left the house quickly, as if fearing this chance might slip from their fingers.

"Thank God," Kordula groaned. "I never thought the two of them would leave. I didn't have a single client today."

"Neither did I." Hiltrud sighed. "And Hedwig could only come out of her hiding place in the sweltering heat for a few minutes. Now she can finally have something to eat."

"I'll tell her they're gone." Marie climbed up into her room, stood up on her chest, and pushed back the two boards blocking the entrance to the hiding place. Hedwig quickly stuck her head out. Beet red, with sweat streaming down her face, she looked about to suffocate.

"Just in time," Kordula joked. She felt sorry for Hedwig but didn't conceal that she was disturbed by her presence. Just then, she saw a man walking by the house, wearing a Bavarian cavalry officer's uniform, and she rushed out to talk to him. Marie climbed down the ladder and tugged at Hiltrud's sleeve.

"It's possible we'll have to clear out fast. Someone recognized me."

"Who?" Hiltrud put her hand to her throat, breathless with shock.

"Linhard, my father's former secretary. He saw me in church and called out my name. If he tells Rupert or Utz about it, we're in real danger."

Hiltrud wanted to know everything. "We have to be ready to flee at any time, but what will you do about Hedwig? If you bring her along, she'll have to work as a prostitute."

Marie had no answer. If Mombert was executed for the murder of young Steinzell, Hedwig would have no other choice. In the meantime, Marie had gotten to know her cousin well enough to suspect she wouldn't be able to bear a harlot's life for long. She wasn't hard enough and would drown herself before the summer was over.

"You say he's now a monk?" Hiltrud was seized by a sudden thought. "Then perhaps you're sensing danger where there is none. Linhard may have recognized you, but is it certain he would also betray you? That he's entered a monastery could mean he long ago regretted his crime against you and means to atone for it for the rest of his life."

Marie had not considered that, but even if Hiltrud was right, they were far from being safe. Linhard might unintentionally tip off Rupert, or it was possible the counselor was keeping an eye on him and already knew what had happened. Marie realized she was inclined to imagine things, but when it came to her former fiancé, she was inclined to assume the worst. For a few minutes she wavered between fleeing and staying, but she finally decided that running away in panic wouldn't do her any good. If she wanted to destroy Rupert, she'd have to risk her own life, if necessary.

She smiled bitterly. Rupert had made her a prostitute, but in so doing, he had also created ways for her to bring about his downfall. If he had put her in a nunnery, she never would have met Brother Jodokus or Count Eberhard von Württemberg.

IV.

Over the next few days, Marie's moods changed faster than her customers. Sometimes she was afraid of her own shadow; other times she told herself that Rupert and Utz hadn't yet recognized her, even though she was a well-known figure all over town, and they probably didn't connect the well-known harlot from the Ziegelgraben with the young Constance woman whose life they had destroyed, five years before. In these more optimistic moments, she reveled in her plans for revenge and imagined herself leading her uncle triumphantly out of his dungeon while casting Rupert and his henchmen inside. But this feeling of confidence never lasted long.

She had to admit she feared the future. No matter what happened, she was beyond redemption, like dirt in the street that everyone walked over. But before she met the same miserable end as most other harlots, she wanted to see the man responsible for all her misery go to his grave.

The next time she visited Württemberg, she begged him again to finally do something about Konrad von Keilburg and his brother. Count Eberhard raised his hands regretfully. "I'd love to do that, my girl, but at the moment my hands are tied. The kaiser is so occupied with his own plans that he would be annoyed if I summoned my troops and began preparations for a feud with the Keilburgs. He suspects resistance and treason and is very quick to anger. Now that John the Twenty-Third has been declared unworthy and removed from the list of popes, the kaiser must act against the next representative of God on earth."

Eberhard von Württemberg laughed, and Marie wondered whether he was making fun of the quarreling popes or the kaiser.

Though she wasn't interested in high-level politics unless she herself was in danger, in hopes of finally convincing the Württemberg count, she continued. "What does the kaiser plan to do now?"

"Next he plans to depose Pope Gregory. In addition, Master Jan Hus is a thorn in his side, and he views Hus's inflammatory rhetoric as a threat to his crown. Don't forget that Sigismund is also king of Bohemia, and it appears Master Hus is summoning the Bohemians to rebel against the holy church and its protector, the kaiser and king."

Again it wasn't clear if Eberhard von Württemberg shared the kaiser's views.

Marie looked at the count with a frown and shook her head. "According to everything I've heard, Master Hus doesn't preach against God and the divine order. When he decries the immorality of the prelates and the pompous behavior of the abbots and bishops, he is no doubt speaking for every true Christian. After all, these men have been elected to be Christian shepherds, not the church's jailers."

Count Eberhard smiled indulgently. "Don't let anyone hear you talk like that, or you'll also be considered a heretic. Views like that threaten the authority of the princes of the church, and thus the pope and the kaiser as well. The mighty see their position in the world and their task differently than you and Jan Hus, and perhaps even differently than common people. I, too, have heard Master Hus's sermons and approve of much that he says. The church must be renewed from the ground up, and its representatives must be put back in their proper places, but Master Hus errs in believing his sermons can bring that about, and that someone standing high up in the clergy will willingly allow himself to be demoted. His greatest error, however, was in trusting Kaiser Sigismund's promise of safe conduct. If the kaiser believes Hus has outlived his usefulness, then that promise is worth nothing."

The count's coarse language and bitter laugh told Marie how much he disliked having to pay homage to such an unreliable man. "If Sigismund of Bohemia were a sovereign ruler, then I could speak openly with him, but the Keilburgs stand in his favor, and Rupert Splendidus has been able to ingratiate himself as well. It is revolting how this upstart bows and scrapes before the kaiser and his close advisers."

Suddenly falling silent, the count stopped, as if he'd already said too much. Nevertheless, Marie understood. Eberhard von Württemberg didn't dare oppose Konrad von Keilburg because he didn't know to what degree the kaiser wanted to see justice done. Worst case, he would approve Konrad's theft and elevate Rupert's standing even further. She felt like the ground was giving way beneath her feet.

The next morning brought news that spread like wildfire through the city. Pope Gregory XII renounced his title and withdrew to Recanati as Cardinal Bishop Angelo Correr. It was said that the kaiser, though unable to force this resignation militarily, had purchased it with generous concessions in order to secure his position as the supreme monarch of Christianity. The next person the kaiser had set his sights on could no longer hope for such concessions and mercy, however.

Jan Hus steadfastly proclaimed his views in his sermons. Many lower-class people and servants admired the combative master from Prague and prayed for him. The kaiser and the cardinals, however, didn't like being branded as leeches and oppressors of the people, and had secretly condemned him.

There were so many rumors concerning Master Hus's trial that those who had heard his sermons were still hoping he'd receive mercy even as the knight Bodman and the bailiffs of Constance led him to Brüel Field where he was to be burned at the stake. To humiliate Hus, the chief prosecutor in his trial ordered all the prostitutes in the city to accompany Hus to the stake. Most of the harlots just shrugged their shoulders, having been humiliated so often that they were happy to see someone worse off than themselves.

Marie would have loved to disobey the order but didn't want to risk being dragged in front of the furious cardinal and whipped. People in town wouldn't want to miss such a spectacle, and Utz would recognize her. Surely Utz had talked to Jodokus's landlady in Strasbourg and learned that the monk had amused himself with a strikingly attractive blond prostitute shortly before his death; Utz would have made the logical connection between the hasty departure of this woman and the disappearance of the documents. Her life wasn't worth a thing if he recognized her.

Hiltrud and Kordula lamented the imminent death of Master Hus while cursing the merciless judges and above all the treacherous kaiser who had broken his promise. Just the same, they went with Marie to the church square in front of Saint Peter's where a huge number of harlots were gathered.

They went over to join Madeleine, but didn't have much time to talk, however, as the bailiffs soon appeared and ordered them to exit through the Scottish Gate, then line both sides of the street to allow Jan Hus to proceed toward the execution site. Marie was shocked to see Hunold among the bailiffs, passing so close that his elbow brushed against the breasts of the woman in front of her. Retreating, Marie hid behind Helma and Kordula. Hunold didn't notice her, however, as he was eyeing Madeleine.

"Well, pretty little bird, how about getting together and having a little fun this evening?" he asked her.

The woman examined him disdainfully. "Gladly, if you can pay a gold Ecu. Otherwise you should visit the penny whores. They'd certainly enjoy a visit from you."

Madeleine's ridicule hit Hunold hard. Blushing, he glowered at her and uttered loud threats. When another prostitute demanded to know if he was aware he had just insulted a high French nobleman's mistress, he quieted down and ran to catch up with the other bailiffs.

Hunold was a brutal, highly opinionated fellow, but Marie realized with a certain malicious glee that the bailiff only bullied people who couldn't defend themselves, and bowed and scraped in front of higher-placed nobles. At any other time Marie would have asked herself how she could make use of that knowledge, but just then she wasn't considering that. Instead, she joined all the other harlots and followed the bailiffs through the gate, standing so as not to attract the notice from the people accompanying Jan Hus.

Behind the harlots, so many ordinary citizens pushed through the gate that the bailiffs weren't able to keep the crowd under control. Marie saw Michel in brightly polished ceremonial attire marching at the head of his foot soldiers to make room for the condemned man and his escorts. Though the soldiers pushed people back with their crossed spears, they still couldn't keep order in the crowd. Even Count Palatine Ludwig tried in vain. When the count's horse got stuck in the crowd, he ordered the knight Bodman, leader of the city guards, to close the city gates and allow onlookers out only in small groups. The condemned man and the court officials had to wait until the crowd had dispersed before they could leave town.

Little remained of the line of harlots that were intended to mock the renegade Bohemian Jan Hus. Marie, like other courtesans, had jostled up into the front rows next to the execution site, but she didn't realize how exposed she was there until Rupert Splendidus passed by in the retinue of the bishop of Constance, Friedrich von Zollern. Fortunately, Rupert was interested only in the higher noblemen and paid no attention to the common folk. Trying to hide behind one of the tall horsemen, Marie watched him until he had smugly taken a seat on one of the benches for the high-placed council attendees.

His gaze wandering over the crowd, Rupert took pleasure in having people enviously watch him and see how Bishop Friedrich and the other noble guests treated him as their equal. It wouldn't be long before he would be a frequent guest of the kaiser's, perhaps even accepted into his circle of advisers. Rupert had even heard that some bishops and counts valued the younger son of Heinrich von Keilburg as a polite and agreeable nobleman in contrast to his uncouth brother. He assumed that many of their neighbors and most of his brother's opponents would be relieved when he took his brother's place.

Indeed, he would soon be able to carry out his plans to dispose of his brother. *I succeed in everything I do*, he thought to himself with a feeling of elation. Suddenly he remembered that there was a matter of great importance where he had met with unexpected resistance, though he still hadn't been able to detect the culprit. Irritatingly, Mombert Flühi, his former adversary in the trial, was still alive, and his daughter hadn't been found.

Hedwig's disappearance, however, wasn't Rupert's fault. Smirking, he remembered how Abbot Hugo had confessed his plight and begged for his help. Why hadn't the ass been able to wait? More than likely, the girl had been attacked by mercenaries, then dropped into the river, along with the false extradition order.

For a moment Rupert thought about the reason for Mombert Flühi's persistent accusations. Hedwig looked a lot like Marie Schärer and had probably reminded him of the loss of his brother-in-law's fortune. Marie had been a true beauty, but Rupert hadn't cared about the girl's fate. On the contrary, he was proud he could control his lustful desires. If he wanted to continue to amass wealth and esteem as the Keilburg heir, he couldn't afford any human weaknesses.

Involuntarily, Marie watched her former fiancé, practically choking on her hatred. Drumrolls announcing the condemned man's arrival tore her away from her murderous thoughts. All eyes now looked at the gate.

Walking behind a few monks carrying a cross and swinging censers, armed foot soldiers led Master Hus from the city. When the procession arrived at the open space around the pyre, Marie was able to get a better look at the Bohemian preacher. Standing tall, Jan Hus had an earnest face that betrayed no sign of fear. Dressed in a black robe of shame symbolizing hell, he also wore a yellow cap that showed two devils drooling at the mouth and the Latin inscription *heretici*.

Reminded of her own punishment, Marie felt an almost unbearable burning and itching on her back, and her gaze unwillingly wandered to Rupert. Unlike Hus, he had committed so many sins that Marie almost expected the earth to open and swallow him.

The condemned preacher was led to the stake, where Constance bailiffs tied him to the heavy logs and post in the middle. Hunold checked the condemned man's shackles, spat at him, and jumped down from the pyre. Together with the other bailiffs, he dragged bundles of branches up to the pyre and piled them around the larger logs.

Just as Hunold selected a burning torch from the iron brazier, the count signaled him to wait. Horses' hoofbeats could be heard on the pavement, and Imperial Marshal Pappenheim and three of his guards rode through a narrow passageway that the palatine foot soldiers were struggling to keep open. Just before reaching the pyre, Pappenheim reined in his horse and turned to Hus.

"His Majesty Sigismund, kaiser of the Holy Roman Empire, king of the Germans, and king of Bohemia, offers you the mercy of returning to the bosom of the holy church through renunciation of your heresy. Recant and you will live."

A murmur went through the crowd, and some people applauded. But Marie had talked with Eberhard von Württemberger about Hus enough to recognize that Hus was being set up. Neither the kaiser nor the church dignitaries were interested in turning Hus into a martyr. They had simply shown him what they could do and were now giving him a way out. Yet if Hus recanted, then the power-obsessed abbots and bishops would have won. He would save his own life, but his followers would turn away and return to the Roman clergy on bended knee. If he didn't recant, he would be burned at the stake as a warning to everyone else spreading similar heresies. Marie believed that Hus was right but doubted it was worth dying for. The strange smile on the Bohemian preacher's lips revealed that he felt differently.

Hus looked at the Pappenheims and laughed. "No, I won't recant! If I did, I would be admitting that truth is a falsehood and a falsehood the truth. Moreover, I'd free the kaiser from breaking his oath." With that, and for all to hear, he was referring to the promised free conduct that was being broken.

"Search your soul and repent," Pappenheim ordered again. Instead of a reply, the condemned man raised his arms heavenward and began singing a hymn.

The officials looked uncertain. The count palatine steered his horse over to the imperial marshal, and they spoke quietly for a few minutes. Finally, Pappenheim nodded with a grim face and pointed at Hunold next to the pyre, raising the torch ostentatiously in his hand.

"Bailiff, do your duty!" the count ordered, and steered his horse away from the flames. Hunold had carried out punishments for many people, but mostly they consisted of floggings of prostitutes and petty crooks. He had never burned anyone before, and he believed that tossing that torch into the pyre was the high point of his career. Now he was an important person who would be treated with respect by patricians and wealthy merchants.

As the flames rose higher, Jan Hus continued to sing. Moved by the sound, some people joined in, without paying attention to the cardinals and bishops who shifted restlessly in their seats and didn't seem to know whether to order the soldiers to drive the people away or let them continue. Marie looked away to avoid seeing the pyre. She wanted to escape, but being so boxed in by the crowd, she could scarcely breathe, let alone walk away.

Eventually, Hus's voice died away, and only the crackling of the flames and the restlessness in the silent crowd were audible. Marie looked at the clergymen's bench and could see that not everyone there looked satisfied. Even in death, Jan Hus stood taller than the church towers and had publicly branded Kaiser Sigismund as a perjurer.

People stayed and stared until the fire had burned out. The count then ordered the bailiffs to douse the smoldering embers and collect the ashes in a large iron bucket. A man standing near Marie told the bystanders that the remains of the heretic would be thrown in the Rhine.

"The bishops no doubt fear that a bird could carry a beakful of Hus's ashes to Bohemia and give them to his followers," he added with a smirk, and turned to leave.

Most people shook off their discomfort quickly and were able to laugh again as soon as they'd entered the city, but Marie remained near the blackened execution place, deeply mired in her gloomy thoughts.

Hiltrud had also left the field but returned from the city gate when she noticed that her friend was missing. Seeing Marie's stony face, she tugged gently at her sleeve. "Wake up, Marie! You can't remain standing here where every passerby will stare at you and wonder. Come on, let's go home."

Startled out of her reveries, Marie nodded. Hiltrud pulled her along and made sure they passed through the Scottish Gate hidden in a crowd of people. The guards paid no attention and didn't stop them as they entered the city.

Hurrying toward the Ziegelgraben, Marie was still preoccupied with the Bohemian preacher's execution. Never before had it been so clear that justice on earth was the justice of the powerful or, as Lady Mechthild would say, the law of the jungle. She felt completely dejected. Was it even possible that someone as weak and insignificant as she could get her just revenge on someone like Counselor Rupert Splendidus?

Approaching their house, they found the door ajar and assumed that Kordula had arrived ahead of them, but it was Wilmar who was sitting on a chair in Hiltrud's room and holding Hedwig by the hand. Next to him a boy was tied up, and he stared at the two women defiantly as they entered. Perhaps only sixteen years old, the boy was clearly frightened, and Marie saw that his jaw was trembling. If he hadn't been gagged, he probably would have screamed in fear.

Wilmar was hugging a visibly upset Hedwig, and he greeted the two women cheerfully. "There you are, finally! What do you think about this? I caught Melcher. I looked for him for weeks without finding the slightest clue and was almost ready to give up when I noticed him boarding a ship in Lindau, headed for Constance. Like so many others, he wanted to watch the Bohemian master burn at the stake. I found him sitting in a tree not far from the field, and I shook the tree so hard, he fell to the ground like ripened fruit."

Marie stared at Wilmar in amazement. "How did you get him into the city?"

"I tied him up, gagged him, and stuck him in a sack. I was going to tell the gate watchmen that I'd bought a pig, but there was no one there—they had all run off to Brüel Field to see the execution. So I didn't even have to pay customs' duty for my little pig." It was clear that Wilmar was overjoyed with his success.

Hedwig beamed at Wilmar. "Now we'll be able to prove my father's innocence, won't we?"

Wilmar nodded enthusiastically, but Marie tried to restrain his exuberance. "It's not going to be as easy as that. We'll have to hide the boy with Michel's soldiers until the trial begins. Wilmar, make sure that Michel picks him up tonight, and have Michel also find you a place to stay. Hedwig, go back to my room. It was foolish of you to come down here where passersby might look through the window and recognize you."

The two young people looked so alarmed that Marie almost laughed out loud. As she watched Wilmar helping Hedwig up the ladder, she could feel her anxiety gradually giving way to elation. Now that the kaiser was no longer busy dealing with the Bohemian preacher, he might be more inclined to fulfill the Württemberg count's request for a just trial against the real murderer of Squire Steinzell.

Throwing a shawl around her shoulders for warmth, Marie ran to Eberhard's house to tell him of Melcher's capture.

V.

Eberhard von Württemberg was not at home when Marie arrived. The friendly doorman informed her that the kaiser had summoned all the noblemen of the Reich to discuss the next steps and asked her to return the following morning. Marie felt as if she had hit a stone wall. All the strength she had mustered to convince the count to act slowly ebbed away. Despondently, and with sagging shoulders, she returned to her little house, wanting only to find a place to hide and go to sleep.

But when she climbed the ladder to her room, she found Hedwig and Wilmar sitting on the floor and holding hands. Such mutual affection was something Marie had never been allowed to experience, and envy sprang up inside her. Instead of following her first impulse to throw Wilmar out and shoo Hedwig back to her straw sleeping sack beneath the eaves, she climbed back down to the first floor and helped Hiltrud in the kitchen.

As she approached the count's house the next morning, the doorkeeper tore open the door even before she arrived at the threshold, clearly relieved to see her at that early hour.

"Thank God you've come, Marie. My lord is unbearable today."

Indeed, the count's angry voice could be heard from the street. The moment she stepped in the house, she heard footsteps hurrying down the stairs, followed by a loud crash. A servant had dashed down, barely dodging a chair the count had thrown after him in a fit of rage. Marie wondered uneasily what might have caused his anger and was about to return later, but she set her jaw firmly and went upstairs.

Count Eberhard von Württemberg was standing in the doorway to his room, holding a silver platter in his hand, evidently preparing to toss it at the next person who came in. When he saw Marie, he dropped the plate, and pulled her toward him in a wild gesture. His sour breath and flashing eyes told her he had had too much to drink. His shirt was open, and a button on his pants had been ripped off. It was clear to Marie that something unexpected had happened, and she looked at him questioningly.

"To hell with the kaiser," he said as a greeting.

"Did you quarrel with him over something?"

"Quarrel? If I'd dared to speak a single contradicting word, he would have declared me an outlaw, stubborn as he is. Ever since he sent the Bohemian preacher to the stake, he can't stand being in this city and wants to leave for Spain as soon as possible to come to an agreement with the monarchs there concerning Pedro de Luna, or shall we say His Holiness Benedict the Thirteenth. That's currently more important to Kaiser Sigismund than anything else. When I asked him about some outstanding matters he should have taken care of long ago, including that of Squire Stenzell's murder, he rudely cut me off. In the course of our argument, it was revealed that he had already referred your uncle's case to the episcopal court in Constance on the advice of the honorable Counselor Rupert von Keilburg. I had to struggle to control myself. He actually referred to him by the name Rupert von Keilburg, the wretched bastard. May he roast in hell. Now all that's missing is for Sigismund to declare

Konrad von Keilburg the Duke of Swabia. He's powerful enough already."

Marie clenched her fists in helpless fury. "I'm starting to think the devil is helping Rupert and his brother to gain power through their treachery. In the eyes of the episcopal court, my uncle will be a dead man even before the trial starts."

Pulling her to him, the count stroked her hair and tried to console her. Marie wanted to push him away at first, as she was too agitated, but she gave in and leaned against him. "I had hope again, because Wilmar found the apprentice Melcher who could prove my uncle's innocence."

The count waved her off wearily. "That would help us only if the kaiser himself were the judge and we could present to him all the other evidence against Rupert Splendidus. But to change Sigismund's mind, God himself would have to come down from heaven."

Eberhard released her and walked to the window as he often did when he was at odds with himself.

Marie walked over to him, helplessly clinging to his arm as if he were the only person who could sustain her in a world in which all her wishes and hopes had been dashed. Staring down at the throng of passersby, she caught sight of a group of prostitutes she knew who were talking animatedly as they turned the corner heading toward the Ziegelgraben. For a minute she wondered in annoyance if there was going to be another meeting at her house, as she was getting tired of the senseless whining and complaining. But then it came to her. She took a deep breath, collecting her thoughts. Only after Eberhard had released his arm from her fingers and playfully kissed her did she realize she'd been rigidly standing there for quite a while, digging her fingernails into the count's arm.

Patting his arm apologetically, she gave him a mischievous smile. "As of yet the kaiser has not left the city. Come to early Mass at the cathedral tomorrow and bring some of your people along. I will see to it that a miracle occurs."

The count frowned, looked at her closely, and realized that she was serious.

"Very well, girl, if you gain the attention of the kaiser and interest him in our concern, you'll be worth your weight in gold."

"I'll do my part." Marie curtsied and was about to say goodbye, but noticing his disappointed expression, she pulled off her dress and fell onto the bed. It was better for him to face the next day relaxed and happy.

VI.

As Kaiser Sigismund and his retinue rode to Mass the following morning, a number of harlots streamed toward the cathedral and gathered in the two church courtyards. At first no one paid the women any attention, but as they began blocking the church doors with their growing numbers, the city guards became restless. Their commander, the knight Bodman, ordered some servants to clear the prostitutes from the main entrance.

Madeleine stood in front of the men, placing her hands on her hips. "We want to speak with the kaiser." Cursing and gesturing angrily, the soldiers tried to force them to move, but the women crowded even closer together with such determined looks that one of the men returned to his commander.

When he reported Madeleine's words and asked for further orders, Bodman's face flushed dark red. Spurring his horse up the steps, he then quickly withdrew when he realized he would be hemmed in by the now-constant flow of women entering the square. He shouted angrily, but the women knew he didn't have enough men to deal with them. One man suggested getting help from the foot soldiers of the palatine guards, but the messengers who were sent to find the guards came back empty-handed.

One of the women giggled and tapped Marie on the shoulder. "I saw your friend moving out with his entire company earlier. It's nice of him to stay out of this."

Marie nodded happily, for Michel had been able to keep his promise. He would act when the time came, but not the way Bodman expected. Marie knew that her friend was taking a great risk, since if something went wrong here and Rupert won, it would cost him his head.

When another large group of penny whores started marching up the street toward the cathedral, Bodman ordered his guards to bar their way. Some of the courtesans standing on the church steps ran down to block the guards' advance, showering them with obscenities and curses. Some of the women even raised their skirts and bared their backsides at the men.

As the stunned commander watched helplessly, the new arrivals slipped through the ranks of the city guards to join their friends. Bodman became visibly nervous; judging from the singing inside the church, the Mass was coming to an end. He turned his horse toward the whores once again, stood up in his stirrups, and raised his arms to get their attention.

"What's the reason for all this uproar? The kaiser will be leaving the cathedral soon. Do you want him to think you are all mad and drive you from the city?"

Madeleine smiled sweetly, but her words made a mockery of her expression. "We'll stay here until the kaiser has heard us."

The knight swallowed hard. "But you can't block the kaiser's way. Be reasonable and leave, or I'll have the guards chase you away."

Madeleine laughed in his face. "If there were no whores here, you and your men would be in sad shape. You can tell your people that anyone who beats or harms any one of us will find our doors closed to him in the future."

"Are you trying to extort me, woman?" Bodman raised his fist as if about to strike Madeleine, but lowered it again feebly. The knight wanted to order his men to drive the women away with spears and halberds, but he knew he would then forever be the laughingstock of his colleagues. Furthermore, after Madeleine's loud pronouncement, he could no longer rely on his men.

"I warn you, the kaiser will be very angry," he pleaded, but all he got in reply was a scornful giggle.

Just then, the mighty cathedral doors swung open and young squires exited, followed by six soldiers of the imperial guard in gleaming armor. Arriving at the bottom of the church steps, they found themselves facing the dense crowd of harlots. Helplessly they turned to the kaiser, who was just leaving the church at the head of a procession of noblemen and dignitaries.

Kaiser Sigismund first looked astonished, then annoyed. He was accustomed to seeing many people in the cathedral square, but until now everyone had bowed reverently before him and formed a path for his procession. This time he found himself confronted by a woman who neither greeted him in his accustomed way nor made any signal to retreat and open a lane through which he could pass. Looking at the seething crowd, he stared accusingly at Bodman. The knight gestured helplessly toward his men and shouted that the crowd of whores could only be driven away by a force of arms.

Meanwhile, Madeleine had pushed her way through the throng to stand directly in front of the kaiser. Curtsying daintily, she looked at him with a smile that was half-apologetic and half-provocative. "Your Majesty, we must speak with you."

The kaiser glanced at her open cleavage with a look of revulsion and passed his hand over his royal robe, its purple material adorned with golden embroidery. Standing up straight, he stared at Madeleine as if she were a repulsive insect that had dared to crawl across his path.

"What do you want, woman?" Madeleine noted with a faint smile that Sigismund's question suggested he was ready to make some small concessions in order to be permitted through.

"We courtesans have a number of justifiable complaints. Your governor refused to hear our concerns, and so we must trouble Your Majesty in person."

"If you have reason to complain, you may go ahead and plunder the money from my loyal vassals." The kaiser had listened to the satiric verses of Oswald von Wolkenstein often enough and therefore couldn't take Madeleine seriously.

The French harlot looked at the kaiser with a piercing gaze. "We have reasons to complain. You probably think we'd take all that money out of pure greed, but that's not the case . . ."

"Oh no? It has come to my attention that you're behaving like harpies and aren't even content with double the established city price!" The city councilman Alban Pfefferhart stepped between Madeleine and the kaiser, interrupting them heatedly. Evidently he wanted to spare the kaiser of the Holy Roman Empire any further embarrassment of having to speak with a whore.

Madeleine cast a disdainful look at the man. Though dressed in his best finery, Pfefferhart looked like a common partridge among the golden pheasants of the magnificently clothed nobility. "Your bakers and butchers don't stick to the established prices when they see a prostitute coming, but instead demand four times as much for a loaf of bread or a sausage. The prices you've set ensure a decent life for the noble class while we courtesans must pay whatever is demanded if we don't wish to go hungry."

Pfefferhart bit his lip. "I will see to it that from now on people don't take advantage of you." He thought that would be enough to mollify her, but she turned to the kaiser again.

"That was just the first item on our list of complaints, and one of the least. We courtesans are also troubled by the unfair competition from local women who lift their skirts for council attendees and their retinues, and ruin our prices. Most courtesans have been declared dishonorable for the slightest offense and condemned to a life of whoring. Others have been sold to brothels like a sack of flour while they were still children and pay for it the rest of their lives with society's scorn. Yet, we ask ourselves why Constance maids can do the same work we do to put together a dowry for themselves and why middle-class women can profit from fornication and still be considered honorable."

The kaiser looked at Pfefferhart as if considering him personally responsible for this embarrassing state of affairs. "Is this the truth?"

The councilman turned pale. "Well, surely there are a few kitchen maids who sell themselves to a monk or a soldier for a few pennies. There's not much we can do about that."

Madeleine laughed scornfully in Pfefferhart's face. "A few maids, you say? There are more Constance residents who go whoring than there are courtesans in all the bordellos of the city, and they do it mostly with the knowledge and approval of their husbands and fathers. Since their costs are less than ours, they undercut our prices and steal our men."

An old penny whore who had pushed her way through the crowd to Madeleine pulled her dress over her head so the kaiser could see her back scarred by lashes. "That's what they did to me when they caught me in bed with someone other than my husband! After that, I was driven out of town without a coin in my pocket and nearly died in a ditch at the side of the road. If the ever-so-honorable women of Constance take my living away from me now, I won't survive the next winter."

The kaiser stared at her unsightly back, and, judging from his irate tone, seemed to be blaming the councilman for this complaint, too. "Is it true that honorable citizens and virgins are engaged in fornication here?"

Pfefferhart raised his hands in exasperation. "Excuse me, Your Majesty. I know nothing about such things."

"Then perhaps you should keep your ears open, Councilman," Madeleine told him. "Look in Balthasar's house in Ringwilgasse Lane. A lot of interesting things are going on there."

Pfefferhart snorted. "The citizen Balthasar Rubli runs a completely legal bordello there."

"Where he employs his wife, his daughters, and his maids!" one of Madeleine's people called from the back of the crowd.

"Anyone who is a harlot can no longer be considered honorable." The kaiser's words displayed a nobleman's complete contempt for the dregs of society. "I have taken note of your complaint and order forthwith that any women or girls in Constance convicted of prostitution, whether citizens or maids, must be treated as prostitutes. They will be whipped and driven from the city, forbidden to ever set foot in it again."

Even before Sigismund had finished speaking, the prostitutes burst into cheers, extolling his wisdom. Since local women and girls now had more than just their reputation to lose, they would think twice before spreading their legs again. Though the chance to turn a quick trick might be appealing, the wretched life of a wandering whore was not.

In the meantime, other attendees at the Mass had exited the cathedral, wondering why the kaiser was taking so long to leave. Marie recognized Lütfried Muntprat, the city's richest man, and Rupert Splendidus and Abbot Hugo von Waldkron at his side. Rupert seemed amused at how the kaiser gave in to the harlots' demands, but the abbot clearly wished he could order the soldiers to undress the women and whip them.

Marie shuddered, realizing how close her cousin had come to falling into this man's hands. She knew it was time to carry out her plan if she wanted to take advantage of the commotion she had helped arrange. As the women started moving aside to make way for the kaiser, she stepped alongside Madeleine and raised her hand.

"But how about the girls who have fallen into the hands of evil men and lost their virginity by force?" At the sound of Marie's voice, the crowd surged forward again.

Seeing a crowd of curious and expectant eyes upon her, she straightened up and climbed the cathedral stairs. She also saw her former fiancé, and he looked as if the earth had spewed out a demon in front of him. Her first accusation, however, was for someone else.

Turning her back to Rupert Splendidus, she stood in front of Alban Pfefferhart. "I want information on the whereabouts of my cousin Hedwig Flühi, daughter of the master cooper Mombert Flühi."

"What's this girl's problem, Master Alban?" the kaiser asked abruptly.

Alban Pfefferhart chewed on his lip nervously. "Your Majesty, that's a story almost as puzzling as it is unpleasant. A few weeks ago, Hedwig Flühi was arrested for possible complicity in a murder and thrown into the tower, but she disappeared without a trace that same evening. It's all a great mystery."

"Really?" Marie pulled Abbot Hugo's scroll out from under her dress and held it out for Pfefferhart to see. "You no doubt know more about this matter than you care to admit."

While Pfefferhart stared at the document in confusion, Abbot Hugo let out a surprised shout and pressed his way through the crowd of men in front of him, trying to seize the paper. Just then, however, he was surrounded and stopped in his tracks by Count Eberhard's bodyguards. Meanwhile, a bewildered Pfefferhart passed the document back to Marie.

"I didn't write this! Someone has played a dirty trick and signed my name." He was so agitated, his voice almost broke.

Swallowing hard, Marie wasn't sure how to proceed. It seemed that Pfefferhart had indeed not prepared the order to extradite the girl. But before she could respond, the kaiser beckoned her over, taking the document from her hand and giving it to the bishop of Constance, who then read it aloud and looked questioningly at Pfefferhart.

"That's a vile counterfeit," the councilman said again, holding his hand up to his throat as if his collar had suddenly become too tight.

Marie glanced over at Waldkron, who had gotten himself under control again and was now wearing a placid expression. He was evidently certain that no one would connect him with the document.

Throwing back her head, Marie smiled at Pfefferhart. "Perhaps I can jog your memory. A friend of mine took this document from Abbot Hugo von Waldkron's personal servant, a fellow by the name of Selmo, after he had taken my cousin Hedwig from the tower."

"So the girl is still alive and unharmed?" When Marie nodded, Pfefferhart breathed an audible sigh of relief.

Abbot Hugo shook his fist at Marie and bellowed, "Slander!"

Marie was about to ask Pfefferhart to interrogate the tower guard, when a group of Michel's palatine foot soldiers came marching toward the cathedral. In their midst was Selmo, shackled and screaming, and with them the tower guard, waving his arms as he ran alongside Michel. When the tower guard caught sight of Pfefferhart, he ruthlessly shoved his way through the prostitutes, who let out a torrent of curses. As soon as he reached the councilman and pointed at Selmo, however, the crowd fell silent.

"Sir, that fellow in the cassock is the monk who took the girl. I recognize him with absolute certainty."

Pfefferhart looked Selmo over as the soldiers escorted him through the crowd of women, who backed away to make a clear path; he then turned to Michel, puzzled. "Who is he?"

Marie answered for Michel. "That is the man I have just accused. He calls himself Selmo and is the servant of Abbot Hugo von Waldkron."

Pfefferhart ran up to Selmo and shook him. "Where did you get this document, you scoundrel?"

"What document? I don't know anything about it! I was illegally taken prisoner and dragged here . . ." Selmo's voice was so indignant that he almost sounded innocent, but the look in his eyes as he glanced at Hugo gave him away. Pfefferhart pointed an accusing finger at the abbot. "This forgery comes from you! How did you get hold of the official seal of the city of Constance?"

The abbot's face turned dark red, and he addressed the kaiser. "I don't have the slightest thing to do with this affair, nor does my servant. This is a conspiracy, Your Majesty, intended to harm your most loyal servants and thus the crown."

Looking uncertainly at the men, the kaiser seemed ready to believe the abbot, when Count Eberhard von Württemberg, who had been standing inconspicuously in the background, stepped up.

"It's one person's word against the other, but a falsified seal is just as despicable as perjury. There's a simple way to exonerate the abbot. You need only search his quarters here in Constance and his house in Maurach. If you find nothing there, it's possible he is in fact a victim of slander."

The kaiser nodded and seemed relieved, as that opened the possibility of finally dispersing the crowd. But before he could give the order, Rupert Splendidus stepped forward.

"Allow me to carry out this search, Your Majesty."

Sigismund opened his mouth, but before he could speak, Count Eberhard's voice echoed across the square. "No, Your Majesty, don't do that! That would be like putting a fox in charge of the henhouse!"

Clenching his fists, the kaiser cast an admonishing glance at Eberhard, who bowed apologetically and pointed at Rupert. "I accuse Counselor Rupert Splendidus of perjury, forgery, slander, and incitement to murder, and I have enough proof to convict him. For one thing, he arranged the theft of the testament belonging to the knight Otmar von Mühringen and replaced it with a forgery that transferred Müringen's possessions to Konrad von Keilburg, his half brother. In addition, through forged testaments and perjury, he has seized the domains of Dreieichen, Zenggen, Felde, among others, and turned all the land over to his father, Heinrich, and his half brother."

Marie was now smirking, and Rupert stared at her in disbelief, putting his hands to his head, and emitting a hollow-sounding laugh. "It sounds like you had bad dreams after enjoying too much to drink last night, Count Eberhard, or you wouldn't be taking these fantasies seriously."

The Württemberg count didn't deign to even glance at Rupert. "I have incontrovertible proof of these and other scandalous deeds carried out by the Keilburg bastard."

Marie was glad to have the count as her spokesman. If she had accused Rupert, he would have torn her argument to shreds, making her look ridiculous. But here, he couldn't oppose the word of Eberhard von Württemberg, whose power and influence were even greater than that of Count Konrad von Keilburg. Just the same, she wasn't willing to let the discussion turn into a noblemen's quarrel over land and castles. Tugging on the kaiser's coat, Marie curtsied and pointed at Rupert.

"I accuse this man of murdering my father and depriving me of my honor and my inheritance."

"That is ridiculous," shouted Rupert. He raised his hand and moved forward to strike Marie, but a few soldiers from Eberhard's retinue quickly seized him.

Alban Pfefferhart bowed before the kaiser. "Allow me to go search the abbot's quarters." After Sigismund granted the request, the councilman beckoned to Bodman to follow with some of his men. They were soon joined by Michel and some of his foot soldiers.

Casting his eye over the dense crowd that had since doubled as curious citizens arrived, the kaiser gestured at his followers to go back inside the cathedral. Count Eberhard made sure his soldiers brought Master Rupert and the abbot inside, too, despite their furious objections. Marie watched them enter and didn't know what to do. A nod from the count relieved her from having to decide.

Inside the cathedral, people looked around at a loss, and only the kaiser's silent, grim presence on his throne kept them from loudly erupting into discussion. Count Eberhard von Württemberg, considered by some the instigator of the turmoil, garnered many curious and angered looks, while others stared at Marie, so out of place amidst the Reich dignitaries and Constance patricians in her yellow harlot's ribbons. Some onlookers also excitedly nudged their neighbors, reminding them that Marie was the count's regular bedmate.

The Constance bishop, Friedrich von Zollern, stepped to the altar and began to pray, more to have something to do than out of a need to commune with God. Nearly an hour passed before the councilman and Michel finally returned with their retinues. As he walked in, Pfefferhart gingerly held a long wooden chest out in front of him as if afraid its contents would soil his clothing, and he laid the chest before the kaiser. After Sigismund gestured for him to unpack its contents and place each item on the bench, Pfefferhart removed seal after seal from the chest, each one seemingly an offense to him and the gathered noblemen.

"The Abbot Hugo von Waldkron not only has the city seal of Constance but also those belonging to several noble families. It is highly unlikely that he acquired any of them legally."

Abbot Adalwig von Ottilien, who was sitting with Sir Dietmar and Lady Mechthild in the back of the south nave, stood up and hurried forward. "In the last twelve years, the Waldkron monastery has received an unusual number of large gifts that came as a surprise to many heirs whose families had been left in dire straits. I'm convinced the seal was used in the forgery of documents."

This accusation brought a number of noblemen to their feet, since many of them had been forced to give up good land and sometimes productive villages to the Waldkron monastery. They loudly proclaimed their demands, and it took quite a while before Eberhard von Württemberg and Bishop Friedrich von Zollern managed to calm them down.

Pfefferhart beckoned to several of Michel's palatine foot soldiers, and they brought in a secretary desk whose elaborate lathe work and inlaid wood had not held up well to their rough handling. Shouting angrily, Master Rupert tried to pull away from his guards.

At Michel's command, his men set the secretary desk down in front of the altar. "Since Master Rupert Splendidus was also accused of forgery, it seemed necessary to me to search his possessions as well. In so doing, I found this little secretary desk, in which we discovered several hollow secret compartments. Breaking one of them open, here's what we found." Michel handed Count Eberhard von Württemberg a document with a number of seals on it.

Quickly glancing over it, Eberhard smiled as if all his assumptions had been confirmed. "This is the genuine testament of Kunos, a knight and uncle of Gottfried von Dreieichen, who was said to have bequeathed his possessions to Heinrich von Keilburg."

Marie was probably the only one to notice the hint of relief in Count Eberhard's voice. This finding established Rupert's guilt once and for all. Marie, too, was overjoyed even though she couldn't help wondering why the man hadn't destroyed the incriminating document long before. The obvious answer was extortion. Rupert could use such a document as a weapon against his half brother in case Konrad got weary of Rupert's services.

Kunos von Dreieichen's testament wasn't the only treasure in Rupert's secretary desk. When servants smashed the valuable desk into pieces at the kaiser's command, other documents appeared along with a bound volume of fine, handmade paper more than half-filled with Rupert's clear handwriting.

Sigismund looked at it briefly before handing it to Bishop Friedrich. "It appears to be Latin, but the words don't make any sense to me."

The bishop frowned, staring at the first page, then muttered something and continued leafing through the volume. When he heard the kaiser impatiently clearing his throat, he looked up, startled, and closed the book with a resounding thud.

"The text is written in a code like that used by the clergy for secret notes. Rupert Splendidus kept diaries, entering detailed notes on all of his actions. This document is a journal of his crimes. Yes, the man is guilty of everything as charged, along with many other illegal activities."

"Then we shall prosecute him and his accomplices." Pounding the bench to reinforce his word, the kaiser ordered the guards to tie up both Rupert and the abbot and take them to his quarters.

VII.

The following days were one long nightmare for Marie. Locked in a room in Kaiser Sigismund's quarters in the Petershausen monastery, she was given two meals a day and some water for washing, but was not even once allowed to leave the room. After her long years of wandering, she felt stifled within those four walls, especially since no one told her what was going to happen to her or even why she was being held. Was it because of her ties to Rupert Splendidus? Or her involvement in the prostitutes' insurrection? Or could it be for some other reason? Imagining the worst, she saw herself once again tied to the pillory, being slowly whipped to death as Rupert looked on triumphantly in a nobleman's clothes.

If anyone had been allowed to visit her, her imprisonment wouldn't have been so agonizing. After much urging, one of the taciturn nuns who brought her food told Marie that a courtesan whose description matched Hiltrud's had been turned away several times at the door. On the third day, just as Marie thought she would go mad, Michel was able to get close to the locked door to her room and tell her that the kaiser had put off his departure for a few days in order to personally preside over the trial of Hugo von Waldkron and Rupert Splendidus.

Count Konrad von Keilburg and some of Rupert's accomplices had also been taken prisoner, including Utz, Hunold, Linhard, and Melcher. Michel told her that as soon as Utz had seen the instruments of torture, he'd admitted his crime against Marie as well as a few other misdeeds he had carried out on the counselor's behalf. In addition, Linhard had confessed remorsefully, but Rupert and Utz still disputed everything despite the overwhelming evidence against them.

The noblemen surrounding the kaiser, however, seemed less concerned about the just punishment of the criminals than the distribution of rich lands that the Keilburgs had seized. Marie had already guessed this, since she was able to hear the noisy quarreling of the noblemen from her room. These men were only concerned with their own well-being and in gaining even more power, and she loathed the way they treated everyone else as pawns in their game. Angry at her exclusion from the trial, she felt it was highly unjust— after all, her fate was also at stake.

From time to time, when her fury subsided a bit, she would stop and wonder how it would all end. After the men who had violated her and condemned her to an itinerant harlot's life had been found guilty and punished, her goal of these past few years would have been realized. What would happen after that, however, hung over her head like a threatening, black cloud. No matter what happened, she would not go back to working as a wandering whore. Yet for a homeless, dishonored woman, the only other way out was death.

The fourth day began the same as the three before it. Awakened by knocking, Marie saw a nun open the door and bring in a tray of porridge. Without saying a word, the nun placed it on the table, reached for the previous night's dishes, and disappeared just as silently as she had come.

Marie was picking at her food when she heard another knock on the door and assumed the nun was back to bring her a fresh chamber pot and pick up her half-empty breakfast plate. Pushing away the rest of her porridge, she stood up and, to her amazement, four nuns in the garb of the Second Order of Saint Francis entered. Their faces seemed earnest, indeed a bit solemn, but not unfriendly.

"Marie Schärer, we have been ordered to dress you and bring you to the judge." The head nun nodded with the hint of a smile, but the very words sent a shiver down Marie's back.

Had she been indicted because she had been so bold as to return to Constance? Did they want to punish her as one of the ringleaders of the prostitutes' insurrection? Squaring her shoulders, she told herself she wasn't going to be executed, since the pious sisters, not the bailiffs, had come for her. She took off her robe and was handed her best dress, but it had new, freshly dyed yellow ribbons on it. Putting it on and buttoning it, then defiantly jutting out her chin, Marie indicated that she was ready. The four nuns surrounded her like guards, leading her through endlessly long, deserted corridors until they reached the interior courtyard of the monastery where a covered travel coach was waiting for them.

When Marie hesitated, the mother superior put her right hand on Marie's shoulder and pushed her toward the vehicle. The coach was large enough for them all and, to Marie's surprise, had upholstered seats since the nobles who ordinarily used this coach seemingly weren't fond of bruised backsides. Trying not to worry about where they were going, Marie peered through a crack in the window leather and was surprised to see that the wagon was taking them over the Rhine Bridge into the city. Before long it stopped, and Marie recognized the place she hoped she'd never see again—the Dominican monastery on the island where she had once been tried and convicted.

She noted that separation of the sexes was no longer strictly observed in the Constance monasteries. This became apparent as the nuns escorted her through the huge building to the same place where she had been sentenced more than five years before. It looked just as she remembered it, except that this time every seat was taken and court bailiffs and noblemen's servants stood along the walls.

The kaiser had taken his place on the throne decorated with the Reich's symbol beneath a small baldachin. The golden coat of arms with the Reich's black eagle that the kaiser wore on the chest of his long red surcoat seemed to stress how seriously he took this case. His face, however, looked impatient and weary, something that could not be said of the nobles around him.

Directly next to him sat Count Palatine Ludwig and the bishop of Constance, who was cradling his head in his right hand as he looked at the new arrivals with a strangely detached but not unhappy smile. Alongside the count palatine, Marie caught sight of Eberhard von Württemberg, who winked at her, then gave her a guileless smile. "We did it," he seemed to say, nodding toward the defendant's bench where Rupert sat alongside his accomplices, Utz, Hunold, Melcher, Linhard, and three other men Marie didn't know. All had been dressed in penitent's robes and bound in chains, except for Linhard, who was clad in his monastic robe and seemed to be meditating, hands folded in prayer.

Marie turned away from Rupert's look of hatred, instead staring straight ahead at the judge's bench. For a minute she thought her heart would stop, for there sat Honorius von Rottlingen, the judge who had condemned and sentenced her before. His assistants were also the same, and she even recognized the court clerk, though he had aged visibly. Father Honorius did not look as arrogant and repulsed this time, but instead seemed grim and determined, as if standing in judgment on himself.

The judge motioned to a bailiff, and Marie was led to a seat alongside the judge's bench. Now she could see the spectators sitting farther back in the room, where she caught sight of Sir Dietmar, his wife, and Abbot Adalwig of Saint Ottilien. Michel was also there, standing near the door, in his dress uniform, appearing oddly lost in thought.

After the four nuns had stepped back from Marie, Honorius von Rottlingen raised his hand to call for order. He gave Rupert a furious look, as if blaming him for all the problems he'd ever had or would have, then bowed to the kaiser and briefly to the bishop of Constance, with whom he seemed to be on unfriendly terms.

"We are gathered here today in the name of the Father, the Son, and the Holy Ghost, to render justice." His tone suggested he was almost choking on the words. "The accused, Rupert Splendidus and Utz Käffli, are found guilty of many crimes and will be executed at Brüel Field tomorrow. Rupert Splendidus will be put to the stake, and his ashes shall then be strewn into the Rhine so that on the Day of Resurrection there will be nothing left of him. Utz Käffli will be tortured on the wheel."

Emotionless, Utz accepted the judgment without comment, but Rupert jumped up and cursed the judge. Within moments, he was seized and gagged by two bailiffs. Melcher, Hunold, and the three others looked up as if hoping for more lenient punishment, but collapsed again on hearing what followed.

"Hunold, the bailiff, is condemned to death by strangulation for rape of a virgin, perjury, and other crimes that will be revealed in the course of the proceedings. The cooper's apprentice, Melcher, will be given the same punishment for complicity in murder, as will the ferryman, Hein, for theft and complicity in murder. So too will the same punishment be given to the merchant's assistant, Adalbert, and the former monk, Festus, for document forgery, accessory to fraud, and theft.

"The last defendant, Linhard Merk, who now goes by Brother Josephus, has confessed and shown remorse for his sins. He will therefore be kept under guard in a monastery until the end of his days. All these men were accomplices of the principal defendant, Rupert Splendidus, and have assisted him in his monstrous crimes."

Honorius von Rottlingen was silent for a moment and then looked at Marie uncomfortably, as if about to swallow a poisonous toad. "It is the will of His Majesty, the kaiser, as well as that of all the assembled nobles of the Reich, that you, Marie Schärer, daughter of Matthis Schärer, citizen of the city of Constance, shall receive justice. Sister Theodosia, do your duty."

One of the nuns who had accompanied Marie to the courtroom handed a pair of scissors to the mother superior while the two others brought in a brazier of burning coals. Walking over to Marie, the mother superior gingerly took hold of one of the yellow ribbons, cut it off the dress, and with an expression of revulsion threw it into the brazier to be consumed by the fire. Though she continued to grimace as if picking disgusting caterpillars off a grapevine, she didn't stop until she had thrown the last yellow ribbon into the fire. Then, with an audible sigh of relief, she motioned to the other nuns to continue. They unfolded a white robe, slipped it over Marie's old dress, and led her to the judge. Father Honorius made the sign of the cross, scooped up some holy water, and let it trickle down onto Marie's head.

"In the name of the Holy Trinity, I absolve you, Marie Schärer, of all your sins and declare you as pure and innocent as if you had just come out of your mother's womb."

"So be it," the bishop added with a smile.

Friedrich von Zollern had personally insisted that Honorius von Rottlingen should grant absolution to Marie. The arrogant abbots and monks of the island monastery had all too often harassed both him and his predecessors on the bishop's seat of Constance. Now

Friedrich had succeeded in humiliating the most imperious abbot of all, and with him all the monks in the monastery.

At first Marie didn't understand what had just happened. Was she innocent? Even the priest's words couldn't allow her to believe that, but if the citizens of Constance accepted the verdict and gave her back her citizenship rights, she could use her money to buy a little house and live here as a respected townsperson.

She was startled out of her thoughts by an evil laugh. "You can go ahead and absolve the whore," Utz shouted in the chamber, "but she'll never forget all the men that she's had, and I was the first!" Utz tried to continue, but a court bailiff pressed a gag between his teeth so all he could do was grunt.

Utz's words were like a splash of cold water in Marie's face. Though she had briefly clung to the hope that the events of the last five years had been erased and she could continue to live in Constance, she now realized her fellow citizens wouldn't forget her past. Men would look at her as easy prey while women would shut their doors to her. Briefly she thought about how Utz had told yet another lie. He had not attacked her first; that crime belonged to Hunold, who was now whimpering and trembling on the defendant's bench. She had yearned for the conviction of these men for so many years, and now that it was over, Marie felt no pity but also no particular joy.

Instead, she had felt as if she were standing before a gaping chasm, desperately searching for a way across the abyss. Her only hope for the future was her money. Yet even her riches couldn't buy her citizenship rights in some small, faraway city, where she might live modestly for the rest of her days in a house with two goats. Sighing, she thought of the fortune her father had once amassed. If she was given just a third of that amount, she could fashion a decent future for herself and Hiltrud.

Still pondering her next steps, Marie was again sprinkled with holy water and blessed by Father Honorius. Marie had thought it was all over, but then the four nuns came toward her again and over her white shirt placed a dark blue dress decorated with rich embroidery and fur trimmings. Marie could tell that it was made of the finest Flemish cloth similar to the clothes that the richest and noblest Constance citizens wore to Sunday Mass. She was uncomfortably hot in her three layers of clothing, and the sweat running in streams down her back was making the scars from her whipping itch dreadfully. She saw Mechthild von Arnstein coming toward her and wanted nothing more than to ask her to scratch her back.

Instead, the lady took her by the hand to Abbot Adalwig and remained standing there, holding her hand. A palatine knight then led Michel forward to stand next to Marie. Abbot Adalwig smiled at them warmly. When he began speaking, Marie didn't understand what was happening, as he was pronouncing the nuptial blessing without even asking her if she approved. Marie turned toward Michel, but since he raised no objection, she didn't dare protest.

"And so I declare you man and wife. Amen." Abbot Adalwig was visibly satisfied with himself for officiating at the marriage without stuttering or making any other errors.

During the short ceremony, Michel had watched Marie's astonished face. She seemed as bewildered as if he had dragged her off to the pillory, and he couldn't help feeling annoyed. After all, marriage with him was not the same as being condemned and whipped in the market square. Then he remembered that he had felt equally dazed the previous day.

Less than twenty-four hours before, he had accompanied his liege lord, the Count Palatine Ludwig, to a meeting with Count Eberhard von Württemberg. In addition to his host, the meeting had included the Constance bishop, Friedrich von Zollern; the councilman Alban Pfefferhart; and the Arnsteins.

After a brief greeting, the Württemberg count had gotten right to the point. "What's going to happen to Marie?"

Alban Pfefferhart had waved his hands dismissively. "It's hardly possible for her to remain in Constance. We can give her back her citizenship and a house to live in, but night after night shiftless men would come to her house in hopes that her morals remained loose enough to give them a night of pleasure. The municipal authorities, of which I am one, therefore suggest assisting her in acquiring citizenship in a distant city where she can live in peace."

"That would suit you rich Constance merchants just fine," Count Eberhard von Württemberg had scoffed. "But I question how a single woman might live unmolested in any city of the Reich."

At this point Michel had decided it was time for him to speak up. "Marie needs the protection of a man, and I will therefore ask her if she will stay with me."

"As a mistress?" The count's voice had sounded sharp, but then a broad grin appeared on his face. "No, I won't allow that. You will have to marry her."

Lady Mechthild had shaken her head indignantly. "Michel Adler is an officer of the count palatine and one of his ministers. He cannot marry a prostitute."

The Constance bishop raised his arms in a conciliatory gesture, as if something amusing had occurred to him. "There is a solution for this, Lady Mechthild. Allow me to do my part in making an amicable arrangement."

"Then we're in agreement," said the Count Eberhard von Württemberg, indicating he didn't want to hear any further objections. Walking over to Michel, he patted the man on the shoulder. "This will work out well for you, young fellow. If you marry Marie, I'll make you a castellan in one of my cities. Then if any fellow says anything bad about your wife, you can throw him in the tower with my blessing."

Staring at the count, Michel hadn't known how to answer. Then he looked at the count palatine who looked like he didn't know whether to laugh out loud at the whole matter or start a fight. Finally, the man walked over to Michel.

"You have a reputation for arranging marriages, Count Eberhard, especially when it concerns your cast-off mistresses, but Michel is my liegeman and will remain so."

Michel had a hard time shaking off the memory of that scene and tried to accept that Marie now belonged to him before God and the world. Judging by the dismissive look on her face, however, she was now even less accessible to him than in the five years she had been out wandering the roads and he had been rising through the ranks of the palatine guards. Before he could say a word to her, Eberhard von Württemberg and Count Palatine Ludwig stepped up and shook their hands.

The smile of the Württemberg count made it clear to Marie who was responsible for this last little trick, and she was tempted to give him a piece of her mind. She wasn't a puppet whose strings he could pull, and Michel deserved a better wife than a wandering whore. But she didn't have an opportunity to complain to Count Eberhard, since more and more people came up to congratulate them. Sir Dietmar was so embarrassed that he didn't dare look at Marie, while Alban Pfefferhart seemed delighted that by this marriage a stigma had been removed from him and from the entire city. Even the kaiser deigned to place his hand on her and Michel's shoulders, wishing them a happy and fruitful marriage.

That entire time, Marie didn't dare look at Michel, and she sighed heavily in relief when Lady Mechthild took her by the arm and led her into the hallway. Briefly looking back at the room, Marie saw the count palatine handing Michel a cup of wine for a toast. Then the door closed, and Marie felt as if she'd once again been damned to an uncertain fate.

She turned to Lady Mechthild. "This is ridiculous. I can't marry Michel."

The lady pointed down the hallway toward the main door. "Come now, someone is waiting for you and we must hurry. As for your marriage, you are now Michel Adler's wife before God and the world. I understand that you feel manipulated, but it seemed like the best solution. You are no longer a young woman, but you're not a widow, either, and it is highly unlikely you could ever have married any other man without first telling him about your past. To spare you the embarrassment of such a situation, Count Eberhard suggested that you be married to your childhood friend, who has been your constant shadow these past many weeks. The Constance city council was happy with this solution, and Herr Muntprat as well as Herr Pfefferhart will even present you with a considerable dowry. Michel has not married a poor woman, Marie. If you include the compensation you will receive for your lost fortune, you are actually very rich."

Lady Mechthild's voice sounded a tiny bit envious, but her cheerful smile made up for it as she took Marie by the hand toward a waiting carriage, where they climbed inside and sat next to each other.

"I would like to apologize to you, Marie, for I have wronged you. When you came to us a few weeks ago, I was convinced you wanted to take my place again in my husband's bed, and I was jealous. I also thought you were making up a fanciful story to somehow use us to suit your purposes. We have learned from Count Eberhard that you did in fact bring the real testament back for us, and we now have sovereignty not just over Mühringen but also over some of the land formerly belonging to Felde Castle, which nicely rounds off our territory. My husband and I are very grateful and would like to reward you. If there is anything you wish, whether it be farms, forest lands, or vineyards, just tell us."

The carriage began to move, but this time Marie was not interested in where it was taking them. She was thinking of Hiltrud, who had saved Marie's life years ago and reluctantly supported her in her plans for vengeance. She owed it to Hiltrud to help her also find a better life and a bit of happiness. Though it might not be possible to revive the winter romance between her friend and the goatherd in Arnstein, it was certainly worth a try.

"If you really wish to show your gratitude, Lady Mechthild, give my loyal companion Hiltrud a farm and let her marry Thomas, the goatherd."

Lady Mechthild seemed pleased with the idea. "Gladly. Shall the farm be in the Arnstein realm, or would you rather have your friend closer by?"

Marie laughed. "I'd love to have Hiltrud close by, but I really don't know where life is taking me."

Lady Mechthild put her hand in her lap and gave her a conspiratorial smile. "Your husband has just been appointed castellan of Rheinsobern by Count Palatine Ludwig. That is one of the best properties the count will receive from the Keilburg estate."

"Very nice for him." Marie shrugged off this news but was curious enough to pose a question. "Was there no heir to lay claim to Rheinsobern?"

"The Keilburg counts forcefully seized many lands and made sure there were no heirs to contest their ownership. We were lucky, but without the protection of Count Eberhard von Württemberg, we would also have been their victims. Count Eberhard acquired ownership of Keilburg Castle with all its land, and others were given back property."

Giggling, Lady Mechthild continued. "The only one to come away empty-handed was Friedrich von Habsburg as punishment for his angry outburst at the kaiser." Lady Mechthild also told Marie that Konrad von Keilburg had been sentenced and put to death by the sword, as had Hugo von Waldkron.

As the lady recounted who had benefited from the breakup of Konrad's holdings and Abbot Hugo's lands, Marie soon lost interest in who acquired what and instead looked out the carriage window, wondering what life at Michel's side might be like. Before she had thought it all through, however, the carriage passed through the market square and turned into the narrow lane beneath the columns leading to the upper market.

"Where are you taking me, Lady Mechthild?"

Lady Mechthild gave her a friendly smile. "I think you'll be happy to see your relatives again."

Only now did Marie realize that she had been so caught up in her plans and the trial that she hadn't thought of her uncle once. The lady told her that her accusation against Rupert had saved Mombert and his wife from being condemned for murder. Tears of relief welled up in her eyes, and she could hardly wait for the carriage to stop at the entrance to the Hundsgasse. Lady Mechthild smiled as she watched Marie jump from the carriage, run down the lane, and open the front gate to Mombert's yard.

Delightedly, Marie burst into the parlor where her relatives had gathered. Mombert and his wife must have only just been released, as they didn't seem to able to comprehend the surprising turn of events. Both appeared pale and emaciated. Wina, who was standing beneath the painting of the Virgin Mary, held Hedwig tightly in her arms while Wilmar, shifting his feet anxiously and staring at his master, watched as Marie entered. When she smiled and nodded at him, he gave a big sigh of relief.

Mombert stood up and walked toward his niece. Trying to speak, he started sobbing instead—not for the first time that day, judging by his reddened eyes. He finally embraced her, burying his face on her shoulder like a child.

"What a joy to see you." He was so choked up, he could hardly speak. "God sent you to us, Marie. Without you, my poor wife and I would have been tortured to death, and Hedwig would be enslaved by a perverse scoundrel. You saved us all."

Marie glanced briefly at Wilmar and shook her head with a smile. "Don't just thank me, Uncle Mombert. If Wilmar hadn't set Hedwig free and found Melcher, there wouldn't have been much I could have done."

Breaking free of Wina's grasp, Hedwig hurried to her father. "There you have it, Father. It was because of Wilmar that I'm here now and unharmed." Her pleading look was obvious.

Mombert pushed his daughter into Wilmar's arms. "If that's the case, you both have my blessing."

Full of gratitude, Wilmar beamed at Marie, but she didn't return his gaze since her focus was now on her father's old housekeeper. At first, Wina had scarcely dared touch her, but when she saw Marie's smile, she wrapped her arms around her and swore tearfully that this was the happiest day of her life. Rocking the old woman in her arms, Marie patted her fondly. It was nice to have someone who loved her.

VIII.

The kaiser departed the next day, seemingly glad to finally leave the city. The hour when Marie would leave was also fast approaching. Though she wished she could secretly slip away at daybreak, Pfefferhart had made it clear that it was her duty to attend the punishment of the men responsible for her shame and her father's death. The hangman made short work of Hunold, Melcher, and the other accomplices, slipping a rope around their necks and pulling until they stopped moving.

When he got to Utz, however, he crushed his bones, then broke him on the wheel while the condemned man was fully conscious. Utz didn't scream or ask for a quick end, but ridiculed the court and boasted of his crimes, seemingly proud of the misdeeds that earned him a place of honor in hell. Shouting out the names of the knights and other nobles he had murdered, mentioning Sir Dietmar's uncle Otmar among many others, he finally claimed he was supposed to murder Konrad von Keilburg for Rupert, and regretted he had not gotten that chance.

While the carriage driver was still yelling out details of his misdeeds, Rupert was being led to the stake. He whined plaintively, begged for his life, and offered his services to the bishop of Constance, Count Eberhard von Württemberg, and any other of the noblemen who would save him from a fiery death. But all that got him was the mockery and contempt of the Constance citizens, and finally the street urchins, who threw dirt at him from the front row. The hangman's servant had to carry him to the stake and hold him tight in order to tie him up. Unmoved by his pleading, they heaped wood and branches on him and set fire to them at the judge's order. As the flames rose around him, his screams rang out eerily over Brüel Field.

Marie lingered only as long as was expected of her, then ran to her father's grave in order to say her first prayers there. Though Michel had been following her since early morning, she had hardly looked at him, much less spoken to him. Now, joining her, he also knelt down to pray at the gravesite.

As she stood up to return to the city, he pulled her to him and led her, despite her objections, down to the harbor and onto a boat that seemed to have been waiting only for them. This anticlimactic departure from Constance irritated her, since she was looking forward to spending a few days with Mombert and his family even though the tearful gratitude of her relatives was a bit taxing. To her surprise, she saw Mombert and his family sitting up in the bow and watching the boatmen. Freeing herself from Michel's arms, she started walking toward her uncle, then paused and remained at the back of the boat. She wasn't ready to speak with anyone yet.

It wouldn't be easy for her to become accustomed to her new life as a castellan's wife, which would bring with it a number of unfamiliar duties. First off, however, she'd have to realize that the goal she had set for her life had actually been achieved. For five long years she had yearned for Rupert's death with every fiber of her being, and with her revenge complete, she felt empty and burned out.

She sighed as the current caught hold of the ship and the walls of Constance quickly disappeared behind them. Though she didn't regret her hasty departure, it felt strange not to have Hiltrud beside her. She wanted to share her thoughts with her friend, even though she knew doing so would have earned her another scolding. But Hiltrud wanted to leave for Arnstein with Lady Mechthild to pick up Thomas. Marie would see them both again in the fall. Kordula, however, had decided to stay in Constance in order to earn as much money as possible. She then intended to follow Marie after the council ended, and with her help open up a tavern in Rheinsobern.

Michel suddenly walked up behind Marie and placed his hands on her shoulders. Just as she was about to push him away, he began to talk. At first he avoided speaking about the two of them, but instead told her that her uncle was tired of Constance and had received permission to settle and set up a master cooper's business in Rheinsobern. Accompanying the family were Wilmar, who would become Mombert's son-in-law, and Wina.

As he began describing the place they were headed, she realized she hadn't been treating him as he deserved and lowered her head in shame.

"I'm sorry, Michel. About the marriage, I mean."

"I'm not sorry." Michel pulled her to him with a sigh of contentment. "Marie is mine! I've always loved you but never dared hope that the two of us could be together."

"But will you be able to forget all that has happened over the past five years?"

"No, and I don't wish to. It was a hard time for you, and you have proven yourself brave and courageous, exactly the qualities you will need as a warrior's wife. Those years were not easy for me, either, but we've both made the best of them. After all, you are marrying an officially appointed castellan of Rheinsobern."

"Who is stuck with someone like me." Her voice sounded bitter.

Michel chuckled. "I owe what I am to you, too, Marie. If I hadn't been so madly in love with you, I never would have left

Constance. Marriage with you brings much to me. If it hadn't been for you, I might have become a castellan of a ruined, drafty castle in a distant mountain forest after fifteen more years, and not the castellan of such an important castle as Rheinsobern. Ordinarily, one must be of noble birth to obtain such a post. I'll admit, I wouldn't be so happy with my promotion if Rheinsobern had been awarded to the Württemberg count, but Count Palatine Ludwig is our lord and Count Eberhard is very far away."

There was a touch of jealousy in his voice that even surprised him, and he fell silent. Smiling lovingly at her, he absentmindedly played with a lock of her hair shining like gold in the evening sun. As their hometown disappeared behind them in the east, he led Marie forward to the bow of the ship.

"You must not look back, dearest. Look forward to the future, and you will see the two of us there, the beautiful and wealthy wife of the castellan on Rheinsobern, and me, your husband."

Marie laughed. "Husband? You're already starting to sound like Lady Mechthild."

"Why not? The next time we meet her and Sir Dietmar, we will be sitting at the same table. And who knows, perhaps one day a son of ours will marry one of their daughters."

Those words seemed a bit far-fetched to Marie, but she did have to admit they had a very pleasant sound.

HISTORICAL NOTES

The year is AD 1410, and the Holy Roman Empire of the German Nation and the Catholic Church are both in turmoil. King Rupert is dead, and the two cousins Sigismund and Jobst von Mähren are involved in a dispute over his testament. Sigismund will eventually prevail, but even he is not able to put an end to the feuds and power struggles among the nobles that pose almost irreconcilable problems for all of Christendom.

Three princes of the church lay claim to being the legitimate followers of the apostle Peter, and are in an all-out war with one another. At the same time, the clergy is in decline. Monks and priests have become flesh-peddlers and abbots and bishops territorial lords who care less about the souls entrusted to them than their own wealth and status.

In England, the preacher John Wycliffe raises his voice against the scandalous situation in the clergy, and in Prague, the Master Jan Hus rises to denounce the rulers. But no one who has reached the pinnacle of success ever wants to permit his demotion to a lower status, and none of the three popes—Gregory XII in Rome, Benedict XIII in Avignon, nor John XXIII in Pisa—agrees to step down and make way for the unity of the Catholic faith.

For this reason, Kaiser Sigismund convenes a council in Constance. Only one of the popes, John XXIII, appears personally, and he expects support from the kaiser against his two adversaries. Gregory and Benedict merely send representatives. But how can the kaiser break the impasse and settle the competing claims when the Spanish empire supports one pope, France the other, and the kaiser himself the third? After long negotiations, John XXIII is finally declared unfit and removed from the list of popes. The name John falls into such disrepute that for six hundred years no pope will choose that name again. Not until the twentieth century will Cardinal Angelo Giuseppe Roncalli take this name, becoming the true John XXIII. Gregory XII finally renounces his claim voluntarily while Benedict XIII clings to his title for the rest of his days, though his influence shrinks to a small group of supporters after Oddo Colonna is selected as the compromise candidate, becoming Pope Martin V.

Though the Council of Constance solves the papal problem, it fails in other significant respects. It does not bring an end to the pomp and immorality of the clergy nor set up an honest dialogue with church critics. Jan Hus, who came to Constance trusting in the free conduct promised by the kaiser, is put on trial before an ecclesiastical court, condemned to death in a questionable proceeding, and burned at the stake on Brüel Field. The consequences of this betrayal were the long and ruthless Hussite Wars and the alienation of people of German and Czech descent in Bohemia.

More than one hundred years after the Council of Constance, a Benedictine monk will nail his ninety-five theses on the door of the church in Wittenberg, thus continuing and extending even further the work of Wycliffe and Hus. He cannot reform the Catholic Church, but his protest will open a schism in the church, reaching far beyond the Reich. The conflict with the new confession will, however, not remain without consequence in the clergy and monasteries, and will change them more in the hundred years following than in the thousand years before.

During the Council of Constance, morality became so loose that the minstrel Oswald von Wolkenstein mocked the town as a whorehouse extending from one gate to the other. Newly arriving prostitutes therefore resorted to radical means to fight the unfair local competition. Many of the nobles simply took any girl they liked, as Count Eberhard von Württemberg did, seizing a Constance citizen's daughter off the street and then taking her on horseback to his quarters.

The city of Constance had to struggle with the consequences of this for many years. Even a generation later, the term "council child" was the worst insult any citizen of Constance could fling against another.

Such were the realities of the times faced by Marie Schärer and others like her forced by circumstance to struggle for survival and dignity in the harsh and often cruel world of medieval Europe.

ABOUT THE AUTHORS

Iny Lorentz is the pen name for the husband-and-wife writing team Iny Klocke and Elmar Wohlrath, historians whose tales of medieval action, adventure, and romance reflect their academic interests and love for each other. Together, they've written more than thirty-five books, almost all of which quickly became bestsellers and which are also available as audiobooks. The five-book Marie series, perhaps their most popular, has sold more than five and a half million copies in Germany alone and has been translated into fourteen languages. The first book in the series, *The Wandering Whore*, introduced the captivating and beloved character Marie, whose story has since been made into an award-winning German television movie called *The Whore*, starring actress Alexandra Neldel. Elmar and Iny live and write in Poing, near Munich.

ABOUT THE TRANSLATOR

 Lee Chadeayne is a former classical musician, college professor, and owner of a language translation company in Massachusetts. A charter member of the American Literary Translators Association (ALTA), he's been an active member since 1970. He presently serves as editor of the ALTA newsletter and as a copyeditor for the American Arthritis Society newsletter. He is a scholar and student of both history and languages, especially Middle High German. His translated works to date focus on music, art, language, history, and general literature; notable works include *The Settlers of Catan* by Rebecca Gablé, *The Copper Sign* by Katia Fox, and the bestselling Hangman's Daughter series by Oliver Pötzsch.